BOOK THREE

AUSBUND

VILLEINS
A TRILOGY

BRETHREN
VILLEINS
AUSBUND

JEREMIAH PEARSON

The characters and events portrayed in this book are fictitious. Any similarity to real persons, living or dead, is coincidental and not intended by the author.

Text copyright © 2013 Jeremiah Pearson

ISBN-13: 978-0-9895467-2-0

DEDICATION

Dedicated with all my love, to my wife Velvalea, who inspired and urged and nurtured this book into being.

War is delightful,
to those who have had no experience of it.
…Desiderius Erasmus

CAST OF CHARACTERS

The Mission Cell of Brethren Reformers

Kristina, orphaned at 12 when her parents and sister were burnt at the stake for heresy; raised in a convent by radical Sister Hannah who fled with her to Kunvald, where she is further educated to become a teacher of literacy

Marguerite, known as Grit, once a beautiful stage singer and absinth addict rescued by Brethren, now a devout reformer and papermaker and printer

Frieda, sheltered pretty daughter of Brethren Johannes and wife, Rita; trained to be a teacher

Dolf, converted ex-magistrate, now a teacher of literacy

Symon, escaped villein and Dolf's best friend; printer

Veterans of War

Lud, of Giebel, villein, disfigured and widowed by pox, illiterate yet of restless and penetrating mind

Waldo of Giebel, Dietrich's groom, mute, will not tolerate unkind treatment of horses, father of wild daughter, Kella.

Mahmed, Ottoman Janissary cavalry commander, fourth son of physician, intellectual, chess master, taken hostage as war prize

Ulrich, mercenary, Landsknecht cavalry commander, and professional duelist

Ambrosius, grandson of cobbler and harness maker villein Ferde, dreams of learning to read

Little Golz, tall son of potters Deet and Berta

Steffan, tiller parents, oldest pikeman
Jakop, plowboy
Kaspar, miller Sig's son, loses a leg during the war
Linhoff, apprentice of blacksmith
Max, jester, cynic
Tomen, son of barley farmers

At Wurzburg, the City and the Fortress Marienberg, Southern Franconia, the Holy Roman Empire of Germany

Konrad von Thungen, Prince Bishop of Wurzburg
Tilman Riemenschneider, artist, city councilman
Brother Basil, monk in confidential service of Konrad
Martin Luther, priest, sensationalist reformer, best-selling author

At Giebel, the Geyer Estate South of Wurzburg, From 1519

At the Castle

Witter, a man of many secrets, printer, artist, intellectual, master of languages, now a teacher
Lady Anna von Seckendorff, pox-scarred widow of Dietrich, mother of Florian Geyer, taught literacy by Kristina
Lura, maidservant to Lady Anna
Leta, laundress
Vogler, aged castle guard

In the Village

Father Michael, estate priest
Arl, weaver, baby catcher, mother of Fridel, Hermo, Greta
Greta, villein, daughter of Arl, once betrothed to Kaspar
Ruth, villein, mother of Matthes who was killed at war, candle maker
Merkel, villein, smithy who demands to be taught to read
Sig, villein, miller, father of Kaspar
Ferde, villein, cobbler and harness maker, grandfather of Ambrosius
Deet, villein, potter father of Little Golz

Berta, villein, potter mother of Little Golz
Huber, steward, driven out by Lud
Peter, infant born to Kristina at Giebel
Old Klaus, road pushcart peddler, distributes broadsheets
Steinmetz, impoverished knight; living in the woods, foraging
    with his followers

The Peasants' War, Holy Roman Empire, 1525
100,000 villeins from across Germany, including miners, weav-
    ers, tillers
Goetz, leader of Gay Bright Troop of villein rebels, who betrays
    Florian Geyer
Stoller, knight of Lupfen
Balthus, knight loyal to Konrad
Muntzer, radical priest, foments revolt of villeins
Prince Georg Truchsess von Waldburg, leader of the Imperial
    Army

**At Vienna, the Imperial Court of Maximilian von Hapsburg,
    1526**
Konrad, having fled the fall of the Fortress Marienberg
Maximilian, Emperor of the Holy Roman Empire
Archduke Ferdinand, war financier of Imperial Army
The Duchess, admirer of Paulina
Cardinal von Wellenburg

At Passau, on the Danube, 1526
Paulina, formerly the Brethren Frieda
Willy, a turnkey bribed by Witter
Davo, Passau commercial printer of pornography
Gunther, luthier hired by Witter to transcribe Ausbund

The Prisoners of the Oberhaus
Ruta, seamstress seized for heresy
Hans Betz, Swiss Brethren, printer, teacher of literacy
Elizabeth, wife of Hans, printer, teacher

George, Swiss Brethren, printer, teacher
Marta, Swiss Brethren, typesetter, teacher
Leonard, Swiss Brethren, printer, teacher
Schneider, Swiss Brethren, printer, teacher, and known composer of some of the hymns of Ausbund

KRISTINA

The night's storm had turned to steam with the morning sun warming the ancient stone ramparts of the castle. From the casements she could see the land sweating clouds of fog into the sky.

In the bedchamber at the dressing table with Lady Anna, Kristina sat stiffly, and read aloud the frightening Veritas broadsheet, again and again. She felt her sheer gown clinging where her skin began to sweat. She trembled, but not from the heat of the rising day nor the damp of passing night.

"Must I read it again?" Kristina said.

Lady Anna paced about Kristina's stool. The lady wore only a day slip and no veil with her hair pinned back, and she could have been a serving maid, herself, for today she was careless of appearances.

"Yes. Read it once more, Kristina."

As if in reading it one more time, the meaning would somehow change, or hints of possible amnesty could be teased out. A fly alighted on Kristina's arm and she brushed it away. She did not want to read those words again, nor have them form in her throat, nor fly from her tongue.

"Once more, I say," said Anna.

Once more then, Kristina read it, aloud. She felt the unpleasant tingle where the fly had landed.

When she had read the Veritas broadsheet all again, there was a long, ugly silence, and finally Lady Anna said, "Nothing soft can be found. The Veritas publicists have damned Florian, and our estate, in every way conceivable."

The story denounced all of Giebel as a nest of vipers and evil. Florian was hell borne of serpents in a nest that must be burned out as one burns out a leper's cave; a vicious apostate who had insulted the honor of his betrothed and of all good Christians of the Holy Empire.

The broadsheet did more. It announced terrifying news—that three days from this printing a force from Wurzburg would seize Florian and take him alive if possible. If Florian were already dead by some desperate hand in that estate, it would save none; they would all be punished for harboring sedition. And, like Florian's English hero Wycliffe, who had translated the Bible into English common vernacular—held up as a crime so heinous—Florian's body too would be dug up and burned. The holy word could only be interpreted by holy men, not common folk.

A force was being sent from Wurzburg. They were coming. Veritas announced it boldly. It was as if no force on earth could stop them.

Kristina prayed, seeking guidance, and it felt like begging—

I am so afraid. What am I to do, Lord? What of my brothers and sisters? What of Lud? Most of all, what of my child?

"We shall not dwell upon this," said Lady Anna, rising suddenly, as if emerging from a spell. "This is a falsity of some kind. Konrad would never do such, and we shall trust in God."

Then, so oddly, the daily work went on.

Kristina cleaned and sewed and helped Leta with the wash and Lura in the scullery, as if this were any other day. Leta and Lura seemed stunned, refusing to speak. Kristina went back to Lady Anna's chambers with fresh linens.

Florian had locked himself away to meditate and to write his last will and testament.

"Let no sweet sounds interrupt our wretched deliberation," said Lady Anna, when Peter wanted to play the harp.

Peter screamed when the harp was removed from his reach to a place up high on a wall hook, where he leaped for it again and again. Kristina lifted him bodily and carried him out, down the stone stairs, outside into the sunlight. He wriggled free and spat at her and ran away like a little dog.

2

Peter, Peter, Peter…

What would happen to him if she were taken? How would he survive? Who would give him food? Who would shelter such a child?

She did not know how but she only knew that she had to stop this. Everyone and everything she loved was here.

She went to Lud and found him in the stable grooming his horse, Ox, but he could not help.

Said Lud, "You have two days to run. Take your child and food and a wagon and run. All men are brothers," accused Lud. "Is that not what you wanted, always?"

"Not this way, not with death and murder."

"Do not try to keep the people from fighting. You do harm to them. You want peace? You think love can save us? Pray to God and see how long we live. Will God bring down lightning bolts on the soldiers when they come to take us?"

The next words she spoke came from so deep in her that she fought to bring them up, to give them to him now…

"I care, Lud."

He did not stop brushing the horse.

"Everyone cares," he said.

"No. It is you. I care about you."

She saw him slow the brushing, saw him stiffen, and he took a long, deep breath before he spoke again.

"Your soft heart will get you and your boy killed. It is too late for saving such as me. This is the world of men, not God. Take your reformist dreamers and run. A few of us at least will put up a fight but it will be short. They will take a few days with tormenting and rapine and burnings."

"Lud, I cannot bear this. Will you die?"

He threw down the brush and turned to look at her.

"You say you care. Do you truly care?"

"You see that I do."

"You are a pretty woman, get away from this coming nightmare. Use that time to make distance. Think first of your little boy. While you can."

"Please, do not go out and kill and die, please."

Now he took her by the shoulders. She thought she would shrink back, wanted to shrink back, but she let him hold her. He came close and she saw only the liquid depths of his eyes, not the scars that encroached them.

Then, finally, he spoke—

"If you would let me, I would spend the rest of my days trying to make sweet that sad smile of yours."

"What are you saying?"

"I care for you. You know that. I know you know it. Tell Witter he must protect you to the end."

"Witter?"

"He is your man, and he must fight for you now."

She sensed that Lud feared what she would say next, that she loved Witter. She prayed that he wanted to take her, know her, have her forgive him for everything he was and had done. To love her as she did love him. More than flesh. That their souls would mingle, merge, become one soul.

"But Witter, he is..." she began to say.

Lud crushed out her words with his embrace and held her, long and gently and sweetly, and she let him, with surprise at his tenderness, at her own willingness, and at the feeling that went down through her to the core.

"Please," she said, "please do not go."

If I said I would not go, would you come lie with me? His eyes seemed to say this. She knew not how she felt it, knew it. But she did know. He thought it, but did not say it, for he loved her and knew she would not lie with him for that reason. And if she did lie with him, he would go anyway. She felt and realized all of this at once. He would go and fight and kill to try to save her.

"Tell me," he said, "that you will pray for me to kill many, before I die."

"I cannot pray for you to do murder."

"If you love your child, you will pray so."

"I pray for you not to go, not to kill."

"Pray that God is on my side, a little," said Lud.

4

"I pray that you will be on God's side."

"He made me for killing, your God. I will die before I see them hurt you or your child."

She thought of her mother in that moment and felt the old sense of being abandoned—her mother turning from her, leaving her; her mother going with the magistrates, and the monks begging her to recant; her mother leaving her forever. And why did it have to be?

Destroyed by cruelty, for resisting the forces of cruelty, with only the force of reason and love...

Lud turned from her and was gone from the stable. She wanted to chase after him but when he turned away it was as if he were rejecting her, quitting her, leaving behind anything she might feel or say or do now, now that it was all too late.

She went back to the castle to try to make sense of this fate that was coming to consume them all. She could never leave her child the way her mother had left her. And yet, if she did not, that would mean her mother had died in vain. Or did it? Was she wrong or was her mother wrong?

At the castle, Lura had put Peter to bed and he slept snoring on a cot in the kitchen. Lura, baking loaves in the oven and preparing a meal as if it were any other day, cutting up onions and potatoes with red eyes, told her what many in the village were saying. She looked worn out, and Kristina pulled on kitchen sleeves and an apron to help.

Said Lura, "Leta has not been back since yesterday. The villagers are fearful; that or outraged. Florian tells them he wants us all as his equals. He spouted fine words to them, and they ask how will the castle be served? How will the shares be done? Who will decide who gets what? How will votes be cast? How will a bishop be met and turned away? Some believe the end days have come, and those who read quote from the book of Revelations...a pale rider upon a pale horse..."

"Enough!" shouted Lady Anna. She stood on the kitchen steps and came down into the kitchen scullery.

Lady Anna swung between moods of black fury at her son's foolishness, and despair at a fate that could not be turned back. She shook her head and her long hair hung in her veiled face.

"Shall I go crawl and beg Konrad for mercy? My son is my lord, and to do such is betrayal of all. But not to do so is ruin."

Kristina said, "Lady, I cannot say."

"Speak your mind, girl."

"If killing can be averted, anything is wise."

"Anything, you say? Anything?"

"Lady, my only fear now is for my child."

Lady Anna paced beside the big bakery oven fire.

"Konrad loved me once, but long ago. Before my beauty was so ruined I might have softened his heart. He loved my Dietrich, I know he did, and he is godfather of Florian. How could my son have so wrecked our ancient estate? In one generation he has sunk us into such terror and sorrows."

"Lady, when people learn for themselves, when they learn to read, each becomes equal in awareness of right, and good, and faith. Your husband wished for that very good awakening. He said so as he died."

"Good? Is ruin good? Dietrich insisted our son be schooled in England. And how I fought it. But as a woman, I had no final say. Now we are left with absolute disaster. Florian will never bend, and we are all to serve as a grim example of Konrad's justice, and proof of his fair hand, even in the unspeakable cruelty surely coming."

"Cruelty," said Kristina.

"Yes, cruelty, the price of pride and folly."

The lady looked at her not with disdain but with the caring eyes of a mother. Kristina saw her fear making her weak, making her softer, and yet more honest somehow.

Kristina said, "Only love can conquer hate. Hatred cannot conquer itself. More hate breeds ever more hate."

"Love?" Lady Anna pulled back her veil and cautiously felt her face, her fingers moving over the corrugations that the pox had left there. "What can love do with cruelty? You urged communal sharing and that made them want more. You taught them to read and that made them unhappy. Your mother's example was not enough?"

Kristina stood and glared down at the despairing woman. The mention of her mother this way put fire in her.

"My mother taught others to read. To learn for themselves. She believed that the love of Christ could banish all cruelty from this world. And for that they destroyed her."

"You, too, are a mother and you must not be so destroyed."

So Kristina was silent.

She tried to take Peter with her when she left the castle but he clung to Lady Anna, and she waved Kristina away. Peter bounced on the lady's lap. Pulling her veil, her hair, her scarred nose.

"The bright child wants me. I love him being with me, playing for me, dressing him as I once dressed Florian, who no longer cares for me or anything but his sacred pride. Now he locks himself away to meditate, when all is threatened with doom. And here is Peter, one little person who truly cares about me. He will be here when you return. You and your people have to decide what you will do."

Witter and Grit and Dolf and Symon were already meeting together in the old stone barn where the printing press lay in a shattered heap.

They were arguing. Kristina could hear that no action could be agreed upon.

"Things are worse and worse everywhere," said Witter. "Desperate people rise up and are crushed back down. It seems that we are to be made an example of, to quell any possible rebellion."

Kristina still could not believe this was happening.

"Before we came, before they learned to read, they were ignorant of all that they have since read. We roused them from slumber. Can it be that teaching them to read has brought them to this willing violence? Is the terror to come to be laid for eternity, priced upon our own souls?"

"We roused them from blindness," said Grit. "What comes, comes. We do as we must. Teaching them to read was our duty. Now they must look to their own duty. Each bears one's own cross. Each must choose."

Said Witter, "I can tell you that they have no mercy. If they say they will destroy us, they mean to do it. I have come to know them only too well, too closely."

Kristina felt the world closing in upon them.

Said Dolf, "All the Giebel men are angry, even though afraid. They say we all have to fight or run. There are no other choices, they say."

Said Grit, "To fight and kill is to burn for eternity."

"We have two days on them," said Dolf. "We can go far in two days' hard march."

"Go where?" said Kristina. "Where will I go with my child as he is? How far must I go to protect him? And what of these folk? Do we abandon them? For eight years now, they have protected us from the outside."

Added Grit, "Taken us into their homes and many into their hearts. And we taught many to read. Our ideas have changed them. Much of what is coming is upon our heads, too."

"You take up a knife then, an axe?" said Symon.

"Foolish talk," Grit said. "Ask Witter, he has seen them."

Said Witter, "They have their magistrates and the Marienberg guard garrison, but all the Landsknecht mercenaries are away training in the field, and not that many of them anyway. The wealth extracted from the estates and guilds and city councils, in shares and in taxes, has engorged the military, and with the people's own sweat the princes build their power over all. That is how it always was and will ever be, anywhere you try to live."

"I read war accounts in the broadsheets," said Symon. "Is not the emperor Charles's army away fighting in Italy against Francois, the French king?"

"True," Witter said.

Said Symon, "Witter, what are the people saying in Wurzburg? I mean, the word in the street?"

Said Witter, "That the emperor is busy with his foreign war, his own backyard is open to foxes. He has his brother the archduke Ferdinand, up in Wurttemberg, running the league now. But they do not hold much authority over the princes who comprise the Swabian League. Wurzburg only joined the league upon Konrad becoming bishop. Their mercenaries are spread thin, from their headquarters in Ulm, from one end of southern Germany to the other. Florian knows this better than anyone. But if there is an uprising, the league will muster a new army no matter what the cost, be sure of that."

"Dear God," said Grit, upset. "Let us not read broadsheets of war, nor debate the random forces of murder."

"Then we do what? What?" said Dolf. He was choked with emotion. "Will God make their dogs lick me and their magistrates love me? Their soldiers not impale me, burn me? I say we run."

"I am not a fighter," said Witter. "But to run is to be hunted by dogs like wild animals and run down and butchered anyway."

Said Grit, "If we fight, we all die anyway, and then go burn forever in hell. If we run, we starve and freeze to death, unless the dogs and men take us and do with us the things they will do. We must save our souls and all those souls within our reach, however we can."

"However?" sobbed Symon, breaking down. "However? No matter what they do to us, when we are taken?"

Kristina felt Witter's hand gently touch her arm. She looked at him and he was looking at her with an unmistakable longing. There was love and fear in his eyes. He was so the opposite of Lud. In his soft, dark eyes was a tender sorrow, whereas in the defiant eyes of Lud was a fierce love.

And she realized she feared more for Lud's life now than for his soul. He would fight. Of that there was no doubt. If he fought he would die. Losing him would be terrible. Everyone, all, were going to die.

Yet she must save little Peter.

Said Witter, "There is only a chance, if we separate, all, in ones or twos, and depart in every direction at once, so that they cannot track us all. Some will be taken. Some may escape, once far enough away."

"No," Kristina said. "Peter could not last."

Said Grit, "We cannot abandon our brothers and sisters here. They will need us more than ever before. We must persuade them not to fight, not to harm others. We must fill them somehow with the loving will of Christ, and even if they submit and are cruelly used, to kill is worse, and we must help them in this fear."

Kristina closed her eyes, bent her head, and clenched her teeth, trying to accept Grit's words. But she could not. Whatever she had to do, whatever she had to submit to, she would save her boy, her Peter. She would. She must.

"But Peter, he is innocent, I cannot see him perish."

Grit put her arms around Kristina, holding her close.

"Did we come here to die?" said Dolf, as if it could not be true. "Is this to be our end?"

"Our end will be in the glory of heaven." Grit put her arms around Symon. She looked at them all. "I vote this—we stay and wait and trust God and hold fast to our faith. We are being tested. How we stand up to our fear, that is our trial, and our testament to others, and to Christ."

So they prayed.

And that was how they voted to stay.

It was not out of faith, Kristina realized, but truly out of not knowing any better way, for there was no escape.

Witter's way was impossible: to die like wild beasts. Kristina had been hunted before, with Witter, and she would never expose Peter to such terror. And yet by staying, she could not protect him nor save him, if they destroyed everything and everyone.

The thoughts rushed one upon another, unbearably real. She would never marry again, never know love again, never have another child.

Then she felt a terrible guilt, that along with her fear she held resentment of her boy, Peter...

And what of him? Does my faith hold for him, too? Does my pain stand for his pain, my life for his life? He will suffer from what I do. He is innocent. And what of him if I am gone? Will they put him to the sword? Burn him?

She realized that Grit had reached out and was holding her hand and singing, and then reluctantly, dolefully, Dolf and Symon were singing too...

"He makes wars cease to the ends of the earth,
He breaks the bow and shatters the spear,
He burns the shields with fire..."

10

LUD

The cocks crowed as if it were any other morning, yet the village was shut down as tightly as it had been years ago with the pox, when Lud and Dietrich had returned home with the boys from the border war. People had withdrawn behind closed doors. Only their dogs ranged about. Their owners had let them all run free and bark if strangers approached, to buy a little time.

The Giebel boys alone had taken some kind of action. They took turns posting themselves on the road at the edge of the estate. They took turns with the same horse, one Waldo had lent them from the stables. As if a few boys who had once carried pikes could stop what was surely coming.

It was the second night before the third morning and Lud spent hours readying himself for battle. It did not matter what others were doing. Perhaps some were doing the same. Others might have already run away, he did not know. It no longer was his concern. Whoever stood would die, therefore there was nothing left to lose.

He would stand between Florian and whoever came, whatever came, whatever numbers came. He would make his stand, it would be his last, and then his bad luck would be over.

No more longing for Kristina. From across the fields he had heard them in the old stone barn, singing their songs of peace.

He felt pity for them now. But none for himself.

He thought of Kristina's child, Peter—how she had named him for Simon Peter with his sword, whom Christ made into a pacifist— and how all things ended in death, by design. When he had learned to read and had read the Scripture story, he found it too hard to love a God that would let his own son be tortured to death. And Kristina's death was one thing he would never be forced to watch, or that of her poor sweet, yet almost uncontrollable, child.

He thought of the sweetness of kissing her. And of her confronting words pushed at him like daggers:

"I cannot pray for you to do murder."

"If you love your child, you will pray so."

"I pray for you not to go, not to kill."

All that had to be forced from the mind.

It would be all business now. No more grieving for what might have been. No more wearing the scarred mask of a face. But he would make the bastards pay. He would kill as many as he could before they cut him down. They would see what a Giebel man was made of. And some, at least a few, would take the true story of the fight back to the barracks. Soldiers had a way of finding their own truths.

His mind, as he armored up, ranged down the road and along the forest turns and the watering places, thinking which would be best for ambush. He had never been a good steward, but he would give them a very bad bargain in the matter of trading his life for as many of theirs as he could.

Layer by layer the armor came to protect his body. The quilted tunic first, then the mail shirt, then the outer breastplate. He thought of the big breastplate for Ox, and his head plate, too. Like his own armor, the overlap of the plates was critical, and the leather straps had to pull tight, so that no bolt or ball or blade could go between. The longer it took to kill him the more of them he would take.

It was the good black armor that Dietrich had given him years ago, dented and pocked like his face. Many points of iron and lead had sought his life but the old sheet iron had saved him. A smile crept upon his face and he felt it there. He realized he was almost beginning to look forward to this.

They would come arrogantly in formation on the road, not cautiously through the woods.

The best luck would be if the fortress guard, in their finery, were sent. They had not trained for months, if ever. They were soft and spoiled from the city, used to parading, and they would not want to die.

The officers and monks would be back behind the vanguard. He would let the vanguard pass first and then take the monks, who would be easy to take. Then the officers would come to defend the monks, and all would be in disarray, and he would take as many officers as he could.

But if they sent mercenaries, even half-trained ones, that would be much harder. Still, they would not be ready to die, not willing to die, as he was. And that gave him an incredibly powerful edge. He would move fast and kill many. Then he would be dead. They would have no chance to torment Florian. No chance to snare and torment either of them. It would all be over. He would not live to see everyone he loved destroyed.

God's whims would be finished. Or maybe he would discover there was no god at all. That it was all random, meaningless, and that the universe had never meant him any special harm. That would be disappointing, for he had many complaints to take from this world when he left it.

Lud finished tugging the last harness straps. He stretched and swung his arms and made last adjustments. The range of motion was good. He was harnessed and began arming himself. His weapons lay together on his straw bed. His little family of steel. Always faithful.

The little gutting dagger for last, the long sword for a clash, a crossbow first for possible ambush. He was feeling the weight of too much metal and realizing he needed more balance for better speed.

Waldo was at the door. Mutely he knocked, then he was making signs. Gesturing urgently.

Someone came to the stable.
Someone took a horse.
Florian took a horse.
Florian rode out.
Out toward Wurzburg.
Armed.

WITTER

Witter saw the world changing, as if he were watching through the peephole of his weeping room all those years ago.

People learned to read and realized too many things, and now demanded freedom and equality. They would fight and die for it. The greatest irony was that he and the Christian pacifists like Kristina and Grit had taught them to read. And what they read had incited them—not to peace, not to love of all men, but to violence.

Worse, he had broken his most fundamental rule of survival— allowing himself to care for the life of another.

Kristina would not run with him and he had tried all night to unclench himself from thoughts of her and to make himself go away from this place. The more time that passed, the less distance he could put between himself and the oncoming disaster. There still had to be some way to make all of this stop; some way to save Kristina. But he had nothing but his brain and his dagger, and both were impotent.

He had left the others praying and singing in the printing barn. Alone on his knees in the hut of the village square, he had tried to pray to Yahweh, then to Judah, his father, for guidance. But it had been as expected. He heard nothing come back but that echo of his own mind's voice. They had all given up on him.

Finally, Witter forced himself to go to the stables.

He was going there to try to make himself take the Marienberg horse and ride away. But near the stables, he stopped. He saw Lud come running, cursing, creaking in his battered old armor, with his weapons. Lud had taken his own big warhorse and ridden out like a madman.

Witter stepped behind a stable wall until they were gone. The village dogs outside were barking like mad.

Then came Lady Anna. Lura was with her, holding a lantern. In a sleeping robe, Lady Anna ran from house to hut to house banging on the doors, her hair and scarred face appearing wild, screaming…

"Florian has gone to fight them, my Florian! To arms! Come out!"

And then, quickly, Witter wrapped his riding cloak tight, sashed it, pulled up the collar, and got his own horse saddled.

As he pulled open the big doors of the stables he saw villagers pouring from their homes. The young ones and old ones, too, both men and women. Some had lanterns, and most carried weapons, old swords, harvest knives, farm implements, scythes, axes, hoes, shovels. Sig hefted a huge grain flail and Merkel carried his big anvil sledgehammer.

"Help my Florian!" Lady Anna kept shouting.

The mob roiled and shouted in confusion. He saw Grit and Kristina come out among them, arms raised beseechingly, and try to reason with them.

"No, friends," cried Grit, waving her arms, "do not give yourself to this madness, stop with us and pray!"

It was no use. Grit tried to throw herself in front of some of them but Kristina pulled her back, for they shoved Grit aside, as if not even seeing her.

Witter heard Kristina shouting at him.

"Help us stop them, Witter!"

But he too felt the urge to go. The villeins were swarming as if compelled by some primal sense that hearkened back to tribal energy, ancient and pure and wild. He felt himself part of this. It held a tidal power, sweeping them all forward together in one fierce collective resolve.

Some held back and tried to stop others, but most were moving. Children were trying to join the rush but women and the older villeins were fighting them and holding them back.

"Giebel!" they shouted. "Florian! Giebel!"

The horse was jerking, startled by the shouts, and Witter was swinging up in the saddle and trying to get up the reins, with the nervous horse turning round and round in confusion, when he heard Kristina again cry out his name.

"No, Witter, no!"

But he leaned over the hard-muscled neck of the animal and goaded the horse's flanks with his heels, hard once, and it plunged forward and away, quickly leaving behind the surging mob. He went out of the gates and down the road, like a hawk flying low over the road, feeling light as air.

Out in the open, the big horse stretched out, opening its stride and taking speed, as if glad to escape the noisy, milling human mob. It dumped dung from its lifted tail and its head was pumping up and down, its breath in loud reports.

Riding fast, the air was much colder. Ahead, Witter saw moonlit dust from other horses, sparkling in the frosty air over the road. Lud was up there somewhere.

The small and great are there; and the servant is free from his master...

A great weight had fallen away from him. Witter rode out hard, filled with that same impossible emotional anger, that state of crazy grace that had driven him that day he had run down the two magistrates. He had been on this same horse. The city mob had cheered. His exultation had made him a free man, even if only for a few minutes.

The nausea of fear was gone. He had simply let it go. The sense of release from all his dread and fear made him feel as if he had taken something incredibly sacred down from the altar of his father.

After a few miles, he saw a pack of dogs running ahead. No doubt they had run with Florian and then Lud until the horses left them behind.

Witter quickly overtook and passed the dogs, startling them, and they broke up to dodge the big thundering horse. Looking back he saw them form a pack again behind him. Two or three big dogs led out front and all kinds and shapes swarmed together, like a school of fish. His fast horse quickly left them behind.

Riding was natural to him now and he leaned over the horse's big pulsing neck and let the horse have its head.

Witter heard himself shout—

"*Yaaa! Yaaaaa!*"

Insane sounds. Bursts of rebellious joy. Rejection of everything that had ever constrained him.

The horse went even harder, with surging long strides. He knew that Florian had ridden out to die and now Lud and Waldo were riding hard to join Florian, and he too was riding after them. He had no idea what he would do when and if he could catch them.

He would defend. He would put himself between the force of killers who were coming and Kristina. He was living moment to moment. And he knew only one thing—that whether he lived or was about to be killed, he felt liberated from his reasoning mind that had held all his fears.

For the first time since he had been a child, Witter felt free. Free of the fear that had been his master.

I am a free man...

LUD

Riding hard, Lud focused on the road ahead, but his thoughts plunged inward the way they did sometimes when life was too strange. He thought of a book he had read, from Dietrich's library. He had chosen it because it was so worn and he knew Dietrich must have loved it well. It was *Psychomachia*, and Dietrich had penned on the title page that this meant "the struggle for the soul." Inside, there was a passage Dietrich had framed with his quill and ink, and so Lud had memorized it....

> *First of the fighters to face the field*
> *and the doubt of the duel's fate,*
> *Faith came forward, disheveled and messy,*
> *dressed like a farm girl from far in the country:*
> *bushy hair untrimmed with bowl or beautician,*
> *shoulders bared to give biceps an airing.*
> *Heat to get glory had her boiling over*
> *all of a sudden, in fact, for this new deed.*
> *War nor weapons nor girding of armor—*
> *she paid no nevermind.*
> *Trusting the might*
> *of her heart and her hands, raging and reckless,*
> *she challenges battle-chance, meaning to smash it...*

Why this came to him now, riding hard to his certain death, he could not know. Only that it felt important, as if it held prophecy of relevant meaning, like a dream that tries to explain a misunderstood event, or an event soon coming.

Now the road twisted and ahead he saw Florian in the middle of the road. Florian sat his horse there, at the edge of the Geyer estate and its fields, where the road went into the great forest.

The moon was almost down and the first purple light of dawn was coming, with streaks of gold in the east. Florian, he saw, was not wearing the shiny new armor. He wore the old black gear that must have been his grandfather's.

Lud slowed Ox to a walk and Waldo came behind.

"So you found me," said Florian. "And you wear your Turkish sword. Did you come for a fight?"

"I did not expect you to come alone and face them alone, and act the fool," Lud said. "You were always the one who quoted all the wise men."

"Is it the fool who makes a stand?"

"Pride is not enough, Florian."

Florian looked at the faintly dawning sky. "It is the dawn of the third day. When Konrad's broadsheet said they would come to take me. They will be here. Go home, Lud."

"Did you think that your death alone would satisfy them? They are coming to take all, everything and everyone."

"This is not your fight."

"The hell it is not my fight. I wait with you. Or we go together and intercept them."

"I wait here. At my own border. My own land. Go home. Go away. I order you."

"You said we are brothers now. Your orders mean nothing, unless you lied when you said it."

"Take whoever you love and go away."

"I will make you a bet, Florian. You go in the woods to the left and I go into the woods to the right, and I wager I will kill three flankers for each one you kill, before they turn."

"How can we settle the bet? In the next world?"

"Geyer credit is good with me, even in eternity."

"I will save a nice hot rock for you."

Waldo made a sound.

Lud turned and saw Witter coming. They all turned and stared. Witter rode up, breathless, wearing a winter robe, unarmored, unarmed. He pulled in his horse and it turned sideways to the other horses.

"What in the hell do you think you are doing here?" said Lud.

"I do... not... know," said Witter, gasping.

"If prayer is your weapon, do ride back the way you came," said Florian. He handed Witter his short sword, the kind that line troops jokingly called *monk-gelders*, and Witter took it as gingerly as if it were a snake. "Take care, that edge will shave hair."

"Better he pray," said Florian, with a smirk.

Said Lud, "Your father, Dietrich, always told me, 'Pray before a battle and rejoice after.'"

"He believed in life. Pray for us sinners now and at the hour of our death, the priests say. Not my father."

They shared a wistful smile.

"Would that he were here now," said Florian.

Lud said, "All he had he put into his son."

Florian reached out and laid his armor-gloved hand on Lud's armored forearm. There were no words to say what would have meant more to Lud than the look that Florian now gave him.

"All men are brothers," said Florian. "That was father's fondest dream."

"Perhaps, someday," said Lud.

Then came the pack of village dogs. Panting, tongues hanging out, they went running past the horses, then they all turned and gathered around the horses, sniffing the horses, the men, and one another. They wagged their tails and whined and squirmed for approval from the riders. The horses stirred but were used to dogs. Then one of the smaller dogs lifted a leg on Ox's hind leg and peed, and Ox's tail whacked it away, yelping.

Waldo laughed. He was mute but he could laugh. His laugh broke the grimness and their tension eased.

Lud laughed.

"We make a fine sight," said Florian, and laughed.

"The bastards will fear us now," said Lud.

They laughed again, louder. Even Witter laughed.

Lud's laughter cleansed him and he felt as if he coughed out a filth of evil spirits, and then he realized that it was fear that the laughter chased out.

"I think the whole village will be coming," said Witter.

"What?" said Florian.

The laughter stopped.

"Your mother roused them to arms," said Witter.

Florian rolled his eyes. "Dear God in heaven above."

"Good," said Lud. "Good woman."

"Yes," said Florian. "Yes, none finer. But the villagers, they are villeins, tillers, how can they fight, with what?"

Said Lud, "This time they let the dogs run out. Are they less than their dogs?"

"Dogs and all will be killed. It is my fault."

"For not begging?" said Lud.

"Yes," said Florian, evenly, "for not begging."

"Hear your father's words, from me. Many say that it is better to die on your feet than to live on your knees. But your father would say it differently—better to die fighting than any other way slower."

Now Witter spoke. "Each owns his own honor until he gives it up. My father taught me that. Or he tried to."

"Truly," said Florian.

"Enough philosophy and posturing," said Lud. "There are good narrow places ahead to trim their flanks. Our only chance is to kill their commanders. But this time they will be back in the train far behind the vanguard."

But it was too late.

There was sudden movement in the tree shadows far ahead on the road.

Lud leaned forward on Ox, squinting, staring hard. From the deep forest shadows emerged a single figure. Carrying an axe. Running toward them. Then two more.

The shapes emerged in dozens from the deep tree shadows and took form in the road light, hurrying behind the first figure, trying to catch up to it. The first three forms ran like devils escaping hell. Then Lud recognized the first one.

It was Linhoff, tall and lanky and running scared. Lud cranked the old crossbow, careful not to wind it back more than six turns lest the ratchet slip. It creaked with increasing tension and then the pawls clicked and the trigger set. The horse pawed, hearing the pawls clicking.

The dogs began barking at the distant shapes.

"Linhoff?" said Florian.

There was shouting now. From up the road.

"What is he saying?" said Florian.

Then Lud realized what they were shouting—

"They come! They come!"

WITTER

Seeing Lud and Florian and Waldo turn their mounts and draw their swords, he realized that something had changed him forever.

The old blackish, crawling fear was gone. There was no fear at all, only that mad exultation of being a free man. Free of his dread. Free of all that had enslaved his soul.

He could hear the marching drumbeat now of approaching troops. Then he saw the cavalry vanguard riding out front, all gold and red pennants and flashing armor. The road was narrow there and they rode only four abreast.

Linhoff and Ambrosius and Max reached Lud and Florian and ran past them, but stopped behind the horses.

"Report," said Florian, simply.

Linhoff panted it out, "Ten...horse...forty...foot...and... monk's carriage in the van..."

"That is all?" said Florian.

"Plenty enough," said Lud.

"I will ride forward and try to negotiate," said Florian.

"No," Lud said. "They will take you."

"I said I will try."

"I will gut your horse first, young sir," said Lud. He hooked Florian's reins in one hand and held tight.

"Let go of my reins, damn you," said Florian.

Said Lud, "You say all men are brothers, we stay together and fight together and die together, if damned is what it is to be. Together. That was your father's way and it is my way. So damn me all you will."

"Then damn us both together," said Florian.

The horses began to move and the pack dogs moved with them.

A revelation pierced his mind with an astonishing force: when one was willing to die for love or dignity or beliefs, or even anger, one was absolutely free, and nothing could harm one further.

His horse took speed under him. Ahead of him, Lud and Florian and Waldo were riding forward, swords out, straight at the oncoming force. He had the leather-sheathed short blade Florian had given him and it flapped on his saddle where he had thrust it under the girth strap, futile, something he would never use for any reason.

It was not madness, thought Witter, goading his horse. All his life he had feared taking action. He had dreaded all such impulses as surrender to insanity. But this was freedom. This was sanity. Like letting go of an anchor that had been dragging him down into a bottomless blackness. Like shedding the weight of the coins in his cloak that night years ago, in the river, and clawing his way back up to the world of air.

He had feared such men all his life, had loathed and despised and dreaded them, and now he had joined himself to them.

All seemed crystal. All was clear now. He let everything go, on the back of this horse with the first comrades of his life, all of them flying in the teeth of fear, with this freedom such as he had never before known—something no philosophy nor wisdom had ever taught him, no religion nor prayer had ever given him, this wonderful liberating sanity.

Looking past Lud and Waldo and Florian surging ahead of him in the pounding dust, he saw the dogs with their happy jaws askew, tongues red and teeth showing, and ahead of them the force of marching men and pennants and cavalry stopped, their poise lost as they pointed and shouted.

One way or the other now it is done...

Then there was screaming and he was screaming, too.

LUD

Twenty of horse and sixty foot, he reckoned. The monks would be behind, with the squadron of magistrates and their capture wagons of chain and yokes. On their flanks came pikemen, but their pikes flew gold pennants—all bore the bishopric cross, twined with a vine of thorns, signifying Christ's suffering for the sins of this world. All of this Lud took in at an instant, his mind seeing then rejecting everything except their number and formation and the weakness of their flanks.

He drove Ox hard and shouldered Florian's mount aside, so that he was just ahead of Florian, to give Florian a better chance to live a few moments longer. Twenty yards ahead, the Giebel dogs collided with the Wurzburg war dogs in a snarling mad scramble. Ox ran through the dogfight, straight at the Wurzburg men of horse.

He expected now to be killed. A lead ball would pierce his armor, or a steel bolt. As Ox drove forward, he knew he should already be dead from musketry and crossbolts but he was not dead. Then he saw why. Their ranks were breaking into disorder.

Now he saw the bolts flying from the trees into the mass of Wurzburg men. Their column was being attacked from the woods on both sides. Lud glimpsed ragged shapes and black armor and he suddenly realized who it was.

The band of Steinmetz was attacking the Wurzburg force. They were in the woods on either side of the road firing crossbows into the flanks of the oncoming column. Cries and shouts erupted from startled soldiers and monks and magistrates.

It was the rogue knight and his bunch he had met one day in the far wild woods of the estate, and who had let them be.

Under the withering flanking attack, the Wurzburg column was folding back upon itself, breaking ranks, the whole formation balling up backward down the road.

Beside him, Lud saw Florian with his sword out but hesitating, not cutting down men with backs turned. Florian had never butchered men before.

He drove Ox forward, sword high.

"Drive them!" he shouted at Florian.

Ox crashed into the front of their line where their line of cavalry had turned away to the flanks. His crossbow took one of them and he threw it at another.

Lud drove Ox deeper into them, using his sword, cutting them down, every one of them he could, back or front, but avoiding their pikes farther back in the bunched mass. He saw Waldo on the other side of Florian, silently cutting and hacking, and then Florian was doing his share, screaming at his own work.

Under the horses' hooves the big war dogs were killing the Giebel dogs, but the war dogs were outnumbered and being mauled. Some began to run away and some were dead.

Three pikemen rallied, he saw, and one gutted Waldo's horse. Waldo was pinned by their pikes, lurching in his saddle. Florian was in a sword duel with a Wurzburg cavalryman and did not see Waldo.

Lud turned Ox and tried to reach Waldo, but he saw Waldo falling and the pikes driving through him. Waldo's horse raced away disemboweled with its red guts looping behind, bouncing on the road.

In the swarming fight up the road, Lud saw Linhoff and Ambrosius and Max using their pikes together as he had taught them years ago, and Florian was on his horse using his sword. Lud saw the ragged knights in old black armor among them. With pike and sword now they were working in one strong line, fighting as comrades in good order, driving the mass of Wurzburg soldiers back. Now the magistrates were swinging their chains wildly and trying to make a stand.

Old Steinmetz shouted in beats like a war drum.

"Drive them! Drive them! Drive them!"

Lud's horse stumbled on the bodies of men from the Wurzburg column, and he saw a pike coming and jerked Ox away from the stabbing point, and Ox reared and Lud went tumbling off the horse's back, falling and rolling and losing his Turkish sword. He fell hard onto dead men and dead dogs.

In the bloody dust he struggled for breath and rolled away from the thrust of a pike. The three Wurzburg pikemen were chasing him along the ground, and he was crab crawling, his dagger out, trying to scramble to his feet.

They were experts, veterans, he knew now, and they worked as a team. Spreading apart, they surrounded him on three sides and he knew he could only kill one before he died.

Suddenly a horse came charging through them.

Witter—leaning low with no weapon, but running the big animal straight into the three pikemen, to break up the deadly tripod trapping Lud. The pikemen whirled to dodge the horse and to spear it, and Lud got to his feet.

Pikes just missed Witter's face.

Witter's saddle hung half off and it knocked one of the pikemen aside. Lud got in a dagger thrust at the pikeman's ankle tendon, and the pikeman fell shrieking. Lud blocked a pike thrust with the dagger but it was knocked from his hand. He sidestepped, grabbed up a fallen pike, and faced the other two. They came right at him without hesitation, good soldiers with his killing in mind. He tried to see where Florian was, and that was a mistake; he tripped backward over a dead dog. The two pikeman came at him.

Witter turned his horse and came charging back. Now the pikemen turned at Witter, lifting their pikes, spearing Witter's horse, both pikes going deep into the neck, the horse tumbling and Witter flying off, and from behind, Lud cut the throat of the closest pikeman.

The third pikeman hurried to catch Witter, but Witter was scrambling away, and Lud caught the pikeman first, grabbing his hair from behind and jerking him backward off his feet, killing him with a neck twist.

"Look!" cried Witter.

Suddenly, Lud heard behind him some great roaring, louder and louder. He turned to face whatever it was. Then he stared and could not believe what he saw.

Half of Giebel village was coming, a mob on the run, some silent, some shouting, all of them waving tools and shovels and axes…

KRISTINA

K ristina hardly recognized anyone now.

Armed with anything metal they could find, some only with wooden grain flails and bull clubs, men and women alike came pouring down the road in one shapeless seething mass of resolve. Their faces jerked and twisted.

Grit had begged and pleaded with them not to violate the holy command of Christ, to not do murder, to love their enemies. Only Grit tried to argue, to beseech.

"Your souls, Brothers and Sisters, your immortal souls!"

And now they all had gone out there to defend the others or to die. Only the eldest stayed back, and they were busy keeping the village children in check, pulling them back into huts and houses.

Kristina had stopped with Grit by the village gates and tried to speak.

"Brothers, no, Sisters, wait…"

They did not listen. She did not want Lud to die. She did not want Witter to die. But they were surely being killed or they were already dead by now.

"Me go!" a child shouted somewhere. "Me go!"

Kristina recognized the cry and felt as if her heart were being ripped from her breast. She turned and saw, up on the castle chamber balcony, Lady Anna standing with little Peter. The lady wore no veil now and her face shone with tears. Peter was shouting and trying to break free, but Lura was there, too, helping hold the child fast. Wherever others ran, Kristina knew, Peter wanted to run with them. Kristina felt torn apart between the urge to run to her child, and her desperation to stop the madness that was consuming the whole village now.

"Madness, madness," said Grit, despairing. "It is like trying to stop a flood. They have all lost their minds, their souls."

"They all go to kill or to die," said Dolf.

"Their village is their whole world," said Symon.

Kristina looked at him. Dolf and Symon stood by the village gates, staring in wonder.

"And Witter, too," said Grit.

"And Lud," said Kristina.

"They are victims," said Grit. 'They have all been maddened by the evil of their fear. Whatever we can do, we must help the wounded."

"Not I," said Dolf. "No use, not this time."

"All will be slaughtered," said Symon.

"We must give mercy," said Grit.

Dolf gripped Grit by her arms. "No, Grit."

"Let me go."

"Please, no," said Dolf, his milk eye rolling in fear.

"Damn you, Dolf," Grit said.

And Dolf released her, shocked.

"Forgive me," said Grit, "I did not mean that."

Kristina felt as if the whole world were crystalline and fracturing as if dropped from a great height, breaking apart relentlessly, crack by crack, around her.

"Brother, do forgive me," Grit said again, not moving.

"It must be the End of Days," said Dolf.

"We are sent here for a reason," said Kristina. "But what is it, truly?"

Said Grit, "We stand in an abandoned village. A madness has seized our brothers and sisters and they are gone to do murder. All of our years of work here, all our teaching, has changed nothing. The command of Christ has changed nothing. Nothing."

Kristina stood there as if pinned to the spot and she looked up past the great old linden tree at the balcony where Lady Anna and

Lura held little Peter. Peter was struggling and the two women wore tragedy in their faces.

Said Symon, "We can do nothing. All will be dead."

Kristina's mind flashed upon her encounter with Lud in the battle so long ago, how she had feared and loathed him then. And then, under Dietrich's command, Lud had fought a death match—challenged by the linemaster—with knives, to defend the Giebel wagon. And if Lud had lost, she and her sisters would have been given to the soldiers. She and Grit and Frieda.

And now again Lud was rushing headlong to his death, in yet another defense. And Witter was hurrying away to join him.

Lud and Witter. Witter and Lud.

Suddenly, Kristina felt an overwhelming urge. She realized that she was running down the road. Running hard.

Please do not let him be dead…

Peter's shrill voice was shouting, receding behind her.

"Kristina!" called Grit, coming after her.

Then they were running together. Her goatskin housework slippers tore and flapped and flew off, one then the other, and she ran barefooted on the hard, gritty road, churning up the cold dust.

In her heart there burned a sharp stabbing heat, and one man's name compelled her.

WITTER

Witter sat slumped, as if he were dead, against the side of his dead horse, the animal's ribs still hot. His long cloak was soaked with sweat. It hung as slack on him as the wet hair that stuck to his face. The horse lay staring with the broken pike half through its neck. It had been born in Giebel and groomed by Waldo, and now all that was over. Its long-lashed, unseeing brown eyes were already turning milk blue, unblinking to the flies.

What part did I have in this?

Around him and the horse, three pikemen lay askew, like fallen dancers frozen in absurd postures, marionettes with their strings cut. With their armor now stripped and gone, they looked foolish, pathetic. And things had been done to them, so Witter made an effort not to look directly at them.

What is my share?

The air stank. It was the same stench of the hog and lamb slaughter days in the village. The bend in the road was pocked with pools of dark red blood, and dusty pieces of human bodies—a hand, a head, a foot. One dead man lay with his legs entangled in pink ropes. Witter, staring, realized the ropes were his insides.

Not since Spain and the worst days of the Inquisition had he seen anything like it, nothing even close. The villagers prowled among the dead, some cursing, some weeping. All of the force from Wurzburg was dead or dying—hacked into silence with shovels and grain flails, pounded with hammers, cut with stock knives and cleavers. Some of the injured were still crying out for mercy. The farmers who broke the earth now broke their enemies with the same husbandry, the same resolve.

His mind tried to refuse all of this but here it was. He remembered something Maimonides had said about reality, and it only increased his sense of not being here...

You must accept the truth from whichever source it comes...

So this was truth. Weapons and armor were being pulled from fresh, limp, hacked corpses by a priest and by unknown ragged men, some in old black armor. Witter tried to fix it into logic but it was all fragmented and too strange to reckon with. He knew he should feel horror. But nothing came. In hell, all seemed normal.

There was a priest.

Witter stared and realized that the priest was Father Michael. It could not be—but it was him.

Witter sat there on the stilled rib cage of the animal, feeling like an island. No longer did he feel part of the village. He no longer recognized the village or anyone in it. Strangeness and death were all he saw. And the metallic stench of blood made him sink to his knees and then he retched out all his insides into the bloody dust of the road.

"You saved my life," said a voice.

Witter looked up from his retching, up into a shadow with arms hanging wearily.

It was Lud. A dagger hung from his right hand.

"The horse did, not me," said Witter.

"You wear the look of shame."

"Leave me alone."

"You were a man, when you did what you did."

"I helped you kill them."

"I was a dead man."

Witter struggled to his feet. Lud stood with slumped shoulders. He looked smaller than he had before, somehow. His scarred face was coated with dust and spots of blood.

Behind them, the last of the killing had stopped and now the village women wailed over their dead. Some of the men were doing obscene things to the dead monks and magistrates who had come to arrest them.

"How can you allow this?" said Witter, sickened.

"They are not soldiers. They have lost friends and loved ones. Such killing is new. It has shocked them."

"But not you."

"Each in his own way. That is not my way."

Witter reached out a hand and touched Lud's shoulder and Lud jerked as if waking from a dream.

"Lud, if you are grateful, for God's sake, make it stop. Why are you not making them stop?"

"There's the priest, Michael, he was with the knights doing much of the killing. Ask him why."

"It is all lunacy," Witter said.

Lud turned to move away. Then he said, "That was a good horse. Waldo would have wept for him but Waldo is dead. Next time, use the blade."

"There will be no next time," Witter said.

"Hell has come home, Witter. Run away, Witter. Run or fight."

Then someone else stood there. Witter looked up.

It was Florian, with a bloody hand on Lud's shoulder. Witter stared. They looked almost like brothers, Lud the older, Florian the younger, with the scars of time and war making Lud seem ancient, yet his eyes still young. Lud shied from Florian's hand on his shoulder, and stood away.

"You saved my life," said Florian.

Lud said, "We have started something here that will not end until we are all dead."

"You are wrong," said Florian. "On this day, we have begun a change that the world shall never forget."

Lud motioned up the road with his hand. Witter saw the magistrate wagons being turned upright and horses hitched. The village was loading up its wounded and dead. Some were weeping, some cursing. They moved wearily, like shapes in a dream.

"Tell that to them," said Lud.

KRISTINA

Turning the corner of the road, hurrying, panting, she saw where the fight had been, ahead. Bodies everywhere. People loading dead and wounded into wagons.

"They are not all dead," said Grit, "but many are wounded."

Beside her, Grit began to run again.

Now in the distance they saw the first stripped bodies of magistrates among the tangled bodies of dead dogs and horses.

"Do you see Lud?" said Kristina. "Witter?"

"No, nor Linhoff," Grit said anxiously.

Kristina looked at her, hearing her. Grit's voice bore a soft deep urgency that Kristina recognized as caring, desperate and urgent caring. It was the sound of love, the needful sound in a voice that only one woman can hear and know in the voice of another woman.

"My Linhoff," said Grit, "dear God, I must find him."

And then Kristina stopped. She saw the first dead man up close, his body askew, stripped naked, and closer, she saw the terrible wounds and some looked like mutilations.

"Dear Christ," panted Grit. "Oh dear Christ in heaven…"

Kristina could not tell if the wounds were from fighting or after, but they were all shaped by madness.

Grit said, "We should have been here trying to stop it."

"Who has done this?" Kristina whispered, aghast.

"Do not ask. They were not in their right minds."

"We should have been here."

"Yes. We should have been. Beseeching on our knees, sobbing and praying. Like an island in the nightmare, hoping our prayers could stop this, until we, too, were cut to pieces. Now we are here, so let us give aid."

Lud, thought Kristina…

For the next hours, Kristina saw the world as she had never seen it before.

First, she found Witter sitting on the dead horse with his head in his hands. She knelt beside him and tried to take his hands but he would not even look at her.

"Witter, thank God, praise Him, I feared for you so."

Witter shook his head and shut his eyes against her.

"Go away. Do not look upon this. Go."

"Is Lud… slain?"

"Alive when last I saw him," said Witter, eyes shut.

And Kristina felt her heart leap.

"Does that make you so happy?" said Witter. Now he opened his red eyes, and glared at her, and she felt an unfathomable pain coming from him.

She touched his arm.

"I thank God you are alive, Witter."

Witter shook off her hand and waved a hand toward a mass of men up the road. "He will be with the other killers."

"Who are the men in black armor?" she said.

"Rogues. Beggar knights. Living in the woods. Now go away from me. Do not look at me. Go."

And she hurried up the road, past the dead, trying not to look at them, but glancing so as not to step upon any.

She hoped that it was the rogue knights, not the villagers, who had cut the throats of the wounded magistrates and soldiers.

She saw the villagers had gotten most of the weapons and armor and the men looked like bandit rogues in the odd gear worn over their farming robes. Half a dozen villagers were wounded. Those in the formation from Wurzburg were all dead, save one who took a message back to Konrad.

The people of Giebel carried or dragged all the bodies into the woods. The soldiers they stripped and left for wild beasts. The beloved dogs were wrapped in the cloaks of the dead, and with lolling tongues and staring eyes, buried with prayers. All tenderness was lavished upon them, as if from the earlier savagery some goodly love could be salvaged. Many wept.

Kristina did not know which way to look. In all directions the terribleness was so relentless. And yet she searched for Lud.

Waldo was dead. She could not believe he could be dead, such a force of life, but there he lay, with women kneeling over him, cherishing him.

A man cried out and Kristina turned and saw Ferde, the cobbler and harness maker. He had gone half mad and was talking to himself, led about by Merkel like a child. Ferde's grandson, Ambrosius, had a head wound that made him fight and scream, and Max and Linhoff held him down until he finally died.

Please God, help them, help this, make it stop...

Kristina looked at the surviving villagers and at the men in black armor. She saw the priest, Michael, then Florian, and she wondered who of them had done the terrible thing to the dead of the force from Wurzburg.

And then she realized it was not yet finished. Moans. Growls. Cries. The scrape of steel.

"Some are killing the wounded," said Grit urgently. "Lud is over there by himself, he does not stop it."

Lud stood away by some trees, leaning on one, and Kristina looked at him. Lud saw her. He turned his back to it all, and to her.

The last of the Wurzburg wounded were being slaughtered on the ground. Some of the older men who had been Sig's friends were doing most of the killing now, Merkel leading them.

Kristina stood back and tried to hold Grit back.

Kristina dared not interfere but she screamed at them.

"Brothers, stop, he was alive!"

"Help me stop them," said Grit.

Grit moved now and grabbed to pull the men away from the dying man in their midst, and they raged at her and threw her back hard and Grit stubbornly tried again to stop them. Kristina stood there too afraid to move.

They punched Grit, sending her onto her knees. Kristina helped Grit up and Grit was stunned, her nose bloody. She was not angry but devastated, and Kristina felt terror now. She did not know these people. They were as savage as the dogs that had run her down in the woods so long ago.

"Enough," Lud's voice said.

Suddenly, Lud was there and it all stopped.

"Save your blows for the fights to come," said Lud to the men who stood there. "You are all marked men for the rest of your lives and you will be fighting to stay alive until they hunt you down and kill you."

The men stood panting, wild-eyed, their hands bloody up to their elbows, as on slaughter day.

"Tell those women to stay out of our way," said Merkel.

"Let us tend the wounded," said Grit with her nose leaking blood. "Please."

"Our true Giebel women tend our wounded," said Merkel. "You do not belong with us. All your talk of peace and love only weakens what we must do now."

Kristina pulled Grit away and sat with her on a fallen tree at the roadside, in the deepening shadows.

Lud looked down at Kristina.

"I am so glad to see you alive," said Kristina. She stood and wanted to put her arms around him, to embrace him, but he stared like a tree, his eyes hard in his dark face.

"Why are you here?" he said, his words hard, too. "What draws you to this?

"I was afraid for…"

"Witter is unwounded," said Lud, cutting off her words. "Go to him. Make him take you from here."

I was afraid for you, Lud…

"Are you not a mother? Why are you not with the other mothers and their children? Why are you not with your child? Take him and run where none can ever find you."

Then he turned and walked away.

"He is so hard, so cruel," said Kristina.

Said Grit, "Let us do whatever there is to be done. I am all right. In my old life I was hit much harder. They are not themselves. Do not judge them, Kristina."

No one was burying the dead from Wurzburg, so Grit and Kristina took shovels and began to dig holes in the woods.

Dolf and Symon came and had shovels and began their own holes, digging silently.

Kristina's shovel was splashed with blood and she dared not think what murder the farm tool had done.

Grit began to sing softly as she dug,

"When the last trumpet's awful voice,

This rending earth shall shake,

When opening graves shall yield their charge,

And dust to life awake…"

Merkel looked weary and streaked with blackish blood. In the waning light his eyes gleamed and Kristina hardly recognized him.

"We heard you," said Merkel. "You sing a prayer for them who would torture and kill us and our wives and babies? Those who had yoked us down so hard we can barely feed our little ones?"

"They suffer," said Grit.

"They came to kill us all, and worse," said Merkel.

"They had mothers, too," said Grit. "They were made by God just as we all were."

"Sig is dead," said Merkel. "Others are dead or wounded. What will crippled Kaspar do without his father, Sig? What will any do without their good fathers and sons?"

"All of those who take up swords," said Grit, "will die by swords. Why did you do those things?"

Merkel spat at her and said, "For freedom, for survival. I have nothing to do with the likes of you people."

Grit looked up at them without acrimony. Wiping Grit's face, Kristina saw only pity in Grit's eyes.

"Brothers, we love you and will pray for you."

Said Merkel, "Dolf and Symon, are you not our brothers? Will you dig like those women, like you live, on your knees? Or join us and fight for what you believe? Are you men or not?"

Grit shook her head. "Murder has no good sides. Christ said all murder is wrong."

"Are your men not allowed to speak for themselves?"

"Let us be," said Dolf, digging harder.

"What about you, Symon?" said Merkel. "Do the women keep your balls in a jar for you? Do they make you cowards?"

"It is not like that," said Dolf, looking ashamed.

"Me, I do not know," said Symon, digging, shaking his head. "I pray and pray but now I do not know."

Merkel spat again, and he and the others went away.

"Do not listen to them," said Grit.

"You, too," Dolf said, "let me be."

Kristina dug harder through the roots and rocks until her nails split. When she pulled the heavy limp weight of a man, when she felt the damp, chilled flesh of those she helped bury, she tried not to look at their faces and wounds. Sometimes her fingers slipped into a wound and in horror she wondered again and again which of the people she knew, or thought she knew, had done the terrible things to these dead, and brought harm therefore to themselves.

I do not know them, none of them...but I know that they all had mothers, all were beloved children once, and now all will be wept over, mourned, and their brothers and fathers will hate and kill in their turn of vengeance, and all shall happen over and over again, endlessly...

Someone came and stood over her and watched, and she looked up and saw it was Witter.

"Witter," said Grit. "So good to see you alive."

"I found another shovel," Witter said.

Silently, Kristina kept digging.

Witter began helping them dig.

Linhoff came and he already had a shovel.

"Grit," he said.

"Linhoff!" said Grit. "You live!"

40

Kristina saw joy glow in Grit's weary eyes. Grit stood shakily, and Kristina saw that Grit wanted to reach out and touch the young man, but did not.

"Can I help you dig?" said Linhoff, smiling.

"Yes. Dig, Brother. To help yourself, not me."

Linhoff went to work, hard, and helped Grit dig her holes. Kristina saw them trade glances, saying nothing to one another. Dark stains of blood streaked both of Linhoff's arms. He looked embarrassed and he dug with a powerful urgency. She saw him now as a total stranger.

All are unknown....

Kristina worked through it all in the same frenzy, digging violently, trying to fight the strangeness that was so overpowering and frightful.

She tried singing, but she felt nothing of God.

It was after dark when she broke down and could do no more. Lud's words tore at her...

"Are you not a mother? Why are you not with the other mothers and their children? Why are you not with your child? Take him and run where none can ever find you..."

She was on her knees beside a half-dug grave. The shadows were deepening and night was coming fast. Torches were lit out there on the road and the loaded wagons were moving out.

I want my child, my Peter...

She knelt, sobbing, covering her face with her earth-covered hands, and then she felt Grit's hard, firm arms around her.

"I cannot do this anymore. No more."

Grit stroked her hair. "Hush now, little sister, hush."

"Nothing will ever change, it only becomes worse and worse, no matter what we do, always worse."

She no longer cared about Lud. Nor Witter. Only Peter. She wanted her child, to take him and hold him close and to run away, to live like other people, anywhere that people did not hate and kill one another.

"I want my baby," she said, getting up, shoving away from Grit. "They are all evil. All."

She ran.

Who were these people? These villeins? How could she have ever thought she knew them? Oh, how they had rushed to the fight, to the killing.

Kristina made her way through the darkening woods, running past the new humps of earth, out to the road. A sliver moon was up with the star companion. She had seen that somewhere before, and remembered Mahmed's tunic, dark blue like a night sky, embroidered in gold threads, the crescent and star. Mahmed was a killer, too. Lud, too. Even Witter. She knew none of them.

Her running slowed, finally, to a walk.

It was all suddenly so clear, so cruel and plain. All men were killers. Women brought life into the world and men destroyed it. Her child Peter was yet a boy, infected with the poisons of men, and she must save him.

Then she realized that Grit was walking at her side. Grit was panting and Kristina knew she had run to catch her.

"God has sent us here, little sister."

"We are not sisters. Stop calling me that. Kunvald sent us here, not God."

Grit wiped her nose. The bridge of it was swollen where it had been broken by the fist of some man.

"It is here we must serve God. All men are brothers."

"All men are brothers," said Kristina. "Brothers in killing. There is no love."

"It is a difficult birthing. I worry for Dolf and Symon. I fear they are tempted by the other men to do violence."

Kristina did not care. It was strange, too, not to care, but there was no room in her for Dolf or Symon now. Only Peter.

"Let each do what he will. I belong with my child. I want to live and I want Peter to live."

Walking beside her on the dark road, Grit took hold of Kristina's hand and would not let go. The bones of Grit's palm were locked tight around her own.

"*His name shall be called Wonderful*," sang Grit softly.

"Counsellor, God, Strong,
Father of the world to come,
A prince of peace.
And his name shall be called
Marvelous, Counsellor, God, Strong,
Father of the world to come..."

"Prince of peace," said Kristina sadly. "Always the world to come. Never saving the world here and now."

"I believe that to love is to serve," said Grit softly.

"I am not as strong as you."

"None a tyrant over others," said Grit.

"I know the Scripture. But it is all pride, pious pride. I shall not serve strangers anymore. I only want to be with my child."

"Hush now, little sister," whispered Grit.

"No more, Grit. Just stop. No more Scripture, no more prayers. No one is listening. Just shut up."

Then she felt Grit shudder. She looked at Grit and saw tears gleaming in the moonlight.

"You are not the only one in conflict, little sister."

"What do you mean?"

"Linhoff asked to call me Marguerite, not Grit. He says Grit is too harsh. Says I am too...lovely for Grit."

"Were you alone with him?"

"He keeps coming near," Grit said. "I know not what to say to him. He is like my little brother. Yet I am sure that this day he did murder."

"Like Lud. Nothing we do can change them. I am through with all this. Only Peter matters to me now..."

"We will pray through this together."

"No. You do not have a child. You do not understand."

She wanted Grit to be silent. And Grit did not speak again for a time, walking beside her up the shadowy road under the moon.

But then, when Kristina was sinking deeper and deeper back into her own thoughts, drowning deep in her dread and her fears, Grit spoke once more, this time with a wounded hurt low in her voice, as if her words came up from hiding in some deep place, confessing.

"Once I did. Once I had a child."

"Once?"

Grit said no more, all the way back to the village. She said no more, but then she sang for a little while…

"Leave off weeping,
My white little sheep,
Fear no evil,
While thou doest sleep…"

They walked together with their moon shadows falling ahead, on the silvery dust of the road. She expected the men to be coming back on horse and foot, and to pass them on the way to the village, but they did not come.

Grit's calloused fingers were strong, and still would not let go of her hand.

KONRAD

Dawn prayers in his little fortress chapel cleared all fear constrictions from Konrad's chest. His breath flowed cleanly, easily, bravely.

Service was his sacred path, his life. As Prince Bishop of the ecclesiastical state, he served God. As prince, he served the state. With much prayer, and divine guidance, he had grown from the callow schemer he once was. Now he felt himself grown so much stronger in his faith. He was a selfless servant, and in prayer, God reassured him that he was blessed. All things in one man.

Surely, he had grown far beyond his desire long ago to be a man as strong as Dietrich. His father would not know him now. He was fully strong in God's will.

After prayer, Konrad let his monks dress him in the sacred robes, and he went down from the Marienberg by carriage to the great cathedral. On his knees at the Riemenschneider altar, he prayed and planned for Advent Vespers. Then, in the candlelit shadows of the gallery, the boy's choir sang its achingly sweet choral feast, for spirit and mind and ear.

An hour later, he was back in the Marienberg, changed from the robes of the church into the golden armor that bore the cross, to serve now in the secular world.

With his four garrison captains, he took a surprise tour of the walls and found the watch nervous and alert. Like spectators, pigeons cooed up high on the foggy ramparts as if this were any other day. But Konrad knew now that history had turned a page that would never be turned back, no more than he would ever again wear the sleeping robe he had once so cherished, gifted from Anna, her beauty destroyed by the pox.

So many things were transpiring suddenly against him. And against the good order of the entire bishopric, and of all Swabia.

As the sun burned away the fog of dawn, a Swabian courier brought word of village uprisings to the north and the east, including one in his own estate. Villeins were refusing to serve their rightful labors. They were demanding a higher share. His own steward had been killed. The courier reported that other courier riders had been taken and their messages lost.

Basil reported that the radical monk Thomas Muntzer had inflamed the silver and salt miners and the weavers as well. The mutiny was spreading throughout all lower ranks of common folk and artisans, not only the villeins of the farming estates. Wherever literacy had reared its ugly head, wherever those low of rank had learned to read, rejection of rightful law was spreading.

Konrad felt that God was sorely testing him. Never had he needed more resolve. And in prayer, God told him that the strength needed was in him.

But it did not stop. It was like an avalanche of wrongs.

Then came a demand much closer to home, from the Wurzburg City Council. Their new mayor, Riemenschneider, requested an urgent private audience.

"I shall meet him alone," Konrad informed Basil.

"Do you not wish my transcription of conversation?"

"What I will say to this upstart artist is not fit for bishopric historical record. Alone, I said."

Konrad met him just after breakfast; not in the good greeting chamber for favored guests, but in the unheated and unfurnished antechamber, where the bishop sat in the only chair.

Basil saw Riemenschneider in. The artist-mayor was as tall as ever but more bent by time. And he wore less gold than before, though Konrad knew he had amassed great wealth. His deep, dark-browed eyes looked strong but wary. In his fine dark red robe he looked like a would-be cardinal.

"Your face is longer than ever," said Konrad. "We have not met since you were elected mayor. "

"Regretfully, no, your grace," said the tall, gaunt man, without kissing the bishopric ring as he should. "Not since our dear prince-bishop Lorenz died. The city council has often wished you would attend at least once, to lead us and guide us. I have requested such many times but the reply was always negative."

"Then it did not reach me," said Konrad, recalling all the times he had instructed Basil to make some excuse. "You were a good friend of Werner Heck, were you not?"

"Heck was a good man, your grace."

"Indeed? You share his heretical sentiments?"

"I am here to help restore order, your grace."

"You are here to whine and snivel about equal votes and other issues of power and control, a duty that is rightfully mine alone, and my cross to bear."

"Your grace, as mayor, I am appointed to speak for many others. Times are rapidly changing and our wish is only to head off dire disasters."

"I see. Is that a threat?"

"By no means, your grace. The opposite, I assure you. It is no secret that unrest is fomenting across our lands and in the city here, too. The citizens bear too much want and trouble, and relief is all that can stop a great tragedy, I fear. I am here to offer our help."

"You stand here in your typical arrogance, masked with shallow humility. You were Lorenz's favorite sculptor and painter, and he gave you many fat commissions for monuments. Do not expect the same easy favors from me. The needs of my people come first before my vanity for flattering devices of art."

"I do not come seeking commissions, your grace."

"What then? What is this help you offer?"

"The people," said Riemenschneider, "have a demand of common rights, and it has been set out in twelve articles for you to consider and in good faith to agree, we hope."

Konrad felt a flare of anger but kept his face cold. His hands tightened on the deeply carved lions that capped the ends of the chair arms. He pressed his thumbs into the orbs of their wooden eyes.

"Articles? What are they? Who set them out?"

"The city council and the guilds all respectfully request that you hear the articles in person, in open public meeting in the city hall, at a time of your choosing."

Konrad sat forward. "I do not meet others. Others meet me. When I say they can. You tread heavily. Beware."

"I wish only for peaceful resolution. Will you not listen, your grace?"

"If threat is all you have to convey, we are done here. Go before I have you taken and severely questioned for heresy. Only because my good Lorenz loved you will I allow you now to depart."

"Threat? Heresy? How, heresy?"

Konrad got up and went out, leaving Riemenschneider standing there, looking foolish and disappointed.

In the outer chamber, he told Basil, "See the upstart out. Put him on the radicals list. And get hold of a copy of these twelve articles, whatever they might be. Let us see what outrages they plan to request. I want all the names. And then we shall arrest them all, for sedition and possible heresy."

"Even Riemenschneider?" said Basil.

"Why not him? Is that upstart not a radical? Has he not challenged us, thereby challenging the very authority of God?"

"Indeed, but he is the elected mayor, your grace."

"Exactly so. A radical elected by radicals. That is proof of the fallacy of votes by lower ranks. I will personally attend his questioning, and I cannot express how eagerly I look forward to it. Whatever is brewing must be quenched, and quickly. Things that begin to fall soon crash down."

He could not have been more right. His prayers had warned him well. For, that same afternoon, the situation became much worse.

First, he sat and read through the Twelve Articles. They were simple and direct. And impossible. At first he almost believed it

48

must be some sort of parody, a comic invention to mock all things holy.

His eyes darted through the demands like a fox through a field full of snares—

Every municipality shall have the right to elect and remove priest...

It is devised by the Scripture, that we are and that we want to be free...

All the woods shall be given back to the municipality so that anybody can...

The nobility shall not raise the villein's rent...

Community land must be at the disposition of all members...

Never again shall widows and orphans be robbed contrary to God and honor...

Konrad read with increasing horror and disbelief, and then a growing burning sense of rage.

"Villeins? Who do they think they are, if they would not be villeins, as they were born to be?"

All men neighbors with equal rights, each voting equally, each taxed equally, none obeying another, nobles and villeins having the same legal rights, all alike.

Accepting these would mean the end of the Holy Roman Empire. The end of civilization itself. All good things tumbled from their rightful places, crashing down to become the mixed mud of common ground. All would be reduced to scum. All the same.

It was all pure anarchy, pure heresy.

The weight of his duty came heavily upon his shoulders and he felt the world drifting like a great wandering force, unmoored under him. He almost fainted and choked back retch that bit his throat and burned.

For hours, then, he fought the nausea and prayed in the cathedral for divine guidance.

Guide my heart and my hand for the good of Thy people, O Lord, and gird me against mine own softness, lest I fail in my great obligation to bring order to disorder, light to darkness, and to preserve the good, no matter what the cost...

Then, as if in cryptic answer, a strange message did come. But not one that Konrad had ever expected.

About noon, a battered cavalryman had come riding to the Marienberg, so beaten and exhausted that he had fallen from his horse at the very gates. The guards carried him inside. Wine and hard slaps brought him back to answer.

The entire garrison was called to muster.

Now, with drums beating assembly, the courtyard of the Marienberg was lined with silent helmeted men in mail and armor, all standing in formation, staring. They were the Bishopric Guard, the soldiers who manned the gates and ramparts, and his own body-guard. Many were second or third sons of nobles and this fashion-able and relatively safe employ was a gift for some favor granted, and to bind the soldiers' fathers' loyalty.

The drums stopped and Konrad came out.

He sat on the back of Sieger, and the magnificent white horse wore its best gold-filigreed armor and red-fringed horse robe. The sun was almost blinding, flashing off all the armor. A special leather cap, intricately tooled, had been crafted to fit under Sieger's tail, a catchment for any unexpected excreta that might erupt, and impi-ously lessen the impact of Konrad's authority.

A special broadsheet had been issued by Veritas Press regaling Sieger's virtues, his special diet of oats and barley, comparing him to the great spirit of the Holy Roman Empire.

With long poised steps, like a God, Sieger moved. In gold armored gloves, articulated like a crab, Konrad held the gilded reins, forcing Sieger not to hurry. In this way, Konrad could look down upon all the faces of his fighting men. He passed in review of the line, until he reached Basil and the wretched cavalryman wait-ing under the wind-whipped banners at the review stand.

There, four footmen took hold of Sieger, and Konrad twisted and slid down off the fine saddle, with the help of many strong and careful hands, ever respectful.

Konrad then stood and steeled himself for bad news. He had dressed for the occasion in his own intricately pleated tunic with bloused sleeves, the fine red waistcoat, and his filigreed golden breastplate with the cross. There was no doubt now of serious fighting to come. He, of course, would not be personally engaged in combat, yet his troops must be properly inspired. Softness had no place here.

Now, in the great courtyard, the cavalryman was kneeling on the stones, and blubbering out the news of a shocking ambush on the road at Giebel forest.

"You sent out no flankers, no forward scouts?" said Konrad.

"Your grace, our captains saw no need."

"No need? With banditry everywhere, you did not observe the most basic rules of march?"

"Forgive me. We were the Marienberg guard, sent to arrest some country trash. And they—they were nothing but a village of villeins and low-rankers."

Slumped on his knees before Konrad, the cavalryman broke down and wept like a baby.

Konrad stared down at him with contempt. Now bloody and ragged and sobbing, this cavalryman was usually tall and handsome, the shallow sort Konrad saw in the parades, the perfect public figure of a professional man of horse and sword, the kind that Konrad, as a child, had so admired and envied. The kind his father had so wanted him to become someday. And with his disgust, Konrad also felt a shiver of fear—that simple country villeins could so humble an officer of horse.

"They charged at us, at first only three or four of them, coming straight on, right at us, with a great pack of mangy dogs, and we formed properly in front to take them, our horse moving out and our muskets shaping a line, and, and…"

"And what? What?"

"We unleashed the war dogs but their mongrels engaged them, outnumbering them five to one. Then we took the worst shock."

"What shock?"

"Ambush, from the woods. Both sides. Bolts flying. Both flanks."

"Bolts? From crossbows? Who were they?"

"Men at arms, shabby rogue knights. A priest was with them, raving like a madman. Then the rogue knights formed a line and cut

us in half, driving our men like cattle, they did. The priest screaming and ranting them on."

"What priest?"

"I did not know him. Michael, they called him."

"Go on."

"Four on horse were coming at us. In the flanking attack distrac-
tion they charged our front ranks, cut into us, driving past our own
confused horse...back into the formation...cutting through the
monks and magistrate wagons in our rear."

"You could not protect even the monks?"

"There was no order, your grace. The empty wagons meant
to bring prisoners back to your justice, their teams broke and ran
into the formation, too, causing much confusion, and there was no
order to be had..."

"Twenty men of horse and sixty foot. And this handful of common trash tore you apart?"

"We did turn, and volleys got off, but the riders cut through our center
and the rogues came cutting in with their swords from the flanks, and
then...then when I thought it could be no worse, came their villagers."

"Villagers?"

"Maybe a hundred, even two hundred, with axes and flails and
scythes and pikes and knives and shovels. They were strong. People
who work hard. Wild, shouting in their wrath and glee, like fevered
rats they were, and decimated us, and they took down those who ran."

"That the villeins punished cowards is the only good thing you
have said to me."

"Your grace, I did not run."

"Then how are you here, alive, in one piece?"

"I fell and would have been chopped to pieces, but their priest, the
one called Michael, he saved me. Then their leader, Florian Geyer, he
sent me to tell you all of this. I told him I would rather be dead."

"Yet you live."

"To do my duty to you, your grace, and report, even should it
cost me great suffering in my shame."

"They are villeins, low-rankers, commoners. How? What happened? What rallied them to such fire?"

"Many had one of these, your grace," said the soldier.

"One of what?"

The soldier pulled a wrinkled wad of paper from his tunic.

"Florian Geyer, the apostate, the traitor, he sent a verbal message with this, your grace."

Konrad handed the wadded paper to Basil. Basil took it in two fingers and carefully opened its folds as if a spider or demon might spring forth. The monk flattened the sheet out on his belly. He tried to hand it to Konrad, but Konrad did not wish to touch anything that had touched Basil's belly.

"Do not touch me with that heresy. Read it."

"But it is only our own broadsheet, your grace."

"Ours? Which of ours?"

Basil sounded confused. "The broadsheet that Veritas Press printed and spread everywhere. Florian's excommunication. His sins, his villainies. His defiance of the Holy Church and his traitorous beliefs against the state."

Konrad looked at the soldier, who was bent lower than ever over his knees.

"What was the heretic's message?" said Konrad.

"His words, your grace, not mine, please."

"Your life hangs by a thread of my impatience."

"His words, not mine. 'Florian Geyer sends his most sincere thanks to your grace, for denouncing him in printed words across all of Swabia.'"

"His thanks? And how should he be grateful for such lawful damnations?"

"His words, your grace not mine..."

"Say that once more and your head shall fly."

The man cringed so low now that his face touched the courtyard stones. Men were muttering vaguely in the ranks. Konrad looked up, and their gazes flicked away from his.

"Answer me," he said, and had to strain to hear the defeated man speak—

"Your grace, the apostate Geyer says that, with Veritas Press… 'you have rallied the whole countryside to his cause, which is the cause of freedom…and to their own liberation surely so soon to come.'"

Konrad stood there, his face stinging with disbelief.

God had sent him yet another test of his faith.

It was his own press, Veritas, and his own broadsheet that now had rallied the people to Florian.

He looked up at his castle guard. Two hundred in all. Neither Emperor Charles in Vienna nor his brother, the archduke of Wurttemberg, had regular reserve troops to send anyone. The entire regular army had gone to fight in Italy.

Konrad stood there in his gold armor and he had never felt more alone. All his men at arms stood silently waiting.

What shall I do? What must I do, Lord?

Three pigeons flew down and landed and walked about, strutting. To Konrad, at this moment, the wild birds seemed like a sign—of villeins going as they pleased, doing as they pleased, taking whatever they pleased. Konrad felt shocked, and hated those birds.

"What are your orders, your grace?" asked Basil in a whisper.

His distress over the pigeons went away. In its place remained an empty need. He had to decide something. He had to say something to Basil. And whatever he said would be done. And so it must be something right.

Then, as Konrad began to feel the deep squirming of panic, God sent him wisdom, clarity of mind, strength of heart; God whispered to him what must now be done to regain order. He must crush those who endangered the good.

"Promote this brave man and bonus him, for fighting his way out of the heretical trap."

The battered cavalryman looked up, astonished.

Said Basil, "But he was sent by them, your grace."

"I say he is a hero. Let the men see it, too. See it done. Double the tower watch. And bring the magistrates back from the city to patrol the grounds outside our walls."

"There will be anarchy in Wurzburg if we remove the magistrates, your grace."

Konrad laughed bitterly. "What do you think is there now? You are not usually so slow, Basil. Agree to their council meeting. We will meet and hear their Twelve Articles. Send word to Riemenschneider."

"But your grace, the city is too dangerous now for you to go among the people. And the council, they are seditious. Half the countryside estates are out of control. Must you leave the safety of these great walls?"

"I did not say I would go."

"But, I thought…"

"You and your monks shall go. You will demonstrate your faith in the holy protection."

Basil's face drained of its blood. "But, your grace…"

For the first time, Konrad put his hands gently upon the shoulders of the little monk. Basil tried hard to be good and loyal, but he was unused to physical danger. Konrad felt pity for him, and almost something like love, just for a moment.

"God is with us, good Basil, not them. Such a meeting will be dangerous, you are right."

"Must I go? Must I?"

The little monk shuddered. He tried to put his arms around Konrad and Konrad stood back abruptly.

"Dangerous for them, not you. Yesterday I called back the Fifth Landsknechts to return by forced march, day and night, from the field. You shall be the bait in God's trap, and we shall end this great evil."

LUD

Lud dismounted and tied Ox where he could graze on a patch of fresh, tender grass. Michael came to him.

The man was changed. His softness was gone. There was no sad lingering look. Something firm had replaced all the despair that had once eaten the man to his core.

"Michael," said Lud.

"It is good to see you alive," said the priest.

"Your face is harder than before."

"I am just another plain man, trying to learn."

"So what have you learned here, in all this death?"

"That this is a beginning, Lud, only a beginning."

"There are ends to every beginning," said Lud. "Now we will all be hunted till the end of our days."

"Once you told me to go out and find some real suffering, if I must, some honest suffering. And I have done so, and seen much, too much now, to ever go back to that self-seeking creature I was before."

They regarded one another silently. Nothing would be said of what had happened in the church that night when they had last met. It seemed like another lifetime. Lud read the solid face of the man he now hardly recognized, the sad and lonely priest who had taught him to read; who had lectured and taunted him; who had kissed him and then tried to hang himself, before running away like a child. But they did not take hands, nor embrace as they might have in the past. Only their eyes touched.

"In the city, Muntzer and all our brothers, they await Florian," said Michael. "They knew he would be coming, for I told them that

I would bring him to lead them in support of the city council's demand for Konrad to sign the Twelve Articles. All our brothers in the Marienberg dungeons must be released."

"Have you taken to calling all men your brother now? Even cut-throats and madmen?"

"I have. For that is the truth."

"Konrad, too? Is he your brother?"

"You know what I mean, Lud. Riemenschneider, the mayor, will present the articles. It was brother Muntzer who sent me to bring Florian. We meet in the city hall tomorrow at noon, Judica Sunday."

"Black Sunday," said Lud.

"Passion Sunday, yes. Only Germans call it Black Sunday. But it is fitting, for all crosses and icons are covered in black, to signify the dimming of glory during Christ's passion. He knew his earthly body was soon to perish."

"His earthly body?" said Lud.

"Yes," Father Michael said.

"You would think Christ would be glad to leave this place," said Lud. "After the way it had treated him."

Father Michael looked at him and said nothing.

Late in the night, some of the old men and women from Giebel had arrived in the camp with carts loaded with grain and sheep and smoked meat and bedrolls.

There had been much sobbing and laughing and rejoicing in loved ones and family finding one another still alive. The dogs that had survived the fight, some of them half crippled, came licking and wagging for scraps. A flock of children had come behind, too, but they had been chased back home. Lud had no part in any of this. He had no family, no loved ones. He was part of the village, yet not a part of its soul.

The wounded were sent back to Giebel on the wagons with the few old women who would go, but most of the women came with their men. They were strong people.

At the break of dawn, Florian took a final voice vote. It was unanimous. Men and women, all voted to march to Wurzburg to hear the articles read and to support the new rights of man.

Elated, half-rested, they marched toward Wurzburg.

"It is the fourth week of advent," said the priest, Michael. "Let us sing the songs of Christ's coming, as we march ahead together."

Their voices droned, the men's low and broken, the women's high and some of them angelic.

Lud heard them only dimly, as a traveler hears a nearby river rushing among rocks. His mind ranged far ahead…

Of course, Florian was right. What began could not be stopped. There was no going back now. There was never any going back, not in this life. Now there was only going forward. Many men wore armor and all carried good weapons. Florian told Lud to put them into some kind of marching order, and he had done so. Many of them had served once in years long before. They knew how to march. And the young pikemen formed at the flanks.

Life was surging, pushing them all ahead.

After the collecting of weapons and armor and valuables from the Wurzburg dead, which was the fair lot of victors in any battle, the woods knights flocked around Florian, and Lud saw Florian's pleasure, mixed with good surprise.

"If there is no hope for us to live in peace, there is nothing to lose by risking death altogether," said Steinmetz, the knight in his old rust-stained black armor. "Your man Lud made us welcome in your far woods, and we will stand with you as brothers in arms."

If there still had been doubt among the men and women of Giebel, Florian and the priest had finished it.

A big fire had been built of broken wagon planks around midnight, and in the orange light of flames, first Florian had spoken, then Michael.

Each had taken turns preaching to the crowd. Lud watched, saying nothing, but he could feel the tremendous sense of excitement among all the people here. They hushed, and only the crackling of the big bright bonfire could be heard, and the words being spoken here, which would decide all their fates.

Said Father Michael, "The people of Wurzburg want change. They back the city council. We must join them. The whole countryside is rising, place by place, for the truth is setting the mind of man on fire. Who can stop us?"

Said Florian, "The emperor's army is away in Italy fighting the French."

"They are professionals, Landsknechts," said Merkel.

"Yes," said Florian, "and they are away in the field, still training, and green as grass. In a border skirmish with Poland and a dispute at Wurttemberg, I officered them. The bishop has only his guard garrison and his magistrates in Wurzburg. This is our time. This is the time for men to free themselves and make a new world."

Father Michael waved his arms for attention.

"Do we not have good fighting men, too? And they have been professionals of war. Can they not be our cavalry?"

"With enough of us, we can," said Steinmetz. "From the road peddler Old Klaus, I read to my men the Veritas broadsheet—the one of Florian's excommunication and his struggles against the wrongs of the bishopric and of all things the way they are everywhere, when equal rights should be free to all. That broadsheet was all the encouragement we needed. It even told us that the force from Wurzburg was coming. There are many other villages and estates rising, we know."

Then Merkel spoke up and said, "I think I speak for many when I say, never again do we wish to live in want and fear."

"We have news," said Michael, "that will change everything. There are the Twelve Articles—a bill of the rights of all men—being drawn up by the leaders of the common workers in cities and on the land."

"Yes, Florian told us," said Merkel. "But, what leaders?"

"Thomas Muntzer, for one."

There were impressed looks all around.

"I have read his broadsheets," said Steinmetz. "Muntzer has a great following in the cities."

"Is Muntzer not a crazy man?" said Linhoff.

"So says Veritas Press," said Michael. "I know him for the bravest, most inspired man I have ever met. He is dedicated only to the brotherhood of all, equally. The Twelve Articles are to be read under a bishopric truce, Friday, at noon in the council hall."

"If all are brothers, why have leaders?" said Merkel.

Florian said, "There must be a leader or there can be no order, no consolidation of efforts against our foes. Each will vote, equally. We shall always choose our own leaders. That is the new way, the right way. The way of brothers."

Merkel said, "Twelve articles? Of what demands?"

Lud, watching all this, saying nothing, saw their energy rising like the fire eating the broken wood. And he thought of that night years ago, when the orange flames had danced across the face of Dietrich, as they worked to sort out the dead and bring order following the battle in the storm. Florian's face was looking, as ever, so like his father, and he had that same gift of bringing others eagerly to his mind.

"The articles grant freedom," said Florian. "Freedom of equality."

Said Michael, "I know the men writing them."

"But are not men born with unequal gifts?" said Merkel.

Said Michael, "I only know one article, the one I love best. Shall I tell it to you in my own words?"

"Tell it," said Lud. "Make it clear, for the cost is high."

The priest blinked. Slowly and carefully then, he said it: "It has been practice so far, that so-called common men have been held to be born as villein, which is pitiful, given that Christ redeemed all of us with his precious bloodshed, the shepherd as well as the highest, no one excluded. Therefore, it is devised by the Scripture, that no man is more common than any other, that we are all children of God, and that we want to be free."

"Free," said Leta. "All villeins free."

Lud looked at her. Leta, who washed the castle linen day in and day out, her arms and hands always red and raw. She stood in the firelight, holding a pike brought here by some Marienberg man now dead in a hole. And then he saw Symon and Dolf standing behind Leta.

Said Linhoff, "None born to be villeins? None born to be lords? How will this work?"

Father Michael lifted his arms high. There was the self-importance of Muntzer in him that Lud did not like to see. All harked to him.

"No more the rich grinding the poor with all blessings of Church and state. No more rents raised and wages lowered and shares ever reduced to pay for armies, weapons, foreign wars. Your own Florian, and Dietrich before him, tried to lessen your burdens. But they too were being crushed. No more church and state working hand in hand to enslave those who do all the work, Brothers."

"As I told you in Giebel," said Florian, "all men shall be brothers. When the articles are accepted by all the lords."

"That makes no sense," said Linhoff. "You say no more lords, but they are lords, yet, which must agree."

"Unless we smash them down, make them not lords," said Steinmetz. "And we know many impoverished knights, most good men driven to desperate means, all of them veterans of war, many with horses, who will flock to this fight."

Said Florian, "And we shall be there to see no harm is done to the council who put forth those rights."

"We can never go back from this day," said Michael to the crowd.

"Lud," said Florian, "you have been silent. What say you?"

"You have words enough for all of us," said Lud.

Lud sat on Ox and looked at Florian, and he saw there was no use trying to talk him out of this. They were all drunk on it. Besotted with their willingness to die. Words were one fine thing. But too often they led to much killing.

For a long instant Lud debated whether to ride away and leave them all here.

Ride away and back to Giebel and take Kristina—by force if need be, tie her if need be—take three horses with Kristina and little Peter, the two of them ponied on two horses behind Ox. Take them and ride as far and as fast as the three horses would take them. And do what he had told her—spend the rest of his days making sweet that sad smile of hers. Remove from her willing shoulders the crushing weight of the world's sins. Teach her child the ways of a man. And become a man himself, by loving them both...

But the bright instant passed. The dream of Kristina was gone, like a twinkle of light when one draws from a well at night and sees the reflected stars floating deep down on the black water, and then the bucket drops and the stars shatter.

Lud looked at Florian, son of Dietrich, and he saw the son in the father, and the father in the son. He knew that he would end his life in service to that blood, in the circle of life where he had begun.

And so, at dawn, three hundred four in all, by Lud's rough tally, the people formed up and went down together toward Wurzburg.

Lud goaded Ox and left the column; not back to Giebel, but on ahead, as he always did in war, to scout, to try to see death before it saw him.

It was not yet noon when Lud, riding Ox, scouting a half mile ahead of their little column, encountered the first contingent.

First he saw the glint of steel radiant in the risen sun, and pulled Ox to be blocked among the trees along the road.

Then, as they came on, their shapes materializing in better light, he saw who they were.

WITTER

All rules had changed.

Around a big campfire, the people of Giebel were gathered together like some ancient tribe. They were deciding who they were now. There had first been the bragging from euphoria, the exultation and sheer amazement that they had fought magistrates and men at arms and had won.

"They sat so proud, but fell like wheat!"

"Are we not Giebel? Did we not see our justice?"

"Cowards threaten, villeins fight!"

But after the boasting, then it had settled in, the knowledge of the aftermath certain to come, of the Church-state's wrath. Power was as relentless, they knew, as the seasons changing. The Church-state had always been. Would it not always be?

So now, the villagers and knights were like hungover drunks after some forgotten orgy, weary with excess and sick of it. All was wanton and quiet. All weapons and armor were being shared out in common. The bond of village was there, and more—the killings had made them blood brothers in their fate. They ate the bishopric rations together, rich city food from dead men, and some slept on the ground under wagons and trees, many arm in arm on the ground. But others still searched the trees and roadside for their dead.

Somewhere off in the dark, a woman wailed. Witter saw a woman kneeling in some trees, sobbing over a body she held cradled in her arms.

"Greta...my Greta!"

It was, Witter saw, Arl, the baby catcher and weaver, who had long ago lost her twins, Hermo and Fridel. Now Arl held her black-haired daughter, Greta. In the faint glow of the distant campfire he saw the white nape of Greta's neck where a wound gaped like an open mouth.

"Not Greta!" Arl cried. "Not my Greta!"

Women from the campfire now came hurrying over to try to comfort Arl, but she pushed them away, hunched over her daughter, inconsolable.

He needed to be with Kristina now.

Only that thought gave him any sense of hope in his life. Just to see her and be near her would be enough. But he could not find her here. He pulled Leta away from the women trying to help Arl and asked her where he could find Kristina. Leta's eyes were wild and strange.

"Kristina went back to Giebel, to find Peter," said Leta. Then Leta shoved him away and went back to Arl.

In the night, alone, Witter took one of the bishopric horses from some two dozen warhorses still in war harness, near the looted magistrate wagons. The Giebel men had tethered them for use in whatever they might do next. He picked a big black one that looked steady.

He slipped the tether loose from the halter. The saddle was still on the horse; no one had bothered to unsaddle him. Nor did the horse care who used him.

Now, Witter rode back toward Giebel.

The horse quickly became lathered, huffing with its strides, and with its airy sweat came the stench of blood. Its rider had been killed in this war saddle, big and square like riding a hard wooden box; the heavy loops for weapons were empty and flapping.

Witter rode alone, alone as always, whether with himself or with others, armed like an amateur highwayman with his little dagger and his mind, always so alone. Witter thought of the magistrate or horse guard who had ridden this horse only hours earlier, no doubt with a somewhat bored certainty, and never imagining he was hurrying to bleed out his life all over his mount and be cut to pieces and dumped into a hole.

Riding the big horse, a laughing fit took Witter. Bitter and irresistible. He rocked on the saddle until he choked with laughter. Then it was gone, like a quick angry spasm, leaving him even emptier than before.

Lurching on the back of the horse, he passed through the flickering moon shadows of the road, and he tried promising God—if He was listening—that he would never be part of killing, never again. His fear was now of himself. He knew men *in extremis* regressed to a childlike state, atheists believing anew, hard minds crumbling and begging, and still now he wanted to bury his face in the bosom of God, as he had buried his face in his father's bosom as a boy, when other boys had taunted and mocked him.

Perhaps Judah could intervene for him. He did not deserve Judah but he had no one else.

Father, hear me...

He feared the seductive freedom, yes, the joy, the release of his own fear that he had felt amid all that killing. Now, with a dread of falling, he stumbled along the very edge of a great, deep pit. The pit perhaps was his discovery of his own true nature. He was surely just another beast, feral and evil. No doubt Judah had disowned him, and loathed him now, as he deserved.

Father, do not despise me, help me find my way...

As if in answer, Witter felt a shudder under him and realized that the horse was laboring on the road. It slowed and began to wheeze and stumble.

Witter got down, twisting clumsily to the ground.

In the silvery light the massive beast stood there, head down, and then he saw blackish blood dripping from its nostrils, big drops pattering upon the moonlit dust. He ran his hand over its neck and then he found the puncture in the coarse hair at the base of its throat. Something had pierced the muscle there. Then his finger felt the splintered end of a bolt that had been broken off. So the stench of blood had not been from its former rider killed in the saddle. With motion, the bolt had worked its way in deeper and deeper and now had found the life of the animal.

The horse moaned and sagged down onto its front knees. Witter stepped back, startled and dismayed, as though seeing a wall that might collapse. Then the horse looked at him and rolled onto its side, still looking at him; and, as if trying to understand why it must die, it heaved a last long shrill cry of breath and then was still. Still staring.

He had lost Waldo's horse in the battle, and now this horse, from the Wurzburg force, accepting him without complaint, even though it was wounded.

Horses were such noble creatures. Strong and never complaining. Witter realized that he had never known his other horse's name. That name died when Waldo died. Waldo, who loved horses. Now this one too was just a great dark mound, and Witter marveled that it could be dead. So gentle, eating grass. Not living by death, never consuming others. Many times stronger than any man, yet living the life of a slave. So much nobler by design than any man.

Witter went on, running, shuffling, hurrying toward the village. His breath came harder and harder. His sweat, once cool, was now hot, and his hair stuck to his face and his cloth to his damp and clammy skin.

Where did life go? How could it simply vanish?

That was why one had to try to believe in a world after this one. If one did not, nothing mattered here in this world.

Take Kristina and the child and run...

His father's voice told him what he must do. It was the first time since he had run down the magistrates that Judah had spoken to him. The thought of Kristina filled him with warmth and hope.

He hurried his steps toward the village.

The others were all going to their deaths, marching to Wurzburg, hurrying to their destruction as if the anxiety of waiting were intolerable. They were full of hope and anger that had risen like water behind a crumbling dike, and all that Witter knew was that a great bloodshed was coming, coming on fast, like an unstoppable wave at sea.

He kept seeing the surprised faces of the magistrates he had run down outside Wurzburg, that day of Muntzer's speech, and then the pikemen he had run down to save Lud, their screams and the sound of their breaking bones under the crushing weight of hooves. Surprise made hard men's faces go soft like boys' faces.

Like anything else he did, it had been much stranger the first time, and much less strange the second time. A person got used to the idea of killing insects, then animals, then men, too, for all were creatures that sought pleasure and avoided pain, that tried to breed the like, and tried to avoid death. And it felt so good to be giving fear instead of cringing and hiding.

So he had found the way to evil, the easy way, the cunning and efficient way—the slide to hell. As his father had warned.

Suddenly something was coming at him and he stopped. A gang of boys rushed past. He saw Peter running with them.

"Peter, stop!"

Then they were gone up the road toward the encampment where the fight had taken place.

He hurried on toward Giebel, and saw the scattered lights of the village ahead, and again he promised Judah—

Father, until the end of my time in this wretched world, I swear I shall never take part in harming another, no matter what happens to me, never again…

A pinkish glow was in the eastern sky as he finally came into the village. The gates stood wide open. His shadow ran before him on the ground.

Inside the village gate he saw a dozen old women kneeling at the great black linden tree. Some pressed their slack bosoms to the wood as if suckling it, opening it to their pleas. Their withered hands caressed its gnarled trunk, and they were chanting, heads bent in prayer to their old gods, he thought, thinking that the new Christian God had failed them now.

Witter hurried on through the tree shadow, past them, past the well, past the chapel, to the castle. The castle gates stood open. There was no one at guard.

"Peter!" he heard.

It was Kristina's voice, urgent, shrill with fear.

"Peter! Where are you? Peter!"

To him, it was sweet, that sound, that voice, as if he could taste the very air passing across her tongue and lips. Then he saw Kristina running toward him.

"The boys are all out on the Wurzburg road together."

"The old folk," said Kristina, "had them all in one hut, but the boys broke out and want to be with the men."

"Wait!" Grit shouted from the stables. "Help me fetch a cart or wagon. We can pick them all up."

"No time," Kristina said, and then she was hurrying out of the gates and up the road.

"Help me and we will pick her up," said Grit. He turned and saw Grit struggling with a mule on a rope.

Witter knew Grit was right. She was solid and sane amidst all this blood and death. He could help with the wagon and mules and they would soon overtake Kristina and pick her up and then move fast to find Peter.

The second mule was finally hauled around, nipping at the first, and both were chained to the wagon tongue. They got out on the road, Witter driving the team. The sun was already coming up.

"How long has it been?" said Witter.

"Too long," Grit said. "But she cannot have gotten far."

Witter snapped the reins but the mules had their pace and shuffled along without haste.

And for miles on the road, there was no sign of Kristina.

LUD

Morning broke and the sun came up like it had every other morning. But Lud knew his world would never be the same.

Urging his horse out of the screen of trees, he came out onto the open road. On the road ahead, a crowd was moving toward Wurzburg, and he saw they were villeins—tillers, villagers, people like the folk of Giebel.

The little horde stopped and stared at him. He rode toward them, and they backed away a few steps and then stopped again. Then they raged at him with threatening flails and axes and hammers and shovels.

Lud stopped the horse, lifted his hands and showed open palms.

"Lud?" one called. "It is Lud of Giebel!"

Now he recognized some of the men from Lupfen village, having seen them at the Wurzburg market and in service in the border war. They saw him and asked for Florian, and then came Florian, riding and catching up. His style was elegant, Lud saw, his poise in riding well-studied and, somehow, just a bit vain.

The people of Lupfen made a great fuss about Florian, but at least Florian seemed rightly embarrassed and modest, not basking in their fawning attentions. They too had read the Veritas broadsheet. Some rogue knights were with them, in their ragged tunics and random armor.

The people of Giebel came up and the mass commingled, and then with Florian at its head, and Michael just behind, they were on the move toward Wurzburg.

Lud had seen so many act foolishly, throwing themselves forward into the magistrates, screaming and swinging their farm tools. Tomen, who had run away from the battle with the Turks years ago, now stood blood-smeared, proud, for this time he had not run.

"I did not run away," said Tomen.

"Next time do not run forward, either," said Lud.

A hard old man on a plow horse rode up beside Lud. Across his lap was an axe.

"You are Lud," he said.

"I am." Lud was surprised. "You are?"

"Stoller. We marched right behind you and your boys those years ago, when we ended it in the great storm battle, and all hell fell upon us."

"I remember. Lupfen. You fought well and lost half."

"Lupfen. We were villeins, but no more."

"What happened?"

"We took charity from your village priest, as other villages did also, because your lord, Dietrich, wished to be a good Christian. But other lords were not so good of heart, you know that. In Lupfen we revoked our ancient obligations—all that broke our fathers and grandfathers, through all remembered time, forever. Now we are free men, as long as we stand aboveground and breathe air. Now we follow the son of good Dietrich, your Florian, for if he has dared the bishop Konrad, as the broadsheet says, we love him for that."

"They gave us no choice. Kill or be taken. And you?"

"Our old countess of Lupfen, since her husband died she would not heed our troubles. Hunger brings sickness to children and old folk and many died last winter. Then last week, she ordered us to collect shells in the forest and fields, snail shells. The same forest where we may not hunt, or lose a hand or an eye, or worse, by her steward and gamekeeper."

"Snails? For her table?"

Stoller laughed bitterly and shook his head.

"No, man, the lady only wanted the dry shells. So she could wrap thread around them."

Lud just stared at him.

"You cannot know how we laughed at ourselves, and despised ourselves, crawling about for snail shells. We were starving, our kids crying from want, and so we said no to the steward and he too said no to her, and we quit all that was no longer tolerable."

"How did you quit?" said Lud.

"By filling my belly. I killed the steward and we ate his stores and my woman and I drank his wine. Others came and joined us. At first I thought they came to try to take me for my crime. But all of them were done. We took the castle stores and wine, too. Put the old lady out. Wailing, she was. Sent her away with her maid in a donkey cart, down the road to the Benedictines in Mannheim. Gorged ourselves till we were sick with food and passing out from drink. Then we sobered and gathered our wits. That is when our fear came. What could we do?"

"Whatever you must," said Lud.

"That is it. A road peddler had brought the broadsheet damning of Florian, so we knew there was only a fight to come, to change it all. As with you, the robber knights have come out of the forests like hungry bears to throw in with us. All feel there is nothing to lose and much to gain. No more villeins. No more lords."

In the late afternoon shadows, they came out of the great forest, and Lud saw people encamped along the Main River, on the approach to Wurzburg. It looked like a dozen villages of people were in ragged clusters there.

Lud had forgotten the day, the month, almost the year. None of it seemed to matter now. Time was of no importance the closer to the end of it you came.

So tomorrow they would go to the great city hall.

Lud considered the strange portents…

Tomorrow was Black Sunday—Judica, the fifth Sunday of Lent, like Father Michael said—when church icons and crosses were draped in black cloth to signify the Passion diminishing the glory.

He had read Dietrich's Bible, in the German language, through and through. Now he remembered David's plea from Psalms: *Judica me, Deus…Judge me, O God…*

They would go to the city hall where men were judged and came to judge others. Commoners would present their righteous demands for equality and demand new laws.

Villeins would tell the lords to stop being lords.

As if the reading of some words on paper, some demands for rights, would turn back steel and shot. There, he knew what they would face—the bishopric garrison and at least two hundred city magistrates. Konrad would arm his civil servants, too. They would face every vassal whose power, great or small, depended upon Konrad. And those men would be just as desperate to save themselves as were all of these gathering here.

Michael stood on a log and lifted his arms high:

"Brothers, by the grace of our true lord Christ, when that false lord Konrad sees us in our numbers, and he realizes the power of our mighty resolve, he will agree to all the rights we demand, and in all the other great cities, such will be the same. How fitting, on the fifth Sunday of Lent."

Lud looked at the mob and he indeed felt its vigor, sensed its intoxicating optimism, saw hope in all their faces.

And yet, far beyond this gathering, rising in the distance beyond the river, stood the Marienberg Fortress, with its walls and towers dominating the high ground above the spires and roofs of Wurzburg.

"And," said Lud, "if Konrad does not come out? If he withdraws into the Marienberg? What then?"

Said Michael, "Then he is in his own prison, Brother."

"Calling us brothers will not make it so," said Lud.

Then Florian was there, putting a hand on Lud's shoulder. Half a dozen people were following him, watching with bright eyes whatever he did, listening eagerly to whatever he said. And there was Steinmetz and a dozen other impoverished knights and their footmen, staying near Florian, for the knights were as clannish as any villagers.

Said Florian to Steinmetz, "You say there are many more good knights starving and robbing out there, then go ride out, bring them back, tell them a new day is here, but we must fight for it together, as brothers."

"Knights will not come for brotherhood," said Steinmetz, "but they will come for their pride, for the old honor that has been so long lost. It has been asked whether enough knights could become the cavalry of this horde."

"If it could become a people's army, with leaders."

"If we had the numbers, would you lead us?"

"If voted to lead, I would," said Florian. "I am young, but I am studied in all the classics of war. And I have served in Landsknechts for the league, and know all their tactics well, to foil against them."

"What force would we need?" asked the old knight.

"As many as would come," said Florian.

Oh yes they will come, thought Lud, saying nothing, *they will come for the spoils, like wolves to a kill...*

Said Father Michael, "When our numbers join the city mobs, the bishop will sign the articles."

"Why would he not kill us all instead?" said Lud.

"He will bend as he must," said Michael.

Lud argued no more. No use. The sea will drown any man, and argument against fate was folly. But it was Florian who next spoke. Florian, whom they all believed now.

"All men are brothers, Lud. Once we take hands, in our great numbers together, none can withstand the world we bring to all."

All heads turned when Florian spoke. People all around stopped their doings and talking and harked and stared. Lud was amazed that it was so.

"Pride is not enough, Florian."

"Not pride," said Florian. "The might of our will shall make it so, in faith, united together."

Only much blood could ever make it so, thought Lud. *And faith cannot take the place of blood...*

Steinmetz and his men got to their horses and left the camp. Many villagers waved them good-bye and some handed them up loaves of bread or chunks of smoked meat.

But Lud stood staring in the direction of Wurzburg. Low clouds moved past the defensive towers of the Marienberg Fortress and he could feel the eyes watching from there. Looking up at those towers, at the blind mass of the thing all gray and black and faceless, Lud felt a deepening sense of dread slowly coming over him like a premonition. As if that stone monster could rear up, become animate, and leap, crashing down upon all of them...

That was when a rush of ragged boys went racing past him, with sticks and stones in their fists, playing war. Imitating things they had seen done, no doubt.

Lud heard a familiar squeal of anger. He turned, his eyes seeking the source. Then he saw what could not be. But it was.

Little Peter, Kristina's Peter...

Filthy and laughing and wrestling and fencing with his stick, beating back a larger boy while the wild faces of the other boys all screamed encouragement, Peter was yelling—

"Beat him! Gut him! Kill him!"

KONRAD

From the high ramparts of the Marienberg, he no longer felt impregnable, he felt trapped. A scum-like sea of humanity surrounded the fortress as ants upon a corpse.

That horde had swarmed up out of Wurzburg, chasing his guard—what was left of it—back across the bridge up the hill to the Marienberg. Only the narrowness of the great bridge had saved Basil and the last of the Landsknechts.

Now the bridge was littered with dead that the villeins were throwing over the side, like garbage, into the river. Some of his guard had been trapped when the gates had come down and some had died fighting with their backs to the closed gate, but many others had lifted their weapons and joined the uprising, and Konrad had witnessed the obscenity with his own eyes from his tower vantage point: villeins and guardsmen embracing as comrades. He knew there would be bitter resentment among his guard that some of their friends had been blocked by the closing gate.

Now he wore his dress parade armor and stood with other armored men on the high ramparts, idling with his commanders, pretending not to be daunted, no matter how foolish and posturing the ritual armor made him feel, as impotent as a cheap actor in a backstreet play.

"They have no order, nor big guns," said his commanders. "Our stores are in plenty for a long siege."

Then there came a mass cheering from below.

"What are they howling about now?" Konrad said.

"Do not look, your grace," said the commander.

"Do not look at what?"

And then he did look, and would have given anything to have not seen what was down there. Each of Konrad's breaths came like fire, searing up with each gasp, closing his throat, making him need to bend his back, as if God were bending him down upon his knees to beg.

How could this be?

Two hundred feet below, impossibly, amid a crowd of jeering villeins, Sieger's fine white head stared up at him. The eyes were open and milky blue, the tongue hanging out of the soft lips like a black rag. The beautiful head was on a pike just planted there.

Konrad, peering over his tower battlements, saw a thousand villeins farther down the hill, now roasting the rest of Sieger on an open spit. It was a dance of devils from an altarpiece triptych. They danced and laughed.

"They are scum, your grace," said the commander.

"They are my children," he said thickly, for he knew that whatever he said now would always be remembered. "My sad, greedy, lazy, misguided children."

"You are a saint," said the commander, and crossed himself.

Konrad stared at the scene below him with forced dignity, until God began quenching the fire, until his breath began easing a little. He would not react with weakness. All of God's faithful depended upon him now, and he knew he must not fail them.

"Can ball or bolt reach them?" he asked.

"Only by the most skilled, your grace."

"I am not all saint, I am also a man," Konrad told the commander. "Five florins for the ball or bolt that strikes any one of them near the head of my Sieger."

From the ramparts, downward, his guards fired both arquebus and bolt. Most missed wide, but one bolt pierced the leg of a villein, and the crowd cursed and scuttled back down the hill, among the roiling mass of human filth. But then a lead ball struck Sieger's nose.

Konrad screamed for his guards to stop. Now Sieger's head was left all alone on the pole, forlorn, staring up at him.

Dear sweet friend, forgive me, forgive me…

For the first time in weeks and months, he went into his tower and began drinking wine. He had a full flask down him when Basil reported.

On his knees, Basil reported to him, between pants and sobs:

"In the city hall all was ready, your grace, and we heard the Twelve Articles, which amounted to them taking all power from the Church and the ecclesiastical state. They would be born as free men, not villeins as their fathers.

"They would usurp all the rights of nobles, by force. To live where they please however they please and share in the bounty reserved for the rightful Holy Order of things. But also there were guildsmen, artisans, even university students and professors, clamoring for a new order.

"Just as your grace did instruct, our Landsknechts moved in from the outbuildings, and I tried to arrest Muntzer and Riemenschneider and the other chief evildoers…but they fought our men, and many villeins at first dropped but many more then fought back. And of the villeins there were too many, far too many, and many itinerant knights, led by your godson, Florian…"

God was truly testing him now. Konrad again felt his breath come fiery in his throat, the wine boiling up, his heart jolting. His own godson, Florian, arising to destroy all of God's kingdom.

"… all made great slaughter of our goodly men, and only by a miracle of the Holy Mother did any of us escape back here alive…"

"By running away," said Konrad, in one breath.

"I am but a humble monk, your grace, not a warrior."

"And why…was my Sieger…so exposed?"

Basil groveled, kissing Konrad's boots. "He was stabled this week outside the fortress, at upper pasture enjoying the young fillies, your grace, just as you wished. He is so well known as yours, a symbol of your grace, white and noble and strong…"

"Do they all hate me so, my foolish children, to hurt me this way after all my sacrifices for them?"

"It is said the villeins were incensed that he ate better oats and barley than did their children…"

He cut off the monk's words with a hard jerk of Basil's sash and dragged him kicking to the stone rampart. He heard howls of the mob far below, torn in the wind, like the screams of the damned from hell. He forced Basil to peer over the edge. The monk's eyes bulged, pouring tears.

"Do not flatter. Or I will have you lowered over that wall into the loving hands of that horde."

"They punish dear Sieger as they wish to punish your grace. Satan is surely hunting us now."

It was true. Even this fool Basil saw it.

He released Basil and turned from him. There was no more breath to waste in simple rage. He had much praying to do. Within the great stone walls there was silence and the clamor of the damned could not reach him.

His fortress chapel was a sanctuary of lit candles. Only in conference with God would he know his right path now. Prayer always brought surcease from the grip of fire, which surely was the hard hot hand of Satan himself, searing his throat. It could not be the grip of a mere demon. He was bishop. In prayer he could hide from it all.

But not forever.

Later that day, the report came from his garrison commander that in full, even counting magistrates, only two hundred and twelve men at arms now manned the fortress walls and gate. That meant that fully six hundred guard and Landsknechts and magistrates had been lost, murdered by the mob, or perhaps had deserted. Many bishopric retainers lived in the town. Many no doubt had relatives and close friends in that horde. Others, too, might be greedy to sack and loot the wealthy houses and monasteries. They were all scum.

"How many joined them?" Konrad asked, probing.

The commander lowered his face and said nothing.

On his knees for the next hours, Konrad prayed for guidance and for deliverance and for word to get out to other members of the Swabian League. He prayed for the plague to destroy the mob, for all the plagues that had chastened the Egyptians. He prayed for the mob to turn upon itself like a dog to its vomit and he prayed for the soul of his dearest Sieger, to be accepted, even though he was a horse, into the golden gates.

And so, he was besieged. Inside his own lifted gates, he and the survivors of his force were trapped inside the great walls of the Marienberg.

Yes, Konrad thought, *imprisoned...*

Not by an army of Turks, not by invading Swiss nor French, but by his very own flock, his spiritual children, the filthy mob which he had given so much of his adult life to sustain, to nurture, to protect from the temptations of knowledge and selfish will.

He begged God to undergird him...

Doth Thou not see me sorely beset by Thy enemies? Does Muntzer not preach violence and utter ruin of the Holy Church?

Do not their Twelve Articles of equality reduce Thy kingdom to a spawning ground of common evils?

Do their preachers not teach doctrines contradictory to the Bible, even the sanctity of good works? Has not Luther removed books out of the Bible? Yes!

Hebrews! James! Jude! Revelations! These holy books do not fit Luther's radical and corrupt theology!

Is not our sacred purpose to preach the true Gospel, instead of wrongs the ignorant wish to embrace? Is that not the demonic path of anarchy?

But he heard nothing back, and he realized that he was not beseeching, he was demanding. He was raging, because he felt betrayed. He was not sufficiently humble.

At nightfall, word came from the gates that a delegation from the horde had come under white flag of truce to demand the release of all Marienberg prisoners."

"All the scum, thieves, killers, rapists, heretics, all?"

"Many have kinfolk under sentence, your grace."

"Is that their only demand?" asked Konrad.

"Releasing prisoners is a small thing for us, and often done by castles under siege, when concessions are offered."

"And you say they have no cannon?"

"No, your grace. They cannot breach our walls."

"No cannon. Tell them we will pray upon it, for now. Tell them my heart is wounded by their infamies. My horse's cruel murder is a perfect symbol of their ignorance and savagery. As one humble earthly representative of Christ and of our emperor, I shall pray for their souls, and consider the prisoners like the good shepherd I strive to be."

So at least he had a card to play. In a tiny measure his prayers were answered. He could have the prisoners thrown over the wall, for all he cared. They were filth.

His rage was collecting from all his extremities, rising into a volcanic fury that burned and bubbled somewhere just behind his eyes. His chest began to constrict. His breathing shortened and sweat came hot and stinging into his eyes.

He retired to his chambers to lie down.

With prayer and as the first night hours passed, the heat of his rage was spent and, with the tight pain in his breath, he began to feel the stealing of fear. It first came sneaking from behind, down his spine and coiling first in his bowels, making him need to void, and then up it came straight into his heart, more wormy than serpentine, like a rot.

The more he resisted it the worse it became. He went to pray. At the prayer rail his knees were numb like stones. He was shivering in his bishopric robes. His hands fluttered like crippled birds. The rage was gone but something much worse replaced it.

Konrad was terribly afraid. While he napped, he had dreamed of his own head down there, on another pike, alongside Sieger's.

As the Marienberg bells tolled the midnight hour, he tried a desperate new tactic, pleading for the safety of others, in hopes God would hark to such a plea…

Not for me now, I beg of Thee. What of our monasteries and abbeys and nunneries and convents? How can we protect them without your Almighty intervention?

But he was still alone. He was definitely being tested. Oddly, now, searching through his collection of fears, Konrad thought of his dead cousin, Dietrich, the bravest man he had ever known. Dietrich had spoken to him so often of moral values, of good and evil, right and wrong, and in those years, so long past, Konrad had smiled, feeling superior. But he had matured. And now Dietrich's words came flooding back…

Cruelty is always caused by weakness.

It had been when the beaten army had marched back to Wurzburg, with Mahmed as its prize, and they had debated the future of man. Dietrich had spoken Seneca's words, and Konrad considered them now. Perhaps, if a man were weak, he must employ cruelty? Yes, of course, that had to be the meaning. And there was something else Dietrich had said…

Fear is the tool of doubt and evil.

And now Dietrich's own son, Konrad's own godson, serpent seed of ingratitude, was out there championing fear, as if the seal of the Apocalypse had unhinged and a sea of devils was pouring out hungrily upon the land. He wished he had not burned Anna's sleeping robe years ago, for now he could have thrown it down into Florian's face as a taunt.

Now, in that instant, Konrad knew. So this was the way God answered him, with Dietrich's words from long ago.

All doubt vanished. God was training him for some greater destiny. The tightness released from his chest. His breathing cleared and he took in deep, strong breaths of the fresh air of day. God's meaning came as crystalline as a spear of ice through his mind—

He who withholds his rod hates his son, but he who loves him disciplines him diligently.

It was his fault, all of this, and his to remedy.

In a stunning flash that sent him onto all fours, like a beast prostrate before the altar stones, a revelation devoured him. As powerful, he thought, reeling from it, as Saul's revelation on the road to Tarsus. This was God's true voice, not words but knowing, steeling his soul against all doubt and fear, and his true journey as the hand of God, the living will of God on earth, was only just beginning.

Had not Saint Paul made this sacred duty clear?

Fear and trembling to all who do evil...

Whatever happened, they would all pay. He had been too lenient, too kind; too remiss in wielding his shepherd's staff, to control
the unruly flock, for its own good.

He would not die at their hands. He knew that now. And he
would spend the rest of his life achieving their just torments and
damnations, and thereby save many souls.

He swore a sacred oath to God that he would never be weak,
never again. If cruelty were the right weapon, as Dietrich had said,
then let it be so.

LUD

It was worse than bad luck, it was stupid. Like a falling wall is stupid. Its own weight bringing it down.

Driving the bishopric forces back into their own fortress instead of cutting them off first at the bridge. Stupid. Now they were up there in that enormity of stone, looking down from their high ramparts, the approaches to the fortress high upon those steep hills. Stupid, the way the radical priest Muntzer was raving and stirring the mob.

Everyone knew that the Marienberg was designed hundreds of years ago, built by engineers of war to be impregnable from assault, to repel organized invaders—much less this growing mass of folk that was pouring into Wurzburg from all the villages and estates. And it was stupid to think it could be brought down by new ideals and high hopes.

Stupid to have killed a fine horse and put its head on a pike. Stupid to anger the bishop so, and taunt him. Stupid to defy instead of negotiate. Stupid, the way so many were plundering the taverns and monasteries for wine, and reeling through the streets, bragging and strutting in their mob-like excitement, men and women both carrying weapons like one sex of brotherhood, unleashed.

He knew that the league had couriers on the roads night and day, and some riders might be taken but not all. Some would take back the word of this siege. Some of the fleeing bishopric men would cry alarm in Munchen, in Ingolstadt, wherever the league had castles and power.

Hell was not coming, it was already here. A plan of survival was what was needed. All else was stupid.

Fires were built in the coming darkness of night. There was the wail of hurdy-gurdy and fiddle and singing, laughing, and whole herds of folk dancing together. The soldiers who had come over to this side danced with country folk, and even university fops were among them.

The country villeins, obvious from their scruffy beards and simple cloaks and belts and shoes, stacked their weapons and farm tools. Some danced, waving their scythes and hoes and flails. Despite the Lenten rule against eating meat, or perhaps in open defiance of it, many were eating chunks of steaming flesh from the bishop's horse, waving them in salute of one another, and laughing.

Gangs of kids chased and grappled and stole meat, and some took ale. Lud kept looking for little Peter. He was sure he had seen him once with the other Giebel boys, but then they were gone.

Once, he saw Big Merkel carrying his forge hammer. Lud grabbed his arm. "Go home, man. Go back to Giebel, find the others, take them with you while you can."

"We are here to finish it, Lud."

"You cannot break that wall down."

"All my life I am called Big. Big Merkel. All my life I must try to live up to the name, Big Merkel, big man. Now I shall go on with it. And my hammer."

"You are a smithy, not a warrior."

Merkel jerked his arm free. The cords and muscles of his arm felt like iron bands under the greasy, thick skin.

"Then with my good hammer I shall fight like a smithy."

The excitement was like a plague infecting them all.

Lud pulled Florian away from a clutch of his new admirers, most of them city men and villeins, but also the itinerant knights, including old Steinmetz.

Aside, he told Florian, "This is all stupid. There will be none to survive the first attack from any force that comes against us, not without bringing order to this horde that some are calling the People's Army."

"Exactly what the knights are all saying," said Florian. "But there will be no force coming against us from outside. The Twelve Articles were read in every bishopric. In all the great cities there is much uprising. Muntzer has set into plan the taking of the castles in every city. His horde of miners are marching in the thousands, attacking cities to the north and east."

"Some miners would be nice here, to dig under those walls, but it would take months. We do not have months. They will find mercenaries to send against us. We cannot take that fortress, Florian. Do as your father would do."

"And what would my father do, exactly? Have you consulted him from the next world?"

"Tease them out into an open fight. Use the knights for cavalry. Form ranks of villeins. Give them their chance to strike those they so despise."

"Against my will," said Florian, "they taunted Konrad with his pet horse but they are seasoned men and will not take such easy bait. The fortress must be taken by storm."

"All the gold and the silver from across the seas could not buy armies enough to take that fortress without great cannon to breach those walls."

"I am not my father. And God is with us."

Lud felt stung, taking the easy words as insult—Florian talking down to him as he and Witter had done on the long ride back from England.

"God is with us. Do you say those cheap words for the others, or do you believe such a foolish thing?"

"It is truth because we shall make it so. We shall take the Marienberg by storm, without cannon, and it will be our citadel until the rights of all men are recognized, once and for all. We who see the future are in a unique position to change our world now, and such a chance may never come again in our lifetimes. Have faith, Lud."

So there it was.

No use arguing with someone who imagined he could see the future, especially a future he wished for, which had to be paid for in much suffering and tragedy.

Yes, his bad luck was the one thing he could always count on never failing.

God is with us. Believing that was the worst folly of all, since every side thought the same ridiculous self-defeating thing.

At least Kristina was not here. At least God might really be on her side, for she did no harm in this world, only as much good as she could manage.

He thought again of little Peter, how he had chased the boy like trying to catch a feral dog and had lost him in the pack of crowding people.

Muntzer stood on a wagon bed above the crowd and Lud saw him, robed in black, hair wild, eyes glinting in the firelight, teeth flashing. If killing Muntzer would have stopped all this, Lud knew now he would do it, but all was folly and there was nothing stronger than folly.

Munzter shouted for Florian to join him.

"Florian! Florian Geyer! Knight and brother!"

So now, with bonfires lit in the night darkness, Florian climbed onto the wagon bed. He stood over the multitude of faces that had shouted for their hero to come up and speak.

Lud, by old habit, posted himself on watch. He stood in the front of the mob, between the wagon and the host of people in revolt, and he watched them for signs of any who might sneak an attempt to kill Florian.

When all was folly, the cunning often had their way.

He trusted no one. There could be a bishopric spy angling for a reward, or just a madman seeking fame, and Florian insisted upon mingling openly with all. Just another folly in this growing plague of follies. Life seemed obvious and solid, but Lud knew that was an illusion. Death was always closer than one thought, until it was too late.

As he had been flag bearer for Dietrich, acting as footman bodyguard in the city, Lud naturally took that role now, guarding the son who looked so like his dead father. Life just kept pushing everyone forward toward the edge. The end was always somewhere lying in ambush.

Lud palmed his stubby dagger under his tunic hem, held low and ready. He watched the faces of the crowd, not Florian, as Florian began to speak, and a magical quiet fell upon the host. In the faces was awe, and more; they loved Florian. Now and then passed a familiar face—Linhoff, Max, Tomen, and then he thought he saw Dolf, but the crowd kept shifting as all tried to see Florian better, their hero.

Said Florian, with raised arms, as if embracing them all:

"My brothers and sisters, comrades all, there are only two kinds of people. Those who work and those who do not. You are those who work. Those in that fortress do not work. And your work, all of it, belongs to you!"

The crowd erupted, cheering, interrupting Florian. He waited, smiling, nodding, approving. Then went on:

"We are entering the most important time in our human story thus far. With printing and reading, our world has become one of equals in power structures, in social structures. Their armies travel by forced march, with their gallows wagons and whore wagons and monks selling indulgences for killing! We shall march each in the cause of freedom and equality, with no evils driving us, no doom at our backs! We shall take control of our world. We are our own future!"

Muntzer raised a pike. At the end of it on top was a simple villein's floppy leather shoe. The screaming crowd loved that.

Muntzer said, "Here is our standard! Our signet is the common shoe, raise them up high so that we know who to follow in battle!"

Shouted Florian, "Not the fine boot of the lords! But the shoe of men who love liberty and equality, and the love of God for every man and woman equally!"

The crowd roared and danced. A drum started booming. Lud sensed the pressure mounting in them, all the pent-up hard work, all the unjust labors, all the starving decades and generations of slaving for others, yoked and helpless, all of it powering this angry rush to the abyss.

Over it all, Muntzer shouted, "In every great city of our land, our brothers and sisters are standing as we now stand! All monasteries and castles must give themselves over and share all their riches, and all so-called lords and nobles must live as brothers with us. For what is truly noble? No more shall there be villeins! Only equal brother-hood is noble in the sight of Christ!"

Booming cheers. Flails beat against shovels and hoes.

Muntzer lifted his arms high, and said, "Tomorrow we storm the Marienberg! There lives the Antichrist! That evil cur Konrad! Tomorrow we trap and collar him like the beast from hell that he is! Bring every ladder from the city and lash them together! We shall take that fortress and release all prisoners, and seize God's true freedom for all, to secure the sacred rights of every man and woman!"

Lud stood there like a rock as the cries of joy and pride came pounding past him, and he could not stop the crush of bodies that rushed forth to raise Florian upon their shoulders, dancing him away as if he could fly.

So, after all, it was about plunder.

They would empty out the wealth of the castles and monasteries and share it all out. It made sense. The wealth had been extracted from the slavish toil of villeins in the first place.

He saw Father Michael trailing Muntzer, like a faithful puppy. He saw him blessing villeins who bowed, on their knees with heads bent.

Lud wanted to pull the priest aside, to taunt him, *is suicide not a folly? Is it not a mortal sin? Is this not a mass suicide? What difference between your blessings for war and the monks' blessings for the empire?*

But he knew what the answers would be—the same God-is-on-our-side lie that all sides always used, that Muntzer and now even Florian used. If God were on any side, there would be no war.

Now occurred something truly remarkable.

A great vote was taken, among the entire horde.

"In our People's Army, one man, one vote," shouted Florian. "Each vote equal to any other. You shall fight in your village or guild or miner units as you assemble that way. Therefore, vote among yourselves in your group and vote for the man who shall lead you in formation for battle. This man will be your sergeant. Vote for a fair man you trust, not the popular one but the solid man of experience who will not quail at the first flight of balls or bolts. Vote also for the leader of this war, and your sergeant shall vote that name for you."

There was great consternation and rumbling and a sense of excited conferring among the many groups in the horde. It did not take a full hour and it was done.

The groups put forth their sergeants, and the sergeants cast an almost unanimous vote, shown by taking sides. Over a hundred stood together for Florian, with perhaps a dozen standing apart for Muntzer. Florian was voted leader.

From somewhere came a flag waving on a pole—red and white strips of cloth with a black cloth shoe sewn on it.

Florian made another speech to great cheering, rousing the crowd even more, but Lud hardly heard any of it now. Florian had the gift of good speech, he was learned and brilliant, but speeches that sent men to fight did not win their fights, despite the popular stories of glorious heroes.

Lud turned away and went out of that thronging mass, until he was alone. Fog was rising from the slopes beneath the Marienberg, like veils.

So it was now true, each man had had one vote equally. Never had he imagined he would see the day when the vote of a villein would carry the same measure of destiny as that of a knight or a priest. His mind could not follow the sense of where it would all end. Would votes be needed for every great decision? If men could vote, could they take back their vote if things went bad? And did they not go bad always?

Now Lud stood looking up into the stone heights of the fortress, where watch lanterns burned high on the ramparts, and he felt the hard appraising eyes of professional men at arms, readying themselves to do their life's work: to kill. In that moment, he wished he were among such seasoned killers. Instantly, that thought shamed him.

He turned away from looking up there.

In the fire-lit camp, the dancing had stopped. Ladders were being brought and lashed. Tools were being honed on the rocks that jutted from the ground.

These were his people. They were good, strong people. They had always deserved better, and in their strength, hardened and loyal, maybe they had a chance.

He wished Dietrich were here, not Florian. He wished he were not part of this great stupidity. He wished he did not know the heartbreaking things he would see tomorrow.

Late in that night he heard a woman singing.

He thought it was Kristina, somehow, but she was not there. It was an old woman, singing some exhausted men to sleep.

"This night, this night, every night and all,
fire and fleet and candlelight,
may Christ receive thy soul…when thou from hence away art past,
every night and all,
To heaven thou come at last, may Christ receive thy soul…"

Listening to her sweet voice, seeing the faces of men softened in sleep like children, Lud knew that—as sure as the sun would rise and the cocks would crow—he would be running at Florian's side, leading, pushing the stupid ladders, with all hell raining down upon them in the hottest forefront of the first assault.

So, in the deepest dark before dawn, there was nothing left to do but to strip himself down, to crawl, worming his way up the slope toward the fortress.

Up he went, out of the firelight of camp, past a final picket line Florian had ordered posted. The men were drunk, half of them asleep, and Lud easily slipped through them unseen.

Keeping to the low places, the darkest places, he found the stone drain that ran with sewage to the river, then he came up along the old contours of ancient earthworks, grassy ruins from some long-forgotten war.

Low in the muddy grass, sliding and squirming, he saw something half visible in the dark; he realized it was the impaled horse head, its ears droopy now and the eyes beginning to shrivel. That folly would cost many lives, he thought, moving again. Something rustled to his left. He froze, flattening himself, unable to see what or who it was. A rabbit came past him, saw him, and fled.

The sun will be coming, move faster...

With muddy, slimy wormlike progress, Lud slithered along, scouting the great walls turn by turn. Now as he came around the side with the great gate, he saw lanterns being lowered on long chains from the ramparts, sweeping the walls for any sign of intruders. Sometimes he could hear distant rustlings.

He came to the verge of the deep fortress ditch, a black gulf at least twenty feet deep, running along the immense wall. Many would die faltering here, Lud thought. The ladders would be fumbled, the men would slip and fall and showers of bolts and balls would eviscerate them here.

He crawled along the verge of the great weedy ditch, hoping to see some place of crossing, and saw none.

Now and again, invisible bolts came sailing blindly down. One slammed into the mud inches from his right foot. They must have plenty of ordnance, he thought, to waste their bolts so. They must be saving their musket powder for daylight.

He felt them up there, sharp and alert, professionals methodically preparing their killing tools. They knew the strength of their great walls, the power of its design. They knew how deeply they were hated. They would be desperate, knowing the hordes wanted everything. And they would be resolute in their desperation.

He lay there looking up from the dark at their winking lantern lights on high, their watch changing in the great tower battlements. And he understood those desperate men better than he did the hordes encamped so joyously below.

Up there, they were trapped. Some were inwardly despairing of their own bad luck. Some had religion and secretly cursed, hoping God would not notice. Others had no religion and yet now, for the first time, they prayed.

All of them were hard trained men, trained in killing, ready to kill as many as could be killed. They were Konrad's personal guard, handpicked, and they believed they were in the right. They had wives and mothers and children somewhere, too, to live for. No men would be harder to fight. Any of them taken alive would be tormented to death, slowly, as they themselves would torment those who had cornered them, if they could.

Far better to die fighting. Unless you had a reason to live.

Kristina, he thought, *Kristina…*

If he could have her, somehow, he would do anything to keep her. He would even want to live. He would run and hide with her. Anything. But he knew he could never have her, wherever she was now.

Crawling backward, he looked back up a last time at the black stone mass above him. That was his destiny, not Kristina. That was his luck. His fate.

If only he could detect some weakness, perhaps discover some blind spot between towers, but now he saw the first glow of dawn in the east and the cocks were crowing in the city below, so he squirmed back down the steep slopes in the slimy weeds, and despaired of finding some antidote to the great sadness of the oncoming days.

Night assaults should be tried first, on this west side, this one blind spot between the towers. If the night attack faltered here, there would still be a chance of retreat when the sun was yet low and shadows heavy at dawn. But the ditch would catch many, far too many.

He could only report that to Florian. There was no other good news here to be squeezed from fate, only bad.

KRISTINA

She was exhausted, but continued running along the road in the breaking daylight, her slippers long gone, hurrying and stumbling. In the rising light she saw a dead horse and ran past it.

The sun was up and still she had not found Peter or the gang of boys. They had to be far ahead, with all the others of Giebel. The road was full of tracks. Horses, wagons, feet.

She felt as if she had lost her child forever. Now there was only Peter. Her precious gift from God. Her inheritance from Berthold. Peter was her rock, her purpose, her salvation.

What happened to Giebel or Anna or Grit or Lud or Witter or anyone else, it was all behind her now.

Please let Peter be all right, please, please...

They would all be going to Wurzburg, all to kill or be killed. She no longer cared about Lady Anna who lay like one dead, curled up on her bed like a despondent child, staring at the empty wall and refusing to respond. She no longer cared about the wounded brought back on wagons from the fight on the road, nor the wails of women and children.

Behind her then, overtaking her, came a short wagon, pulled by a team of plow mules jingling in their crude work harness.

Grit and Witter.

"Kristina!" said Witter. He jumped down to help her.

"My boy," Kristina said, hardly able to stand.

"Get up, Sister," said Grit.

Witter said, "We will find Peter with the others, even if we have to go all the way to Wurzburg."

Witter helped push her up, and then he climbed back onto the wagon, too. Holding the reins, Grit snapped them and the mules moved down the road with the shuffling, slow pace of mules.

"Your feet," said Witter, reaching toward Kristina, "they bleed."

She pushed his hands away and crouched forward, staring past the mules as the road came and passed, as if staring hard enough would make the world turn faster underneath the wagon. The left mule was young but the right one was older and slower, and the cart kept pulling to the right, as Grit constantly fought the reins.

"Dolf and Symon are gone, too," said Grit, though Kristina had not asked, did not care now. "May God help them if they have joined the horde going to Wurzburg."

"Peter," said Kristina.

They did not understand. No one understood.

Oh God, please save my child until I am reunited somehow by your grace again with him, with my arms around him this time I shall never let go, forgive me my trespasses, help me now, O Lord...

"We will find your boy," Witter kept saying.

"Walk on, mule, walk on!" urged Grit, making them hurry. "We must find them. We must do what we can. If you see Linhoff, tell me, if I find Peter, I will tell you."

"Linhoff?" Kristina said absently.

Said Witter, "Think of it. You can say whatever you want, wherever you want, as much as you want, and none will torture or burn you for it."

Said Grit, "Not this way. Not this evil way of death and cruelty. Not this way of the devil."

Grit muttered prayers and jerked the reins. It was not until they were on the approaches to the Main River, with the spires of the city visible in the full-rising sun, and then on the river road leading to the great bridge, that they heard the roar, a booming rumble that first sounded like rolling thunder but then kept repeating. And Kristina suddenly knew that the roar, rising and falling, was the screaming of thousands of voices in one outraged cry.

It was the sound of battle. The sound she had heard on the day she first met Lud and Mahmed.

"It has begun," said Witter.

Kristina thought, *What good is freedom without my child?*

"So much death," said Grit. "I feel it, we must go help those who suffer. Oh, my poor Linhoff, Brother Dolf and Brother Symon, please do not kill."

Grit stood up on the wagon, trying to see better. Kristina stood. Witter stood.

Kristina saw great black clouds rising from the heights around the Marienberg and swarming shapes like schools of fish rushing up the slopes.

"Oh no, oh dear God," said Grit, hurrying the mules.

The older mule now stumbled and the cart jerked and stopped.

Kristina leapt down and was running barefoot, hard and fast toward the bridge where Heck had hanged himself, where Berthold had led her first into Wurzburg.

And in her mind a song came and she sang it with all her heart, in her mind only, a beseeching song of her fear:

Preserve my child, O Lord,
please God,
forgive me my sins of neglect,
O Lord, please...

LUD

The worst nightmares are the ones that repeat themselves. Lud always knew how bad it would be, and sometimes it became even worse.

Two assaults on successive nights had both failed.

It was madness to attack such walls where there was no breach. The fortress ditch was filled with dead and dying, and its defenders would allow none to rescue the dying, showering them with balls and bolts.

Now the third assault, at daybreak, was failing.

Lead shot and iron bolts rained down from the high walls of the Marienberg; scathing fire that harvested the People's Army like so much winter wheat under the scythes.

There was no order, more a kind of swarming. With drums beating and their standard of common shoes on pikes waving, the villeins yelled as they broke and stormed up the slopes that were the great bed of the Marienberg. It seemed to slumber in a silence of contempt, on its heights without reaction. Then as the horde reached its base, down came the rain of lead shot and steel bolts and iron canisters and baskets of broken stones.

There was a madwoman shouting, raving, screaming for them to fight harder. Hoffman, someone called her; they said she was the wife of a bookseller who had been drawn and quartered years ago.

Lud, riding close along the ranks, passed behind her, and as she whirled around he stared—*Arl?*

He recognized her in a flash of disbelief. Hoffman was Arl, the weaver, the gentle baby catcher, not the wife of any bookseller. Arl, whose twins Fridel and Hermo had died years ago in another war under his command. Arl, whose daughter Greta had been killed in the fight on the road. That had broken her, he realized.

Now she was Black Hoffman, driving others, perhaps to take revenge for all the wrongs in the whole world, screaming at them as one who had lost her mind.

Bolts and ball flew about Hoffman, and her long black sleeves were pierced but she seemed magical, impervious.

Lud flashed upon all this in a single thought and then the battle surged, pushing him on up the line. He looked ahead and saw confusion, which always means disaster.

The horde was breaking apart against the gulf of the great ditch around the fortress wall. At the base of the Marienberg, a great slaughter began choking the assault's momentum and filling the ditch.

Ladders tumbled over bodies and yet some were getting across to the fortress. In sheer numbers they ran across ladders and bodies and all hell fell upon them from the fortress wall.

Lud marveled at their mad courage.

Under that relentless downpour, many ladders went up. Brave men, angry men, screaming men, some women, too, with farm and artisan tools and pikes and swords, pushed upon the shaking, wobbling ladders, breaking some, others half-reaching the ramparts, speared, stabbed, shot, pushed over. Those working hardest stopped screaming. Then they broke and all fell back together.

A hundred—too angry to go back—raged and clawed at the wall and were killed on the ladders. Some of the ladders were taken up by grappling hooks from the ramparts, others pushed back over. Lud saw it happen and ground his teeth, for there was nothing he could do.

They gathered into a solid horde again.

Standing out of range, Lud stared at their losses scattered between them and the stone fortress. Its massive sides showed white in flashes of lighting, then black again.

A wind came up from the west, pushing the black gunpowder clouds from the fortress and blowing away the shouts of battle, so the scene seemed even more dreamlike to Lud, as he watched so many dying in that muted violence on the stone walls.

The only concession Lud had won from Florian was that Florian would not lead the next ladder assault.

"Brothers or not, men still need leaders. They must see you riding as a knight rides," Lud had persuaded. "With the ladders you will fall in the first five minutes, and they will have no hero, no leader, none but Muntzer, who knows nothing of the order of battle."

Again they went.

So now Lud stayed close to Florian, both on horse, trying to focus the attack on the west wall, that one blind spot Lud had seen scouting in the night. There the fighting portals were spread too wide between the side towers, leaving an angle where the ladders might have a slight chance.

Florian rode too close and was almost killed in the first assault, his horse shot out from under him, and in the next two assaults Lud was kept busy holding back Florian from riding too close to the walls. Steinmetz and other knights on horse rode with them, but the horde had its own mind and there was no use for cavalry, for there was no enemy on the field. Lud saw Arl running, yelling, falling behind.

But again the ditch began to fill with new bodies.

The bishop's men stayed on their high ramparts and did much killing safely from there. Once, a monk called down at them through a shouting cone—

"Our good Konrad, our prince-bishop, forgives you, his children, and begs you save your own immortal souls from eternal damnation! Go back to your homes in peace, and all sins shall be forgiven in this world and the next!"

"When we reel out good Konrad's guts!" some wit shouted back, the horde jeering up at the men on their high wall. Then bolts and balls came raining down in answer.

"Bastards, cowards," said Florian, seething.

Lud said to him, "Look at them and learn. Your father said there is always much to learn, especially from a losing fight."

"Losing? We shall not lose this fight."

"You have no breach in those walls, no cannon, so they have no fear of us. The fight was lost before it began, Florian. Bring them back. Use them better than this."

Just below them on a lower slope, Muntzer stood like a wild man on a wagon, back from it all, waving his long sleeves and shouting prayers for victory. Each wave came tumbling back down all bloodied, and he leaped down, pale, furious, and harangued them to go again.

Florian and Lud rode up to him.

Said Muntzer, "The new Franconian troop has been formed. Our brothers of Mergentheim, Rottenburg, and Anspach. They are all on the march and bring a cannon! Nothing can stop us now! God is good! God be praised!"

"A cannon," said Florian.

"Yes, thank God."

"Call them back from those walls," said Lud.

"You are our Black Host!" raved Muntzer. "You knights of Christ in black armor! You shall drive the evildoers before your horses. Never in history have knights' cavalry brothered with commoners, for the glory of Christ!"

Lud wanted to shut him up.

This unwashed priest was brainsick, Lud thought, mad or brilliant or both, and even Florian seemed to defer to his frantic energy, for the horde loved him.

They rode back up to the slopes where many were helping the wounded back down the bloody trails. Others were rallying and screaming and shaking their tools and weapons, looking up at the impassive hulk of stone that was the Marienberg.

"He is insane," said Lud.

"Muntzer is inspired, not insane," said Florian.

"The Black Host, they call us?" said Steinmetz, riding aside now. "If my armor were not poor it would be the Silver Host. This is all poorly done. A waste of good people."

"The enemy will not take the field," said Lud.

"I must lead the next ladder assault," said Florian. "I was wrong to listen to you, and sit upon this horse."

"Did you not hear me?" said Lud. He blocked Florian's horse with his own. "What you must do is call them back and plan better. Wait for the cannon."

"Listen to your man," said Steinmetz.

Florian's face was strained and he looked much older now than he had when making his heroic speeches to the horde.

"By God, Brothers, are you with us or against us?"

"I am with you, Florian," said Lud.

Steinmetz said, "They must be trained. Trained and led in good order. Else they give their lives for nothing."

"My fault, all my fault," said Florian.

The slopes crawled with wounded coming back down, leaving the dead, hundreds of them, where they fell.

The wind of the coming storm shifted and the wails and moans of the wounded came drifting down on the wind. Many who had retreated now turned and started back up to try to help. Then the first big, fat drops fell, and it began to rain.

Lud heard the beat of distant drums.

Not from the Marienberg, but from the approaches to the bridge.

"Look," said Florian. "Look, just as Muntzer said."

More hordes were coming. The whole countryside was on the march. Lud had never seen anything like this. Could not have dreamed it, nor imagined it.

A cheering arose from the defeated group, and just as quickly, the whole sense of defeat became one of new hope, of unreasoning optimism, even of victory, as if the baleful Marienberg had already been taken and none had died.

"They shall bend to God's people now!" screamed Muntzer, shaking both fists at the fortress. "The Antichrist trembles. I feel his fear! Behold the dreaded might of holy brotherhood!"

Lud rode down to see the new force. They were led by a dissident knight, old Goetz von Berlichingen, bald and monkish, with a great white beard. Dietrich had known him. Lud remembered Goetz from long ago.

"Eight thousand foot!" some were saying in the crowd. "Three thousand guns! And cannon!"

Goetz led scores of knights who rode with him, but in flashy armor, not the cheap black armor of Florian's impoverished knights. They wore a dozen different tunics of all colors, bright and garish, wearing them inside out so the signets of arms from their former wearers would not show. The mounted warriors looked like a wild troupe of carnival fighters, and had taken their gear from dead men, he knew.

Then he saw their infantry of foot soldiers, many with shouldered muskets, marching behind the riders. They carried a crude banner with a signet of broken chains and a shoe, and the name boldly sewn—Gay Bright Troop.

Many of the men of foot were a horde of miners, but they marched in good order, like troops, pacing truculently, their bodies sturdy and hard, determined faces with the grim stubbornness of miners. Lud admired their toughness. He saw nothing gay nor bright in their aspect.

They made the city people appear incredibly soft, welcoming the hard miners, chanting, many with shoes on poles and pikes, everyone joining the cheering, then embracing. The miners waved the red and white flag, sewn from strips of cloth, with the black cloth shoe displayed.

Florian rode up beside Lud.

"Gay Bright Troop. Look at their good order and pride. We too need a banner and a name. Look how they shine."

"Our armor is black," said Lud.

"Black and old."

"Then let us be the Black Host, as Muntzer called us."

"A good, honest name. So we shall be."

Here came Muntzer shouting praises to God.

Lud sat his horse and stared, as the new horde flowed around the clutch of knights in black armor, pressing them with flowers and jugs of ale and wine, and Muntzer praising them and blessing them loudly, all in Christ's name.

Even all these new, hard, determined bodies would not break down those fortress walls, Lud knew.

Then Lud heard a rumbling of great wheels farther back in their march, and a wide grin, much more of relief than of any kind of elation, broke across his face for the first time in many days.

He saw the great, long tube of the cannon first, then as it came nearer, he saw its massive caisson, pulled by oxen, designed for only one purpose—to breach walls of stone. Thousands poured across the bridge, drumming, and the monster rolled on its huge caisson, and many stroked the long bronze barrel and pushed at the big wooden wheels.

The horde of Wurzburg roared at the sight of the big gun. But Lud could not make sense of the picture before him. Watching from his horse as the cannon train passed, he realized what was missing—no ball and powder wagon came behind the big gun.

Then an hour later, to renewed cheering, came the Tauber Valley Horde, four thousand of them marching across the bridge. Lud watched them occupy the hill opposite the Marienberg. They had brought light cannons designed for infantry assaults—four culverins and thirteen falconets, light guns not for the breaking of stone walls, but they set about firing at the Marienberg from hill to hill.

Already, the miners of the Gay Bright Troop were digging into the Marienberg hill well away from the bombardment. Lud saw this and shook his head. Tough as they were, the best miners would need at least a month or more to dig their way under those walls from there, and breach them by collapse. There was no month to spare; the emperor and the princes of the Swabian League would be sending forces long before a month passed.

But at least it kept the miners busy, he thought. And the small-bore cannonades and mining would frighten the bishop, no doubt of that, even if much precious powder was being wasted.

Lud and many others sat on the bridge approaches and watched the show. The light cannons leaped and gushed fire and smoke spouts; the balls flew in arcs, some breaking on the wall stones of the Marienberg, some bouncing off, flung back down the slopes as if the fortress were shrugging mere hail from her massive stone shoulders.

WITTER

Near the bridge into the city, the little farm wagon had been pushed out of the road by chanting men, and Kristina had thrown herself into the mob that crossed the bridge.

"Peter, God help my Peter," she kept saying, with Grit trying to hang on to her.

Witter knew Kristina only wanted to find her child and nothing else mattered to her now. He moved in front of her to try to fend off the surging bodies, to protect her.

"Kristina! Stay close to me! We shall find Peter!"

But as they were jostled through the choking press of humanity, narrowing at the city gates, he was pushed so hard that he lost sight of Grit and Kristina.

The horde was tidal, irresistible. There were miners, tillers, city men, serving women, people of all kinds, children swarming underfoot. There was an infectious festival air of freedom unlike anything Witter had ever experienced.

The big Abbey of St. James, the monastery off the square, was broken open, all the Benedictine monks thrown out, and its cellars torn open and wine casks rolled into the street and axed open. Monks and nuns, too, were being shoved and mocked. Some nuns led shy orphans like flocks of geese. Others knelt and prayed and others tried defending the abbey and were beaten down. Witter moved through it all as if invisible.

A broken cask poured the red blood of the grape across the pavers and he stepped over streams of wine and remembered his foolish words to his father so long ago:

"Without Ceres and Bacchus, Apollo dims."

And Judah had gently, urgently said, *"Son, wine is a holy beverage of great power, reserved for the sacred occasions, not for carousing with your friends when you should be deep in study and meditation."*

Chaos rolled clanging through the world and it had taken away his family, and wherever he went he saw that it rolled through other cities in other ways, and now it was here.

Suddenly all was changed. The world had no rules. Wurzburg was flooded with these new people of all kinds and their sense of brotherhood was festive. Witter was swept along in it all. No one harmed another. Many shoved jugs of ale or wine at him. Women kissed him and men hugged him.

Everything was upside down. He realized he still carried the bishopric pass coin—now a death warrant instead of a safe passage token—and covertly he palmed it and slipped it into an open cask of red wine. Having nothing was now the badge of safe passage.

The thunder of cannonades rolled now and again. Sometimes it made a cracking report, sometimes it rolled like distant thunder. The violent noise seemed to excite the mob even more, somehow, ever increasing the crowd's audacity of trespasses. People did what they wanted now.

Witter stayed out of the way. He saw other abbeys sacked. Icons lay in the streets and frantic nuns of all ages prayed and wept. A cursing man pissed on a carving of Saint Stephen and another man beat him down senseless. The nuns tried to stop them both and were flung away.

Witter interfered in nothing and kept moving. He was the ghost that he had always been, ever moving.

Monks fled the Holy Redeemer, and St. Andrew's, and some fought outside St. Stephens and were beaten down by the mob. Their treasures of gold were pulled out into the streets and loaded into carts, some said for revenue to arm the villeins for war, some said to buy cannons, others said it was every man for himself.

Some monks followed the cart as if lost, chanting: *"Vicit agnus noster, eum sequamer…"*

Witter knew the Latin: *Our lamb has conquered, let us follow Him...*

Then a great mob came pushing through and swept the monks and him and many others away, by its sheer mass.

In the core of the mob, a big cannon was being hauled by teamed oxen, the wheels pushed by a hundred men and women, out of the city, and Witter followed until they had it in view of the fortress, its great log-like barrel tilted up at the Marienberg.

Casks of wine were rolled up beside the wheels and men pretended to be loading the cannon. But there was no carriage of ordnance, no projectiles.

They have no balls for the big gun! Witter realized.

It was like everything else about all of this. A pageantry of unrestrained folly.

The old order was being deconstructed and the new order had nothing yet to put in its place. There was only the theatrical threat of the miners digging away, their light cannon whose balls bounced off the fortress, and now this big gun with no balls.

"By God," said one, "the cringing bastards behind those walls will soil their hose and release the prisoners now."

For the next hours he searched the mad city for Kristina. And all around him were scenes that often stopped him, and he stared in pure amaze.

There was a gang of men looting the shops one by one. Their leader was a short, stocky, bald man and Witter stared because he recognized him but could not place him at first. Then he was sure it was the old Giebel steward, Huber. Witter ducked into a side street.

He passed Heck's print shop, which had become Veritas Press. All the windows were smashed out, papers drifting everywhere, sacked. Witter thought of the arrest of Heck and the old ones, and how the bishopric magistrates burned books here.

Old grudges were being settled. There were no magistrates to stop anything. He saw a fight to the death, three men against one, with knives. He saw a woman being chased by another woman with an axe. No one bothered about him. All seemed obsessed by their own unleashed concerns. But he was wary lest someone recognize him.

Searching the city, he made his way down along the tavern row with a fear of encountering Frieda, or "Paulina" as she was now known, for she might denounce him to the mob as a bishopric man. But a riotous crowd of drunks was there. The taverns were sacked along with the rest. The entertainers were all gone.

Then there were the street preachers—wild-eyed as Muntzer, but raving of their own accords, as if each wished to be leader of their own sect. Witter did not pass long enough to listen, nor did many others.

And throughout the day he kept moving, hoping to see Kristina around every next corner.

Only the Jewish Quarter was barred to him. His weeping room in the alley, with his peephole, was long gone. He knew they were inside, hiding behind the high walls, the men ready to defend that gate with everything they had. They had spent their money well. The thick iron sheets and beams were scarred from futile attempts to break in, no doubt by rogues, thieves. This strange struggle was villeins against lords, nothing to do with Jews, for once. They were trapped in there, praying, waiting this out, supplicating to Yahweh, and yet safe in there, too, for they were outcasts and took no sides and the city mostly ignored them.

Standing in the alleyway, Witter looked at the strong gates and had one of his quick flights of thought. It was of the wary rabbi and his beautiful daughter—what was her name?—Rachael, yes. And how terrified they would be now if he tried to beat on the gates, tried to enter, and why would he think he belonged with them?

If this were a fable and he were writing it for a broadsheet story, he would have the Jews take him in and bless him, and the wise rabbi would give him his beautiful daughter Rachael, and there would be sweet honorable bliss. But this was not a broadsheet and he did not know nor love the rabbi's daughter. He lived in this world, where men hunted one another. Where there were those who prayed and those who killed and those who took whatever they wanted from those who were weak. Where people like Kristina and Grit—who believed in universal love—were doomed, savaged, destroyed.

A tumbrel came rolling past, pushed and pulled by a crowd of shouting men. It was full of monastery treasures. Nuns walked behind it praying and some were sobbing, and no one paid them the least attention.

So Witter kept moving. He knew Peter was here, somewhere, near the army, with the pack of boys. Kristina would search for Peter. She would come here, be here somewhere. He had to find her. His feelings for Kristina were his last thread to sanity.

The cathedral and courts and university and all else stood open, and people did whatever they wished and took whatever they wished, as if righting all ancient wrongs, as if collecting debts, and some who tried to stop them were struck down.

Fine clothes were thrown flapping down in bright bundles from windows, and many clownish poor put them on, strutting mockingly. Piles of books came down from rich libraries. Gold icons from the cathedral and from wealthy houses were stacked onto a cart guarded by tough men under the sign of the shoe on a pole. The plunder was returning to the plundered.

"I am Mayor Riemenschneider," shouted a tall man in a good black robe. His face was long and narrow with sorrowful eyes, and he stood in the way of the treasure cart with lifted arms, like Moses parting the waters. "This is roguery and thievery, hardly the right path to equality!"

"Brothers need no mayor!"

They shoved him unceremoniously out of the way.

"By order of Muntzer and the Christian Brotherhood, all wealth shall serve all, shared out in common and used for good common bread."

"You do violence in the name of Christ, just as does the bishop!" cried Riemenschneider, again trying to block them. "You know I have stood for the new way, the right way!"

"Artist!" They spat at him and threw him aside.

Witter pushed on, searching for Kristina, or Peter, or Grit. Dark clouds were building to the west and they looked leaden. Rain was coming.

He saw people pushing carts.

"Books! For all who can read!"

He stopped at one of the carts.

"From the houses of the wealthy," said the youth, obviously a university student from his flashy attire. "Books should be for all, not just the rich. Take a book, Brother, take more, if you can read. Open your mind. Books for all!"

Witter picked up one gilt-edged volume. The carts moved on, trailed by people of all kinds, taking books from them. Some carried many, running away. Others stopped right on the street, to read—pausing and savoring, just as Witter now did.

The first splatter of rain came and Witter sheltered the book under his cloak. He moved into an alcove and the rain came down hard on the streets. He removed the book and stared at it.

It was an old friend, this book. In the alcove, Witter leaned upon a brick wall. Despite himself, here and now, he smiled. It was *In Praise of Folly* by Erasmus.

Quickly he thumbed through to the part most suitable for this day's turnings...

Is not war the very root and matter of all famed enterprises? For of those that are slain, not a word of them...

Then Witter looked up. People were shouting. In the street, Witter heard the word pass from one to another, through the horde like wildfire—

"The fortress gates stand open! Its prisoners have come out!"

In the rain, they surged down the street in one excited body. They were laughing, splashing in puddles.

So the threat of the huge cannon had won.

"The bishop has abdicated! He has fled!"

"Wurzburg is declared an open city!"

Witter joined the rush to see. The rain ended and the sun came out, brilliant on the wet mirroring surfaces of the world. People were embracing, kissing, dancing. Some even went to kiss the barrel of the great cannon.

The word raced through the crowd that the bishop had sent word to Florian, promising he would abdicate, if permitted to leave with his personal guard. And as Konrad's godson, Florian had fought Muntzer and other hotheads to make it so.

Then the fine sense of merriment was suddenly over.

Some said the bishop had left in the night from the gate like a thief with his gang. Florian and the knights had seen him safely away from any of the horde sober or awake enough to care. There was much resentment of this leniency toward Konrad. Witter heard many curses passed from mouth to mouth in the streets. Some wanted revenge, for there had been foolish talk of having Konrad drawn and quartered in the square.

But Witter heard others, cooler heads, who were incredibly relieved that more assaults would not take place against that fortress. As was he himself.

Then word raced through the horde that the Marienberg prisoners were being released. Many had family there, fathers, sons, husbands.

Witter ran to see the prisoners. They came down stumbling through the crowd, some half-blind, some hardly able to walk. Some were helped by friends and relatives who recognized them. Some could only crawl, for a number of them had eyes put out and pieces cut from their bodies. But all moved in a weakened state of cringing afflictions.

People began to sob and embrace the released prisoners—miserable, confused, ragged, and wretchedly filthy—and pressed them with bread and ale and wine. Others shouted in rage at the sight of their loved ones so abused.

Then Witter stared.

One of the prisoners was familiar. He knew the man.

Who is he? How do I know him?

The man was rail-thin and covert, trying to shrink from the welcomers, his eyes obviously searching for some way to disappear into the greater mob. As if terrified of some discovery, some threatening danger.

Mahmed!

It was the Turk. An impossible sense of recognition flashed upon Witter.

Mahmed's rags were torn and stained yet somehow better than the other rags, and he was doing everything to blend in and escape the crush. But there was no mistaking the depth of his eyes, the wary intelligence hiding there.

Witter pushed his way to intercept Mahmed and he put a hand on Mahmed's arm from behind, and Mahmed whirled, gasping as if stabbed. Mahmed tried to jerk free but was too weak, swaying and almost fainting with the effort of coming down that long slope.

"It is all right," said Witter.

A stench came from Mahmed, of body rot and filth.

"What?" said Mahmed, startled, eyes wide; dark, hunted eyes.

"Chess," said Witter, then, "Ibn Tufail."

"Ibn…?" Mahmed opened his eyes wider at Witter.

"However this happened, they cannot hurt you now."

Witter pulled Mahmed away from there. No one cared. The horde kept churning upon itself.

"You would help me? Knowing who I am?"

And Witter's heart went out to him, for in this horde that called themselves brothers, only Mahmed, hunted and alien, seemed at this moment to be Witter's truest brother. This horde hated their oppressors, yes, and Witter knew they all hated Jews, yet Turks even more.

Jugs and open wine casks lay in the street. In an alley, out of the crush, Witter brought Mahmed to sit and gather his breath. He brought a clay jug of wine.

"Is that monk's wine?" said Mahmed, not taking it.

"Tavern wine. Why? Wine is wine."

Mahmed blinked and shook his head at Witter.

"Some wine is not wine. Some has been made into blood, as some bread is made into flesh. And that is cannibalism. Forbidden."

"This is not Communion wine," said Witter, appalled.

"Good. Good…"

Mahmed gulped the wine down. He coughed and panted, collapsed there against the wall. The stench coming from him was worse than any filth pile.

"They released you with all the others?"

"Perhaps by mistake, for all were thrown out. I had been put in a common cell the past two years, to rot, only taken out sometimes for their hated games of chess. They knew the walls could withstand the smaller cannon, and that the miners would take too long to dig under, but they dreadfully feared the big cannon."

"They have a big cannon, yes, but no balls."

"No balls?" Mahmed lifted his eyes to heaven, rolled them, and his drawn face twisted, and he actually smiled. "Too bad. The big stone-breakers they call Monks' Balls would have been fine to see, shattering those infernal walls."

It was disturbing that Mahmed smiled about such things, and good to remember this was a killer, a soldier captured in war, and even in his weak state, not a man to trifle with.

"Anyway, the sight of the big gun was finally enough to blanch the bishop out. He has abdicated and fled."

Mahmed tried to laugh; it came out as a dry cackle.

"The cannon set me free. Yet I am a dead man out here. Is that not irony?"

"No. Not if you become who I say you are."

Mahmed shoved himself upright, trying to face Witter like a man now, and Witter saw him sag, and put out both arms to help him stand.

"Whoever you are, or why, my life is in your hands. But why? Why would you help me, knowing I am a Turk?"

"You are worth a great deal to me."

"If I am found out, you too will not be treated kindly. "

Mahmed's life was a great treasure God had put into his hands. And Witter meant to use that life to the utmost.

He had not yet found Kristina. But God, at last, had not only heard him, had not only seemed to forgive him, but had answered half his prayers.

"When last did you eat?'

"Days. I know not how many. Water I drank from rain dripping in the window bars. In so long I have not bathed, I am unclean and wretched before God."

"We must feed you," said Witter, "and examine you for wounds. In some place of safety."

"Why? Why do you do this? I am worth no ransom, I tell you this now, if it is your greed that redeems me."

"My own freedom is your ransom."

Mahmed sank down against the wall again, this time to his knees, looking up at Witter. His waxy skin was drawn tight in a pallor of creatures long in darkness, his hair stuck to his skull like a black cap shot with gray spidery strands. But his eyes seemed to burn with the insistence of strong life.

"I know not how you mean that, but Allah has found me at last," said Mahmed. "May His will be done."

"Witter has found you," said Witter.

"And you are Witter?"

"Yes."

They shuffled along together, staying to the side streets.

"Witter," said Mahmed, "how do you know Ibn Tufail's writing?"

"I read."

"How many languages, Witter?"

"It does not matter. A few. It is not necessary to always say my name."

"You speak the way that men who speak many languages speak, with no accent, yet there is just a hint—perhaps of the Moor?"

Witter did not answer, but his heart was racing. No one else had ever detected any such accent in his voice.

"Where did you study?" said Mahmed.

"Later," hedged Witter, feeling probed, pursued, wanting to stop this keen train of thought, for Mahmed was of much sharper mind than Witter had anticipated. "Now, we must find a place to rest you. A safe place. And food."

"Food," said Mahmed, "and a bath, *Inshallah...*"

"Say 'God willing,' not *Inshallah.*"

"You understand my language? How?"

"Speak only German here," warned Witter. "Or better, play the mute. My mute comrade, wounded and ill."

"Who are you, truly?" said Mahmed.

"Later," said Witter.

But in the next alley, Mahmed stopped and would not move. "I will not go with you farther. Denounce me, kill me, but I do not move until you make sense to me."

"Kristina," said Witter.

"Kristina?" Mahmed's eyes narrowed, searchingly.

"She told me how she saved your life. How you paid her by inoculating her against pox, and we must find her now."

Mahmed's eyes warmed and his tormented face softened, the deep lines relaxing in the sallow flesh.

"You know Kristina? She is alive? She is here?"

"Perhaps. Yes. I think she will be."

"She goes where there is suffering," said Mahmed. "As she did when she saved my life, in war, and healed my wounds."

"Now Kristina has a child, and this has changed her deeply. Now she goes where her child goes. We must now keep moving."

"How do you know her?" asked Mahmed.

Witter said nothing more, moving, leading the weakened man along, wondering how he would negotiate what he must. How he would use Mahmed to achieve the scheme he had crafted, how he would put it all together, and make it work. So many variables. So many pitfalls…

Witter had not gone past two more streets when he heard a harp being played somewhere above him.

Witter stopped.

He looked up, with Mahmed leaning upon him. The town mansion was broken open and some broken furnishings lay in the street. The harp notes came out upon the air above them, drifting like moths, rising and falling.

"Beautiful…" said Mahmed, blinking.

It was a bizarre and serene perfection, that melodious harp, sweetly playing in this devastated place.

Above them, a window casement was broken open.

Witter looked up and realized…that sound came from up there.

KONRAD

This godless anarchy was the true inheritance from the permissiveness of Lorenz—that feeble man who had tried to charm and buy the weak-minded people with his monuments and his appeasement of their ever-increasing demands.

Leaving Wurzburg to the hordes was the worst humiliation of Konrad's life, but God had protected him, letting him live, at least. The screaming scum along the bridge had actually spit at him, and worse, thrown vile things that he bore with hauteur and cold dignity, head high. He had withstood the light cannonades and the threat of the miners. The night assaults had been thrown back. But once the great cannon had been reported, he had no choice. It was only the mysterious will of God, whom he had so faithfully served.

He knew now that he truly was a tool of Christ. For God had surely saved him for some yet unrevealed purpose.

Konrad had used his connection with his godson, Florian, enabling him to leave unmolested. And that proved that Florian was foolish and soft. Dietrich would have never let him go. But he knew now that Florian did love him, truly, and it hurt terribly to think of one day seeing Florian taken and tormented and burned.

It rained now as he rode in the center of his personal bodyguard, what was left of them. In a herd they rode, their mounts slipping and strung out along the muddy tracks. They stayed to the hills, as the roads were too dangerous.

Konrad had sent Basil north, with a small force of castle magistrates, to secure his estate and protect his foolish villeins from their own pride and folly. Perhaps they were safe, yet unreached by the filthy mobs that were rising everywhere. Perhaps they were already dead. But he knew the princes would go to Vienna to rally there. For one thing now was paramount—if the Turk saw opportunity to attack Vienna, now, during such instability, the capital of the Holy Roman Empire would fall, and all would be lost forever.

The four monks who stayed to attend him rode just behind. They carried sealed in oilskin wrappings his holy vestments, and his father's *Psalterium Benedictinum* of 1459, with its psalms, canticles and hymns; also his gold-bound *Vulgate*, his little *Book of Hours* from his boyhood, his illustrated *Nuremberg Chronicle*, and a gilt-edged pilgrim's map of Nurnberg to Rome bequeathed to him by Lorenz. These things were sacred reminders of who he was and must be. The monks treasured them against the rain.

He prayed for all his little people as he rode, sending his humility up to God, praying for his steward and his servants and his villeins. He prayed for their lives if they lived. For their souls if they did not. He prayed and yet, strangely, he could not see their faces upon the mirror of his mind. He saw his cousin Anna as a fresh young girl, teasing him along a pond of lilies, and him not daring to kiss her. Again he saw Lorenz, squatting in the baths, sucking his teeth in argument, and arrogant Martin Luther in his carriage cheered by the mobs. It all mocked him now.

Konrad clenched his teeth and felt a sharp regret of not having Martin Luther killed on the road as Basil had wished, come what may. He had always been too weak. But now he would remedy that weakness for all time. He saw his cousin Dietrich staring at him over a tankard of ale, on a dusty roadside table with a defeated army sprawled about them. He saw Dietrich's low villein cut up a renowned cavalryman in a duel. He saw Sieger's fine white sleek head staring up at him from a pike, the eyes like blue beads, and he knew that the devil was assailing him with all of these miseries, these terrors, these longings, picking his mind apart stone by stone.

Under the iron-gray clouds they rode cross-country, taking whatever forage and food and beds they needed from estates and farms—many half-abandoned by the angry villeins joining hordes, and their fleeing lords. Often a plume of smoke came up from some estate, pillaring out to the horizon.

"We must reach the Danube and secure a barge," said Balthus, his tall, gravely quiet captain. He had promised the man an estate. There would be many to seize and dispose when all was done.

Always riding southwest, they headed toward Vienna, Konrad knowing the closer to Vienna, the closer to the emperor and his core army in residence, even if it were a skeleton force reduced by the ruinous war in Italy.

Chasing foxes when wolves are in the house...

Many thoughts tore through his mind as he rode, head bent down under his hood, encased in his armor, where cold rain trickled down inside the clammy quilted tunic.

Twice in the first hours he was bent double on his horse, choking for breath, and retainers took him down and he hid his face in his rain cloak and wept, his throat on fire with the asthma and the humiliation.

The rain hid his tears, and when at last his breath came better he came up from his knees and shoved his men away and got up and was riding again. It was self-pity, he knew that. He reviled himself for indulging.

He remembered the asthma advice of Mahmed, handed down from some ancient Turk or Jew, and he relaxed, prayed, rode the horse more easily, and the fire subsided and his breath came well again. If it were blasphemy to use such infidel advice, God would not have made it work so well.

Mahmed, rotting in a dungeon cell, unrepentant. Brilliant in his way, knowing of chess and philosophy and more—even of medicine, easing his constrictions—yet still the fool. Damned eternally. No doubt released to the mob with the rest of the prisoners, and torn apart by the mob, whenever they finally realized who he was.

Why did people not take the open hand of grace?

He thought of the strong spirit of his cousin Dietrich, his mind ranging far back to that sunny day on the road where he had met the defeated army returning from its fight on the Ottoman border trade route.

How Dietrich had been faithful, even then, with all his disgust at being so misused. Dietrich, the dreamer, who yearned for literacy and equality for all, yet who went to every war when called and would never have raised his hand against the holy Church-state.

And who did he have? Basil. Sent ahead down the river, on a barge under cover of night, with Basil's most trusted monks carrying all the bishopric's uncollected tax accounts, which would be settled if this thing were won. Those records of taxes due were the treasury to rebuild Wurzburg and the army.

Good Dietrich. The land had no more good Dietrichs. Only their spawn, like Florian. The evil seed. Florian, so like a serpent, biting the hand of his own godfather and prince-bishop. Throwing away his own estate, lowering himself to be the equal of a villein, even to the ruin of Florian's own mother, Anna.

Konrad thought of that girl with her incandescent smile seared away by pox, a girl once so beautiful that Konrad had caressed himself to sleep wrapped in her gift robe, with aching fantasies of her. But that venal sin was the passage of a boy. Now he was a man, driven from his own city, wet to the bone, yet unbroken. No, stronger. Stronger than ever.

The land rose into hills and they stayed in the valleys, with horsemen scouting ahead. In a village they took fresh horses from terrified villagers who pretended to kneel in loyal respect. Their eyes like darts stinging him.

Villeins were all scum. Konrad knew that now.

It angered Konrad that loyal men of the empire would be threatened on the road, for new hordes of villeins were on the march everywhere, demanding equal rights and equal wealth with their betters. And so he often cursed the torture of the saddle, as his guard crossed the rain-swept hills. Protected in their center he rode a black horse now, and longed for Sieger, whom he had loved, and tried not to think of his woeful staring head on the villeins' pike.

But he was hardly alone in his failure at Wurzburg.

The uprising was endemic. They met a courier also riding cross-country. He tried to ride away, not knowing them, but his horse was lame. A dozen cities had fallen, the courier said. Only the league of princes could save the emperor now, and save themselves, by spending every florin in their treasuries upon mercenaries, whatever men at arms could be bought.

In Wittenberg to the north, broadsheets were out from Martin Luther, condemning the villeins in revolt, and urging the princes to crush them down; not surprising, since Luther was only saved from the stake by his protector, the duke of Saxony. The only good news in all this was that an Imperial army was indeed being raised by the league. The exhausted courier fell in, to ride with them. The wretch had no other place to go where he would not be killed.

His captain, Balthus, the picked man promoted by valor in previous wars, rode up beside him and said, "Ahead is the wide Danube. It will take us the rest of the way to Vienna, your grace. We shall seize a safe, dry barge where no villeins can reach, where you may travel secure in a warm cabin."

"Do you trust your men?"

"As well as any can be trusted, your grace."

"Our faithful ones will be given rank, and titles, every one. You do this for the greater glory of God."

"Your grace," said Balthus, and he sounded sincere, "you have promised me land, but I do not serve you for land. I myself was born a villein, yet advanced my station through service in battle. Seeing the works of God plundered and good monks and nuns thrown out, it boils my rage. If the true order of our world is turned upon its head, how may any of us hope to reach the gates of heaven?"

Konrad felt emotion; he almost wanted to embrace the man and it choked him to feel such loyalty, such true belief, in such a desperate time. This Balthus would surely be his new Basil, an honest man of war, not a sniveling monk of letters. He would be a sword for this terrible season, not a thinking man like Dietrich, but as simple as he was honest.

"Balthus, your words alone raise you in my sight. We shall restore the right order of God's design, believe me."

As so, Konrad rode with his retainers down to the river in the hard rain over the muddy green hills, and when finally he stopped cursing, he prayed and beseeched...

Water ran down his face and it was not all rain.

Make me Thy sword and staff, O Lord, and may sweet Mother Mary guide and steady my good hand, for our Holy Church is our fortress and has withstood all attacks for fifteen centuries, and now from within comes the greatest destruction of all...

In a flash now it all became clear.

Konrad lurched in his saddle, as the revelation shook him like a bolt of lightning from the heavens. His horse even felt it, and jerked under him. His breath came full and his vision became bright and clear. He felt all his weaknesses fall away like dry husks.

This was not tribulation, but a test. This was his time. He was a tool of Christ. His great holy work lay ahead.

For you God, he promised, *I shall see all villeins yoked, and their immortal souls renewed, and the Church-state preserved...*

LUD

Dietrich had once said that every battle began in fear, but finished in exhaustion. When all the dead were reclaimed from the fortress ditch, and many others with ghastly wounds had finally died, their friends and wives and mothers had wept and washed the broken bodies of their beloveds, and had mourned. Their fear and their fury were buried with them. Many villeins wept for hours.

When all the fallen were buried on the green hills above the river, a rough tally was done, numbering four thousand dead.

The cost was appalling to those who had never before been in war. Lud had known, and in this he felt no satisfaction, only frustration at knowing something that could not be avoided. Few had imagined so many would vanish from the earth forever, so quickly. Many women in the camp train took up the weapons of their fallen men, and stood their places in the horde. No one told them they did not have that right.

Lud no longer wore the wrapping that had so often covered his lower face. There were plenty here with the scars of pox. No one cared of such things when so much killing and maiming was everywhere.

Lud watched the hundreds of shovels tearing at the ground, and he remembered—the last time so many dug here had been for the bridge works, when they had returned from the disastrous border fight years ago.

But the evidence of so many dead changed nothing.

More willing fighters kept pouring in every day to join the horde. It seemed nothing could stop the momentum that had broken through all of the parts of southern Germany called Swabia and Franconia. Many had never fought in war nor served in ranks. For weapons, they carried their farm tools and implements of their trades.

"We must bring order to the horde," said Florian, and that summed it up.

The training of the Black Host began.

Foot and horse, both. The Marienberg parade ground was pounded to a muddy bog by thousands of stomping feet, a drill field for the training of villeins—men who were suddenly told that all were brothers, none high nor low. Yet they had to be shaped into one single conforming mass. Each group had voted for their sergeants, who kept the lines mostly in good order, though it was clear that many in the ranks (including the sergeants) had never served anywhere except the bakery or the plow or the tavern.

So, men of horse like Lud, spent much of their time riding the lines and shouting at sergeants.

Across the hills, the Tauber Valley Horde was encamped and servicing their guns. The Gay Bright Troop was now in the city, foraging for stores for the march ahead.

Florian and Steinmetz and the rest of the knights, with their sergeants and retainers, all spread themselves out down the line, and Lud was among them. They were the cavalry, their own horsemen group, and they had voted in their own way, the way of knights. The old chain of command was still in play here, among the professionals.

Shaping up his villeins into rough formations, Lud maneuvered them together in lines, and Florian rode on his horse, shouting, correcting, encouraging, leading. Florian was indeed a natural leader, even more than Dietrich had been, and that was saying a great deal indeed.

"We shall make good Landsknechts of them yet," said Florian to a meeting of his knights. "We shall train them in ways to ensnare the Imperial lines of force."

Lud, not a knight himself, stood back with others like himself, men devoted to their lords, though now supposedly there were no lords.

"With supporting cavalry such as us knights," said Steinmetz, "they will be as good as any. I would have changed my old black armor for new, after the fortress fell, but now I shall not. Your name for our horde is a good one, full of brave fury—the Black Host!"

There were forty-odd muskets from the Marienberg armory, with powder and ball, though much had been destroyed by the deserting guard. Lud made a line of musketeers on the front where the pikes could guard them during reloading drills.

Among the pikes were all the Giebel men together, old and young, Tomen, Jakop, and the rest of them who had joined the fight against the magistrates on the road that day. Merkel had been voted their sergeant, and Linhoff his second, and Merkel shouted and strutted at them, not much different than he was back home.

When Merkel saw Lud ride up the line, the blacksmith tried to smile and hail. Other Giebel men called begging to be given muskets instead of pikes, but Lud cut them short with his own shouting—the standard things cadre had shouted at infantry for thousands upon thousands of years—

"Back in line! Keep good order! The lives of those on every side of you depend upon interlocking pikes all in good order! You guard one another! Be worthy!"

The younger pikemen of Giebel—the once-green youths Lud had trained years ago in the previous border war—knew their business with the pikes, and the older men tried to stay with them in the maneuvers.

I brought all back but three, thought Lud, *but this time will be different, and they voted, and it is no longer on my head, they share all because all voted...*

Merkel shouted at them again and Lud rode on.

Men were spent according to their value in battle. The pikes guarded the muskets and the muskets guarded the cannons, which were the heart of a massed killing machine on any field these days.

Much powder was wasted in training, but it was necessary. Balls flew and bounced. Blue-yellow sulfurous clouds hung about for days. And the old madwoman called Hoffman—who Lud knew was Arl—raved on a nearby hill, always urging them on.

Nervous farmers in fast-load drills forgot to ignite their loads. They double charged their muskets and burst the barrels like unraveling iron ropes, killing three men outright.

Then Lud saw two familiar faces, men standing at the end of one group of pikemen—Dolf and Symon. Symon's limp had caught his eye. He rode down there at once.

"What in hell are you doing with fighting men?"

They saw him and looked sheepish, trying to act like anyone else. Lud drove his horse in hard, and routed them out of the formation.

"Where do you think you go with those monk stickers?"

"To right the wrongs," said Dolf, trying to sound bold.

"In brotherhood," added Symon, hopefully.

"You? Fight?"

"I am brave, I have even been racked," said Symon defiantly.

"Racked? What has that to do with bravery, fool?"

"I did not cry out."

"Then you lie, you were never racked."

Lud realized, with wonder, that the two Brethren had been swept away by the passions of the horde. After all their years of pacifism, now they wished to be treated like any other men, but he mocked and berated them, knowing this the best way to drive them off.

He had to make them go. For he saw Dolf and Symon as protectors of Kristina and Grit and Peter.

"Go back to Giebel, find those women and protect them, you men of peace and brotherhood!"

Lud yelled from his horse, leaning, driving the two men out of the ranks with a slap of the flat of his sword.

The formations laughed, as Lud knew they would.

"You do not belong among these brave fighting folk!" he shouted, as Dolf and Symon went hurrying away, bent with humiliation.

You owe me your lives, thought Lud, watching them run away, *you lucky ones...*

The armed camps became villages, the villagers clannish as flocks of geese. Around the campfires, there were grumblings along with the bragging of how the fortress fell.

In one camp, Lud caught a man berating Florian for letting Konrad go unmolested, but at the sight of Lud, he praised Florian for taking the Marienberg without another assault.

In another camp, he saw Arl, in her black cloak, like a demon lit in orange firelight, urging cruel reprisals upon all who came against them. Her words rattled from her and he pitied her for losing all her children, even Greta. He knew she had gone mad, yet her wildness roused them somehow. This was a time when madness ruled.

Late in the night, there were command meetings of Florian, Muntzer, and Goetz and their appointed captains, several villeins voted to lead by their hordes.

Around the campfire, campaign strategies were debated, but among those who had actually fought in war, one dread fact was solidly agreed on.

"The Imperial Army will be coming, and they come with cannons, always," said Steinmetz. "We must meet cannon with cannon, and if they have cannons, we must have more cannons and the powder and balls for them."

"Then we must march and fight and win and take more cannons," said Florian. "We should march and meet them on our own terms, our own ground."

Said Goetz, "An army of villeins will grow as we march. In numbers is our victory."

Said Steinmetz, "We cannot hope to seize cannons from those who have more cannons with which to resist us."

"Yes, but our strength is human, friend," said Florian. "We must act. Destroying cathedrals and monasteries along the way distracts our hordes too much from the attacks that we must now make, immediately—attacks to capture the cannons we so desperately need."

His eyes glinting like an actor in some arch Passion play, Muntzer raged, laughing and snarling, as wild in his black robe as a great crow flapping its wings.

"You are wrong! Now is our time to drive the devils from their guilty lairs! If they have cannons I shall catch the balls in my good sleeves! God speaks to me, shows me the way! You must only be men!"

Florian and Steinmetz stared at Muntzer. Lud saw their minds working. Muntzer erased all their logic.

"March forward and take victory by the throat! The Antichrist himself in Rome shall shit his unholy robes! God is with us, Brothers! He has told me so many times!"

Late that same night, alone with Florian in a hut by the river, Lud lay on a straw pallet beside Florian and could not sleep.

"You must get rid of this Muntzer," Lud said. "I could open his throat, sink him in the river."

Florian was not asleep. His voice came, in the dark, sounding so like Dietrich that the sense was eerie.

"I despise the ugliness in your face, my friend, when you say something so foolish as that."

The words stung Lud but he kept his voice level. "The pox, I cannot help. A priest, I can."

"I do not mean the pox. I mean the way your face sets hard, when you think, and men fear to look straight at you."

"The priest will get many willing fools killed."

"We need the priest, mad radical that he is, we need him. The villeins follow Muntzer, he inspires them."

"He rouses them to folly. Lords will not lay down their titles for brotherhood, even at the point of death."

"You have not seen the long view, Lud."

Lud sat up. "You must plan for a long, savage war. Against professionals. They will use every last florin to hire men of war anywhere they can be bought. Some of our own may be bought out from under us as well. That is the long view. And the short view: trust no one."

"I know that, too. Go to sleep."

"No, you listen to me. There is something I want to tell you about such a war as this."

"I have read history of wars, Lud, please sleep now."

"This I saw for myself. Villeins rising against lords. And so I know how it goes, a war such as this."

Now in the dark, Florian came up on one elbow, eyes catching the light of a smoldering campfire outside the hut door. "A war such as this, when? A war you have seen?"

"With Dietrich, your father. My first war. I was a boy. And your father was a much younger man, and you were only a castled babe. I went as his footman and flag bearer, at the age of fourteen."

Now Florian's voice took a sharp tone of new interest.

"What kind of war was it? Where?"

"A war of lords against villeins, like this. This is not the first. And your father and I marched south to help suppress it. Slovenia, south of us here, on the Ottoman borders."

"I knew of some kind of feud there…and the unrest gave opening for the Ottomans to move in, and had to be stopped."

"An uprising, Florian. Not a feud between lords. An uprising of villeins against two brothers. The villeins seized their castles and we were sent by Vienna, with a levy of contingents, to help crush the uprising."

"Vienna then was ally to Slovenia?"

"Princes stick together. Lords stick together. If they hate one another, they hate villeins more. All lords are threatened by the villeins who feed them. It is not the lords who feed the villeins, and all lords know that."

"You make my own point. That is why I lead this war."

"We were told—your father and I and all the rest—that the villeins were evil, mad, and must be crushed. We went believing that. And crush them we did."

"How?"

"They were villeins. They had no cavalry and no cannons. And we bought many big guns. We cut them to pieces with volleys into their massed ranks as they came on, rushing us, and the few who reached us we cut to pieces at our leisure. It was at Celje that we finally crushed them out. Our army of the Holy Roman Empire."

"That was another time, Lud," said Florian.

"Another time? That same kind of Imperial army will be coming down upon us, no matter how many hordes come to fight on our side."

The memory was one that Lud had long suppressed. His first kills. The first shock of seeing another man up close and the hurt in that man's eyes, the surprised dismay. Killing men like himself—villeins, though they spoke another language—brave, wild villeins in the dress of farmers, trying to fight with the tools of farmers.

"My father told me of that war," said Florian. "He liked it no better than you."

"It was like a hog killing. Butchery. Farmers and city guildsmen engaging regulars. Until the arms ached from swinging the sword and the legs ached from stumbling over them to cut down the next one, and yet they kept coming, until the last of them broke and ran, to be hunted down like wild dogs in their own woods."

"We have cavalry. The first time in history that good knights have formed cavalry to fight such a war with men of soil."

"You do not listen, Florian."

"Tell me what you need to say. Tell the worst."

"When all the killing was done, your father told me we had fought for the wrong side. Listen to me. Dietrich said those Slovenian princes were corrupt, fat, evil men, they took many first nights and much worse, they ruled by terror and starvation until the villeins could stand no more."

"My father always did his duty."

"Your father grieved over all the killing of those poor folk, and he wished for better rights for working folk, and after that was when he began to give the Giebel villagers more and more shares, more rights on his own land, and he began to read more and more and speak to me of reading, of truth, of rights for all…"

"Even though he was a cousin of Prince Konrad?"

"Even more so, I think, because of that relation."

"He was a great man."

"Yet even such a great man, he was deceived."

Florian spoke without rancor at all. Lud needed to hear anger, a flare of indignation, but there was only the same half-concealed condescension he had heard from Florian, coming from Oxford, debating with Witter on the French roads, as if Lud's mind were not refined enough to catch the deeper meanings within obvious thought.

Said Florian, "As you too were deceived. You went to war again, did you not? Taking the village boys as pikemen? To fight the Turks for a Konrad levy, in the name of Wurzburg?"

"Goddamn," said Lud.

"That is no argument," said Florian.

"Have you heard me at all? We did fight Turks, and flogged our meat and got our ass whipped. I was loyal to Dietrich. So we went. Our boys strutting like great heroes. Dietrich said we had no choice."

"Am I then so deceived? Did that war so mar you in your youth? There is always a choice."

"Then choose. Do not fight without enough cannons, and enough powder to make enough balls fly."

"Go to sleep. Now I am tired and will hear no more."

Lud felt like seizing Florian by the neck and shaking him. Florian's voice was so easy, so calm and rational.

"You will hear me, damn you."

"You loved my father, did you not?"

Lud felt his heart rise and hammer. If he gagged and tied Florian and lashed him to a horse he could be gone before the camp was up at first light. He could pony him back on a second horse, tail-tied, to Giebel, and find Kristina and Peter there, and commit Florian to the cell under the Giebel castle's keep tower, and hand Lady Anna the keys, and leave. But he knew he would never do that.

"I loved Dietrich," he heard himself saying. "He was like a father to me, too...no...he was more."

"Then be loyal to me, as you were to him."

"If I were not loyal, I would not be here at all."

"Then be as a brother to me now, and go to sleep."

Lud tried another way into Florian's mind.

"Your father gave me a book, and I have certain passages committed to mind. There is one passage we must consider now."

"You recall the very words?" said Florian doubtfully.

Lud rolled his head back, seeing the printed words in his thoughts—

"*When fervent sorrow of the mind stirreth thee up unto vengeance, remember wrath to be nothing less than that which it falsely counterfeiteth, that is to wit fortitude or manfulness, for nothing is so childish, so weak, nothing so feeble and of so vile a mind as to rejoice in vengeance.*"

"Of course, I know it. Erasmus. *Handbook of a Christian Knight*. But, listen, it is not wrath, Lud. I bear no malice. It is justice I serve now."

"Justice?"

"The right side must win, for once."

"Florian, you listen. I was born a villein. You were not. I tell you, there is no justice. They all are the same. What is the difference? The Turk says kill a Christian for Islam. The bishop says kill a Turk for Christ. Muntzer says kill a noble for Christ. They are all the same. What is the difference?"

He waited for Florian to speak again. For a while he sensed that Florian lay awake in the dark, waiting him out, and then Florian finally did speak.

"The sacred rights of men, Lud."

"Sacred? Christ makes you kill? In the Scriptures, Christ says plainly that killing is wrong."

Florian laughed bitterly in the dark. "You sound like your pacifist Brethren friends. They have softened you. Where is the hard man who taught me grappling as a boy, and knife fighting, who keened me to hunting and horsemanship?"

"Killing breeds killing. It never ends. I have read much on all of this and do not know any longer what is right."

"Learning to read has only confused you, old friend."

Lud felt his blood rise in his face and sat up from his straw pallet, but he said nothing, hearing the same condescension in Florian again, hating it. He wanted to slap him, but he did not do it, for all was uncertain, and he would not yield to anger now.

"Friend or fool, which do you mean?" said Lud.

After a time, Florian's voice came again, softer.

"Lud, right is what we shall make right. When all men are equal, that will be right, and nothing less. Then we can go back to gentle Christ and such fine thoughts. We are brothers now, you and I."

"You will not listen."

"Tomorrow we march."

"March? Where?"

"It is decided. The bishop will have fled to Heidelberg or even Vienna. If the reserves of the Imperial Army come on the march, we have no time to waste. We must cut the land into digestible pieces first. We march to Wurttemberg to attack the castle. Then onto the next castle, and the next, until it is done and they are all broken. Only then can we go home, brothers for all time."

The news astonished Lud. The whole thing reeled through his mind like a sudden rockfall upon his head.

"Equal votes, you said. When did I vote on this?"

"It was decided in knights council."

"I see. Decided. And the horde, did they vote?"

"They voted with their cheers."

"Wurttemberg has big cannons and many field pieces."

"And we shall take them."

"Or they shall take us."

"Be in this with me, Lud. Do not think too much and dismay yourself. We cannot stand still. Everywhere the league is hiring mercenaries. The princes have ordered unspeakable atrocities upon all villeins."

Atrocity breeds atrocity, thought Lud, remembering what Dietrich had told him so long ago, *war is the greatest atrocity of all...*

There was something else Dietrich had said, something about faith…yet he could not summon it up now.

Nor did it matter. For, lying there in the dark, now he knew that it made no difference what Dietrich had once said, for Dietrich had given himself to war even as his son, Florian, now gave himself to it. Lud knew he would keep his promise to Dietrich to guard Florian, as he did now, even knowing the immensity of the coming folly.

And that meant fighting atrocity with more atrocity, until the end of time. Because now there was no going back.

As Lud thought upon all of it, his mind torn and aching, his words unable to persuade, Florian's words came again in the dark hut…

"We must stop them, Brother. We shall stop them."

And, in truth, despite all his dread, it was wonderful, the feeling that came, when Florian called him

Brother…

KRISTINA

She hardly heard anything Grit said now.

Grit, with fear for others more than for herself, had wanted to go to the horde that was now marching away, out of the city, to tend the wounded and infirm, to argue against murder, to pray, to beg them not to give themselves to violence.

But when Kristina turned away to search for Peter, Grit came with her.

Never again will I leave my little one, if only you will let me find him now, I beg of you Lord...

Searching for Peter, with the need of her child driving her on, Kristina made her way through the ravaged streets of the city. She was dimly aware of Grit near her, always somewhere near, but she hardly heard anything Grit said, was hardly aware of the tugs on her arm now and then, once when a runaway carriage team nearly ran them down.

The great army of villeins and tradesmen and artisans was out of the city across the bridge, and with those kind of people gone, the last semblance of honest order was gone from the streets of Wurzburg.

Many of another dangerous kind had hidden themselves from the whole ordeal, and now came stealing out from byways and alleys and dark crevices of life. They were the criminals, the underworld denizens emerging like rats from the gutters, come to feed upon the lawless carcass of the city.

"Surely it is the end of days," said Grit, with a stare beyond horrified. Grit looked even more paralyzed with dismay than she had at the battle many years ago.

Riotous drunks filled one street outside a monastery, and Kristina and Grit circled wide around it.

In one alley, Kristina stopped, struck by the scene there. Nuns with torn habits were kneeling and singing and praying to a little herd of the severely afflicted.

Kristina, staring, recognized the order by their habits—the same as Hannah's—they were Benedictines. Their abbess was tiny and ancient, cooing, hissing, trying to calm her nuns, who in turn were trying to calm the cretins, the moaning demented, the grinning inanes, some with pox scars or harelips, others shrunken-faced or armless, eyeless, hairless. Three or four looked like stunned and blind war veterans with faces half gone, empty holes where eyes or nose had been, one with no jaw. They were all the unwanted of this world, valued only by these nuns.

The afflicted ones were crouched, some on all fours, one hopping on stumps, and all, Kristina realized now, were tied together at the waist. They shambled along in one long string that was twisted into knots by their frantic turmoil. When one moved they all jerked and cried out, laughing or shrieking, more the sounds of birds or beasts than human beings. Some crawled and were dragged along.

"Dear merciful Christ," Kristina heard Grit say.

Against the alley wall the nuns tried comforting with song, with gentle caresses, trying to calm them, the nuns of all ages, themselves like stunned children, all in a clutch against one wall.

"Salve, festa dies, toto venerabilis aevo,

Qua Deus infernum vicit et astra tenet…"

It was an old canto that she too had once sung with Sister Hannah so long ago, the praising of coming Easter…

Hail, festal day, venerable of all ages, by which God conquers hell and holds the stars…

Kristina's mind recoiled even as her heart went out to them, thinking of Hannah, sweet Hannah, dear Sister Hannah, comforting her this same way, raising her in love, even teaching her the harp, finally taking her to Kunvald…but her mind tarried only a moment, and then she sharply remembered Peter, wanted Peter.

And suddenly she was moving quickly again, her eyes scanning all the crowds for the face of her little boy.

"Wait, Kristina," came Grit's voice behind her, "we must help them!"

But Kristina kept moving.

With Grit catching up, saying something about the love of Christ, words that Kristina hardly heard now, Kristina kept moving.

Now and again Grit stopped to try to help some battered man or woman, then would catch up with her somehow.

A pack of filthy children ran ahead and turned a corner. Kristina hurried, pulling away from Grit, trying to see their faces. She shouted to them and ran.

"Please, stop!"

She turned the corner and a bearded man—in a rich man's coat that was obviously not his—stepped out and blocked her way. He had yellow teeth, was half-drunk and grinning. He shoved her into the wall.

"Here is a good one," he said.

Three men pulled her by the hair and by her cloak, into an open doorway. With the stench of strong drink and the ugly pain of brutal, groping, hurting hands they wrestled her kicking to the bottom of a dark stairwell, beginning to drag her up the deep shadows of the stairs, already tearing away at her cloak and the binding over her breasts, and she was screaming like a wild animal in a snare.

But then something else was happening.

Behind her something flung itself snarling at the surprised men and Kristina knew somehow it was Grit—like a wildcat, biting, and now in some sisterly instinct of primal rage Kristina too turned biting them and clawing at their eyes.

She had never fought a man before. Their strength was brutal. Grit was being crushed under one man and he smashed a fist into her face and her head jerked back. Kristina bit his neck and tasted salt of blood and felt him fling her off. She went flying backward, kicking.

Then they were all being dragged back out into the sunlit street.

On her back in the street, trying to gather herself, Kristina looked up and there was Dolf, his fist smashing at a big, thick face. Symon took another man from behind and, grabbing his beard with one hand, he hooked his other thumb into a socket and pulled out one of the man's eyes.

Howling, cursing, the men ran away, the one attacked by Symon yipping with his hands over his face.

Kristina helped Grit to her feet.

"Bastards," Grit hissed. "Filth, trash, scum." She was panting, her broken nose pouring red blood down her chin and her bosom.

Kristina looked at Grit, shocked at her words, in this day where shock came upon shock too quickly to make sense. She looked at Symon and at Dolf, and Dolf rolled his milk-blue blind eye away from her, as if he were too ashamed of himself to face her now.

"Forgive us," Dolf said. "But we are here now."

Dolf tried to touch Grit but she slapped his hand away.

"Do not touch me." Grit held her broken bleeding nose and said, "Men are filth, all bastards and filth, fucking bastards…"

They all looked at Grit, shocked almost as much by her words as by the attack just now fought off.

Now Grit took her hand from her broken nose and put her arms around Kristina, and pulled Kristina toward her. Kristina felt the hard little body press hers and hold there as if they were weathering a storm together. Grit was trembling.

"Did they hurt you much, sweet child?"

"No. Are you well?"

"My dear, my sweet young Kristina."

Grit held her that way for a long time. Then suddenly let go and pushed Kristina away. "I am a foolish woman. Biting and clawing like a young wildcat that way."

"Thank you and bless you," Kristina said.

"We must find someplace for the night," said Dolf.

"By God's grace you came," said Kristina.

"No," said Symon, "truth be told, we have followed you this past hour."

"Why did you follow but not speak?" said Kristina.

"Too ashamed," said Dolf. "After we left you as we did."

Symon said, "Lud drove us out of the horde, no doubt by the intervention of Christ, to save us from mortal sins that had tempted us."

"To join in killing our oppressors," said Dolf.

"Hate is our oppressor," said Grit.

"All hate is in the open now," said Symon, "none hidden. Lud saved us from that. But not himself."

"Poor Lud," said Grit.

Lud, thought Kristina, and she wished with all her heart that he was here. *If Lud were here it would be all right. He would know how to find my Peter. He would know how to keep us safe from such men. He would know which way we should go, what we should now do. Lud would never allow harm to come to us. Lud...*

Grit now put her arms around the two men, one bloody hand around each. Symon and Dolf leaned into her and closed their eyes as if their mother had found them lost in deep woods.

Kristina looked at them, but now, again, could only think of Peter.

She turned away and moved on, hunting, searching. The others caught up. Saying her name, trying to comfort her, to rein her in.

They hurried on, hurt, shaken, staying to alleys.

"Peter," said Kristina. "Help me find my child."

Said Dolf, "In this city? We will not find one child."

"Even if he is in the city," said Symon.

"We must get away from this infernal place," said Dolf.

"Peter," said Kristina.

Grit's hair stood out from her head, brown shot with much gray, like spikes of twisted iron. Her swollen little nose ran with blood and she pinched her nostrils, tilting her head back.

Kristina tried to pray: "Though we walk through the valley of the shadow of death, we fear no evil..."

She gripped Grit's free hand in the way they did to pray together, so that Grit would pray with her for deliverance.

"May God forgive all who harm others," Grit said, still pinching off her broken nose, her eyes streaming water and her cloak glistening with blackish streaks of blood. "May God forgive me for my sin of violence, but it was in the attack upon my sister in Christ."

"You have much blood," said Symon.

"Not all is mine," Grit said, "and may God forgive me for the joy I felt in their pain."

Kristina let go of Grit's hand and held herself, arms folded over her throbbing breasts. In their rage of lust the men's hard hands had bruised both her mind and body.

"I wish my fist had been a knife," said Dolf.

"No," said Symon. "No, Brother, do not wish for evil."

Grit shuddered. "Forgive me Lord for my anger, my lapse of vile words, all repented from my former life."

"Dear God," said Symon, "What is becoming of us?"

Kristina felt something inside her, like a strong pull of her heart. She instantly forgot her pain.

She lifted her voice: "Peteeeeer!"

Symon tried to pull her back, taking her arm.

"Kristina," pleaded Dolf, "Do not attract attention to us. Your child cannot hear you, wherever he may now be."

"Let her go," said Grit, tersely to Symon. "Keep your hands to yourself, man."

Symon released her arm.

And she felt Peter. She felt him near.

She pulled away from them. They came behind her, and she hurried into an alley that looked out into a wide street of town mansions with shattered windows and pieces of tapestry and ornate furniture strewn on the pavers.

She shouted her child's name again and again.

"Please," said Dolf.

Alone she stepped into the street, out of the alley. Dolf tried to grab her wrist but she pulled free of him.

"Kristina!" someone shouted from above her.

She twisted and turned. The voice came from above them. But at first she could not find the source.

"Kristina, here!"

She knew the voice well and she looked up. She stared in wonderment, hardly daring to believe what she saw.

There stood Witter, in an upper casement where ornate iron railings were trained with groomed ivy.

And there was her child.

Peter, under Witter's arm, Peter smiling brightly down at her now and waving, as if all were right in this world where evil was not real, but merely an absence of good.

WITTER

W itter had entered the broken door of the mansion, Mahmed just behind him, faltering on the tiled stairs. The beautiful longing notes of the harp came louder and louder as he ascended the dimness, toward the light.

And in a richly paneled drawing room, Witter had found little Peter alone, his little face serene and dirty in a far corner amid the wreckage, his little hands plucking a great gilt harp. Peter had grinned his dirty-faced toothy grin, glad to see Witter, and kept playing on.

No more than an hour later, with Mahmed resting, Witter had heard Kristina's voice calling and now they had all rushed up the stairs. Seeing them, Peter had flown from the harp and flung himself first into Grit's arms, kissing her face. Grit had hugged the boy, then pressed him into Kristina's open arms.

Kristina looked hurt that Peter had gone first to Grit. And now she held onto her boy with such fervent squeezing that the child, delighted but squirming and restless, struggled against her.

She had to let him jump down.

The instant the child was released he was back at the harp, playing strange melodies, some like those from the tavern bawdies, others church liturgies and hymns he might have heard. The tones flowed freely from his hands like pure clear water.

Mahmed had been hiding, apparently, not knowing who was coming, and now he came out.

Kristina and Grit saw him and they all embraced.

"I never thought to see you again," he said. "My sweet angels of mercy, from that long march, a lifetime ago."

"Mahmed, it is truly a joy to see you again," said Kristina, with a sincere tone that filled Witter with jealousy, though he knew it was foolish. "May our Lord bless and keep you, sweet friend. But you need care. When did you last eat or bathe? Do you have wounds?"

Mahmed wept openly, then was too weak to stand, and sagged to the floor.

"He is ill and faint, we must find him food," said Grit.

Dolf and Symon found old food scattered in the ransacked house scullery. The silver was all gone. Only pewter remained, thrown about. A study was lined with bookshelves, all empty now. Like other great houses, it had been sacked, but food lay everywhere. The meat was all bad and no smoked meat was found. They found a barrel of walnuts and a cask of moldy cheese and apples and a broken bread loaf, torn by mice or rats, and all shared it.

"With so much wantonness, there is not much food," said Grit. "But when all becomes spoiled there will be much want. We must gather any that does not perish, as much as can be found. We found a few discarded garments from those here before us. Shoes for Kristina. A cloak for Witter and another for Mahmed."

Mahmed choked down his food, and they went to look for water from the house well usually found in its atrium. As they descended the stairs into the open area in the center of the mansion, doves exploded from the courtyard, startling them. The well was there and they drank their fill.

The open-sky atrium was a garden around the well, and blooming flowers had been torn out by handfuls and lay randomly about. At one end was a door that led through a corridor, to a tiled bath.

They went in and found the water cold. But it was better than nothing.

Witter knew, as always, he would wait until last, so that his circumcision would not be seen by the other men.

They dared not light the boiler, for fear of smoke from the chimneys, but ablutions were done, in the chilly water, one by one, first Grit and Kristina with Peter, for Kristina would not leave Peter.

Kristina said firmly, "I have promised this to God, I must never again leave my child."

From the room where Peter sat at the harp, she pried him away with teasing fondness, and brought him down to the bath, took him inside alone, and when they were done, wet-haired and bright-eyed, she brought him back to the harp room.

"Your child is gifted from above," said Mahmed to Kristina. "Surely Allah loves him dearly, your child."

"Often we have wondered and prayed for you."

Said Mahmed, "You are the only Christians I have ever met who ever helped me. Who ever acted upon the commands of the prophet Christ. To love one another."

"Many are Christian," said Grit.

"Not the bishop."

"It was hoped he treated you well. That you might accept Christ as your true Saviour even."

"The bishop tried to force me to cannibalism."

"Cannibalism?"

"To swallow into my body the flesh and blood of Christ. His priests had transubstantiated the bread and wine he gave me without telling me so."

"And you?"

"In recoil I vomited…and he threw me into the dungeon and said he was done with me."

Grit and Kristina traded strange glances. Dolf and Symon moved closer, agitated.

Said Mahmed, "Do we not all worship the same one God? The old god of the Hebrews? Christian, Muslim, Jew, all the same God?"

"That is the old way," said Symon.

"Christ has come to redeem us," said Dolf. "Would you accept even Jews, who murdered our Saviour?"

Said Mahmed, "Can we not worship our one God with different names? Jews are welcome in Ottoman lands and Christians, too, if they do not come as Crusaders."

"That cannot be true," said Dolf.

Grit stepped between them.

"Brothers, let us talk no more of this now. We are all tired and need rest for whatever we must face tomorrow."

They all took down draperies with which to bed and warm themselves for the night on the floor. Witter longed for the comfort of the hearth fire that they could not have, for fear the chimney smoke might signal others.

Their talk of Jews had unnerved him. He searched Kristina's face for a reaction, and once her eyes met his, but there was no harm in them.

They closed and latched tight the winter casement boards so that the harp could not be heard nor their movements be seen from the street. At eventide, there was sunset light in the atrium casements and then they lit candles in the dark.

Peter returned to the gilt harp.

Grit began to sing softly as Peter played.

Witter realized that Peter was playing some melody he vaguely recognized, perhaps from some hymn or even a popular romantic ballad. But whatever it was, Grit was singing a psalm of David with each note of the harp...

The Lord is my shepherd
I shall not want
He maketh me to lie down in green pastures
He restoreth my soul
Yea though I walk
Through the valley of shadows
I shall fear no evil
My cup runneth over...

Witter was surprised, struck by the beauty of Grit's voice. He noticed the ancient Scripture was shifted in her verse. And then, as he savored the beauty of her song, he recalled some old rumor of her former life as a bawdy stage performer somewhere. How impossible that seemed now. Her nose was still swollen and red from being struck that day, and yet he recalled that Marguerite was her real name.

Finally, Peter peeled himself from the harp and curled like a puppy in his mother's lap.

How they glowed, Witter saw, in the wavering candlelight, bound by the precious blood strand from God. He would have loved to draw them, paint them, but he had left his art far behind, in the wreckage of the hard years.

"We must go tomorrow," said Grit. "We must follow the armies and give whatever succor we can to the injured and those suffering from horrors and so many evils."

There was a silence and Witter saw there was much uncertainty upon what Grit had just said.

Kristina's voice broke the spell: "I will not follow the armies nor expose my child ever again."

"What is happening to us?" said Grit.

"They are all animals," said Dolf. "We cannot stop what they do to one another."

"They fight for their freedom," said Symon.

"Freedom?" said Grit, rising, slapping her fists together.

"None born high, none low," said Symon.

Grit leaned down with her face right in his, and said, "Would you forfeit your soul for all eternity, for what you call freedom here in this brief time upon earth? Would you take life, kill another, for this cheap earthly gain?"

"Well enough for you," Symon said. "You are a woman."

"You think I cannot carve a throat nor any other part of a man? That killing a chicken is harder than a man? You think strong women are not among that army now? You are slovenly of mind, Brother. You will not do murder, for your sister in Christ will not let you do it."

"Nor strike one who molests Kristina or you?" said Dolf.

"For that I bless you." Grit stood away from them.

"I wish God would make Himself plain," said Dolf.

"I said I bless you, not God," said Grit.

Dolf and Symon now said nothing back, and hung their heads like chastised boys, but there was a stubborn cast to their scowls.

Grit turned, and Witter looked up. She was looking at him.

"What will you do? What will Mahmed do?"

"Mahmed is too weak for much travel," said Witter, hedging the question.

Said Mahmed, "I must get away from this place. I cannot stay here."

Witter saw Mahmed look at him, as if waiting for his answer, but Witter said nothing. Not now. Not yet.

"Mahmed," said Grit softly, "do you truly believe that your god is the same as our god?"

"There is one God," said Mahmed.

"Then why is there so much hatred on all sides?" said Kristina. "Did not God command us to love one another?"

No one answered her and the question hung in the air, with the chill of coming night.

Grit left the room then and Witter heard her descending the stairs. When she returned she had brought a pewter basin of water and a linen rag.

Witter watched Grit in wonder, as she knelt near Symon and took each of his feet and bathed them gently. Then she did the same for Dolf. Grit's wild straw-like hair caught the candlelight, like a broom on fire. She looked like a witch in a woodcut as she worked their feet, and yet he saw how her eyes glowed, with the beauty she once traded upon.

Then Grit left them and came humbly to Mahmed. The faces of Dolf and Symon twisted into stares of disbelief.

Said Dolf, "No, Sister, do not touch him."

Grit ignored Dolf.

"He is a Turk," Symon said. "A Muhammadan."

"We are all children of God," Grit said.

Witter watched her looking up questioningly, beseechingly into Mahmed's face.

"This act is grace for me, Brother," Grit said, looking up at Mahmed. "I do nothing to deceive you nor betray you."

"Grit, Sister," said Dolf, not moving.

Grit did not look at Dolf. On her knees, she put her wiry hands upon Mahmed's feet.

"By this, we are commanded, to love one another."

Mahmed blinked and then nodded, and Grit washed his feet, with subtle sounds of water in the basin.

Then it was Witter's turn. She came and knelt at his knees. He had not known how he would react. In Giebel he had avoided the more intimate ceremonies, like foot washings. He saw Kristina watching him.

Grit took his feet into the cool basin of water. Witter closed his eyes and felt delicious languor as Grit's hard little knotty hands so gently moved about the balls and arches of his feet, and he felt sweet solace rising through him. Her head was bent, her eyes never meeting his.

Then Grit went to Kristina and bathed her feet, and Witter saw by their gestures that they had done this together many times, and Kristina then bathed Grit's feet. Finally, Kristina took the basin to the harp, and bathed Peter's feet.

"Is it Thursday?" asked Kristina, oddly.

"I am not truly certain yes or no," said Grit.

Then Witter realized what Grit had done. She honored the day of the Last Supper, when Christ had washed the feet of his disciples; that last Thursday before Easter, the day that Christians believed their prophet arose from the dead, and walked the earth again.

Mahmed went quietly into another room and Witter heard him in his prayers. His soft chanting came ardently, his words quiet, unintelligible, with unmistakable sincerity.

No one spoke of that, but Grit put her hands upon the backs of Symon and Dolf then, and they too prayed. They prayed for all the people killing each other, for the people who had lived in this very house wherever they were now, for all sufferers, all the victims of all sides of sin, and they prayed for the awakening of evil men on both sides who sent others to die in war, in the guise of equality or religion.

Witter saw Kristina take Peter in her arms and she prayed softly with him, but the child seemed only aware of her touch, and he turned his face nuzzling into her caresses.

Witter lay where he could watch Kristina. She slept curled around her child in the moonlight from the inner casement windows of the atrium, as the moon climbed there. He loved watching her, again imagining painting her, to somehow make her his, even in art. He watched how the blue light silvered her and her child in a *pietà* of sweet living glimmer, as if in confirmation of life itself.

Kristina, who knew he was a Jew. Who had known it all these years, protecting him with her silence, never saying anything. Perhaps she would accept him even though he was a Jew. Perhaps her beliefs transcended even that difference.

Witter adjusted his little dagger inside his waistband so it would not hurt his side as he lay down, and he thought of the Jews inside their walls, all the men armed, keeping watch, waiting out the madness outside. He thought of the wary rabbi and his daughter.

As sleep eluded him, Witter's weariness, of soul and body both, surrendered to boyhood dreams of that vanished world that now seemed itself a fantasy…

…A world of Jewish cavaliers in their noble dress and wide hats and long swords, high up on their fine festooned horses, parading down the broad avenues of Córdoba. His father had clucked his tongue at their finery and their haughtiness, saying they were like David—proud men of war more than of humility—and yet they were the only ones who had fought back when the terror began… when everyone he had loved perished in fire and hatred, the hatred from which he had fled, unwilling to face it, unwilling to confront his own cowardice, without the courage of his father and of his father's fathers, abandoning all sane arguments and leaving faith far behind.

Sometime before sleep spelled him away, he realized that Grit and Kristina—these who dared the stake—were of the same kind as his father and his mother, and all those with them that day, who had refused to do harm and had gone instead to be burned inside their temple.

Witter fell asleep sometime during the long night.

When he woke he was curled so near Kristina that his hand was touching one of her thick woolen stockings, which filled out the too-large leather shoes that Grit had found here for her.

He sensed her warm body and his hand felt the living heat of her foot, and he quickly pulled away. The first light of dawn came gleaming upon her hair as he watched her breathe, and he tried not to feel it but ached with love of her.

If only she would go with me...

He knew how he would handle Mahmed. He knew how he would try to make his way out of this wretched Godforsaken land of evils. But he did not know how he would make Kristina go with him.

He only knew he could not live without her.

LUD

S couting alone was what he did best, and now he rode far ahead of the horde of villeins that churned the road behind him. He kept his horse along the low brow of ridgelines, so that he did not make a silhouette visible from afar, yet could crest a hill often enough to see far ahead and reconnoiter.

Taking action always cleared his mind. The farther he could predict any action by an enemy, or other urgent situation, the longer Florian and his commanders would have to try to shape up that horde of idealists that rambled with farm tools many miles behind.

He admired their idealism even as he saw it as a trap in which they were ensnared. He lamented their inexperience, even as he envied it for giving courage to ideas, before all was found to fail and be false.

Only when he stole time to rest did his mind drift back to Kristina, and at such times, especially at nightfall, chewing jerky and drinking rainwater, he felt more fear for her than he did the entire army. He wondered where she might be. And the fear became a hot longing.

If she is even still alive...

At such times, stealing two or three hours of sleep in a copse with his horse and a cloak for a bed, he fought off a bitter regret that he had not seized her by force and carried her far away. Then, upon snapping awake, he refocused his thought yet again upon the urgency of his scouting, the need to know who was where and how many.

He found the whole countryside up in arms.

The revolt was far more widespread than he could have imagined. In village after village, estate after estate, people were up in arms, huge groups of them on the roads marching to join one horde or another. Everywhere they made up flags of red and white cloth with the black cloth shoe sewn on.

It was like a new faith, this brotherhood, and Lud began to wonder if it might indeed have some chance to succeed. Many carried broadsheets of the Twelve Articles of Rights. Others had new broadsheets with horrifically detailed accounts of great atrocities by Landsknechts and other mercenaries hired by the League of Princes.

Lud read of massacres and the defeat of a horde from Leipheim, with many executions. These were ordered by Prince Georg, designated Protector of the Empire, and commissioned by the emperor to crush the revolt.

Lud rode back through a hard rain and brought this news to Florian in the night camp of the Black Host. The picket line was still open as a sieve and he would have to correct that. He found Florian's tent as easily as any assassin could have.

Florian was surprised and pleased to see him.

"We have waited for your eyes, for news of the field.'

"I could have slit your throat."

"Only you would know how to find me," Florian smiled, with that unfailing optimism that swayed people to the core and made them want to smile, too.

They embraced. It felt good to hold him for a moment. He wished to God it were Dietrich, though, and not Florian.

Steinmetz and other knights of the Black Host came. Muntzer and his monks were kept out of it, untold. Goetz came to Florian's tent with his Gay Bright commanders. The most prominent sergeant, Jaecklein Rohrback, a hard-faced miner, quiet and resolute, was invited by Florian to represent the ranks.

In the smoky glare of oil lanterns, Lud showed them the situation on Florian's vellum map.

"The Leipheim Horde was attacked and destroyed with many executions and mutilations ordered by Prince Georg."

"Georg?" said Florian. "Georg, Truchsess von Waldburg?"

"All Imperial reserves are now under Prince Georg's command, by order of the emperor Maximilian."

Lud closely watched Florian's face as he gave this unwelcome news, for it was widely known that Florian had been betrothed—before his excommunication—to Barbara, the younger sister of Prince Georg. Florian's eyes flashed but nothing was said of this personal matter now.

"So," said Goetz, "they all come against us."

Did you expect any less? thought Lud. All the long elaborate names of the cities and nobles and leaders ran together in his mind and boiled into one thing—many would die.

"Well for us they all come," said Florian, "with the Marienberg cannons, and our people righteous and angered at such atrocities. In our numbers and with the right at our backs, we shall swallow them whole."

So, three days later, he was scouting again.

The approaches to Weinberg Castle were wide open. He had reported this back to Florian the night before, as well as the disposition of the castle towers, and a fine hill opposite them, where cannons could be placed to create a breach.

From the scouting point on a ridgeline he sat his lathered horse and saw the enemy castle towers in the distance, and below him on the road came the horde pouring through a valley.

He heard their drums echoing up through the hillsides: the Black Host with the Gay Bright troop on the march.

Despite all his hard-earned reservations, seeing them coming, all together, their makeshift weapons glistening, many chanting and singing, all of it made Lud's heart rise, and he felt a wild moment of pride. He tried not to feel it but it came over him as it had when he had been just a boy, off to his first war with Dietrich, so long ago. The pride was alloyed with a kind of visceral lust, to see that castle fall and all the bastard lords there on their knees, and he thought of all the lives soon to be lost, and he forced his boyhood pride back with a guttural snarl at himself.

Goddamn you, Lud, always a fool, never learning a thing....

He rode down to report to Florian and join the Black Host in their outriders of cavalry.

Florian well understood the restless dynamics of the horde and that it was best to let them act and not think on it too long. So in the attack there were no delays.

The Weinberg Castle was shelled by the big Marienberg guns and breached in a north wall between two towers. Its cannonades returned fire and the hordes assembled in their vast groups, cheering, brandishing weapons of all kinds, with the muskets and pike ranks aligned on the flanks.

The drums rolled and black-cloaked Arl raged up and down the horde, flapping her long black sleeves like a great crow, cursing the castle, urging the villeins to send the "spawn of Satan" quickly back to their dark lord in Hell. And her ravings charged up such an eager furor in the horde that it even amazed Lud, who thought he had seen it all. Somewhere in all the madness the gentle baby catcher was no more. And now even Lud himself, who had known Arl all his life, thought of her as Black Hoffman.

The horde was edging forward, just out of cannon range of the longest guns of the fortress, which fired the desultory volleys meant to discourage an attack, but never did.

Their sergeants ran up and down their ranks, shouting, trying to hold back the wavering, advancing lines.

Here we go, thought Lud.

Desperately the wall defenders pried rampart stones with breaker bars, toppling them into the breach, trying to block the opening. But the falling stones crashed and rolled away, opening the breach even wider in the wall.

The horde throbbed like one great beast, hungry to avenge the atrocities that so enraged them, growing in horror and savagery with every telling. Those on the fortress walls would fight to the death, most of them, knowing what would happen were they taken.

The horde chanted and sang and shook their farm tools and homemade weapons, waving their crude red and white flags with the black shoe, people ravaged by lives from childhood under endless hard labor, strong and willing to wait no longer, impatient now to throw themselves into the meat grinder of that fortress, to pay any price to drag out some of those highborn ones inside, risking death to bring the haughty ones low and make them squeal and weep and beg, as hungering folk had long wept and begged and finally grown dull to their own sufferings. But now they raged, for they had learned to read, many of them, and they were dull no more.

Lud saw Muntzer and Michael and other priests urging them to attack, despite the sergeants trying to hold them back.

Now suddenly, he remembered the forgotten words of Dietrich...

"War is where faith goes to die..."

The cannons of the walls could almost reach them now.

Then the horde broke free. Their roar was a thunder and their flood erupted in a headlong rush and their flesh met fire and steel.

KRISTINA

In the enormous town house, with rooms enough for a hundred people, there seemed a vast unnatural hollowness swallowing her. They were washing their faces at the atrium well. Kristina felt like a thief, somehow. This was not her home nor was it a safe place of refuge.

The rim of the stone well was faced with beautiful colored tiles, blue and red and yellow, as were the atrium walls. Ivy crawled up the tall lead-sealed window casings. The window glass was inset with jewel-like facets.

Grit was helping wash Peter, with Kristina holding his strong little arms while he squirmed, trying to escape, but not biting. He had been happily chasing the birds that came sailing down into the open atrium to drink from a little watering well that seemed meant only for birds, unlike anything Kristina had ever seen.

Downstairs were knifed portraits of lords and ladies and lovely children. Upstairs there was a great mirror in a heavy gold frame. She had not looked in a mirror since serving Lady Anna. She stood there, regarding herself—ragged cloak, stringy hair, face burnt by the sun, lines of fear and darkness—and she did not recognize the burdened face she saw there.

The bedroom chamber with the huge mirror was strewn with powders and broken vanities and remnants of stolen gowns. Its walls were paneled and trimmed in gilt and the high ceiling was painted with sky, clouds, birds, cherubs, and angels. She saw a red hair ribbon in a corner, silk and bright, and she twisted it around her fingers. It was sad and strange, that from this house of great plenty, all had fled. Where were they now? Had they been swept away? Were their children dead? Were they starving somewhere in terror?

Now the house was hers, if only for these few hours.

All morning, Kristina felt a sharp and sourceless regret. Then, while she was scrubbing Peter—wondering whether she could ever teach him to read, to act like others, to learn, to behave—she suddenly realized what it was. Had the teaching of reading caused all of this tragedy? Did she share blame? Did Grit? Had they helped infuriate the people with so much knowledge, too much, too soon? What did God think of them? She put the red ribbon back. It was not hers to take and she wished she had not touched it.

"Surely God is sick of our whining," she said to Grit. "It is all vanity. All pride." Kristina heard herself speak as if daring God to strike her down; half that, and the other half apologizing to God for hubris, in daring so much danger.

"What is happening to you?" Grit looked at Kristina, staring, her gray hair wetted to the lines of her face, like the roots of trees. "Do not say such a wrong thing, Sister."

Grit tried to reach up and touch Kristina's face, to look into Kristina's eyes, but Kristina pushed Grit's bony hands away. It was all mounting, building, crushing her.

"So many are dying on all sides. I just want to be left alone now, and take care of my child."

"You are tired."

"Yes, tired of pretending…wisdom, piety."

"Love is truth. That is the only wisdom I know."

"The world seems made of hate, not love."

"Hatred is darkness, a stench, a vile putrescence of the spirit. Once, I lived in that blight. To be saved, we must keep hatred from our hearts. Our hearts must be sweet inside, a clean warm place of love and light for Christ to wish to come, and to be one within us. And we must help others."

Grit's concerned eyes were soft and loving in her hard face. Its contours looked eroded somehow, as if life itself had shaped her skin to her skull, yet her eyes held their innocence, their belief.

Kristina could not look at her without feeling selfish and inse-cure, ungrateful. And she resented that feeling, too.

"The hate is too strong. Love is too weak."

Again Grit tried to take her hand and hold it, and again Kristina felt smothered and she pulled firmly away.

"Child, be clear, confide in me, please."

"I am not your child," Kristina said.

"We stay together," said Grit, with hurt in her eyes, "my sweet sister, together, you and I, whatever comes."

"We are not sisters," Kristina said, feeling herself crossing a line that was forever tearing herself from Grit. "You are deceived. There has never been anything sweet in me. I have pretended it so, against my nature, against all nature. Now life is clear to me. I am a mother."

"Because God blessed you with your child. We do as God wills, Kristina. Or all is lost."

"Do as you will, I do as I will."

"But our will, it is too flawed to trust." There was a begging sound in Grit's voice, beseeching, pleading. "You say love is too weak? Nothing is stronger. That must be why God gave it to us. Love is where I go when I am too much afraid. It is my rock in a raging sea, and I hold on tight."

Kristina turned away from Grit.

"Kristina, please," Grit said, turning Kristina around to face her.

Kristina no longer cared if Grit loved her. The words came in a hot rush. Words to push back, to push away.

"Does not God make mothers of us? Does not God fill us with the need to protect our own? You said once you had a child. Did you abandon that child the way my own mother abandoned me?"

The flood of bad words came out and then it was too late to pull them back. Kristina stood shocked at herself.

Grit stared. She put her own arms around herself and hugged herself as if with chill. Grit's mouth fell open then, and she slowly shook her head as if she could not have heard the words so inflicted upon her.

"You do not know what you say," Grit said.

"Forgive me," said Kristina.

Grit took a step back from Kristina. Hurt was stamped deep in the hardened lines of her small face, and Grit turned away and went slipping from Kristina.

"Grit, forgive me," Kristina said again.

Kristina knew nothing of Grit's child. But now she knew something terrible had happened, and she saw Grit was wounded, and deeply, as Grit left her alone.

Kristina knelt and tried to pray.

She had harmed her dearest sister. So be it. She must shut her mind away from Grit. Her thoughts could not be too strong for her child. Only her child mattered now.

To remove Peter from danger, I must close myself off from this need of Grit and the others. I must be a mother and nothing more. I shall not abandon my child as I was once abandoned. Let them throw themselves into the fire. My child shall not watch his mother burn. My child shall be protected and goodly loved and not be raised by strangers. God has given me the child and I am not free to perish.

Had she not promised most earnestly to God and to Christ (and so many times to herself) that if by grace she was reunited with Peter, never again would she leave her child? Had she not promised God this?

But Grit was not yet finished with her. She returned with Dolf and Symon.

"Kristina, will you pray with us?" said Grit gently.

Kristina said nothing, but she joined them.

"We praise Thee," Grit prayed. "Thee who healed the sick and cast out demons. We give thanks to Thee who led us to learn and read and think and preach and witness Thy truth."

As they prayed, Kristina opened her eyes and watched the earnest faces of the others straining to reach some higher plane. And now, Grit's eyes took on that glow of strange purpose—as if Grit were looking beyond this life, into the next world. If Kristina had not known Grit so well, she would have thought it pretense, a claim to spirituality. But it was just plain Grit, real and honest as the woman herself.

"We praise Thee who could have ruled all kings and owned all gold, yet warned not to lay us earthly riches, but to lay up our treasures in heaven, and offered his body in atonement for our sins, sacrificed to the sufferings of a cruel death. I pray to lift up to Thee the souls of certain ones, of Lud, of Linhoff, and the others who have meant so much to us. May they not kill. May they see Thy divine light and find peace."

Kristina knelt watching them, and Peter came running into the room and she caught him up. He squirmed and she held him while the others prayed. When the circle came to her she did not pray. The silence was long and loud and Peter began to giggle nervously and he squirmed, pulling himself free. Grit had the same willingness to perish that her mother had given herself to, and Kristina felt that breach, as if Grit had already left her, too.

Inside herself, Kristina sent her own prayer…

For years, Lord, Grit had been my helpmate, my lifeline, in so many ways, when times were hard and strange. But now Grit is a tether to torture and death, and Peter is my child, your gift of life, and I must protect him…

So, when the others had all prayed upon it, it was just as Kristina knew it would be—Grit insisted they must follow the tide of war and do whatever they could to ease its monstrous sufferings.

So, Kristina refused to leave Wurzburg with them.

The others were ready to leave the shuttered city house at nightfall. They had used the day to gather whatever food could be found, and often Kristina saw Witter conferring privately with Mahmed, and Grit in a corner shelling walnuts and munching with Dolf and Symon, their heads bent.

But she stayed through the day with Peter in the corner as he played his harp, softly, for she had plied a muting strip of wool flannel serpentine between its strings.

The boy had fretted as she wove the soft cloth between the strings. He plucked the strings louder and tried pulling out the cloth and she held his hand until he let go. He sulked but then played gain, plucking as hard as his fingers could pull.

She stayed near her child and took him down into the atrium only for food and drink and ablutions, and would hear none of Grit's arguments for her to go with them.

"We are one," said Grit.

"Go find your Linhoff," said Kristina. "I heard you praying for him. He worships you. Go fly to his arms."

"You hurt me," Grit said.

"Why did you pray for Lud and Linhoff only? Why not Florian? Why not Bishop Konrad? Why not Merkel?"

"Does it help," said Grit gently, "to hurt me?"

Kristina said no more.

It was Witter, near sunset, who finally convinced her to go with them, saying, "To protect Peter you must leave this city. Food will disappear. Sooner or later someone else will break in here as others have before. It is far more dangerous here than abroad in open country."

"Where is safer?"

"By dark we leave," urged Witter. "Make our way together out of the city, to the river, take a boat if we can find one, downriver, down the Main River and with great luck perhaps even on to the Danube, to Passau and beyond."

"Passau?" said Symon.

"An ancient city, the gateway where three rivers join, the Danube with the river Ilz and the river Inn."

"What is in Passau?"

"The center of the salt mines shipping, down the Danube to Vienna," said Witter. "A great commercial city far removed from the troubles here. Once we reach Passau, the war will be behind us."

"Is Passau not a city of the unholy empire?" said Symon.

"They will not be searching their own back yard. The Danube swells wide with the junction of waters there and flows down all the way to the Black Sea, outward through many other lands."

Said Dolf, "Yes, on through many Ottoman lands."

Kristina felt a rising of great hope in her breast. Witter was brilliant, worldly, and more, he was no foolhardy man. And Mahmed was a man of the world, and owed her his life.

If they went down the Danube, she could do worse than take Peter and go as far as Passau with them, at least. Perhaps there she could take service in a wealthy house.

"How can Passau serve our cause of peace?" Grit said. "The people's army marches south toward Weinberg. There are many reports of terrible atrocities by all sides. We have a sacred duty to ease suffering."

"Where is your duty to life?" said Witter.

"Life on this earth is short, Brother," said Grit. "Guard this life too well and you will burn for all eternity."

"The longer you live," said Witter, "the longer you can do the work you believe is righteous."

"Our brother is right about that," said Symon.

Mahmed spoke for the first time, "You say you are pacifists. If you follow your people's army, your men will be forced to fight to protect you. What of their souls? Would it not be your fault? But if you take the river, God willing, you may get clear of it all."

"Turk," said Dolf sharply, "you have no say in this."

"No, he is right," said Symon.

Said Witter, "The army can turn and turn many times, but the river goes one way only. Is the river not safer to follow? And you know if you and Kristina are attacked, we will harm others to defend you, all we can."

"Devils beset us on every side," said Grit, agonizing.

Kristina sat wearily near Peter and pulled her cloak under her folded legs, sinking into herself.

Her mind fell backward, and she remembered the night and the ferry crossing and the death of Werner Heck at the bridge, when he hanged himself on his neck chain, to give them time to escape the magistrates, and then the chase by the dogs in the forest. And the death of poor Berthold, his eyes so surprised, with the bolt through his neck. And Witter, who thought himself a coward, yet fighting the enormous black dog to try to save her.

She thought of sweet Hannah, her doomed Benedictine sister long before Grit had become her sister. Where were the nuns now with their afflicted? Who would help them? Hannah would never have left them in the street that way. She thought of how Hannah had so admired the Benedictine saint, Gertrude, of three hundred years ago, with her visions of her head upon the breast of Christ, listening to the beating of His heart, and Christ piercing her own breast with sharp pains of His divine love. She wanted to curl up that way and never again be found.

"Kristina," Witter said.

Kristina felt a dizzying spin; her mind returned to this place and to this time.

She looked at Witter now, and did not want to part from him. He had been her lifeline in so many ways. He was a Jew and that secret had been kept only between them, and they shared this intimacy as did no others here, not even Grit. And more than that, Witter was wise in the ways of this world. He had seen much.

But what truly swayed her now was this—she knew that he loved her and that she could trust him because of that love. She looked into his liquid black eyes, set deep and always alive with thought, and she saw how much he cared.

"If no boat can be found?" said Kristina, confused. Their plans were open-ended and fraught with mischance.

"We keep moving," Witter said, "until we find one."

"Witter is right," Mahmed said.

"What will you do?" she asked. Thinking of Mahmed pricking her, inoculating her against the pox. How she had mistrusted him for that, and then later been so deeply grateful.

"I go with Witter," said Mahmed. "There is nothing for me here. The river goes toward my own lands and I will take my chances."

And she looked at Witter, knowing he did nothing without sharp reasons, knowing there was more to this.

"Why are you doing this for Mahmed?" said Kristina.

"Why would I not?" said Witter unconvincingly.

"I asked Witter the same thing," said Mahmed. "He knows I am worth no bounty nor reward."

Witter said, "Mahmed is a learned man. Perhaps I can learn something from him. He knows the ways of armies and how best to avoid their maneuvers. Perhaps I will even go as far with him as his own country, if we make it alive."

Kristina shook her head.

"Grit will not take the river way. She means to follow the army by land and try to help the wounded."

Kristina saw Witter looking at Mahmed and their eyes traded some unspoken understanding. Somehow, Witter and Mahmed seemed to belong together. They made a pair, each worldly wise and strange in their own ways, as if from worlds she did not know.

"Mahmed and I go whichever way is safest," said Witter.

Then Grit came over and knelt with Kristina and touched her face. She said, "Do not leave us, little sister. You travel with your child, with us who love you. You need not go down into the valley of death to help others, if we do. But you cannot stay here. There is safety in numbers for all, and Dolf and Symon, as our good brothers in Christ, have agreed to travel with Mahmed until we are well away."

"For now," said Dolf from across the room.

So as darkness fell and deepened, all the shadows of the great ruined house connecting into one blackness, they prepared to leave.

It was only when she pulled Peter from the harp that a last bad thing happened: her child made a yelp of anger and would not release his grip, and she pulled harder and the child and harp both came falling over as one.

Mahmed was close by and caught the boy just as the harp would have crushed him. Mahmed was still weak and the effort sent him slamming down upon his knees, but his thin arms held Peter and did not let him be harmed.

The harp itself crashed to the floor and the neck cracked sharply, loud as a shot, and strings flew out like snakes, whipping the dark air, then coiling up in a great snarl with a hum of finality.

Kristina saw all this like a bad dream passing too quickly to react. She reached for her child but Peter wailed, kicked, struggling. He bit Mahmed and Mahmed let him leap to his feet and scramble free.

163

Grit came quickly and held Peter, cradled him into her arms, stroked his hair from his eyes, and whispered in his ear. In that way only was he calmed again. Kristina felt a pang of jealousy that Grit could do what she could not; that the warm strength of Grit's being somehow had more power over Kristina's own child than her mother's love.

Then, all together, they left the big house by the alleyway through an atrium passage.

Under a rising moon, Wurzburg was ghostly.

No voices, no music, no sounds of work or play. Its houses unlit. Its street lanterns dark. No carriages, no horses moving. No street food sellers, no open-doored taverns. It was as if the city had died and they stole their way through a vast skeleton of stone and brick.

The rising moon raced through high, flat clouds and she saw the twin towers of the cathedral, its dark windows blind but reflecting the silver light.

They passed along the wide street of tall city houses, the great houses of burghers and ministers, and out of that shadowed street they came into a wide-open moonlit avenue of storefronts with smashed windows like outraged mouths. They continued on around the outer walls of the market square, where once Witter had pretended to be a magistrate and saved Kristina from being arrested by a monk for handing out broadsheets.

Kristina held little Peter's hand and he was trying to jerk free, but he was silent, moving along with some innate stealthiness, slowing often to look and listen.

A clutch of men, only shadows at first, came around a corner far ahead, emerging into spots of moon glow.

Lanterns appeared from both sides, and then men's voices.

"Who are you? Where go you?"

Their black mass blocked the way and their eyes glittered in the dirty yellow glare of their lanterns. Kristina shoved Peter behind her and now she saw a group of men with lanterns surrounding them.

"Burghers, city folk," said Dolf, moving to face them.

Said Grit, "Leaving this accursed city as best we can."

They carried swords but were not rogues in stolen clothes, Kristina sensed with relief, from their decent manner and clean faces. Some looked soft and nervous.

"Men with women and a child," said one.

One tall, thin man with hollow cheeks and a great beard wore a judicial chain that hung heavy on his robed shoulders.

"I am Tilman Riemenschneider, mayor. Our citizen patrols are out to restore good order from wantons who pillage and do much harm to our people's cause."

"We will just be on our way then," said Dolf hastily.

But Grit did not move; she ignored Dolf, looking the mayor up and down.

"Riemenschneider, the artist, who has filled the empire's cathedrals with idols of saints and martyrs?"

"Icons, not idols. I am that same Riemenschneider."

Kristina felt the authority of the man, but Grit stood right up to him.

Said Grit, "Do you not lament the evil fruit of your new cause, sir? Must violence breed violence?"

"Pacifists," said a man in armor.

"Christ said that he did not come in peace, but with a sword," said Riemenschneider, looking down his thin nose.

The men started to move on, to Kristina's deep relief, but then, to her dismay, Grit stepped in their way.

"Christ's sword was love, not meant to kill," said Grit, "but the sword of life, of truth and compassion."

"You read the Scriptures, woman?" said Mayor Riemenschneider.

"As all should, I do read them."

"Then do you not know this is what we fight for? The rights of all to read and know the truth for themselves? Do you argue against the very struggle which frees you?"

"She means no harm, sir," said Witter quickly.

"I mean what I believe," said Grit.

Said Riemenschneider, "Almost all good men are gone with the People's Army. Our city swarms with criminal vermin. Be on your way if you wish to rid yourselves of Wurzburg."

"May God keep you safe," said Grit. "But do not forget Christ's command, to love one another."

"Grit!" said Dolf with a hiss, pulling at her now.

"May God keep us all," said Riemenschneider. "A new day comes for all. Birth is never easy, woman. We are doing our best."

The man in armor said, "Do not infect our brave men with pacifism, not when their courage is needed most dearly."

Grit started to speak but Dolf and Symon both pulled her away, down the street, and Kristina kept Peter close at her side, gripping his little hand hard, and then they were moving again.

The city walls opened and Kristina saw the great bridge. The gleam of the river water was below them along the quay.

Now, abruptly, Grit hesitated.

"We must cross to follow the army," said Grit.

"What?" hissed Symon, crouching low.

"We decided against this," said Witter, his voice low. "Please, there is only death there. Let us take the river, think of the others."

There were sudden loud noises then, from out on the expanses of the bridge.

Men were out there, Kristina realized.

"The bridge is blocked," whispered Witter.

Now someone laughed out there, and then came a breaking of glass. A curse was shouted and there was a striking of steel, chain, or some other metal.

"Devils upon devils," whispered Grit sadly.

Grit turned away, crouched, and they crept down the quay. Kristina followed with Peter, as stealthy and silent as a cat, his eyes alert, probing the dark.

They heard the sound of heavy wooden barges riding tethered along the piers. Peter stopped and gripped Kristina's hand harder. She heard his small breaths quicken.

Then they were running along the quay toward the open fields, running though no one chased them.

Her foot caught a stone and she tumbled with Peter falling beside her. Peter yelped like a kicked puppy.

Some man's voice shouted from the bridge behind them.

Hands came and helped them up.

Another voice shouted from the bridge.

"Kristina…" came Witter's raspy voice, urgently.

She saw Witter's moonlit face and he had her hand. Mahmed picked Peter up and she scrambled to her feet, legs muddy, slipping in wet grass. She tripped on roots as they all ran again, into the deep shadows of the river quay.

She hardly realized what happened in the next hour, minute upon minute.

She squatted in the bow of a flat-bottomed boat with Peter in her lap. The child felt cold and they shivered together, slimy with mud. She felt such weariness that she wanted to cry, but Peter was gripping the prow with both hands and giggling in delight. The black current took them downstream.

In the stern, Dolf was standing, grunting, leaning on a big square rudder, with Symon on the other side pulling at the thing, both of them fighting the current that kept trying to turn the little boat sideways.

"Do not let her turn," Dolf kept saying.

Witter and Mahmed had taken up long poles found in the bottom of the boat. They fended off snags and sandbars.

"Watch ahead for any sign of light," Mahmed said to Witter. "Anything of human intention is a danger."

Said Symon, "There will be battles and armies and we must somehow get past it all."

"Pray hard for that, Brother," said Grit. "But keep a good watch even more."

Kristina remembered the spinning ferry that night long ago, when Peter did not yet exist, when Berthold had still lived, when she had never seen Giebel, and that idealistic girl seemed like a child from another life to her now. Her arm kept firm around the waist of her child.

Help me be what I need to be, to save my boy…

That was all she asked. All.

The dark shapes of the land sailed past on both sides as they came farther out into the current.

Grit knelt beside Kristina with an arm around her. Kristina heard whispered prayers vaguely as the water slammed against the rudder.

Witter and Mahmed, holding poles, stood at the sides of the boat like sentinels watching ahead for obstacles, the half-moon gliding above where old walls and structures gave way to the stark trees and hummocks of open land.

Passau, she thought. That was what Witter had said.

So, with the damp air of river blackness rushing at her, she prayed that in Passau, if they ever reached it, there would be a safe haven where she and her child could escape these purity-seeking people. Yes, escape even Grit; escape them all and escape the fear and the madness of willing sacrifice and find a place to be alone with Peter, her child, and work as a maidservant or teach reading or do anything common to not be noticed but to live as a mother with her son in safety.

Let me now live for life, not for death, O Lord…

With closed eyes and clenched teeth, for this, and for this only, now she prayed.

LUD

"Education for all citizens who desire it," said Florian, "that must be one goal of this war. Is that not what my father wished?"

"Maybe that, maybe more," said Lud. "But what drives you truly? If we win will you raise monuments to yourself? Like the ones in Wurzburg?"

"Sometimes, you do talk like an ass."

"Answer me not like an ass."

"Monuments you say?" Florian glared at him, with the patronizing smile Lud hated most. "I wish for each man to make of his life a monument."

"How would they look, these monuments?"

Florian tapped his chest proudly. He wore the gold Geyer ram's head tunic. "My father understood."

"I am but a poor, ignorant man, and ask you again, describe these monuments."

Said Florian, patiently, "Each one a man who liberates his mind through reading, who learns to think his own way, and teaches his children to find their own way, and all free to create a life that is chosen, not branded upon them. That all can vote for their own rulers and for their own laws. Freedom of worship of any kind. No Church-state. No state rule over any church. No church ruling through the state offices. And all think for themselves. For such monuments we must pay any price."

Pay any price. Easy to say, he thought.

They marched with their standard high. They had no standard in dress or in weapons. Their pride was in their brotherhood. Their flag was the red and white, with the black cloth shoe. The shoe of the working man.

But with every fight, one or two less stood in the Giebel village ranks. He tried not to remember their names. In his heart he wished they would all desert by night and vanish back to Giebel. But he knew they would stand their ground.

It was noon, the sun a dull orange eye burning through thin, high clouds.

Lud stood with Florian on a hill and watched the scene in the valley below. The sun's heat was rising and sweat trickled down inside the mail vest under his tunic. Florian's words were in strange disunion with what they were watching.

Weinberg Castle stood smoking across the valley on the opposite hill. Its west wall had been breached and taken by storm. The cost was close to a thousand dead.

In the deep of the castle, many atrocities were discovered, many dead and mutilated villeins. Some poor wretches were found half alive, still splayed upon the dread machines in the dungeon pits under the walls—ingenious machines that Lud regarded with a marveling contempt, that engineers of such intellect could have given themselves to the sole purpose of devising human agony.

There was a shout. Here came the lords of the castle.

The reaction of the horde was fierce and immediate.

Old Count Strieber, arrogant and unbent, had been taken prisoner, as had several of his personal guard of knights.

Goetz, knight and the leader of the Gay Brights, had put forward this humiliating death ritual of running the gauntlet, which had been voted upon the previous night by the council of the People's Army, and Rohrback the miner sergeant had organized its execution. Muntzer and his followers stood praying.

Black Hoffman the hag stood mocking the condemned lords and knights. Lud could clearly hear her words, her taunts and mockeries, and many in the gauntlet were laughing.

"You would slay the innocents! Now stroll proudly to join the other devils in hell!"

One by one the knights went first through the long gauntlet of sharp shovels, swung by miners whose bodies were as hard as the rock they spent their lives breaking, their eyes as deep as the holes where they had spent their lives. Each of the condemned tried a different strategy. Some tried to dodge and move deftly. Others tried to sprint as fast as possible. None lasted long. The first blow set them reeling. Then they were chopped to bits.

The gauntlet executioners were common folk in common rags and they spit and ridiculed in common ways. They teased each one, tripping them, laughing angrily at them, and let them run and fall a dozen times with many devious cuts that only a miner with a life at the end of a shovel could finesse.

Old Count Strieber was last and he refused to run. He strode slowly, without haste, showing no fear, head high.

Lud had attended his public trial by a great bonfire the night before, and listened to the count's sole defense—his thousand-year lineage, with his forebears named one after another, all the way back to Barbarossa and before, protecting the Fatherland.

Then Muntzer denounced the old man to the council.

"There, see their true face in him! I quote the Twelve Articles, for all to remember. 'All castles, monasteries and priests' endowments shall be placed under lay anathema unless the nobility, the priests and the monks relinquished them of their own accord, moved into ordinary houses like other people, and joined the Christian Alliance. We designate all such oppressors and traitors to be killed, their castles burned, all monasteries and endowments confiscated, to give life to the new brotherhood of all men as one.' Let none ever forget the evil injustices which have compelled us to act in the defense of men everywhere."

The old count spit at Muntzer's feet, and Lud saw that the man had chosen pride over everything else. Foolish, perhaps, but that was something that Lud understood.

So now in the full sun of noon, Strieber walked with grave dignity down the open blood-splashed ground of the gauntlet. He stepped over a hacked up body of one of his knights. The noon glare bleached his uncovered hair and beard white as snow. He strode into the gauntlet as if taking a calm stroll in a garden, but his eyes locked with men he passed, first one, then another, and they blinked, daunted.

Lud felt a surge of admiration. He had seen the terrible atrocities inside the castle. And yet, despite himself, he wished the old count would be allowed to live.

At first none dared strike him. They watched the erect old man pass, humbled by his grace and courage. Then one of his fine boots caught on a turning stone, and he stumbled and glanced awkwardly around, and the miners broke into laughter. The old man gathered his air of grace and he bowed to the miners, and more than one of them nodded and removed their caps.

"Cowards!" cried old Hoffman, "Would you honor one who has tormented and crushed your brothers, who enslaves your children, who hoards up your futures?"

Black sleeves flapping, she herself grabbed up a shovel and ran and struck the old count full in the face. He was flung backward onto his back, holding his face and crying out, all his poise broken. As if released from a spell, the others all fell upon the old man. With their farm tools and blades they chopped him to pieces.

Lud looked away. He turned and saw Florian watching it with interest, but not relish.

"This was poorly done, Florian."

Oddly then, Florian said, "Every heir of this People's Army will learn how to read and learn and think."

"You speak of equality in education, while we watch this? Is this the kind of education you mean?"

"You have gone soft," said Florian.

Lud fought an urge to slap him. "You are too soft if you need to prove yourself so hard, Florian. Dietrich would never have permitted such a cruel farce."

"Father is not here, and our time is not his time."

"We shall pay for what we do here."

"The people have paid for centuries already. They do as they voted to do. It is not my choice. And this will make the statement we need to make to be taken seriously."

"What good effect do you think such atrocities will have upon other nobles?"

"They will bend more quickly," said Florian.

And to Lud's great surprise, it was so.

Florian was proved right within the week. But not in the way Florian expected.

The People's Army went on the march toward Liebenstein, the next castle to attack, and Goetz took it upon himself to send out armed message parties with certain demands.

Before there could be any attack, Count von Liebenstein joined what now became called the People's Alliance. He brought many knights and foot pike and cannons and a half regiment of musketeers.

Lud was astonished at how quickly an idea could ripen. There was no longer the horde, no longer the People's Army.

There was great celebration when from the Count von Hohenlohe came an unexpected wagon train with cannons and powder, with Goetz's messengers escorting it in.

Many sergeants and chiefs demanded now that Goetz become commander, not Florian, and the words that Lud heard most often were: "Goetz will bring us all the guns and horses of the nobility."

So there was a vote and Goetz was elected.

Florian stepped into the center of the council.

"The Black Host is departing to take action as we see fit," Florian said. "Vote or no vote, Brothers. If we do not have your confidence, we do not have your loyalty."

In any other camp this likely would have demanded a duel to decide honor. But not here. Lud saw neither man wished to fight the other.

"Good knight, it is your loyalty you discredit," said Goetz, "not ours. You do not honor the common vote."

Said Florian, to all, "We shall fight in the Wurzburg territories and through the Neckar regions, we shall attack all castles and nests of political priests."

"Comrade, you fight your side and we fight ours, all brothers in the same great cause of equality."

And so it was done, the army split. It was agreed that the Black Host should take forty wagons and twenty field cannons and that the armies would communicate by courier, as did the league forces when in the field.

As the horses were being harnessed up, Lud tried a last time to talk Florian out of this.

"Taking the Black Host into the field alone is a mistake. It is always an error to split the army in enemy regions, and all our lands now are enemy regions. Goetz is not the one I would follow but he is the one who shall be followed."

Florian turned on him now with surprising wrath—

"I have said what we shall do, Lud. Our might will force many castles to capitulate without fighting. Our army is the people. We do not pillage poor villagers for our stores, we take it from the rich."

"They took from us, now we take from them. With the wolves, one must howl, is that it?"

Florian regarded him with a look of surprise, almost as a boy who has cut his thumb. "It is not the same. We steal no girls for comfort wagons, we have no gallows wagons to make men fear to desert the ranks."

"And so they do desert, and steal away in the night, every night, back to the life they wish were still there."

"Some always will lose resolve," said Florian, more strongly, as if needing to convince himself. "But more come as well. We shall roll through this land and bring the new day."

"Not without large cannons. Not without discipline. I would trade all your monuments for a dozen siege cannons."

"Already some lords do send tribute cannons."

"Florian, hear me. They lie, they give us light field guns, not siege guns to breach walls. They fend, they shift this way and that, all to buy time to buy new armies. Then they will stab you in the back. Trust none of them. You talk like one who has not seen much war."

"And you speak like some feeble visionary of pitiless doom. Freedom is our destiny. I do not need your fretting."

"What of your mother? Is she safe and well, unprotected in Giebel with the way things are everywhere?"

Florian's face went deep red. "Do you imagine I do not suffer for the thought that anything could happen to her? Is it not sacrifice enough? Are you with us or against us?"

"So there is nothing more I can say?"

"Say that you are loyal and trust my decisions, or go and be damned."

And that was it.

As Lud gathered his harness and weapons and saw to his horses, he turned.

Michael was standing there.

"I am leaving all this," said the priest.

He stood bent and looked forlorn, anxious, weary, but more, he had a look of fright, like a boy discovered stealing. It was the old Michael Lud had known in Giebel. Gone was the new enthusiasm and confidence, all soured away.

"Are you ill?" asked Lud.

"In my heart now I am sickened."

"For now at least, we are winning, is that not enough?"

"This is not what I thought."

Lud felt a sad affection for the priest. He thought of learning to read, how the priest had taught him, had made him stick with it, encouraging him. How the priest had helped him cheat the steward's tally, so that the poor could be fed. How the priest had once kissed him on the lips, pressing, as some men secretly kiss, how he had recoiled, and the priest then tried to hang himself. How the priest had then gone away, following Muntzer, giving himself to this fight; and now that the man saw what killing was, and all the ugliness of war, he wanted to run away. Lud felt an urge to embrace him, to somehow protect the priest from his own idealism.

"Michael, what did you expect?" Lud said gently, without rancor, as brother to brother. "Parades? Joy and flowers?"

"Good-bye," said the priest, "that is all I came to say."

"Where will you go?"

"Away from Muntzer and all this death."

"I thought you worshipped the man."

"He is mad; a brilliant madman. Evil is evil. Paint a flower on an arsehole, its still an arsehole. All of this on all sides of it, all evil. And I see my own evil, truly."

"And yet I have watched you bless the battles, with your hands on the heads of those about to fight, telling them God is on their side."

"And for that I am eternally damned. Better I had tied a millstone about my neck and thrown myself into the deepest sea."

"How did you come to see this?"

Michael sat down and put his face in his hands and sobbed. Lud knelt with him. The horse stood looking down at them patiently.

"A woman was dying. She suffered terribly. Her wound was so terrible, like so many, yet she lived, impossibly. Of course I had seen such things. Many such things. But, Lud, I was alone with her, at the edge of the battle…and she begged and begged me to kill her."

"What did you do?"

Michael suddenly stood and began backing away, shaking his head. Now Lud saw the puffy bleary eyes, red from no sleep or from smoke or from crying, or all of those. He had seen men lose their minds in war. All who fought had seen this. Lud saw it now, a kind of dissolving of the will, of the spirit, when a man forgets the why and the who of himself. Michael turned away.

"Do not look at me," the priest said.

"Tormenting yourself will not change what you have seen and done, believe me, I know."

The priest said nothing back.

And with that, Michael was gone, running back through the crowd of soldiers readying gear and wagons and horses.

Lud watched the priest disappear, and then he returned to his horse and busied himself doing final adjustments to its armor and harness. If the girth hitch was too tight, the animal could not run hard for long. If the breast hitch was too loose, a blow from another horse or lance could shift the saddle sideways. The armor plates that protected the great neck and withers and the headpiece must be free to move yet never chafe nor blind.

The horse held its breath, inflating its chest, so the drawn-down straps would not stop its breath. The horse made sense. The horse knew what was expected, without knowing what could happen. The horse was like sanity itself. Lud remembered when he too was like that, as a boy.

The Black Host gathered, near six thousand by Lud's rough tally by sight, and Florian climbed onto a wagon and roused them to many cheers with words of glorious praise for their honor, as brothers equal each to each and to him as well.

"You villeins who tilled this land from the stones of the earth, you who built cities, you who slaved to feed the rich, now you shall inherit that which you sowed, and all tyrants shall reap the whirl-wind! God is on our side!"

God is always on every side, thought Lud, but the horde sent up a roar that thundered across the hills and valleys.

At the head of the Black Host, they rode out together, with the loyal cavalry of Steinmetz and his impoverished knights, now proud again, restored to their purpose in life.

Behind, came a whole city, the ranked legions of infantry, men and women both, then the cannons, then the wagons of the baggage train, with stores, and many women and children afoot.

The sergeants shouted and kept order in the line of march as they poured out onto the road toward the castles of the Neckar, which would have to be taken one by one, the hard way, unless their lords capitulated, as Florian believed they would. But doubt came, with its cold bony fingers in the gut, when he thought of old Count Strieber and how nobly and arrogantly he had accepted his gruesome walk in the villeins gauntlet, how disdainfully he had died.

Lud twisted round to look back from his saddle.

It was impossible not to feel love for them, despite all his fear for them, too. They were as common as he was, men of many crafts and and walks of life in one great body together, his people, his kind. They were infantry in good ranks for a horde of villeins, drums rolling and men chanting and carrying their axes and scythes and forks, with ranks of muskets and pikes, and in front of their ranks was their standard.

Across the valley on the hills around the ruined castle, thousands of the Gay Bright Band were cheering, too, saluting the Black Host as their brothers.

Florian lifted his fist, pumping it high. They cheered him, they believed in him, and they loved him. And Lud saw, too, how much Florian loved being their hero.

Riding behind Florian, up out of the valley along the old Roman road, Lud looked back where thousands of new muddy graves dotted the green hills.

Perhaps the world could be made safe for innocents like Kristina and Grit and little Peter. Perhaps this was the beginning of a new world after all, the bright, new world of equality of which Dietrich had dreamed.

The priests like Michael would be needed to put the pieces back together, once the killing was all done.

It was like nothing he had ever seen nor dreamed possible here. Yes, he had seen other villeins destroyed in the Slovakian war when he was hardly more than a boy, but that rising had no cannons nor cavalry, nor the sheer numbers of this mighty horde.

It was as if Dietrich's voice spoke to him again— words that Dietrich would have spoken, and Lud could not be certain whether the words now came from his own mind:

Whether you believe in it or not, nothing can stop what has begun. You cannot hope to win a fight you have already lost in your heart...

And he knew he had to try harder to believe.

Perhaps it was possible. Perhaps the people's unleashed might would sweep the land clean.

Until then, his only goal was to keep Florian alive.

WITTER

The broad black river was a sheet of starlight that had taken them sliding through the night. Its turns came almost blindly. The men were exhausted from fighting the rudder and the poles. Twice they hit unseen snags in the dark and the boat turned hard round, the boards groaning like a wounded beast. Only a hard fight kept it from rolling over, that and the alert thinking of the women who shifted their weight to the high side so quickly. Water sloshed about their feet and the women bailed with their hands.

In the first pinkish glow of dawn in the east they had beached the boat and dragged it into a brushy copse of scrub willows, to hide during the day and wait to launch the boat again come nightfall and the relative safety of darkness.

Witter's cloak hung heavy on him, soaked. They all collapsed in sodden heaps and in the wet grass each curled and fell hard asleep.

Dolf and Grit and Symon slept off somewhere apart from one another, each hidden in their own places, and Kristina was with Peter.

Witter did not know the time or hardly the place when he woke in the dusk, with Mahmed leaning down over his face.

"The prick you feel in your throat is your own little dagger," said Mahmed, his voice no more than a whisper.

Witter felt the alarm of utter disorientation. There was early night fog drifting over the high grass and the sunset light made Mahmed's dark face look like that of a demon from a nightmare. Witter blinked and fought his panic.

"No, friend," whispered Mahmed, "do not try to rise lest the blade cut you."

"What…are you doing?"

"I am stronger now. Many thanks to you. Time we had an honest talk, you and I."

He tried to rise but Mahmed pushed him back down.

"Let me up, please."

"What is your game?" said Mahmed, his voice hard.

The quietly grateful tone of past days was gone. The humble meekness, gone.

"Have I not helped you? I do not understand."

"I shall make it plain for you. We travel in dangerous country where armies are on the prowl to destroy one another. You say we head for Passau? How do you plan to use me?"

"Use you?"

"I am a soldier, a killer, a tool, is that what you need?"

"No. I mean only to help you, not use you," fumbled Witter. His mind raced through possible words and actions.

"To what gain for you? What do you need from me? I know all this goodness for me has not been from your kind heart and faith in brotherly love."

"I know," said a voice behind them.

Witter turned his head. Mahmed turned also.

Kristina was there in the shadows, her voice unmistakable. The sun was down now and she stood in the last purple light. Fireflies rose from the high weeds around her and, for a moment, Witter and Mahmed both stared as if at some apparition. Then Witter was afraid for her.

"Kristina, go back, get away."

"Do not harm him, Mahmed, I will tell you."

"No," said Witter, unsure of anything but full of panic. He did not know what she might say nor why. But he felt the sharp tip of the dagger gone from his throat.

"He is a Jew," Kristina said.

She said it gently, tenderly, and Kristina touched his throat where the dagger had pricked him a little.

"A Jew?" Mahmed said.

Witter held his breath, and had no idea what would come next.

Kristina said, "Witter dreams of living where Jews are welcomed. Is that not where you come from, Mahmed? Is it not obvious he wishes you to help him go safely there?"

"You are a Jew," said Mahmed, and whispered a small laugh of knowing.

Witter just stared, accusingly, at Kristina. He had struggled with the manner of disclosing all of this to Mahmed, to express it with a clear meaning, irresistibly persuasive, but now he was at a loss; it was all dumped into the air. By Kristina. Of all people. But why?

"How could I have not realized it?" said Mahmed. "The things you have read, the things you know."

Said Kristina, "Is Passau not on the way to the lands of the Ottomans? And even Jerusalem, farther beyond?"

Witter took deep breaths. Mahmed pulled him to his feet. Darkness was falling fast, and Kristina was hardly more than a lovely shadow. Witter tried to stay between her and Mahmed, somehow feeling he protected her.

"A Hebrew," said Mahmed.

"The others do not know," said Kristina.

"If they accept a Turk why not a Jew?" said Mahmed.

"They do not accept you," Witter said.

Mahmed stared away, to the south. "The Danube flows on past Vienna and then Budapest and Bucharest and on to the Black Sea, but if we could reach even Budapest I would be safe, and you both safe in my authority."

"Not I," said Kristina.

"Yes, you, and Peter," said Witter.

"Why would I go from one unholy empire to another? Both wage war for profits. Both feed on hate and fear."

Said Witter, "But Jews are welcome there?"

"Yes," said Mahmed, "but Kristina is also right, for all empires exist only by violence inflicted upon others. Jews are welcome in the Ottoman regions for many are gun makers, and professors of sciences useful in war. I did not spring from some heavenly estate."

A shadowy shape approached with soft footfalls through the foggy grass; it was Grit. She said, "Is everyone all right?"

The presence of Grit eased the tension Witter felt.

"All right," said Kristina. "Where is Peter?"

"Hungry," said Peter, just behind Grit.

Now Dolf and Symon came stomping through the wet foggy grass.

"The boat," said Symon.

"The boat is gone," said Dolf. "Symon did not tie it well enough and the current came up sometime in the day."

"You tied it, not I, Brother," said Symon.

"The boat is gone?" said Kristina.

"The current did not take it," said Grit.

"How do you mean?" said Symon.

Grit touched their hands, one by one. "Listen to me, my brothers and my little sister, while you all slept, I untied the boat, myself. And pushed it out into the current."

Witter clenched his teeth and looked at Mahmed, and even Mahmed was shaking his head in staring disbelief.

"But why?" said Kristina.

"Yes, why?" said Witter, trembling now with anger.

The boat was everything. It was the river itself. The boat had been the way to freedom, their way down the Danube past Nurnberg, Regensburg, to Passau and beyond, their escape from this ever-expanding anarchy, this war that swept all people before it. Witter could almost not believe the boat was gone.

"The boat was temptation," said Grit.

"Temptation?" Symon said, and whined.

They all sat down in the night, in a circle in the dark grass, with the moon rising over the weedy bank of the river, and the wide moving water below them like silver flowing from a crucible. Their eyes gleamed silver, too.

"Again and again, while half-asleep I awoke," said Grit, "with such a strong revelation, such an inescapable knowing, that I first feared I was not myself. Then I knew it was the spirit reaching to comfort me."

"Jesus Christ," said Symon and rocked on his knees in the night grass. "This is the end of us."

Dolf rolled his milk-eye up at the moon and tears ran down his leathery jaw. "You let our boat go."

Grit put a hand on Dolf's back, like she was petting an old dog.

"Because I too am weak, and knew we must not run away. We must not flee from so many who suffer. We must be who we are."

"I am the mother of my child," said Kristina. Her words came sharp and hard. She was angry.

Witter searched for something strong to say, but Mahmed spoke first, leaning toward Kristina.

"We must travel only by night. The boat was not the safest way, so exposed as the river made us, even by night. I will go with you if you wish."

"Who voted you to decide anything?" said Symon.

"Mahmed is right," Witter said.

"You, Witter," said Dolf, "with your strange ways and your learnings, you were never truly one of us."

Said Grit, "Witter was not one who quit us to join a war. Judge not lest ye be judged, Brothers."

Dolf and Symon traded guilty looks.

"We must vote," said Grit. "Any who will go with me, vote with me. I will go follow the war and do what I can."

"Behind the war may be the safest path," said Mahmed.

"No vote for him," Dolf said, staring at Mahmed.

"Abraham is father of us all," said Mahmed.

"Blasphemer," muttered Dolf.

"All are children of God," said Grit. "All shall vote."

Then, suddenly, Witter saw Mahmed rising into a half-crouch. His hand raised for silence. His eyes scanning the riverbanks below them.

KRISTINA

Mahmed had pushed her roughly, down into the tall, wet grassy scrubs, and she lay blindly and held Peter tight. Mahmed lay panting beside her and she heard him choke back his breath. Grit crawled to them and held Peter and her together. The world had all disappeared in the thick undergrowth that hid them, and Kristina could not bear knowing what was happening. Were they being hunted?

Kristina pressed her hand forward and shifted and peered through a scrub bush...

There were barges coming up the river.

Horses, soldiers, the barges chained together and lit by lanterns. Many strong men with long poles walked from one end to the other in a tireless circle, forcing the barges ahead relentlessly against the falling current.

For over an hour the procession came barge by barge. Then came three much larger barges, tethered by long chains. Big cannons were chained down on the barges. Teams of dozens of horses were on the riverbank at the other ends of the chains. Their drivers walked alongside and lashed them and cursed them as they passed along the bank within earshot of Kristina and her child.

Once—when the teams passed so close Kristina could hear the horses grunting, their drivers' boots slogging in the hoof-churned river mud—Peter squirmed hard, seemed to want to jump up and run to see. It was Grit who pulled Peter tighter to her bosom so his little face was muffled there.

The moon was high overhead by the time the army had passed. Kristina held on to Peter while he stood and peed.

And Kristina thought, *if we had still been in the little boat, we would have gone straight into those barges.*

"Let us vote," said Grit. "Please."

"I am taking my child from here," said Kristina. "Whatever vote is cast, I am going away from the war."

"Get it over with for all the good it may do," said Symon.

He was right. The vote was split. It did not work.

Symon and Dolf voted to go with Grit. Witter waited to vote, and Kristina saw he was watching her, waiting for her vote, and Mahmed was waiting for Witter, watching them both. Kristina held Peter's hand and he tugged and twirled at the end of her arm like a spinning top, singing to himself.

"Sister," said Grit, "there is no safety for you alone with a child out in this open country. Stay with us."

She no longer cared what Grit had to say, nor the others. "You run to your deaths so lovingly, so eagerly. I will go wherever I must and do whatever I must now, to protect the life of my child."

"Stay with us, Mahmed and me," Witter said, "please."

Kristina looked at Witter and never before had she seen how much he loved her. It was naked on his face, deep and strong in the beseeching of his eyes. His hand was poised, reaching out to her hand, but not daring to fully touch her.

A cold-blooded sense of utility told her how best to use Witter. It was survival now. The survival of her child. He wanted her love. She had never doubted that. And whatever she promised now did not matter, only that she protected her child as best she could.

"If you go toward danger," Kristina said, "I shall never see you again. But if you go away from this war, I will go with you."

"Kristina," Grit said, her voice shocked.

"Let them go," said Symon.

But now Mahmed stepped close and looked into her face. Kristina realized how dark he was, how deep the black eyes now searching her eyes, and making her blink.

"You cannot know the safest way now," warned Mahmed. "You cannot escape a thing that turns in all directions. War is a beast with too many heads."

"What will you do?"

His black eyes lingered on her face and a gentleness came to them, and he smiled.

"To you I owe my life, from years ago. To the others I owe nothing. Witter is nothing to me. My life is worth nothing here. Except to repay you."

"Tell me what I should do," Kristina said.

"Why listen to him?" said Dolf.

"Mahmed," said Kristina, not looking at Dolf.

"Witter is right about Passau, if we can reach it. The fighting will be well away from there. But there will be Imperial armies coming from every side, against the uprising, as quickly as mercenaries can be bought."

"Then which way?" said Witter.

"Those hills," said Mahmed, gesturing with a turn of his head. "Take them east and south toward Passau, away from the river. Armies on the march will always avoid hills."

"How do you know so much about it?" said Symon.

"War is my trade. We still have hours of darkness for travel. Time is wasted here."

"How will we guide in the dark?" said Kristina.

"Sirius, the dog star," said Mahmed, and pointed to the brightest point of light, visible even with the full moon.

"I go with Witter and Mahmed," Kristina said.

She turned her back on Grit and felt a terrible tearing emotion. She wanted Grit to hold her as a mother holds her child. But she was the mother, and Peter was the child.

"Pray with me," said Grit, and tried to take her by the hand. "You belong with us, Sister, we must hold together."

She pushed Grit away. "Enough, Grit. No more."

Dolf said, "We must find food."

"Where we find food we find danger," said Symon.

"Like rats we are," said Dolf. "Pray for manna, maybe God will hear us for once."

"Do not blaspheme," said Grit.

"I am damn hungry," said Dolf. "If God sees even the sparrow fall, can he not hear the growling of my guts?"

So, they gathered their meager bundles, with no parting words, with Grit looking stricken. And Kristina knew she had forced Grit to choose between God and her, and that she had lost, and would always lose.

Where Witter and Mahmed went she did not care, as long as it was away from the killing. Even though Mahmed warned that war could turn in any direction, that there was no safe travel, Mahmed was the closest man here to Lud.

Mahmed was a warrior, a man who would kill to keep her and her child alive; she was certain of him. He would keep his word.

And she now was certain of Witter, whom she had so many times caught covertly watching her the way a man watches a woman he wants desperately. She knew he would surely sacrifice himself if it came to that. Now she imagined going with him, with Mahmed guiding them, all the way to the Holy Land, with her child, to safety. For was Witter not a Hebrew? Was Christ Himself not a Hebrew?

She was overcome by a dominating selfishness to save her child. She had promised God. But it was more even than that. She was a mother. If they were caught and taken, at least they would not actively seek the path of death.

So Kristina was resolved.

And yet, it turned out, none of that resolve mattered.

The time came to part, and farewells were said, with averted eyes, with reluctant gestures. Kristina saw that Dolf and Symon wished to embrace her, but she stood away. She reached for Peter.

"No," the boy said.

Peter gripped Grit's wrist and would not let her go.

Kristina had set herself, expecting anything but this.

"Peter, we are leaving. No, let go. Please let go!"

Kristina tried to pull her child free, to pry his strong little hands loose, and she began to cry, and then scream at him. The more she screamed the harder Peter held on.

"You frighten him, Kristina," Grit said.

Kristina let go of her child. She had never felt more confused, more helpless, watching Grit with her arms around the boy, soothing, shushing, and then she too wept.

"Grit, please, help me know what to do."

Grit looked up tenderly. Kristina stared at Grit's tight little face, her wild hair a shining wraith in the moon glow.

"Forgive me," said Grit. Peter held her tightly.

"Forgive you?"

"For my own selfish need to serve strangers, when you are so close to my own heart. It is all right, sweet sister, little mother. I will not abandon you."

Kristina put her arms around Grit's hard little body and felt Peter between them, holding on to Grit. Grit pressed her cheek to hers.

"Why must God endanger my child?" Kristina said.

"Do not blame God for what we do. We shall take the hills together, and stay together. Where God leads us, even away to Passau, we shall try to get far from this war."

"Away?"

"I told you I once had a child," said Grit. "Now God has blessed me with two."

Kristina felt ashamed that Grit so loved her after she had rejected Grit so miserably before. She had never asked Grit about the child she had told her of before, for she had sensed an area where she must not trespass; and now she felt Grit press harder, so hard that Peter squirmed and shoved against them.

"Grit," said Dolf, "we must get moving away from this river, the day is coming."

Kristina looked at them and saw Witter and Mahmed standing apart from Dolf and Symon, all of them waiting, all of them watching. They were all good men. Kristina felt a sudden overwhelming burst of affection for them all. And just as unexpectedly, she thought then of Lud, and she missed him with all her heart.

"We must go," said Grit.

Grit gently took Peter's hand from her wrist, and joined his hand with Kristina's. Then Grit held them tightly together in her own cupping hands.

"Together, whatever comes, whatever we must face," said Grit, "let us face it together."

"The sun is coming," said Mahmed.

Then they were moving, all tightly together, hurrying toward the hills with the sun rising fast over the river behind them, orange and violet, cutting the fog with sharp black shadows.

Witter and Mahmed were just ahead of her, Peter scampering along between her and Grit, and Dolf and Symon behind them. There was a shepherd's path along the ridgeline, a path thousands of years old, deep from countless generations of feet and hooves.

They were pushing through high grass when the wind came up and with it a morning rain. Kristina had Peter against her leg inside the folds of her cloak with only his little face exposed, when she saw flickers of reddish light below them in a little hollow.

They all stopped.

The wind shifted and the wet smoke blew back at them, with a hail of spinning ashes that stung their eyes.

It was a village, burned out, the wind stirring up the fiery embers from collapsed structures.

Something was moving in the smoke.

A black shape was walking, moving away from them, its arms to its chest, holding something. It turned around as if sensing them. Then it was moving toward them.

Within the black cloak was a white face and from each sleeve came a white hand, reaching out to them. Kristina stared, knowing she knew the face yet too startled to grip that memory.

Mahmed had pulled out a small dagger, but Witter waved him back.

It was Father Michael, the priest, Kristina realized. In his arms was something small and pale. He said nothing, staring, but sank to his knees as if supplicating them, offering them a sacrifice from his arms.

Grit ran to him.

KONRAD

The storm had broken, and under the sun the days had been almost comforting, taking them farther and well away from the fighting.

The horse guard had worn itself down, but Balthus had driven them hard, and when they had finally reached the Danube, Balthus had seized a train of three barges to reach Passau, where three great rivers joined.

The very sight of Passau renewed Konrad's spirits.

His prayers seemed charged with new purpose.

The great castle fortress, the Oberhaus, overlooked the triangle of waters. Here, the Holy Roman Empire was in full alarm at the frightful outrages of the uprising of commoners. The Passau skyline was reassuringly spiked with cathedral spires. Konrad felt heartsick, thinking of Wurzburg now, realizing how much more he loved the city than he had ever before known, now that he had lost it.

At Passau he spent one night in the guest chamber tower of the Oberhaus Fortress, which commanded the junction of the three great rivers, the Danube with the Ilz and the Inn. Its walls were covered with tapestries of the Sermon on the Mount, in colors that Konrad found most pleasing.

At midnight he had been unable to sleep, the feather bed too soft perhaps. In a silk gown he had wandered out onto the tower balcony and stared at the moon riding upon the three rivers that enjoined below like the roots of one great tree. He smiled, remembering the lullaby his wet nurse had sung him many times of the moon in love with its own reflection. The horizon glimmered with far distant flashes of a lightning storm, and he was enjoying the mighty display of God's power, when a stench began to drift upward on a breeze rising from the river below. The effect was spoiled and he went back inside and pulled the tapestries over the rampart casements.

"Jews and heretics, your grace," answered one of the body servants, when Konrad asked the next day. "In the lowermost pits, their air vents are below the fortress."

"Jews and heretics?"

"The Jews are left to starve, that no harm be on the souls of our good bishop. The heretics are questioned and mostly they burn, in time."

Konrad, thinking out loud, said, "Undoubtedly, the wealth of the Jews was taken into the treasury to fund some of the mercenary armies so lately needed and bought."

"Forgive us, your grace."

"What?" Konrad realized he had just spoken to a body servant as an equal; it felt humiliating.

The man said, "Usually you cannot smell them so far up here. Shall I dispense fragrances and herbs before your evening rest?"

"No, I am leaving for Vienna today."

Following new grooming baths, then an Imperial tailor for more suitable fresh clothing, Konrad was met by retainers of the archduke of Austria, Ferdinand, and from there escorted on to Vienna.

Down the Danube, in a fine barge guarded by the archduke's own retainers, whose uniforms were elegant far beyond need. Konrad's own weary horse guard was left behind in Passau to rest until further orders.

"Your excellency, the archduke himself wished to convey his compliments," the archduke's captain informed him. "We shall escort you on to Vienna."

He saw Balthus standing by, concerned; Balthus with his stained, bedraggled tunic and rusting armor, and this one from the archduke, in parade finery, looking like he had just stepped out of a coronation ceremony.

Konrad defended Balthus.

"My captain Balthus has matters well in hand."

"Your grace's captain is no doubt most excellent in many ways, but is he not weary? And would not Wurzburg men be made most uncomfortable by the many courtly protocols of Vienna?"

Konrad knew it was true. He was a voting prince of the league and he had voted for Maximilian to become emperor, and yet he himself hated all the protocols of Vienna. He had been tutored in the mysteries of court by both distinguished professors and by suitable Jesuits of high order, and had been to Vienna a dozen times as a boy with his father, and at court since that time.

Passau was a fortified river-junction village compared to the castled seat of the Hapsburgs, where the Romans had once built a great, fortified city, where young Maximilian the Second now reigned as emperor of the Holy Roman Empire, following the footsteps of his father. And, indeed, Konrad was flattered by the escort. Yet now, suddenly, he wondered if it amounted to a state of being under arrest, perhaps for having surrendered his castle to a horde of outlaws and upstarts and heretics.

The thought angered and frightened him almost as much as did the cacophony of names and titles involved at Vienna, with all their intrigues and lines of force and alliances and old slights. Too many names for anyone to ever remember in order of power. There were three that mattered most, the emperor, the archduke, and the cardinal, and their relative power continually shifted from one to another.

"Balthus," Konrad said, and took his faithful captain aside and ordered him to wait and rest in Passau.

"Upon my return from Vienna I will have much need of you to be rested and ready for anything."

"I am ready now, your grace."

"You will take quarters in the Oberhaus Fortress. Your task here is to gather all information possible, of actions in the field, from refugees and others. Keep an especial alert for heretics. They are abroad everywhere, I am sure, feeling free now that anarchy is loose in our land."

Balthus bowed and that was that.

Four days later, he came up from his cabin at dawn, and the river turned and he saw Vienna's towers piercing a morning mist radiant in the sun. The officer of the guard stood at the prow, in all his martial finery, like a cock ready to crow. Konrad thought of Dietrich, the way he cut such a handsome figure, without all the grand trappings. He thought of Florian, and the terrible betrayal of his godson.

"Excellency?" said the officer.

Konrad realized he was staring.

"Is there unrest in the city?"

"None, excellency, we have things well in hand."

"Answer me truly. Am I under arrest?"

"Arrest, excellency? I am at your service."

And when they landed, a small delegation greeted him with flowers and wine and sweets and a fine carriage.

Konrad was not under arrest by any means; just the opposite, to his immense relief and joy.

The streets of Vienna showed no trace of the costs or pressure of war. Great carriages displayed elegant riders and the markets were full. Religious processions and musical pageants and weddings were ongoing. The surly streets of Wurzburg seemed worlds away now.

He was feted as a welcome guest and given private chambers in a Hapsburg town house. He was a prince but had never been attended by so many body servants, and he fretted at his knowledge of high court manners. New bishopric robes, and accoutrements for evening wear, were sent to him by the cardinal.

There was a great high mass at St. Stephen's Cathedral, with hundreds of angelic voices in the boys' choir, in counterpoint to the nuns who sang from concealment.

Konrad longed for vespers in his own cathedral, where everything felt strongly of Lorenz and the Riemenschneider icons, all of it once repellent yet so steeped in fond sentiment now that it was lost. He wondered where all the boys who had sung there were now—were they dying in the villeins' army, that evil that they called the People's Army? Were they being driven out into the countryside to starve, or forced to die in gruesome battles?

That same night, Konrad was guest at a Hapsburg feast.

The guest hall was vast. Never had he felt more insecure, more the country rube himself, despite his princely bishopric rank. Vienna was a maze of splendors. His mind reeled with all the fine points of ritual that royalty implied: too many names, too many titles, too many things to ever recall correctly.

He had prepared all his excuses for losing his own city, Wurzburg. But instead found he was being honored for valor in the cause of Christian justice and rectitude—for holding out so long against such evil violence of such great numbers.

"And," said Maximilian over a grand court dinner, "you bought time. Your valiant defense of the Marienberg Fortress delayed the villeins."

Konrad bowed, and considered his best possible response, realizing the support implied by the emperor's statement.

There was a wine toast in his honor, which gave him time to think. He had already taken two glasses of the heady red wine; its soothing heat was rising through his fear.

It is good that God has been so wise as to not allow others to read our thoughts, thought Konrad. The emperor was young with much white powder covering the pimples of his face, like a mask of white paint on rough plaster, softened only slightly by the candle glow. The painted faces writhing under their stiff powdered wigs were like grotesques from comic opera. The women, when they dutifully smirked at the jests of their lords, had the pained toothy grins of foxes caught in snares. Their men affected hauteur and disdain. The women had refined their art of flattery so well that the men believed it themselves, as they dueled with their wits, trading jibes up and down the table.

Prince or not, Konrad felt very small.

This was a game to be played and won, or all was lost. Konrad realized that the return of Wurzburg to him, as prince-bishop, was at stake.

Maximilian was voted to office by the Swabian League's nine princes, of which Konrad was one. Perhaps there was dissent among the other princes. He was not close to any of them, except by accident of rank and birth. Perhaps his vote was badly needed by Maximilian in the election surely to come following this disastrously expensive war, which was incurring vast debts to both league and empire.

"Tell us," said Maximilian, "we hear they march in a horde? Their standard is a poor villein's shoe on a pole?"

"They take pride in poverty," said Konrad.

"Yet they would steal our wealth," said Archduke Ferdinand. He sat at the right hand of the emperor.

On the other side was Cardinal Von Wellenburg, a heavy-faced man of sour disposition and sour comments meant to sound droll. He wore his red cap over a furry brow so that his eyes peered from a hairy cave.

"Prince Konrad," said the cardinal, "do tell us. Are the villeins as clumsy in war as they are in breeding and tilling? Were they amusing, flailing away with farm tools against cannons? Were they like children in tantrum rigors?"

Much laughter, mostly strained and polite.

Konrad smiled and measured his response. Many faces along the table were staring at him, no doubt eager to hear in what tone he would respond.

Then God whispered for him to speak truly.

"They were vicious," said Konrad. "With the courage of those who no longer value life."

He looked into the gold of his banquet plate where the grease of flesh had smeared the polished gleam. In the mirror of his mind he saw Sieger's head staring up at him from the stake.

"Your courage delayed them," said the cardinal. "Bought us time to raise new armies in God's name."

Said Ferdinand, "The villeins delay themselves."

Konrad looked at him appraisingly. The archduke was sere and thin, almost ascetic in his thinness, and his skin was stretched upon his beak and cheekbones, translucent. His beard was trimmed short except for his receding chin area, where the beard attempted to make a good chin. But he had an assertive confidence that Konrad envied, and noted.

Said the archduke, "Our spies tell us the hordes must even stop to vote among themselves before taking actions of any kind. Even to squat, I presume."

There was laughter among the men. Among the ladies there were teasing little cries of delighted disgust; Konrad knew their game and respected them for it.

"Imagine the confusion," said the cardinal, "in a world where all—*all!*—vote as equals?"

There was again much laughter at this.

Conversation was by rank, yet sometimes also by novelty, and Konrad was the novelty of this dinner, he soon found. Elegant ladies and men of rank were too many to keep track of, but he focused upon the key three: the emperor, the archduke, and the cardinal.

"You are the only one here who has seen firsthand what the horde can do when evil thoughts do overflow."

"First Luther," said Konrad, "now Muntzer."

"Muntzer is a madman and will not be bought." The cardinal took more wine, his ashen jowls jiggling as he swirled it before speaking. "Luther, on the other hand, is for sale. He has issued a broadsheet condemning the villeins, asserting the right of the Church-state and the nobility."

"No surprise there," said Maximilian. "The duke of Saxony keeps him for a pet. They say his broadsheet sales are bigger than ever. Bigger even than those of Erasmus."

"Erasmus is busy defending Anabaptists and other heretics, and promoting reading," said the cardinal, his mouth stuffed with roasted figs. "All the while hiding in England where morals are looser than a villein's bowels."

Laughter.

Konrad laughed low; watching, he sensed the game was changing, though he could not yet detect how or why.

Said the cardinal, "Luther was always clever at keeping himself uncooked, while promoting his sales with tours of cities and his outrageous manuscripts."

Said Maximilian, "Now the monster wisely has concealed himself up the arse of his patron Duke of Saxony."

More laughter.

"We bought Goetz and a number of other horde commanders dirt cheap," said the archduke. "There will be estates of dissident knights and others in plenty to hand out when this business is done. Goetz split the horde they call the Gay Brights, and the bulk of them are crushed in a trap Goetz set for us."

Said the cardinal, "Now to deal with the apostate Florian Geyer, with his horde that they call the Black Host. A name of perdition, surely, for those who serve the Dark Angel of Damnation himself. God is surely with us."

"The Ottomans all say that, too," said the archduke. "Gunpowder and mercenaries do this work best."

"Money does this work best," Maximilian said.

More laughter.

Said the cardinal, "The Ottomans, thanks be to God, are busy with a rising of their own in their southern borders, and God thereby has protected our backs at this time of internal madness. Let us give thanks."

The cardinal stood and gave a long sonorous prayer in Latin. Heads were humbly and decorously bowed, but Konrad stole glances under his lids and observed the scene.

The long candlelit table glittered with crystal and sharp eyes under powdered white wings, and some lords smirked and eyed one another. It was all a game. Some overly pious, others smirking with contempt. Konrad took deep heady breaths, rejoicing within himself, for he felt closer to God now, a better man than these posers and cynics.

"None here have experienced the villeins firsthand as you, dear prince-bishop," said Maximilian to Konrad.

Konrad saw Maximilian's white face powder beginning to crack like wet plaster, in long lines, from laughing.

"They are as madmen possessed," said Konrad.

Said Maximilian, "Can mere words frame such monstrous incivilities? We have spoken here of Florian Geyer, leader of the Black Host, hero to the scum. Is it true he is your own godson?"

The whole table turned to Konrad expectantly. He felt his face grow hot. The game had turned his way.

All eyes were on him, expectant, waiting to see which trap he would step into unaware. He knew this game well enough for Wurzburg, but he was far from his depth here. Best to be honest now.

"True, your excellency."

Said the cardinal, "We read your Veritas broadsheet in which you described his heresies and his excommunication, declaring how you would in three days seize his estates."

"The mind of the villeins was so purloined by wrong thought that our broadsheet, spread far and wide, our denouncements, made Florian Geyer their hero."

"Lamentable, indeed," said the cardinal. "And we have heard that the uprising started there?"

"It began in many places, it seemed, almost all at once. As if the villeins' common mind was an orchard, with evil fruit ripening in an evil season, the same in many trees. Reading has done it. My godson was ruined in England. Many others were ruined in our own lands."

The archduke said, with an accusing tone, "And he let you live, your godson Geyer, he even protected your exit from your fortress?"

"My godson did let me live," said Konrad.

There was a ripple of confusion down the long table, as if he had made a joke too ill-formed to brighten easy laughs.

"The horde screamed for my torments," said Konrad, "but he stood against them and let me go."

"It is normal," said the cardinal, "for a man to love his godson, but surely not one who turns his back upon the Holy Mother Church?"

Said Konrad, "I fear the lust for worldly glory seduced him away from my protection. But he comes from a long line of knights, and his father was my friend, and cousin. They were always soft on their villeins, and now we see the judgment of God upon that inheritance."

"What must we do with the vile remains of this People's Army, when it is over?" said the cardinal.

"Put them back to work, of course," said Maximilian.

"If any are left alive to work," said the cardinal.

"First," said Konrad, "they must be stopped."

"Never fear," said the archduke.

Said Maximilian, "Three armies even now converge upon the villeins. The elector palatine in the south near Switzerland has raised many mercenaries there. He marches north with his contingent of twelve hundred horse and two thousand foot with twenty-four cannons. Duke Georg has raised his own force for our always-faithful Swabian League of princes, and marches south. No doubt he is eager to settle scores with the apostate Florian Geyer."

"Indeed," enjoined the cardinal. "Geyer accepted excommunication, and stained his own betrothal to poor Barbara, the young sister of Georg. As I am her confessor, I must say she has been grievously wronged."

Many eyes glittered and wigged heads nodded at this.

Said Maximilian, "At the time it was a scandal, yet many of us felt the young lady Barbara had escaped a devil in the nick of time. Surely the man is mad."

Konrad felt a sadness now, that he had somehow failed to reach Florian; that Florian would surely wish for mercy, and would find none.

Said the archduke, "Our own Imperial force marches east. We have the villeins in a trap and we shall crush the very devil from those miserable lice."

Konrad was shocked, deeply moved by the power that swirled in this great hall. Surely God had graced him by letting him live to enjoy such company.

There were many toasts and congratulations. Konrad sensed the mood was equally high as the fear that had preceded it. He knew that courtly conversation held many traps for the unwary, and the greatest pitfall was exposing too much before others did.

"But good rulers must forgo self-congratulations and look ahead to aftermath," said Maximilian.

"Ugly," said the archduke, "if you mean our ruinous debt incurred, to pay for this damned war."

"Taxes are in arrears. Do not look to Rome," said the cardinal. "This is what comes of free ale festivals to try to buy off the commoners, yet they hunger to learn the secrets of our knowledge to bring us to our knees."

There was a long silence up and down the table. Konrad saw that everyone waited to hear what Maximilian would say. He was elected by the princes, and his prestige partly rested upon his assumed close relationship to Rome. His father had been a powerful emperor leaning toward new ideas of reform, but this son was far more conservative, and Konrad sensed the young man was desperate to prove himself firm of purpose, yet wise despite his years.

"Truly, the pope has his own wars," said Maximilian. "This uprising is our problem. Reading has brought unsound minds to bear unsound thoughts. When all the killing is done, all the estates will be in dire ruin and neglect, therefore an even greater effort than the war itself will be necessary, to bring new profits from the wreckage. We must all look ahead and consider the best means of persuasion."

"When mules learn to read," said Konrad, "how can you drive them?"

"That, indeed, will be the devil's own puzzle," said the cardinal. "For reading has brought this calamity from the dark ignorance of their minds, proving the evils of acquiring imperfect knowledge."

The archduke said, "We must punish most severely those who teach reading. They are the whipping posts of the devil."

"Too late to stop reading," said the cardinal. "That cat is too long out of the bag, and gone feral."

There was laughter, for many at the long table wished to flatter such a powerful man as the cardinal.

"What says our Wurzburger?" said the cardinal.

Konrad thought a moment, and said, "There is an old saying there, I heard it said. If you have no hawks, you must hunt with owls."

The laughs that came were barely concealed jeers.

"We have our good hawks of war, Konrad, and need no more owls, for those we also have in plenty as you can see here."

Konrad smiled a smile he did not feel.

He thought of Lorenz von Bibra, the one who truly had said it to him. *To hunt with owls.* Like these here at this emperor's table, he had not understood the saying then, yet believed he had.

With all their power, they still had not understood the saying at all. He was not certain that he fully understood it all himself, but it was forming in his mind.

If you could not destroy your enemy by day, you hunted him by night. If you could not persuade him with his own death, you twisted him to your way of mind. You hunted him with owls. You hunted him in his dreams, in the darkness of his ignorance, until his thoughts were turned to your own.

Here at this great table he had first felt small, like a lackey, a country rube not much elevated from his personal guard left behind in Passau, too rough for Vienna customs. Wurzburg was far from Vienna in more ways than roads and the river.

And yet he knew he would prove himself. He no longer felt small.

"Your Veritas Press was known even here in Vienna," said the cardinal. "Many of the broadsheets were quite good, persuasive and clever in damning all Turks and heretics."

"I had no idea we were read so widely," said Konrad, warily, yet flattered beyond all surprise.

The archduke belched. "Yet how unfortunate, that your press and publicists inadvertently made a great hero of this apostate Florian Geyer."

Konrad felt the wine that had rushed into his head. He did not trust the confidence the wine gave him now, and yet his idea felt too imperative to hold back. He needed to be brave now. He needed the courage of Dietrich now. And he needed the wisdom of Lorenz.

"Florian Geyer is my disgrace. Our Veritas Press publicity sought to damn him, to cite his infamies. Inexplicably, many villeins love him all the more. Such are the perversions of the damned."

"But you see, my dear Prince Konrad," said Maximilian, "evil folk embrace evil heroes, and so your broadsheet made your godson their idol."

"Yes, I know, your excellency, well do I know."

Said Maximilian, "The world has been turned upside down by three things—gunpowder, the compass, and the printing press."

"Literacy is the ruin of innocence," said the archduke.

"It is here, for good or ill, and we must find keener ways to use it," said the cardinal. "With gunpowder we shall crush this uprising. With the compass we shall bring the light of Christ to all other lands, and their wealth to the service of our Church-state. But the other—reading—that is all another thing, ever changing, like a curse."

Konrad thought suddenly in a new way of Veritas Press, how its propaganda had scored some successes, yet ultimately failed to conquer the rapidly changing minds of the common people who had learned to read. Where had the failure been? Then he saw it, in a stunning flash of insight.

"We must learn better to twist the words to suit our purposes," he said, struck by the revelation and thinking aloud, even here. "Publicity and propaganda, these are new powerful sciences, and we find our way but slowly. First we must persuade, educate them with our own thoughts, our own histories, make them want to obey, make them think the Church-state is their property, not ours."

"Is that not what they think even now?" said the cardinal. "This Muntzer demands the kingdom of heaven be handed over to him here on this earthly plane."

Said Maximilian, "Konrad makes good points. Educate them with our own thoughts, until they no longer remember that the thoughts belong to us."

Konrad felt encouraged, bold. "Play upon their ignorance, yet have them believe they think for themselves. That comes first."

"First?" said the archduke.

"Shaping their minds must come first," Konrad said.

The archduke stood and raised a gold goblet in a toast.

"First, we must kill them," said the archduke.

That brought the loudest laughter of all.

"First, we must kill them!" cried Maximilian, delighted.

They all stood and toasted.

Konrad saw no joke. They had not seen what he had seen. He forced a smile, distracted by his own deep thoughts, where a new plan was already in birth: a plan that would restore him to his quest for God's greater glory.

In momento, in ictu oculi, in novissima tuba...

In a moment, in the twinkling of an eye, at the last trump, God would have the right way for all men.

Konrad knew now that he had been wrong to fear this court and its elaborate protocols. Yes, he felt deeply out of place here—not less than them, but more. They seemed ever more shallow to him as the long night went on. Vain, sustained by artifice, moved by cleverness, not truth.

His personal knowledge of God was far beyond anything these would ever understand, even this cardinal, with his sneering superiority. Vienna made Konrad realize how much he loved Wurzburg, good old Wurzburg, with its country folk, people like those of Giebel, mad though they were now. But he would burn that out of them. He would crush that out of them. He would sear them in the fires of God and remake them as they must be.

Had he not promised this to God? When all the hawks were dead, he would still be the owl who hunted.

Now he realized that Veritas Press had not failed. Yes, the Florian broadsheet had gone the wrong way. But its very power itself was not in question. That power had gone misdirected, but the power was just as real. Like gunpowder, it needed a direction, a mental lens, like a cannon barrel to focus it at the correct target. That would be the key to future control of ideas.

Lorenz had been so right about so many things. Under Lorenz von Bibra, whom Konrad had so mocked as permissive and weak, there had never been a revolt.

Publicists from the hordes were needed to create a false sense of brotherhood with the Church-state of the ruling class. Publicists would themselves become heroes of the hordes.

And as the wine flowed for the rest of the gathering of elites that night, the archduke quipped many times, always to a new outburst of laughter.

First, we must kill them…

LUD

In a night camp in a pine forest, Lud moved among the sleeping and he tallied the Giebel men and women. The bones of his body ached where they connected at the joints. He was bitterly tired, yet could not sleep. With every battle won and castle sacked, the price was always high, and little Giebel shrank before his eyes. He hoped the missing of Giebel were not all dead. He had not seen some of them fall. Not Big Merkel, who was gone. And surely others who were gone. Many villeins were fading away at night, no doubt returning to their farms and villages, and Lud hoped some were those from Giebel.

Their place in the ranks of the People's Army grew smaller with every battle. Half were gone now, dead or too wounded to not be left behind somewhere that they surely eventually died, in agony of slowness. Villeins from other villages moved into the gaps, for their ranks too were holed with their own dead.

In war, life dropped its mask, and he could do nothing to stop his world from being dismantled piece by piece. The Geyer estate would be no more, even if he could keep Florian alive.

Lud laid his throbbing body down in pine straw and shifted the Turk sword aside and tried to sleep. The sword made him think of Dietrich. Each heartbeat lit the pain in his joints. And when sleep was almost taking him was when he thought most on Kristina. She was gone somewhere, with little Peter.

He hoped they were alive. Lud went to sleep hoping that she lived, and he awoke hoping it, too.

The next day was always the same. Saddle up, ride and scout ahead of the army. Scout for Florian's Black Host.

The horse knights of the Black Host, in truth, were ruled more by Muntzer than by Florian. They rode through the Neckar Region, then the Wurzburg territory, everywhere destroying castles and monasteries. The red and white flag with the black cloth shoe was seen over many ramparts.

In camp at night again, in Muntzer's tent, there were always arguments between the priest and the commanders. Muntzer wanted to wipe out all vestments of the Church and build anew. The commanders wanted to win the war and survive. Lud observed these with a sinking hope.

"We must cleanse the land of priests' nests," said Muntzer. "We shall send the devils back to hell."

"Too many outrages bring new enemies," said Florian.

"Outrages?" said Muntzer. "I speak of justice. All cathedrals must be torn down, and all the symbols of tyranny and idols of the Antichrist."

Said Florian, "The empire has new armies both south of us and east and we could be caught in a vise if we continue savaging the entire countryside."

"Fire burns clean," said Muntzer. "We must immolate the unholy empire and right all its evils. When Eve spun, where were the high lords then?"

Said Florian, "I grow sick of you saying this over and over. It is true enough. But words do not win battles."

"Truth, not words!"

And that same night Muntzer stormed out of his tent and made one of his wild bonfire sermons to the army. Thousands cheered him, sullen at first, then reminded of the injustices that had compelled them, and finally roused to much of their old anger and lust for revenge and justice.

Said Lud, alone, to Florian, "The priest is mad with power. Worse than Konrad or the others. Destroying cathedrals and monasteries will bring greater and greater forces against us, sooner and sooner."

"I know," said Florian, "but Muntzer rules this army.'

"You are the people's hero, speak to them, and bring order to this thing. Do it before all the folk of Giebel are put under the ground."

"There is no stopping it now, Lud. Once the war is won then we shall have order. We must see it through."

Riders from the Gay Bright Troop came with urgent word that the Imperial Army, commanded by Duke Georg of the Swabian League, had trapped them at the town of Neckarsulm. The Gay Bright Troop, hard miners and idealistic tradesmen, had been left leaderless except for the voting heads from the ranks. The troop was still fighting, but crippled in a series of crushing battles. The survivors were besieged and fighting for their lives, surrounded by mercenaries and cannons.

Even worse was the shock that Goetz had defected to the Imperial forces of the Swabian League.

The People's Army went on the march within hours.

In his saddle, Florian said bitterly, "No doubt Goetz sold himself for a great sum of money to lead mercenaries against the People's Army."

"It is Georg," said Lud. "Brother of your once betrothed."

"Yes, it is personal. Barbara was wounded as was I, and yet Georg in his pride feels himself the injured party."

"Do not mix that with all these lives."

"I fight only to win, Lud."

Lud felt no surprise whatever, only the greater pressure of realizing that Florian—as brilliant and brave as a man could ever be— was yet in some sense naïve, and in command of all their fates.

"It is typical of war. Florian, hear me now. We can still get away, to home, and leave this."

"We win or die trying, or we have no home to return to."

"You who went to England, you who studied under the great Erasmus. Do you not recall his words on war? *There is nothing more unnaturally wicked, more productive of misery, more extensively destructive, more obstinate in mischief, more unworthy of man, as formed by nature, much more of man professing Christianity.*"

"I know Erasmus," said Florian with a lifted hand, and finished the quote: *"Yet, wonderful to relate! War is undertaken, and cruelly, savagely conducted, not only by unbelievers, but by Christians."*

"Then what are you doing here with so much killing?"

"We are five thousand strong," Florian said. "A good Christian of course must struggle with the morality of making war. But when we are trapped, when a higher cause is at stake, we Christians must fight."

So there was no use.

Arguing did no good. What would happen would happen. Lud was determined to keep Florian alive as long as he could. Even the hardest headed of men sometimes had their epiphany, and if Florian saw enough killing, maybe he would have his, and they too could go back to Giebel and try to salvage what little was left. And yet, there would be the wrath of Konrad to face, sooner or later.

So there was indeed no use in arguing. It was all doom for those who lost. All that was left was the fighting; to kill as many as could be killed.

Approaching the foothills outside Neckarsulm, the villages were smoldering rubble.

"Behold!" cried Muntzer. "This is the work of the devils of the empire, who march ahead of us now!"

From some of the burned houses and barns came the stench of burnt flesh, like roasted pork it was, yet Lud recognized it as human. His guts recoiled and he lifted his face rag over his nose.

Many elderly villeins hung from trees, old women and children, too. The younger women were found in the fields or woods where they had tried to hide their children, and had been run down and caught and used and killed there.

Said Florian, "See how these wrongs harden the army, making them bitter and eager to fight again."

Lud saw little difference between this devastation and all the sacked monasteries and convents, the wine orgies and monks with throats slit and nuns found outraged.

But Florian was right about the people of the army. Their fatigue became seething ferocity. They cursed and sharpened their farm tools and captured pikes, even as they stayed on the march.

Lud thought of Kristina, and how he had longed to take her and go away, hide with her, anywhere, be with her.

"The young men," he said ruefully, "should have been here to hide them instead of away with us in our army."

"Only together in numbers can we win. You know that. If we do not act together, more and more will desert. Your kind of talk is poison. I will hear no more, or flog you myself."

Lud stared at Florian, his strong but somehow callow young face, the imperious eyes so unlike Dietrich's, who would have never made such a foolish threat. Not without knowing he could back it up.

"You would what?" said Lud.

Florian stared back. He meant it, his face red with confident anger. "You heard me well. I say it for your own good."

"Dark is coming and the moon will be coming up," Lud said. "I go forward to scout."

And he rode away. The urge to strike Florian had been too compelling to stay there.

The risk was great on the night roads, but he had to make time. Scouting ahead, Lud rode slowly into the night.

Sirius the dog star was rising and Lud stayed below it, careful that it would not make of him a silhouette. Then the pockmarked moon was coming up. Lud looked up at that ruined face that was brother to his own mask. In the silver light he watered the horse at a stream and walked him low along the darkening ridgelines.

Long before he saw anything, he heard the cannonades, rolling booms, thundering louder and louder. Now he again left the road. He dismounted and walked the horse up along a foothill, keeping to the depressions in its rising shoulders.

At the head of the ridgeline he stopped and knelt and stared. Below him were the campfires of a vast army. The even rows of tents and the lines of cannons told the story. Professionals. The big guns were shelling the city.

Neckarsulm was a trap.

Inside its broken walls, the red and white flags were rags in the wind. The Gay Bright Troop was being butchered. They could not break out. They could not stop the death that had stalked them to this last corner of existence.

Lud felt a pain in his chest. His heart went out to them, the poor, foolish, brave devils trapped there. Valor meant nothing against the big guns.

Emplacements of smaller guns fired at the breaches in the walls when groups of men tried to fight their way out.

Beyond was a burning hell of broken walls and buildings where explosions sent flaming roofs and wagons and men into the black smoking sky.

"If you are there, God," said Lud, "release us from this thing. Let us go. Make it stop."

But he knew that only death, not God, would make it stop. God had his executioner busy with much work to be done. People started wars but death finished them.

At best he was two full days from the line of march of the Black Host. Lud turned his horse and rode back hard down the dark road, risking a bad fall or worse.

KRISTINA

Michael said nothing; he would not speak. His face was like that of a corpse but sometimes he blinked in the heavy rolling rags of smoke from the smoldering ruins of the little village, so much like Giebel. There had even been a linden tree and a well, but the wreck of the tree smoldered, nothing but skeletal and black now, and people had been dumped into the well.

Kristina held on to Peter; he tugged hard, trying to jerk free, wanting to run to Michael. In the priest's arms was a pale and tiny form, curled tightly upon itself.

Then she saw what it was.

From here she sensed its stillness and saw that the infant in Michael's arms was blue and dead. Dolf tried to pull it from Michael's arms but Grit shoved Dolf away.

"You will tear the babe with your big hands," Grit said.

"It is dead," Kristina said.

"The priest will not let go," said Dolf.

"Michael," said Symon, "Brother. Where do you come from? Which way must we go away from the armies?"

"He is concealed inside himself," said Mahmed.

Closer now, Kristina looked into Michael's brown eyes. The black pupils were like two cave portals, and she knew Michael was deep inside there, somewhere he could not be seen yet could look out and keep watch.

When Grit gently moved him out of the smoke of the village street, Michael stumbled but took firm steps after that. She tried cradling the baby away but he would not let go. Kristina turned away, unable to watch, but whichever way she turned, she saw death and ruin and many tragedies.

It was as if she was dead and in hell now, and did not recall her death. Only the little hand of Peter, held in her own, gave her any sense of life and truth.

"We cannot travel with the priest like that," said Symon.

"We have burials to do here," Grit said. "And search for those who may be hiding, injured, in need of us."

Said Kristina, "We are exposed. There is too much danger here."

But she saw Dolf turning suddenly, then Symon, and she too turned and saw them.

Soldiers coming back up the road.

Peter cried out and pulled hard at her hand.

Kristina felt a hot surge of panic and she turned the other way, and soldiers stepped into the road behind them.

A gang of rogues on horseback was with the soldiers.

One said, "By God, look who we have here!"

It was Huber, the steward that Lud had driven from Giebel many years ago. He was older, fatter, in a better cloak and hat, but it was the same man.

Huber rode up to Michael, who still said nothing.

"The good Father Michael, of Giebel, who said nothing and did nothing to help me, after all I had done for him."

Huber got down. He kicked Michael and the baby fell into the dirt. Grit tried to catch it. Huber shoved Grit back. Symon held her. Michael knelt to try to pick the dead baby up and Huber kicked him down again.

"The baby is dead," said Dolf, as if in apology for doing nothing.

Behind Huber and his gang, cavalry rode over the hill.

She hoped it was the Black Host of Florian and sent a short prayer—not to God this time but to Lud—but the riders gleamed with new armor and they moved in order, their tunics all the same orange and gold, and then she recognized the pennants of the Swabian League.

Hailing a captain in the front rank of horses, Huber said, "These are from Giebel, the same Giebel of Florian Geyer."

"Geyer of the Black Host?"

"Sir," said Huber, "that was his priest, who I reported to be with the devil Muntzer."

"And the others?"

"All from Giebel. All of them heretics. They came just when I was driven from my good stewardship, during the time of pox, and the devil came with them to Giebel."

Kristina had tried backing away, hoping to hide somewhere, but to her astonished horror, Peter jerked hard at her hand and ran a circle around Father Michael, pointing at him with scolding snarls.

The cavalrymen laughed. "Their own whelp denounces them!"

"Sir, hang or chop or burn?" said Huber.

"Bind them up," said the captain. "Heretics, say you?"

Kristina saw Dolf and Symon struggling with some of the rogues who held them and they were clubbed and beaten down. She saw Peter stroking the captain's horse. She saw Grit trying to help Dolf and Symon, and then she was lashed.

"Donkey dicks," cursed Dolf. "Meat beaters."

"They do not speak like saints, do they?" said a rogue.

Dolf was beat down and kicked until he vomited. Among the armed men there was much laughter.

Kristina looked for help, to the sky and the ground; her eyes searched for Witter, but he was not there. Mahmed was gone, too. She had not seen them go yet knew they must have fled before they were even seen.

She felt naked as two rough men came and took her up by her arms as if she weighed nothing.

"We shall keep this one," said the older of the two, with his hands on her.

"No, damn your eyes, I said bind them all," said the captain. "The monks will want them to question."

The captain looked down at Peter stroking his horse. Kristina sensed something, as if she had seen him somewhere before, sensing the memory dimly, as of long ago. The captain smiled and tossed Peter some morsel from his tunic pocket, and Peter laughed and ate it.

Kristina stared up at this all, as if it were some terrible impossible nightmare.

"What of their whelp?" said Huber.

"They have yet to ruin this little rascal." The captain leaned over and gripped Peter by the scruff of his cloak and hauled him onto the saddle.

As the man leaned over, Kristina saw his long, dark hair part at his ear, and she saw a bright scar and a slick hole where his ear had once been. As if sensing Kristina's glance, the officer jerked back, turning his head, and his long hair fell back over the old scar.

And in that moment, she knew where she had seen him before.

It had been so many years ago, when Berthold still lived. It was the duel on the road from war, the duel with Lud, when Lud had cruelly taken this man's ears, with all the Landsknechts jeering Lud. This duelist looked older. He had not been a captain then. But this was him. The snide arrogance was still there.

"We do the work of God," the captain said, "but not to punish innocents."

Peter giggled, and turned and pointed at Kristina, as if her fear and pain tickled him. Her arms were bent around her back and she felt a rope tied down so hard on her elbows that she felt they might break.

The pain drove Kristina to her knees.

"No," shouted Grit, "look to your own souls, Brothers!"

"We are not your damned brothers," said Huber.

Kristina was bent double by the pain that was plunging down from her shoulders and arms like fiery spears into her belly and legs.

The captain rode up to look down at her. Peter was on the front of his saddle, making a mocking sound. The sight of her child up there, smirking and mocking her was more than she could bear; more than the pain of the ropes; more than the fear of the monks when the questioning would come. A swooning nausea came rolling all through her.

"Brother, do not harm yourself," said Grit to the captain. "We offer up our love of the Lord."

Huber backhanded Grit, driving her to her knees. Kristina was tied in a chain, with Dolf and Symon and Michael and Grit, and when Grit fell into the dirt, face-first, they all were jerked forward.

Peter laughed at this, and many of the solders laughed with little Peter, delighted by the wild mockery of her child.

Said Huber, "No one told you to speak, woman."

"These villein trash say anything to try to save themselves," said Huber. "Believe me, captain, I know all their cheating lying cunning tricks."

Ulrich, thought Kristina, *that was his name.*

"You earned extra bonus for these," said the captain.

Grit looked up from the ground. She lay twisted in her ropes. Blood was caked in her gray hair and the dirt on her face. She gasped for breath, panting; yet, impossibly, there was no hatred in her voice. Only sadness.

"I command you, as I have loved you, love one another."

"Dried-up old bitch, be still," said the captain.

But Grit would not be still. She raised her voice, the words cracking. "I beg you, sir, for your own sake. With such violence you endanger your immortal soul."

"Idiot," he said.

"The ropes are ready, sir," said Huber. "Shall we have a dance?"

"Not yet," said the captain.

Now Kristina saw that this captain, this Ulrich, seemed intrigued, shaking his head at this strange interlude on this ruined road, where people hung from trees amid smoking ruins. She debated whether to call him by name.

Ulrich! She might shout, and he would demand how she knew his name, and either wish her good or ill, for that.

It was too great a risk. This captain, here in front of his men, might feel shame that she had seen him humiliated. Or want revenge that she knew Lud, and torture her to find out anything about Lud, where he was now, anything about the People's Army. No, it was much too great a risk.

Kristina said nothing, bowing her head.

Peter was stroking the mane of the warhorse, and Kristina could not look at him.

"Take care, Brother," said Grit. "All war is murder, and all murder is sin."

The captain twisted and slid down from his horse and stood over Grit. Peter now sat the horse alone, as if it belonged to him. Grit's face was caked with dirty blood, her hair as matted as white moss. In his boots and armor, the captain was twice her height. Yet somehow, to Kristina watching this strange bitter thing, Grit seemed unafraid.

"Woman," said the captain, "as you cringe before me, I am not your brother. My own brother is a monk and his monastery was destroyed, and with a life of good works now he is dead. And you dare say all war, all killing, necessary or not, is murder?"

"I shall pray for your brother," said Grit.

The captain looked around at Peter on his horse and at his cavalrymen of horse. None of them had spoken. Huber stood by with the ropes and his rogues, watching. The scene felt to Kristina like a tableau, a spell that Kristina sensed could only be broken by some cruel act of suddenness. She knelt in the dirt and held her breath.

The captain remounted his horse and sat there, stroking Peter's hair. Kristina tried not to look.

"A pacifist," Huber said. "These are the most dangerous sort. Worse than those who take arms against us. For she seeks to disarm our holy cause with blasphemous lies."

"Brother," said Grit, "did not Christ stay the hand of Saint Peter from raising his sword in the garden, against the Romans?"

"You weaken the resolve of fighting men. Is this how you work to help defeat us? If you are such a Christian, truly, did you also seek to weaken the villeins from killing others?"

"Yes, Brother, we tried our best to dissuade them."

"Who of them?"

"All we could reach," said Grit.

"Even Florian Geyer?"

"Yes."

"And one named Lud?"

Kristina thought her heart could not sink deeper, yet now it plunged into utter blackness, the last of her hope gone. She wanted to take Grit by the throat and make her stop talking. Every word deepened the abyss under them.

"Yes, him and many others. They would not listen any more than you. But we tried."

Said Ulrich, "So Lud serves with Geyer and the Black Host."

Now Grit said nothing. Her jaw clamped shut. Kristina saw that she knew she had said too much, gone too far.

"Where is Geyer now?" demanded Ulrich.

Grit bent her head and said nothing.

"Sir, they march east and north from Wurzburg," said Dolf, on his knees. "We fled Wurzburg days ago."

"Sir, the old woman is mad," said Symon on his knees.

"She is no madwoman," said the captain. "You cannot save yourselves this way. She is a thing much worse."

Grit kept staring at the dusty ground and did not look up at the captain. He nudged the warhorse forward, so that the shadow of the huge animal fell upon her now, and for a moment Kristina thought the man would crush Grit with those hooves. Peter was perched up there like a hawk, watching sharply now. Kristina despaired, seeing him so.

Grit lifted her head to look up at the rogues, the man on the warhorse, and those behind him.

"Brothers, all, listen to me, would you enjoy earthly power now only to burn for all eternity?"

"Are you so compelled to speak?" said the captain, irritated. "Do you not see those dangling from the trees?"

Kristina knew they were now about to die. She tried to reach out to God, with all her heart and soul, but her spirit could not reach

Him, as if too weary to climb, too dulled to beseech Him. And had not all those dead ones begged?

"God forgive you, Brother," said Grit stubbornly.

"The old crone will not silence," said Huber, pulling his dagger with one hand, gripping Grit's head by the hair with his other hand, jerking her face back so hard that she cried out. "Shall I take out her tongue before we dance her?"

Kristina wanted to scream. In her head she did scream, a deafening scream that only she heard.

"These we will not hang." The captain waved a dismissive hand.

"Not hang, sir?" said Huber, disappointed, confused.

"Make a daisy chain. More bounties for you. The pacifists are heretics and will be going to Passau for the monks there to question. They all will need their tongues later, to wag aplenty when they have nice quarters under the Oberhaus." The captain looked down from his horse at Grit. "Now what do you have to say, you infernal stiff-necked bitch?"

Peter was leaning over the horse's neck, stroking it.

"I pray…for your…souls," said Grit, in a gargling voice, with her neck twisted back in Huber's fist.

The captain pointed at Grit, and he said, "Stake her jaw."

LUD

Lud rode hard, risking ambush and fatal falls on the bad roads, staying wide of the smoking wrecked villages he passed. He crossed the muddy line of march and found the camp of the Black Host on a hillside, its campfires like fireflies, and passed so invisibly through its pickets that he was glad he did not lead Landsknechts against this loose horde of comrades. They could be taken in their beds like lambs. But there was no time to change things now.

He reported at midnight to Florian, finding him in a fireside meeting with Muntzer.

"The Swabian League Army has the Gay Brights trapped at Neckarsulm. We must move tonight, now," urged Lud, "if we are to save any of them. We can roll up their cannons from the rear."

"We must help them," Florian agreed.

"That Goetz is a Judas," said Muntzer. "He betrayed his own Gay Bright Troop and now they are led by the vote of sergeants. They went their way, and we go ours."

"Then the Black Host will go alone."

"You would split the People's Army?" said Muntzer, as if Florian had committed a mortal sin.

"You divide us," said Florian, "not I. Priests have no business in war."

"Out it to the vote, and be damned. You will not find a vote against me in your own Black Host."

So Muntzer refused, but Florian agreed with Lud and it was put to the vote of all the sergeants. But by the time the vote was done, with much agreement to attack, and the march was organized, dawn was already chasing first light, and Lud knew by now the Gay Brights would all be dead.

It was past noon when they reached Neckarsulm and found the carnage of a great defeat. There was much digging to be done. The army of the Swabian League had already marched on.

Neckarsulm was a killing field. Bodies with bright tunics of all colors, inside out, dangled upside down from trees. Lud walked along the wall of their last-ditch stand, and saw how the cannonades had made red slime from the brave, good men.

"Scout their force," said Florian, finding Lud. "Do not squander your anguish here, put it to use."

So Lud chose a fresh horse from the stabler's line and for the next days, never sleeping, using the dark to the utmost, he fed on his cold, sad rage, and scouted ahead, filled with a despairing fury. Nothing that he did or knew seemed to change anything in this world.

The Imperial Army and the forces of the Swabian League were marching up through the valley of the Neckar and Kocher and Jagst rivers, and the only thing slowing them was their pillaging and the mass executions of any who did not join their ranks.

It was the cavalry that kept driving back the hordes of villeins trying to fight them. Once, a contingent rode past Lud, not seeing him behind a wall, and he was certain he saw Ulrich, with whom he had dueled many years ago.

Ulrich, who had freed Florian from the Landsknechts' training ground, Ulrich, who had promised to kill him when next they met, Ulrich, whom he should have killed as Dietrich yelled for him to do, instead of proudly cutting off his ears to make a great show to those who had so jeered and mocked him.

The Swabian League Army were hired professionals. They marched in strong order. They were outfitted with modern armor and weapons. They were the kind of army that he once would have dreamed of serving. Proud and practical and well paid, trained in all the arts of war, and well bonused for quick victories.

Lud had not the slightest doubt that the Swabian Army would win. They were heading toward Krautheim.

Lud rode back to report all of this to Florian.

Not that it would change anything. Knowing what would come did not mean he could change what was coming. Again and again, through all his years, that had always been the bitterest lesson of his life.

So now the die was cast. Florian had split from Muntzer. The Black Host now was in its own private war.

His scouting report would be simple enough.

The Black Host now would fight alone, against at least three armies of mercenary professionals, trained cavalry, infantry, and massed artillery, big guns served by seasoned cannoneers.

Lud rode back into the west, into the red setting sun, keeping to the lengthening shadows of trees when he could, and down in the stream beds where cover was plentiful.

He rode to find what was left of the People's Army, before they could be trapped. But he rode without hope. He knew too much, had seen too much.

This villeins' war, this struggle to establish a brotherhood of all men, was lost. All that was left was to ride it down like a wild horse, to its end.

WITTER

Witter lay under three dead bodies that stank of old blood and excreta. He lay among them as one dead, and felt the shadows of horses pass over him against the hot sun.

When they had run, the angle of smoldering houses had screened them from the horsemen. When Witter had looked back, he was shocked to see none of the others running with him. He had glimpsed Mahmed running ahead of him and disappearing into the high grass of a ditch.

An unspeakable despair paralyzed Witter, watching Kristina bound and tied to Dolf, then Symon, then Michael, and then Grit at the end of the daisy chain of prisoners. Instead of being hanged by rope they were strung together with rope like tethered animals, their arms lashed behind them.

Now, Mahmed lay beside him in the high grass of the ditch and they watched Grit's mouth being staked open.

Kristina was sobbing. She was on her knees, bent double, not watching. Both Dolf and Symon stared with wide eyes as men who could not believe what they were seeing. Michael was bent double, perhaps in prayer, or just mad. Little Peter sat the horse with the captain. He petted the horse and was not watching what now happened.

From behind, Grit's head was vised between the knees of a swarthy, short rogue, and Huber pierced her cheeks on both sides of her jaw with his dagger. Grit kicked and cried out, her eyes wide with shock.

A rising wind stirred sheets of yellow dust.

Huber broke a short branch from a low tree and broke it to length on his thigh, and thrust it through Grit's face from one side until it came out the other side. Then Huber lashed the ends behind her head with thong.

Kristina sobbed.

Grit's mouth gaped. She coughed and shook her head like a dog with a rat and made a crying baby sound and gagged and blood seeped in her drool. The stick locked her jaw open and Grit convulsed. Her little face had a breached look as one in a cheap comic opera who loudly laughs and will not stop, yet the eyes were streaming tears. In the blowing dust Grit's bare feet quivered like dying fish.

Witter could not look away. His bladder emptied, letting go with a burning rush down his legs.

He could not move his feet.

He buried his face deep in the grass until dirt was in his eyes and mouth and he ground his face hard into the soil until his punished eyes burned and his mouth was foul as he deserved. He sobbed but it did not help.

The captain down there was Ulrich, Frieda's Ulrich, whom he had encountered in the street of Wurzburg; the Landsknecht officer who had taken Frieda as mistress, and called her Paulina, her stage name in the tavern theater where she performed. Perhaps Frieda was in the baggage train of the Imperial Army, waiting to service Ulrich whenever he wished.

Witter lay hidden a long time. Was he any better than Frieda? At least she pretended nothing. He was worse, hiding in all ways.

For a time he consoled himself with suicide. He would use rope down there and hang himself. He would throw himself in a well.

But his own intelligence found him, and mocked him, as laughably impotent as ever...

In your fear you will piss yourself and wait until they are gone to go down there to kill yourself, is that not so? You have not the courage to go down there to fight them, and yet you would instead wait to harm your earthly body?

So Witter lay, hidden.

There were sounds of men and orders given and horse and chains and then there was a long silence with only the wind hissing through the high scrubby grass. He did not move. Finally, even the sense of himself went away.

A hand pressed his back.

Witter jerked up, as if burned, terrified.

"I thought you loved her," said Mahmed.

All he could think of was a retort.

"You owe her your life, you said," said Witter.

Mahmed looked at him with something like pity. "As I do. Fear has made you doltish. All that matters now is what can be done, not what could not have been done."

Witter returned to this world and sat up in the weeds and saw the late afternoon sky, storms in the east with dark bands of rain, and a butterfly roaming the seedy tops of the grass near his face. It was a yellow butterfly with black and blue spots like great eyes watching him as it flapped, eyes that blinked and opened wide, as if in surprise at such a man.

"We must try to do something," he said.

It was not that he knew what could be done, it was that he yearned for Mahmed to tell him what could be done.

Said Mahmed, "I crawled down in the ditch and high grass, as close as I could dare, to hear without being seen or taken."

"You are a warrior, yet you did nothing?"

"We could have done nothing if we were dead, or got them killed as well. With your little dagger I could kill two, perhaps three, of the scores of them, before they cut me down, and that would have been a stupidity."

"God has abandoned us," said Witter, feeling everything against him now, even Kristina taken from him.

Mahmed slapped him, so hard water flung from Witter's tearing eyes. He saw stars in the broad daylight. The wind cut his tears and he saw Mahmed's face swimming as in a dream.

"Blasphemer. You blame God for what men do?"

"I...," said Witter.

"Do not offend God when we need Him most."

Witter blinked, rubbed his eyes. The slap had cleared his brain, replaced self-pity with a rising heat, with anger.

"Never do that again," he said.

"Good. Be more like that and stop pitying yourself," said Mahmed. "You are a brilliant man, but you wet yourself with fear when fear should rouse your better manhood."

The wind blew in gusts that pulled Mahmed's black hair sideways from his head like a long rag. His eyes were black with spidery anguish lines and Witter saw the ancient living blood of the Holy Land there.

"What will you do?" said Witter.

Said Mahmed, "They are bountied for heretics, else they would have been butchered or hanged. I will follow them to their monk's train, but we must try to free them before they are taken into the Oberhaus dungeons at Passau."

"If they live long enough to reach Passau."

"They will keep them alive for the heretic bounty. If there is a great battle perhaps we can try the camp then. It will be less guarded during a fight. From the Oberhaus there is no escape."

Mahmed turned to look across the hills. Witter looked too, rising on his knees, and saw the beaten track of the road.

Mahmed was already up now, moving toward the track.

"Passau is days from here," said Witter.

"When I lay in the weeds, that is where I heard them say they will take them."

Mahmed was up now and moving.

"Wait," said Witter.

"There is no more time to argue. Go where you will."

Witter hurried to catch him.

Below the ridgeline in the trees, corpses swung with limp disinterest in the rising wind. Witter stepped over a ditch where broken people sprawled like field-workers exhausted and flung down in all abandon of life. Their blood was turning brown and black.

Ahead, somewhere up that track, was Kristina.

LUD

Big Merkel was dead. Lud thought the blacksmith had gone back to Giebel, yet there he lay, tangled amongst a dozen others.

It seemed impossible, that the man who had so long tamed iron with hammer and fire, who had swung his forge hammer in waves of battles, lay cold on the ground. Merkel had wanted to learn, and now he was dead. Lud had found him in the aftermath of a cannonade. Others lay scattered in pieces like rags of meat. But Merkel, though filthy, had not a wound on him, no doubt killed by the shock of a blast. The shaft of his smithy hammer was broken but still gripped in his fist, scarred from years in the forge.

When the People's Army moved, Lud rode with the Black Host. Now and again he rode up along the line of march until he came through the wagon train of stores, up through the many contingents from villages and cities, and he rode up to stay near the Giebel contingent, for a time.

The village folk had worked hard all their lives. They were sturdy and strong. But they were not made for war. They were not used to so much death, so much loss. They were raised to farm and to bring things to life, not for the destruction of things. They were tired and would pass a few halfhearted words with him, walking with their pikes and shovels and scythes and flails. He saw the hurt in their faces. And he saw the determination there, too, that came from a life of never quitting something once it was begun.

It shocked him afresh each time he saw that a few more from Giebel were gone; people he had known all his life, gone. And it surprised him that shock could still register upon him, after so much killing and dying.

Merkel, Sig the miller, little Golz—they had learned to read and to think and they had been roused by their emerging minds, to rise up and demand equality, and now, one by one, they were being destroyed.

At Krautheim, the Imperial Army and the mercenary Landsknechts of the Swabian League had caught the People's Army in a vise.

Lud rode scout, as ever, with Florian and the Black Host cavalry, protecting the flanks of the massed horse of villeins as best they could. But nothing could protect the untrained folk from the long range of Imperial cannonades. Their ranks often broke from the terror.

Now and again there came frantic, exhausted couriers from Muntzer's People's Army. In rags, they bore elaborate, beautifully penned letters from Muntzer himself, long sermons denouncing the Church-state and its devils, but little information of value— nothing of Muntzer's tactics nor any long-term strategy.

Steinmetz and a third of the Black Host cavalry had been killed in fierce fighting against relentless charges of Imperial cavalry. Despite their sacrifice, a flanking maneuver forced the People's Army back toward Koenigshofen on the Tauber River.

The sun was going down and the day's march was ended and Lud looked out over the motley People's Army and its smoky camp-fires. Here and there stood high their standards. A common shoe on a pole. The red and white flags of cloth, sewn with the black cloth shoe.

Down there, thousands of weary men and women, some hardly older than children, others almost too old to hold a shovel or pike, were preparing to fight and die if they must.

He felt a weight. It was the knowing of too much. But down there, the people were enjoying the river. Some were washing, others bathing, some playing and splashing. He felt a love for them. They were his family, all of them, somehow. He was made of the same earthen fields as they were, and they were each a part of him. They had all been born together into the same bad luck. And for all that, he loved them. Their lives were precious. Their glimmer was shared with his.

His heart ached at the thought of the devastating flanking maneuver of the Imperial Army, which had pushed them back against the river.

Lud had scouted the maneuver well in advance. But a general vote of all serving in the People's Army was required. When it was finally tallied through all the ranks and accounted by all the sergeants, the decision was the same as Lud's. The vote decided to counter their flank. But too much time had passed. It was too late.

A courier had come with a message from Muntzer, declaring that the People's Army was on the verge of a great victory at Frankenhausen.

"We are eight thousand with thirty-two cannons," said Florian, proudly, on the heights over the Tauber River.

"I shall say this again. The Imperials are joined. The Swabian League entered Franconia and has joined the elector Palantine's force. The vote is suicide. We must retreat."

"The vote is to stand."

"The vote is folly."

"You call the voice of free men, of brothers, folly?"

"Florian, the vote is death. By my tally the Imperials are thirteen thousand foot and horse. Two hundred wagons. Forty-two of artillery pieces."

"Your tallies were never perfect. We took castles, and we shall face this now. Muntzer has crushed the Imperials at Frankenhausen, therefore they cannot have joined forces."

"You believe Muntzer?"

"Surely they will have a great victory."

"You would wrap all fate in a scrawl by a raging priest? What if Muntzer has already lost his army?"

"You vex me too much, Lud."

"We could disperse the army," said Lud.

"Disperse? How? Why?"

"Make them go home. While they live."

"Home?" said Florian.

"Disperse them and they will go back to their fields and their masters will be glad to have them at labor again."

"Once I would have been the new man wedded to the family of their commander," said Florian. "My wife would have been his sister, the beautiful Barbara, and my mother would have been blissfully connected to them at court. Now I am a knight from the noble lineage of many great knights. And I now must try to kill as many nobles as I can, and my army is not men of arms, but common folk."

Lud felt his heart sting, and the blood rise in his face. He had been close to such anger before with Florian. Now he was much closer. Many had died. Many more would soon die. This time the anger was deeper, in rebellion to his loyalty, and he wished for Dietrich with all his heart.

"Common, you say?" Lud said.

"There is nothing common of their willingness to die. Nor their courage to stand. But, if I had real troops, I could clear the field in one day."

"They give all they have, all they are."

"They delay to vote. They delay to sack monasteries and swill monk wine to a stupor. They play in the river instead of digging fortifications. Even if we win, what will such a world look like, if they are to govern themselves?"

Lud stared at Florian as if he had seen him, truly, for the first time. He sat his horse, so superior, young and handsome, he had the jutting jaw and proud thrust of chest, but there was callowness to his eyes, an overdone air of purpose. This was not the little boy Florian that Lud had once taught to fight and grapple and ride and hunt. This was the Florian of the English university. This was the Florian who had debated philosophy with Witter, on the road returning from England, the Florian who mocked Lud's confided thoughts.

Then he looked at Florian's fine boots. They were not the common shoes of the villein, as Lud himself wore. And in that moment it seemed he saw Florian's nature more clearly than ever before. He was a noble, in his heart and soul. He had staked everything upon leading this uprising, and he was a noble.

Lud rode away from Florian before more could be said. He rode down among the people and filled his lungs with their camp smoke and burnt meat and urine, and his mind filled too with their hurdy-gurdy dance shouts and their moans and laughs. His anger had raged up but now it settled, for he was bone-tired.

The horse was tired, too, and needed to be tethered in fresh grass. That came first. The horse in battle was life. This horse was a big bay. Lud did not know its name nor could he hardly recall how many had died under him before this one. The days of Jax and Ox and the luxury of naming horses was long behind him now. The animal did what it was told and they would part when its life ended, or his; whichever came first.

He walked the horse slowly and carefully and with respect among the people—many nodded to him, as they rested and cooked and groomed one another and tended wounds and ate—until he found the Giebel contingent.

Lud dismounted at some patchy tall grass and hobbled the horse with the reins, cavalry-style.

"Lud," said Linhoff, standing.

Linhoff's thin long face looked ten years older than a few months before. His beard was shot with gray, his eyes deeper. Much deeper.

"They voted me sergeant now," Linhoff said.

So it has come to that, thought Lud.

He looked around and saw it was right. So many were gone. Linhoff was the best man left alive for the job.

Sprawled like dead men around the smoky fire were Jakop, Max, Steffan, looking worn-out and old. Lud realized that he still saw them as the young boys whom he had once marched off to a disastrous border fight with Turks. That life now seemed lifetimes ago.

Strangers had filled some of the gaps in their numbers, other faces he did not know. He saw Leta and Lura together, cutting up at an iron pot what looked like a rabbit and foraged greens. They glanced up at him without smiling. They no longer served in a castle. Their hair was filthy, stringy, their cloaks full of holes. But they were still trying hard.

"Now, even Merkel is dead," said Linhoff.

"I know."

"Have you seen Grit?" said Linhoff.

"Nor Kristina nor others," said Lud.

"I hope they are well away from all this," Linhoff said.

"Would we all were," Lud said.

"But we must be willing to die for the right to read and elect our own leaders and make our own laws."

"Waste no time thinking on all that," said Lud.

Linhoff lowered his voice to confide. "Of what should I be thinking? Will they attack us tomorrow?"

Said Lud, "The Imperials and the league are coming, screened behind those hills. They have three times our number, and they are professionals, and they had decisive commanders, and they have many cannons, more than twice ours. This is no place to make a stand. If you can call this a stand."

"This we all know. But Muntzer's last message said he will trap them at Frankenhausen and roll the Imperial cannonballs up into his sleeves."

Lud did not anger now, he was too weary; he put his hand on Linhoff's arm and felt the lines of sinew. "Take Giebel home, Linhoff."

"What?"

"Every night the Black Host loses a hundred men of foot, two hundred. Our villeins steal away and take to the roads. They long for their homes, their crops. You will not be noticed. Take our Giebel people home."

"Home to what, Lud? Are you mad?"

"I was, but am becoming much more sane now."

"You think they would go home now? After all they have been through? After all who have already died? They would slit our throats before they would go home. And Muntzer would dance on our corpses."

"They follow you. They voted for you. Their lives are in your hands now. You can persuade them best. Take them home."

"If we lose this fight we have no home to return to."

"The estates need toil. The fields lay fallow. Nobles cannot kill all the hands that feed them. Linhoff, hear me, while some of our people still live, take them home. When the camp sleeps, take them across the hills until you are past Ingolstadt, and stay to the ridge-line until you reach our river that runs to Giebel."

"Bend our necks again to their yoke, after all this killing? You tell our people this mad thing, if you believe it."

"I am a killer. They would laugh in my face."

"Lud, you taught us how to fight."

"Now I release you from all I ever taught you of killing. I free you from all purposes of killing and being killed."

"You are no priest to absolve anyone."

Linhoff stared at him and Lud wanted to protect him, to save them all somehow, and he knew he could not, but he had to speak.

"Go while you can," Lud said. "Go live your life."

"Where is our hard man of war who once trained up our line of pike? Did Kristina so soften you? I know you love her. As I love Grit. You know that, too. But we are men, and our courage is our last and only hope. Do not weaken us."

"The next battle is the final folly, Linhoff. Take them home. Please."

Linhoff spat.

"Please? Please? You know, I have feared you all my life, but no more. I believe you have become a coward, and it truly saddens me to say this."

Lud returned to his horse and that was all he said. He had done what he could. This was not bad luck, as he had always thought. It was idiocy.

He knew that Muntzer must have been destroyed at Frankenhausen, for he had seen the joined forces coming against them, with his own eyes, and yet he was not believed.

I absolve you from foolishness, he thought. But he could not have said whether he thought it for Linhoff or for himself.

On his horse, with night falling fast and the campfire blazing orange, Lud looked back once and saw Linhoff staring at him, slack-jawed in amazement.

That was the trouble with life. If you did not know, you did not know that you did not know.

But he took no pride in dread of what was coming.

KRISTINA

Consciousness came and went, with pain like fiery clouds passing seared across the sun. She could not be certain whether she was still alive, or if this was the threshold of her eternity here in hell.

She lay in the dark under a wagon in the baggage train. She no longer felt her arms tied behind her. Her feet had been numb earlier but now they burned as if she had walked on fire, the soles of her leather shoes worn through.

Piled against her were the others. The closest was Grit; she could hear Grit's struggle to breathe past the staked jaw, she could feel Grit's bones but not see her. Dolf was tied to her and behind her, and Symon, too, all of them lashed like mules together.

At day's march end they were shoved under the wagon out of the way. Her belly ate itself with hunger and she had no water since they had been allowed to stagger into a weedy ditch at noon, to fall into the mud and drink their fill, before being dragged back out behind the wagon to walk on, and on, and on, the rope from the mule wagon jerking them when they faltered.

In the bed of the wagon ahead were wounded men, some staring back at them with shocked faces. Anything the men said to the mule drivers was met with blows and curses and threats.

But there was one good thing, and she tried to think upon that: her child was not there, and she was glad of that. He could have food and a place to sleep and protection, and it did not matter what the boy believed or did not believe, and perhaps, in that, God was being merciful after all.

The gallows wagon was just behind in the wagon train and three bodies hung dripping there now. Ahead was the wagon where hard impatient men were jostling and joking, waiting in line for their turn at captive village girls. In hell there was no escape even from sounds. Kristina tried not to hear the miserable cries of the trapped girls and the vile sounds of the men that came from up there. She pressed herself closer to Grit's bony back; she felt Grit's breath heave her little shoulder blades and knew Grit was still alive.

Then, the rasping of Grit's breath, she realized now, was faintly punctuated with something else…

"…from Zion…perfect in beauty…God shines…"

Grit was praying, even now, even with her jaw staked open. She was praising God, even now. Even here, Grit was clinging to her Rock in the raging sea.

Kristina thought of the first time she had met Grit.

Long ago and far away in little Kunvald, the night when each of them had met, as one, together, readying to depart for their mission to bring love to the world.

Like children, they were. Foolish, naïve children.

Each had confessed their lives and their pasts and their absurd sacrificial need to do good. Pretty blonde Frieda, her new lovesick husband Ott, mule driver Dolf, farmer Symon, her pompous and pouty sweet husband and teacher Berthold, and tough and resolute Grit.

Grit's real name was Marguerite. She had been briefly a famed stage performer of bawdy song, and her favors had been sought after by men of wealth, and she sold herself and took many gifts, until she had become addicted to wormwood spirits, and that life had eaten her soul until she almost died, and was saved by people of good faith and will. It was impossible to think now that this was the same woman who had braved so much and dared so much and still prayed, even now. Perhaps it was all she had left to believe.

Kristina thought how blind they all were, how vain. Their little Kunvald group, led by Berthold, had journeyed out into the world of war and pain, resolute with faith, determined to do good acts, to alloy evil with mercy, together. Yet that was when she had been her best.

She remembered the battle in the storm, and Grit insisting they must give aid and mercy to those who suffered. She thought of stopping Lud when he would have killed Mahmed. She thought of being captive in another train of war, many years earlier. She had been so much younger in heart then, not yet a mother, and Lud had refused to let them take her and Frieda for the comfort wagon, saying the wagon was Giebel, and Lud had fought a duel. Dietrich had been alive then, too, to protect them. Water and food had been given them then, but here they were worse than the live-stock tethered for slaughter to feed the ravenous army. They were only being kept alive to be tormented by monks in Passau, and only death would end this nightmare.

Life had come full circle to this fate.

Sister Hannah was gone. Berthold was gone. Dietrich was gone. Frieda and Ott were gone. Witter was gone. Mahmed was gone. Dolf and Symon and Grit were soon to be gone. Peter was no longer hers, if he ever had been.

And all those willing folk of Giebel. Lady Anna closed upon herself, strong wise Lura and sweet little Leta both gone to war, and so many others of all kinds, with their goodnesses and their flaws and fears and needs all surely dead by now, swept away by something she could hardly understand, something murderous— the too-potent knowing, too suddenly; anger brought by reading, knowing, learning.

And even Lud was probably already dead. Was he somewhere wandering here, in hell, searching for her?

Lud, she screamed inside herself, *Lud...*

Then something was under the wagon with them—a shape, blocking the firelight, crawling at her. Kristina strained to see who it was going to choose, despaired of what it had come to do. A cook knife glinted in a fist.

"In the name of God do not hurt us," she begged.

"Hush, Mother," snarled a sharp little voice.

Now she saw the shadow was small. Little eyes blinked in the face. It was Peter.

First he was with Grit. He said nothing. He cut the thongs that forced the stick to lock her jaw. Then he cut the wrist ropes behind her back. Grit lifted her freed hands to her face but could not make them work.

Peter cut Kristina free. She felt her arms come loose at the shoulders, but there was no feeling below the elbows.

Grit twisted, panting, and in the deep shadows Kristina saw Grit trying to lift her hands to remove the stick that was impaled through her cheeks on both sides. Peter reached up and his finger gripped one exposed end of the stick, and with a single jerk he extracted it sideways from Grit's face. Grit bent double, choking, convulsing, gagging. Her hands pressed her face clumsily and she sobbed, gasping.

Peter had brought a clay water jug. He pulled it under the wagon. He made Grit take water in her mouth, spilling water down her front. Grit gargled and her breath rasped. She swallowed too quickly, ravenously, and she suddenly choked and her body doubled in a fierce effort not to make the loud sound of coughing.

Peter's little hands splashed Grit's face gently with water and he tenderly rubbed away the caked dirt and blood. Grit winced and wept and tried to caress Peter's face with her own crooked and still-useless hands.

Kristina took water and it was sweeter than anything she had ever tasted. Dolf was cut free, and drank. Symon crawled to them, begging for water, too.

Kristina twisted to look for Michael. He had not moved. His dark shape was hunched upon itself, silently. She reached, leaning over, and tried to nudge him to take water.

"God is great," Symon rasped, between swallows.

"Shut up," said Dolf. "They are everywhere."

Kristina turned from Michael. It was no use. She felt sharp new pains of life run down through her numb forearms, down into her hands, as feeling returned.

Pins and needles stung her waking limbs like wasps. But her soul filled with the joyous revelation that her child had pretended to befriend the soldiers. Her child had acted out a role. Perhaps on impulse only, without any cleverness or plan, still, Peter had acted out his enormous bravery, this kindness, this goodliness. He had charity in his heart and the impulse to do good. More than all those, Peter was loving. She saw Berthold in him now, that shy and tender courage, and she loved God for this.

Forgive me, forgive my doubt, my weakness...

All were flexing their limbs and looking out, fearfully. They lay there, it seemed to her, for a very long time.

Out there in the glare of campfires, Kristina saw the black shapes of men coming and going to the wagon of trapped girls. They were loud, some of them, and others were very quiet. Then there was another hanging at the wagon behind them. Somewhere a drum rolled. There was muttering among the crowd of men as charges were read, of a fight over one of the girls and a throat cut. A monk chanted last rites. Kristina heard the condemned man on the gallows scream a drunken laughing curse upon all man-loving monks, and then he was suddenly silent, his words cut as he swung up kicking.

It was when things settled for the night, much later, after an eternity of waiting—and all their bodies were alive with pain, but feeling had returned, and Grit's mouth could almost close without choking—that they came out from under the wagon.

Peter hissed, crouched like a cat, and pointed the way.

They would have left Michael—Kristina knew that she certainly would have—but Grit would not abandon him. Grit crouched, poking the priest. In obvious exasperation, Dolf pulled Michael out by the hands so that Grit would go.

Then together, legs wobbling, they stumbled and moved like drunks trying to keep their balance. Dolf pulled Michael by the hand like leading a stubborn child.

The camp was a series of islands of men asleep around fires. Between the islands it was darker and there were stones to avoid, and here and there the stump of a tree cut down for the fires.

Kristina saw that they were in the middle of the wagon train but there were horses tethered on a hillside that was much darker, away from the campfires, and that was the way Peter pointed them now, leading the way.

Slowly, in fits and starts, they crawled on hands and knees over rocks and mud. Kristina's knees were torn by sharp rocks and her stiff hands worked like claws, but she kept her child in sight, always, never falling behind.

They crawled between some tents where men snored and one lit tent where men were gambling and drinking. They crawled on past a man who was pissing in the dark.

The horses were on their left and the open hillside behind the horses. Kristina saw stars in the sky beyond the horses. The air was fresher now, and she took great breaths of cool cleanness into her body.

The crushing sound of many boots was coming. Dolf waved them down and Kristina lay pressed into the dewy grass. A dozen guards on picket duty came with lanterns in front and back. They passed so close Kristina could see their lantern-lit armor, their helmets, and the heavy beard of their watch sergeant, who carried the lantern trailing smoke.

Grit gagged. Grit coughed. Kristina twisted round and saw Grit struggling with her mouth. She was fighting herself, not to make a sound. Something seemed wrong with her tongue.

"Hold," said a hard voice. "Who goes there?"

The watch guards halted. They turned.

"On guard, men!" he said sharply.

The watch sergeant pulled his sword and came toward them. His lantern was high in his free hand.

"Villeins may be about."

Grit was gagging but fighting the impulse, as she had under the wagon. Kristina put her arms around Grit and held her tight. But now Grit jerked and then was coughing uncontrollably, little barks of struggled breathing.

Dolf got up and tried to run but his legs crumpled under him. A guardsman kicked him in the face. Symon was crawling and another guardsman stepped on his back to stop him.

Peter was suddenly up, springing like a cat, swinging his cook knife. The startled sergeant blocked the boy with an armored arm, swatting him down.

The entire guard was on them then, and the watch sergeant had Peter by the scruff of his neck, twisting the cook knife from his hand and cursing the cut on his good tunic. He hit Peter full in the face with a blow of his fist. Peter flew back and lay and did not move. Kristina screamed and crawled to her child.

Then Michael sprang up and screamed.

It was the first sound he had made, and it was loud. Kristina and all the others stopped and even the soldiers stared for that instant.

Michael flung himself at the sergeant and gripped the sergeant by the throat.

Michael was grunting.

"Hate and hate and more hate!"

The sergeant was startled, being throttled. He dropped the lantern and was gasping and pulled his dagger and thrust it up into Michael's groin, lifting Michael almost off his feet. But Michael did not let go. He cried out and hung onto the sergeant's neck with both gripping hands like a man afraid of falling. Two more soldiers moved quickly with their daggers and they tore off Michael's cloak and threw him down and butchered pieces from him until his wailings tapered to mere gasps, then nothing.

On her knees, Kristina held her unconscious child and she saw the priest let go, and he went down easily as if his cloak had been emptied of him and fell alone. Nothing was left of the man, of his learning and his glimmer, but a black hump steaming with fresh blood in the cool night air. The mist of his escaping heat created halos around the guards' lanterns.

Kneeling, submissive, Kristina and Grit and Peter and Dolf and Symon all clung tighter in a clutch, awaiting their fate. Grit was muttering, whispering some prayer.

The guardsmen picked up their smoky sputtering lanterns, surprised. They bent and wiped their daggers on the heap that had been Father Michael.

"Feeble swine gave me a start," said the sergeant. He rubbed his throat and laughed at himself. "I thought they were infiltrators. What was the fool saying?"

"Hate, hate, and more hate. I do not think he liked you."

They laughed.

"Cut their throats and be done?"

"These are for burning. Bounty heretics, for the Passau monks. Somebody has got to take the blame for all of this. Get stronger rope from the harness wagon."

The guardsmen cursed the annoyance of tending what they had found. They dragged them all back, Kristina by the feet, Grit by the feet, driving the men at the point of daggers, Peter unconscious and by the hair.

At the heretic wagon—between the gallows wagon of hanging men and the comfort wagon of trapped farm girls—the guards mocked, yawning now, talking of a big attack soon and how much they needed sleep.

And so, Kristina learned one of the most fiendish tricks of hell. The torture of hope. And there was nothing Kristina could do to change hell into something else.

LUD

When the Imperial attack came, it was devastating. It was too late to maneuver or escape. The Black Host cavalry hastily mounted and the horde ran to their formations with their backs to the Tauber River.

"They are as you scouted," said Florian. "Muntzer must have been crushed, with all who believed him. I am the fool now."

Lud said, "All that matters now is to keep them off the flanks, as long as we can."

It was like a play long rehearsed and inevitable. Far off bugles pealed and drums rolled and then the cannonades began their ripping, shrieking thunder. The blasts shook the hills and sent sheens of shock across the river water. Rainbows hung in beautiful mists that moved with the breeze and the next volleys tore them apart.

The People's Army rallied bravely as comrades, as brothers, as equals, in their hordes. But the attack fell upon them with absolute precision, with coordinated and overwhelming force, and the shock ripped their ranks apart.

Knowing a thing would happen, Dietrich had said long ago, did not mean you could stop it from happening. And, as Lud knew would happen, as he had scouted and had warned Florian, the Imperial columns appeared abruptly out of the hills. Their attack was perfectly timed, half concealed by dawn mists, while the People's Army was still rousing itself for the day.

The people fought the professionals with such stubborn courage that the Imperials were thrown back, despite the heavy losses. With their backs to the Tauber River, the villeins fought with the strength of farmers, of laborers used to toil from dawn to dusk; of people used to defeat by weather, by sickness, by famine, by war. They fought on because they did not know what else to do.

Lud had thought that his heart was too scarred to feel what he now felt. He thought he was emptied out, too dead inside to feel it. But this day brought him heartbreaking sorrow, angst that dragged him down as to the bottom of a cold, dark, empty sea.

The people—who were of his blood, of his kind, of his birth—they worked ceaselessly, swinging their axes and knives and hammers as on the spring slaughter at home. They labored hard. But now they did not slaughter animals that could not fight back. Now they were the slaughter. The professionals harvested them. The villeins fell and yet they stood their ground. If they broke and fled they were chased down by men of horse and cut down. But few ran. And the killing did not stop. The ranks of organized professionals terrorized their flanks with cavalry. The steady cannonades burst continually among them.

There was no reason, only the killing. Lud saw cannonades in which farmers were laid down in sheaves like wheat mowed under scythes.

He rode in and out of the shattered ranks and he saw Linhoff lying in a hole blasted from the earth by a cannon. In the hole with Linhoff was Arl, kneeling and wiping the mud from his dead face. There was nothing where Linhoff's chest had been but his face seemed aware.

Lud rode around the hole and stared down at Linhoff, and Linhoff in death seemed to stare back at him from the smoldering hole.

Now Arl saw Lud and she got up and came quickly out of the hole.

"Lud!"

She came running up and threw her arms around the neck of Lud's mount. The horse jerked back but Lud reined him in tight.

"At least you live," Arl said, panting, her eyes flashing at him, her black hair like snakes stuck to her bony face.

"Go home," Lud said. Pulling his horse away from her.

"Take care, my child," Arl cried, "take care!"

Then the old woman was gone, whirling away, with her black cloak flapping like raven's wings in the smoke. For a moment Lud had seen Arl the baby catcher again, the sweet woman who called all those she had birthed her child. Then she was gone. She had birthed half the men of Giebel, who were already dead or were fighting upon this field with their backs trapped against the river. No wonder she was mad. She ran screaming and shaking her fists toward the distant cannons that kept firing.

He heard drums and bugles and saw new ranks of Landsknechts coming to attack. Crowds of villeins shouted and tried to rally around Florian.

In the thick smoky confusion Lud had three horses shot from under him. The Black Host men of horse again and again drove off the flanking Imperial cavalry.

Twice, Florian was recognized.

A shout went up among the Imperials. Despite Lud's pleas, Florian wore the flagrant bright gold Geyer ram's head tunic and made no effort to blend with the other knights. His leadership was obvious, riding in front, directing the attacks. Now that Steinmetz was dead, Florian tried to be in all places at all times, and Lud tried to stay with Florian, riding between him and death.

"Stay on me!" Florian shouted many times, though Lud had been fighting there constantly.

"Damned tunic," Lud raged, "damned pride."

The fighting went on and Lud's arms were like lead. His thighs were like stone. He rode down two horses and fought on in an exhausted delirium.

He kept sight of Florian, always, as the battle lines surged back and forth. But each time the villeins somehow drove the orderly Landsknechts back, new cannonades were the punishment.

Lud lost his hearing in the explosions. He was cut in a dozen places by bits of iron, but his black armor held.

"The day is lost!" Florian began to shout at sundown. Or at least Lud thought that was what Florian was mouthing. Lud's hearing was one loud ringing now.

But there was no mistaking that Florian was riding erratically, trying not to panic.

The big, red sun sank fat on the horizon and then its orange fire melted away. There was delirium; Lud was drowning in a gray fatigue, as the broken ranks were steadily driven back toward the river. With purpling darkness came one great gift—a heavy fog rising from the Tauber, creeping with masking streamers over the obscenity of battle.

Then many were running.

They had all been fighting all day but now they broke, at last, and were running. Many went into the river and were swept away. As if the horde had one mind shared among all, that mind seemed to break apart all at once, almost everywhere on the field. Only the anger and bravery of a core of villeins kept back complete collapse.

"No!" Florian was riding and trying to shout. He had lost his sword and had no voice left and it was a croak. "No! Stand and fight!"

Then he saw a face he could never forget. It was Ulrich, the dagger man, the duelist; Ulrich, in Imperial cavalry harness, red and gold, racing toward Florian with a lance held low; Ulrich's face was bent over the lance, his knees driving the black horse hard, straight toward Florian, and Florian was fighting and did not see Ulrich. Ulrich was attacking his blind side, a killing move with the lance.

"Florian!" Lud shouted and Florian turned in time to see and dive down hard upon his saddle and miss the full thrust of Ulrich's lance. Lud thought the lance head ripped under Florian's armpit but Florian artfully fended off the shaft of the lance with his shoulder.

Lud drove his horse between them.

"You!" Ulrich said, dropping the lance and drawing his sword.

"You," Lud said, with his sword already thrusting.

He fought horse to horse with Ulrich and it was like the duel they once had so many years ago, with daggers—Ulrich a man of greater skill, with cunning moves, but Lud stronger, tougher, and his good mail and armor saving his life. Now Lud smashed his sword against Ulrich's helmet and sent him reeling in the saddle.

But then a cannonade burst among the chaos of fighting and split the air with deafening smoke and Lud saw Ulrich, wobbly in the saddle, whipping his horse away.

Lud's only ally was the heavy rising fog that concealed the survivors with the utter gift of night.

He rode up hard against Florian's horse and gripped the iron bit in his fist and rode Florian right off that field, deep into the river fog. Along the riverbank the ground was covered with the dead. The horses ran through the bodies, stumbling. Lud heard cries from the river.

Florian flailed at him with a fist.

"Lud, no, damn you, stop!"

"Dying is not victory," said Lud back, leaning into his saddle, hauling Florian's horse by the head.

Lud looked behind and saw their horses leading out the strings of limping Black Host cavalry, what remained of it now, behind them, disappearing into the blind safety of the fog.

They were hunted all that night.

On a hilltop, the Black Host regathered, what was left of it, under a full rising moon. There were maybe six hundred left of the Black Host, Lud quickly tallied. All men of horse, most of them impoverished knights and sidemen of knights. Lud knew most of them. They had begun the war together with high hopes of regaining former positions and land taken by the bishoprics. Now they were clinging only to their lives and their honor.

Lud had scouted and knew a strong force of Imperial cavalry was no more than an hour behind them in pursuit. Ahead was the village of Ingolstadt.

"We will encamp and regroup at Ingolstadt," Florian said, and no vote was asked for nor taken.

"We should stay in the open," Lud said.

"They must rest," said Florian.

"We could be trapped."

"Go where you will," said Florian.

"Are you injured?" said Lud, ignoring the insult.

"It is nothing. I can fight."

They rode hard. Only a dozen at most peeled off and faded away into the dark. No one tried to stop them.

Ingolstadt was completely deserted.

In the faint rising of dawn, as structures emerged from the dark, they left their horses and came into the deserted castle.

It was a village so much like Giebel that Lud felt an unexpected longing, a homesickness that took him unawares. There was no linden tree in the square but the church and castle were so familiar. He went to the castle to see what could be done to defend it. It had good walls and a narrow gate and within its courtyard was a castle keep tower. Lud went to the castle, not because its walls and doors were thicker, nor because the simple country church was indefensible, but because Florian went there.

From the old broken ramparts he saw the riders moving in all around the perimeter, closing off every approach. He went quickly back down and reported to Florian.

Florian would not accept it.

"We must break out," said Florian.

"There is no way out," Lud said. "They are out there. By now they are encircling us."

Florian looked around at the exhausted men. Many were wounded. Some had collapsed where they stood.

"They all think it is the end," said Florian.

"Let any man make his stand where he will," said Lud.

"How can we win if even you believe it is over?"

"Florian," said Lud, "I am with you."

Two hundred weary men chose to fight and die in the church, and the other four hundred decided to kill as many of their enemies as they could, and to fortify the castle where they could better sell their lives dear.

Lud stayed close with him. Something was wrong with Florian, more than fatigue, but he would not admit to injury, and he went from man to man, encouraging each.

In the halls and alcoves and ramparts of the small castle, the men of war said nothing now. They all knew what to expect. Their eyes had already left this world. They chose their friends and they made their last stand places in the porticoes and casements and they blocked the passages with heavy benches, and stood the ramparts with their weapons, some falling asleep in their places, others staring faraway.

The attack came in force less than an hour later.

WITTER

In Holland, many years ago, Witter had drifted through the city of Hertogenbosch. That was where he, when still Samuel, first took the name Jan Witter (and claimed a speech impediment to explain his awkward accent). Cutting woodblocks in a Hertogenbosch print shop, he was told that his demons were not "convincing," and the owner sent him to view a triptych, a three-panel painting in the Cathedral of St. John's.

Sullenly, Witter went and entered the cathedral, a vast interior that he perceived as a hollowed-out mountain of cold, dead masonry. As ordered, he stood dutifully, shuffling impatiently in the long line with others, many of them pilgrims whispering prayers. But when he came near the triptych and he saw its imagery writhing in the shafts of light from above, time stood still.

The last panel was the fall of the damned into hell. They were naked, fresh from earthly pleasures, astonished to be seized by demonic insects and crustaceans. Witter never forgot how he had stood there staring, envying the artist for his skill, pitying the artist for the curse of his stunning vision—the fires, the torturers, the plunge into the black void of insanity and remorse.

The vision of the work was expressed so terribly, so vividly, that it had been necessary for Witter, staring at it, to reduce it to Church propaganda. Of course its sole purpose was to frighten children and the ignorant, to impress the weak of mind and make them obey. But he could not reduce it so easily. He had been stunned by the artist's vision because he had seen the faces of the tormented himself, in life. He had seen it like a ghost of his own dead people, remembering the burning synagogue of Córdoba, with all those whom he loved locked inside.

And now in war, in life, with his own eyes, he saw that vision expressed yet again.

With Mahmed, he had followed the Imperial Army, staying to the hills at a great distance. They followed the smoke of campfires and the flies and fleas and open latrines and death in the slime trail of its passage. The land was ground to mud, and when armies moved they did not avoid plowed fields nor ripening crops. All was crushed in their relentless path.

Let Kristina be alive, let her not be in pain…

Twice, at night, Mahmed had left Witter and hours later had returned covered with filth, unable to get close enough to the wagons to search for Kristina and the others.

"I want to go with you," Witter had argued.

"You have no stealth, my friend, no knowing of the order of armies," Mahmed said, refusing him.

It was true. Witter felt a shameful relief.

They were two men joined with the same impossible needs—to find Kristina, to help her, and to help themselves escape—and yet their arguments had become harsher. Mahmed had been a commander of men, used to leading and being obeyed. Witter had been a commander of Witter, and used to obeying, but obeying only himself.

They argued over direction. They argued over food. Hunger and thirst made bad comrades. Wells were not rare but they found bodies dumped in half of them. The stench of death was everywhere.

They had found wild birds in a net snare but they were dried out, too long dead. Then the next day they found bread under an overturned cart in a ditch, and they ate it all ravenously, then and there, Witter choking it down with ditch water.

Mahmed grabbed him by the shoulders, pulled him up from the ditch, made him stop. "Unless a good well or fresh-caught rain, water must be boiled."

"We can risk no fire nor smoke." Witter wiped his mouth. The water was earthy but wet, good and wet. He had not liked the grip of Mahmed's hands on his shoulders.

"Yes, so we must wait for a good well," said Mahmed.

"I am not a child."

"Yet often you behave as one. How have you kept yourself alive so long?"

"By making myself small," Witter retorted. "Unlike you."

"I see. Exactly like a child."

"I am no peacock, it is true."

"You are a gentle soul and indefensible, and I will forget you said that. But never say it again."

Their talk was like life, thought Witter: full of things known yet unavoidable, and none making much sense, after all.

Witter felt feverish and he began stumbling; his bowels let go and Mahmed found a half-burned mill where Witter passed out under the burnt skeleton of a giant mill wheel.

Yesterday, they had lain together on a hilltop with a grand view of the battle by the Tauber. The terrain below was like a vicious chessboard upon which factions moved and pushed and broke and scattered and pushed again. The echoes of bugles and drums and cannonades and the muffled roar of men all came moaning up on the wind.

Mahmed was a professional soldier, an officer of horse, and had called the struggle out, blow-by-blow, attack by attack. Before now, Witter had never understood the logic of battle, had never cared to learn nor known battle had logic.

Mahmed pointed out each attempted flanking move, each rally, each drive of cavalry, and the purpose of the deafening cannonades and their timing that so inflicted such panic upon the untrained and unseasoned villeins. Then, near dark, they had seen the final pursuit of the Black Host from the field in the fog.

The Imperial Army, its ranks glittering and precise, reorganized itself and soon moved again. Its rigid motions seemed inhuman to Witter, so unlike the amorphous ramblings of the People's Army.

"That is why men may never be free," said Mahmed.

"I do not understand."

"It has no soul."

"What do you mean it has no soul?"

"One rule moves that army," said Mahmed, "not the votes of many. Its equipment is new, its ranks professional. It is remorseless. Its only purpose is to destroy. It is a machine of perfect order. It fights without ideals and needs no brotherhood except in proficiency. It is a bought thing, not with honor, but with gold."

Witter looked at Mahmed. More and more he learned about this man and his manner of thought. He kept recalling that Mahmed was a man of war by profession.

"You speak as one who admires them," Witter said, surprised, somehow feeling betrayed.

"It, Witter, it, not them," said Mahmed. "The army is a dead thing. Those within it rid themselves of emotion as best they can. They become the one thing. Like moves of chess, it destroys without emotion."

Like the Golem, thought Witter.

Witter remembered the armies of Spain that swept through, gathering up and murdering the Jews. They acted with the same pure soulless will, the same relentless destruction.

Witter and Mahmed followed, staying far back.

Nailed to trees and posts at some of the main crossroads were broadsheets that read: *"Announcing the Capture of Muntzer and the Destruction (by the Faithful of God and the Holy Mother Church) of Muntzer's Evil People's Army! Six Thousand Villeins Dead in Victory at Frankenhausen!"*

"The world is ever-changing," Mahmed said. "The Imperials must have a printing press wagon."

"Propaganda becomes a force of war," said Witter, "even on the march with the army, to persuade and dismay."

"But only for those who read," said Mahmed. "I do not understand. Is it not illegal to read many certain things?"

"You watch," Witter said. "They will next pass a law that all must learn to read."

Then with the sun going down, they climbed a hill and heard the distant thumps of cannons, miles away, and it was louder and louder, more like a grinding sound as they came through the high grass of the summer hills.

"Big guns," said Mahmed, "and far away. Only the Imperials will have such cannons."

Now, as night fell again, he and Mahmed lay on yet another hill-top and they looked down fascinated, like two little boys, and watched the Imperial attack on the village of Ingolstadt. The attack appeared to be in its second day, for it had taken a full day of weary walking, and time to forage food in ruined farmsteads, to reach the fighting.

The village was mostly a church and a small castle. The church walls had been almost leveled by cannons. The roof was gone. Witter thought of a rotted fruit with its heart eaten out and the shell laid open to the sky. Nothing moved there.

The roar came from the fight that was raging at the castle. In one breach of castle wall, small shapes were like hornets fighting hand to hand.

Said Mahmed, "See how some had fortified the church as a redoubt. A bad choice. Probably those men were villeins and wished to die in church. But those defending the castle are angrier. Probably they are professionals of war, not villeins, but like all men they cling to life. Anything can happen, they think. But they will die there."

The Imperial cannons had breached the castle wall in the area of the gates, but then fired no more.

Drums rolled and bugles sounded. Waves of shouting footmen were assaulting the castle with ladders. Witter saw bitter fighting on the breached wall down there. Many attacking the walls were being killed. The waves of attackers trod on their own dead. But they out-numbered the defenders, it seemed, ten to one.

All of this death…to capture Florian, who had been made the hero of the people by a reverse impact of a broadsheet damning him, from Veritas Press.

Witter thought of the long journey to England, of Florian at Oxford, of the student riot, of Erasmus and the students, Florian's friends. He thought of Werner Heck and the good times, and his weeping room and the rabbi and his daughter, of Kristina and the black dog in the woods and the turning ferry on the river, and of his father, Judah, and his mother and Bianca, and of the synagogue. It was as if a devilish whirlwind were twisting his soul into knots.

He wanted to find Kristina and be with her and be held by her, just once, so that life made sense. He wanted to be loved as he loved, just once.

"The defenders fight hard," said Mahmed.

The words broke into Witter's strangled thoughts.

"The attack does not use cannon. The Imperials wish to take Florian Geyer alive, no doubt, to parade him and prove his infamy with public torments. Their cannons could reduce the old castle to rubble, and crush all inside it, if they wished."

Witter thought of Lud. Surely Lud was down there somewhere, with Florian, if either still lived.

"How long can they last?"

"*Shah mat*," said Mahmed.

Witter thought of his chess game in the square, losing to the brilliant Evil Peacock. *Shah Mat*. The King is Dead.

"Florian is not a king," said Witter.

"He has behaved and led and fought as a king. He has castled himself as a king. Castling can be a trap. But those men are knights and they do not die so easy."

Witter saw an attack on a breached wall. The distant shapes of frantic men were hacking and lunging in the glare of the fires. He felt he could watch no longer.

He got up.

"Where do you go?" said Mahmed.

"To find Kristina and the others. With a fight maybe the baggage train will be left unguarded."

"Their camp will never be unwatched," said Mahmed. "And we do not know where it is."

"It is time to find out," said Witter, moving away.

LUD

When men became too tired, they died.

Wave after wave of fresh Imperials assaulted the old castle of Ingolstadt, and in the last stand in the barricaded breach there was no more delaying of death.

The last of the Black Host were dying.

Florian was wounded and heavy on Lud's back. Lud's legs burned and he stumbled, muling Florian across his shoulders the way soldiers had borne one another from battles since men could remember battle, with head on shoulder, legs hanging, back bent.

"No," Florian said, "no…"

Behind Lud, as he staggered away under his precious load, the new assault smashed and ground the last exhausted defenders down. They fought and fell, cutting and stabbing and hacking and spearing and chopping and hammering and axing and butchering. Carrying Florian away, Lud looked back and saw the shapes struggling in the fire and smoke.

His deafened ears could hear nothing. But his mind echoed the cannonades and slaughter sounds like a horn blast that never stopped. Florian's head hung by Lud's face. Florian's face was bloody from a flying stone in the last cannonades that made the breach, before their final assaults began.

Into a dark passageway, Lud moved like a crab. Lud gripped Florian's hands and kept pulling them down. Lud felt Florian tremble, half in and half out of consciousness, with Lud bent under the unsteady load of the younger man, bearing him like a mule bears wood. He moved down through the rancid fire smoke, down through the stone way he had scouted out two days earlier when first defending the old castle.

The redoubt passageway went deep under the old castle keep. Lud had watched the keep blasted by cannon fire and he knew that above him on the surface there was only a great smoking pile of broken stones.

As one beast held together by Lud's will, he and the dead weight of Florian lumbered and descended down into the dark of slimed stones. Water dripped in the old escape passage. Almost all the older castles had such escapes, but most had caved in or were filled in long ago, and had since been forgotten.

Stones had collapsed on one side at the bottom and here Lud had to crawl lower and lower into black water and then total darkness. He had to crawl down until his head was underwater. He lumbered through, holding his breath, Florian jolting on his back, and then came up again to see a gray faint light far ahead and above, as one sees a hole in a sack. The stones were rising up now and he staggered, slipping, lifting Florian up toward that light.

From his reconnoitering Lud knew there was a garden and then an open orchard field and then heavy woods. Many years of scouting had taught him to always discover what came next. Dietrich had trained him in precaution, teaching him those rudiments of survival when he was hardly old enough to hold a spear.

He came up dripping into a verge of an opening that emptied out where the water was waist deep. It had been cunningly disguised to look like the castle sewer, probably hundreds of years ago, and long forgotten. A stream ran here choked with water moss. Uncut shrubs blocked part of his view of the other side. He groaned under Florian's weight and Florian was becoming revived by the water, the chill, and there was no time to rest.

He froze, staring, hearing hooves. He thought it must be the untethered horses of the dead riders of the Black Host, racing in confusion, masterless and free for the first time in their lives. He thought he might catch one or even two, and he could ride Florian out of here.

But by instinct he stayed low, and then he saw them.

A brace of cavalry rode past on the other bank. They wore the Imperial red and gold. He stayed low and a few minutes later they passed again, the same way. They were in no hurry, patrolling in their set routine. The fight must have ended at the breach, he realized.

The body of the Black Host, and all its magnificent dreams of the brotherhood of men, was dead. But that no longer mattered. Florian was alive.

Lud stared through the snarled thicket and the broken stones, and he marked the patrol's routine. Fatigue blurred his vision. He had not slept in three days.

When the horse patrol passed slowly again, moving with the maddening leisure of victorious men, Lud waited, taking deep breaths. Then in one sudden great urge, he moved fast, slipping and sliding along the muddy bank under the overgrowth.

He was on the other side with Florian moaning now and beginning to struggle. Then running low, his legs wobbling, Lud threw himself and Florian into the untended orchard thickets on the other side.

Moments later the horsemen rode past. Lud steeled himself, not knowing if they had seen him. They rode on past the way they had done each time before.

He moved, panting, crawling, and pulling Florian. He crossed the thicket and then hefted Florian again and ran across a short orchard field, his feet slipping on the untended fruit rotten on the ground, bees swarming up, glittering and gold and drunk on their fruit feasts. Lud plunged through them into the heavy forest.

They lay under a great deadfall of an oak. There were regular depressions underfoot. Stones. Markers. It was an old cemetery, filled with weeds and sunken graves.

Lud's hearing was returning and there was no sound of battle in the distance. He could see the faint whitish oval of Florian's face, and even with his beard Florian looked very young. The water had washed the blood from his forehead. It was swollen.

It was early night with deepening darkness when Lud sensed Florian coming back to his senses.

"So I am only human, after all," were Florian's first words. He tried to smile. "You see, I have learned to mock myself. Erasmus would be proud. But it is a little too late."

"Never too late. We will get out of this. Together."

Florian's eyes widened. "Is this...are these graves?"

"A little rest," said Lud, "and we get up and walk."

"They will have my life. Go. Go and save yourself."

"Your wound is not fatal, your head is clearing."

"Not my head..."

With one hand, Florian pulled open his tunic. Then Lud saw it. Florian was pierced beneath his ribs, twice, one nearer his armpit.

"First was the lance," Florian said. "From then on, I could not lift my arm. With the pain the weakness came."

Ulrich, thought Lud, *that bastard...*

So Florian had not fended the lance completely; it had caught him there. And Florian had ridden on and fought on with that wound. The lower wound was newer, less deep.

Florian could not move that arm. Lud had thought that the blood down Florian's tunic was from the head wound. He took Florian's hands and they were both limp and cold, trembling in the fingers.

"I have something I must tell you," said Florian.

"Be still and rest," Lud said.

"I have something to tell you and then you must do something for me."

"Anything."

"Promise you shall do it."

"Anything," Lud said.

"You must let my blood."

"I cannot promise that." His voice choked.

"You know what they do. They must not take me alive."

"Be still. Rest. Please."

"It is the first time," said Florian, "you have ever said that word to me."

"That word?" said Lud.

"Please."

Florian tried to smile and now tried to sit up, but the effort made him bend and retch. They had not eaten and it was watery foam. Florian's legs kicked in a spasm. Lud held him, pressed him back down.

There was more light, a sheen in the deadfall, and Lud saw a sliver of moon through the branches overhead. It rode a streak of clouds like a silver coin.

"Brother," said Florian.

"You have been like a brother to me," Lud said.

Florian gripped Lud's wrist. Florian's dark eyes shone wetly, gleaming in the dim oval of his face. His hand trembled, but now with emotion.

"Lud. You do not understand. You are indeed my brother."

"Brothers in arms, yes," Lud said without comprehension. "Brothers in equality of all."

"More. My father Dietrich is your father."

Time passed before Lud spoke again.

"You are feverish," he said.

"In his letters to me at Oxford, he told me he would one day tell you. That I was never to say it. That is why he made you steward, why he made you learn to read, why he kept you always near, by his side, against all wishes of my mother, Lady Anna."

Lud stared down at Florian, wondering at the possibility of this. A dim memory sprang up. The old impoverished knight Steinmetz, in the field that day. Speaking, then catching himself.

Your father...

Florian gasped with a sudden pain, then spoke again. He was shivering now. Lud pulled off his own torn tunic and covered Florian's chest.

"I shall be dead before morning," Florian said, with a weary resignation. "You are heir. The Geyer estate is yours. If there is anything left."

Lud swallowed and strove for courage to ask:

"Who is…my mother?"

"Father said, but her name I cannot recall. She is a weaver. And baby catcher, I think father said."

"Arl?" Lud felt a shock.

"Yes. Arl. That is her name. Your mother. Father loved her. Later, she had twins by another man. But before that, she had you by our father. He told me he was her first love, when she was a young girl."

Florian paused, regaining his breath. Lud's heart hammered. "Florian," he said.

"My mother, Anna, would not have you for all to see," Florian said, slower now. "She demanded you be sent away to a convent at Wurzburg, to be raised by nuns. But Arl begged father to let her raise you and Dietrich gave you to Arl. This, my father told me. This is truth."

Arl…Dietrich…Florian …

Under the deadfall of dead oaks, Lud knelt by his brother, Florian, and he swayed and looked up at the rising moon. All the old graves spoke of futility. Everyone died.

Now, he realized, Florian was twisting Dietrich's signet ring from his trembling fingers.

"Take this, wear it well, for you are my brother. Your name is Lud for our grandfather Ludwig…"

The world seemed to turn faster, spinning around him. His father was Dietrich. He was Dietrich's bastard and that was why Lady Anna always resented him so. Even the old knight Steinmetz knew it. Perhaps even many older ones of Giebel knew it or suspected it, yet nothing was ever said. If he was called a bastard he would think it a common slur, and fight or even kill for the insult.

Take care, my child, Arl had said. He had thought she meant it as one of the many she had birthed. Then he had never seen her again. *My child…*

His mother was Arl, Black Hoffmann, forced to give him to the convent sisters until Dietrich would take him at age eight and raise him feral in the stables and train him in hunt and war like a pet hunting dog. Hermo and Fridel had been his young brothers. Greta, his little sister.

The woman he loved, Kristina, was being taken for burning. And this brother he never really knew, Florian, was dying.

"I tried," Florian said. Pressing Dietrich's ring into his hand.

"I know." Lud felt the solid metal circle hard in his fist.

"I tried to do good, Lud. Yet so many died."

"Yes," Lud said.

"Was it all for nothing?" said Florian.

"I do not know," Lud said. "Nothing is for nothing. But we do not live long enough to know very much, I think, nor to see very far ahead of us."

Florian's breath stopped, then started again, in gasps.

"Now you must…keep your promise," said Florian.

"I did not promise."

Lud held his brother up to him and cradled him tenderly and he wept into Florian's bleeding chest.

"Cut my throat quickly, my fear overcomes me."

No, Lud thought, but he did not speak.

Lud turned his head sharply, reacting, and he realized he had heard something moving, a crackling in the brush.

Florian writhed in a spasm of feebleness.

The sound came again from somewhere on the other side of the wood, the rustling motion in the brush. Now Lud knew it was not an animal. And he knew there was more than one. The loathsome dread of being hunted came over him like a shroud, and he fought to clear his mind.

His eyes strained against the faint glare of the moon that limned the black tangles of trees and snarled branches. His right hand found his dagger, his stubby little friend of last resort.

Lud felt Florian press his lips close to Lud's ear. He felt the dry hot breath and the panting desperation.

"Brother," rasped Florian. "Please…"

WITTER

Twice they had tried and the second time they got so close they could hear the guards talking in their heavy guttural accents of fighting men bought from other places. Twice they tried and the last time they were almost caught and ran wildly through the night. Only an open latrine ditch saved them. And the guard that Mahmed killed with Witter's dagger. Now Mahmed had his own dagger, taken from the dead mercenary.

It had been impossible to get anywhere near the wagons of the Imperial Army, even in the deep of night. They were nothing like the loose organism of the People's Army, now dead. Their Imperial protocols were like clockwork. The guard patrol intervals too narrow.

They saw the spires of smoke and foraged ruined farms where the things he saw made him feel dead inside himself, and then they stayed to ridgelines far away and above the moving army.

They began to see broadsheets posted on trees: "10,000 Kreuzers in Gold, for Information or the Head of the Apostate Criminal Florian Geyer!"

"Then Florian lives," Witter said. "It is not over."

Said Mahmed, "The fire is dead. They are merely quenching the random embers. But I shall pray for the soul of the son of Dietrich Geyer, who was good to me and to those for whom I care."

They walked in rain and sun alike for silent hours and snatched a few hours' sleep wrapped in their torn cloaks. They stayed out of sight and followed the army, hoping for some miracle of random chance. When the sun was high, before going to sleep on rocks or in trees, Mahmed knelt in his prayers. Witter went apart for his own prayers.

"I have prayed for a great storm," said Mahmed. "An attack by some unknown force. Anything to break up the formations and give us a chance."

But none such came.

The victorious Imperial Army ground on down the old Roman road, covering it with mud and slime and trash and the hasty graves of wounded who had died, all in its wake.

Witter despaired midday, as he and Mahmed wearily slogged over a ridge, having kept the army ahead of them for many days of ravening hunger and brutal fatigue. He thought of how casually Mahmed had knifed the guard. It had been Witter's fault, as he had stumbled over a tether line of horses. He had run when challenged, and Mahmed, out of nowhere, did the deed and said no more about it, as if it never happened, as if that taken life had no face, no value.

Far ahead, distant towers were rising from the mists where two rivers joined to send the third, the mighty Danube, widening away east and south.

Witter felt a sense of absolute doltish hopelessness.

"Passau," said Witter. He fell to his knees, staring.

Said Mahmed. "We are too late."

"Passau," said Witter.

Below them, the Imperial Army was forming up tighter in its parade formations. Bugles now. Drums rolling. The cavalry was prancing ahead in vanguard, with fresh pennants being unfurled.

The wind crackled up through the high grass, bringing to Witter the celebratory military sounds that he despised with all the depths of his heart. He could see the long train of wagons with infantry on either side.

Somewhere down there she was there. Somewhere down there they were all bound, doomed, terrified, condemned. And he was up here in all his impotence.

"The Oberhaus, there," said Mahmed, pointing.

Above the Passau city towers and spires, Witter saw it. The gray hulking fortress, so like the Marienberg of Wurzburg, yet even larger.

Said Mahmed, "The Oberhaus is where they will take them."

"How can you be sure?"

"It was my business to know every fortress in your lands."

"Not my lands. Not mine."

"Prisoners, both political and heretical, are taken there to be tortured and questioned and sentenced for burning. Nobles to the towers, commoners to the pit. Prisoners of the war will be taken there. After great victories come great celebrations, and spectacles for the hordes."

"We must do something, anything," Witter said.

He thought of something Kristina had told him, something her mother had told her when Kristina had been but a child: *If ever you become too afraid, sing, and God will hear you...*

Suddenly, he no longer cared about escaping this hellish land. The Danube lay before him, his way out, with Mahmed his living passport to lands where he could be free. Suddenly, Witter cared only for what he might do, what must be done there, at Passau—some miracle, some divine intervention, some cunningness of scheme, anything to save Kristina from burning.

If she lives, she is singing now...

"Kristina," he said with a terrible longing, with dread.

Said Mahmed, "Forgive us, dear soul."

But Witter's heart raged against that weakness.

No. Not while you live. Do not forgive us. To forgive us is to lose all hope...

LUD

The land was thick uncut forest where mountains rose from the river valley. It was adrift with villeins who had somehow survived the broken army, scurrying back through the land, trying to reach their homes. The roads were empty of them, but in every heavy forest and ditch and ridge and sheep track, there they were, hiding, crawling, ragged, desperate, forlorn, starving, worn-out from defeat and loss.

Like fleas on a dog, thought Lud.

Lud's mind, too, was fogged and dim, but not so much that he did not shed the ram's head tunic and mail shirt when first he thought of it. He kept moving, with no destination at first, just moving away from places where any force was seen. He saw many others too who were simply lost—men and women moving in the shock of those who have lost all certainty, who cannot recall who they once were, who they were now supposed to be. And he avoided them all as he would the victims of plague.

Near a waterfall, under a fallen boulder, he dug out a damp, rocky hole and closed himself in with brush and slept for longer than he had ever slept in his life. Then thirst woke him with a throat-clenching pain. He stood under the waterfall until his body was numb.

Prowling down into the valleys, he went foraging through every possible place of food, including the bodies that lay here and there, everywhere, like fallen leaves. Their distant stench and the circling vultures made them easy to find. Fleas climbed his legs. Gnats and flies swarmed up in the places where humans had befouled everything.

His mind struggled as he moved again. The Imperials would have taken back the cities with cruel reprisals of martial law. The cities were walled stockades, death traps. On posts and trees he saw the Imperial broadsheet proclamation of Muntzer's trial and his beheading.

The war was done. His world was gone.

Lud, for Ludwig, the name of his grandfather. Ludwig von Geyer, who had once been the most-celebrated knight in Franconia. And what did it matter now? What did anything matter? Everything he loved was gone, and it had not loved him, ever, in return. He was not much more than a flea himself. His death would mean nothing to anyone.

Lud kept attempting to bring order to his mind.

He yearned to return to Wurzburg, for that was the last place he had seen Kristina. He wept, surprising himself, thinking of the things that had surely by now happened to her. And he longed for Giebel, his home. They were surely all dead there, he decided. Only certain death waited for him in Giebel. He was the sideman of Florian Geyer and he would be that to the end of his days. In battle and on march and in Muntzer's great rallies, he had been seen by thousands with Florian. But most of that time his lower face was wrapped, as was his lifelong habit to mask the scarring of his pock-marked face. There were many with such faces.

Outside a devastated village, Lud took a better cloak, dark brown wool, from a dead man he found on his knees. He thought the man was praying but the man had died like that, bent over a big rock. A dead child lay near him. The man had bashed his own head into the rock. A wide hat lay nearby. It fit well. The hat and cloak helped. So he had a chance to move without recognition, as long as he stayed away from places he was well known.

He would live out his life as a thief, moving by night, and live as wild animals lived, and for a life of savagery he was well equipped. He no longer cared about anything, he convinced himself.

He moved like a sick man, dulled with all his thoughts of death, knowing surely all whom he had loved were dead.

He saw and avoided horse couriers in Imperial tunics, nailing broadsheets on posts and trees, announcing the execution of Muntzer. And then he saw another, a broadsheet proclamation that filled him with a strange exultation.

He had to read it aloud to make himself believe it: "10,000 Kreuzers in Gold, for Information or the Head of the Apostate Criminal Florian Geyer!"

For the first time in many weeks, Lud's face cracked into a smile, as he read the reward for Florian. For it proved they still feared him. To them, Florian still lived. He almost laughed out loud to think of the cartloads of heads that would be brought by schemers seeking the reward. But Konrad and his monks would reject them all. They knew Florian's face well enough.

Lud feared hiding himself to rest, for that was when the things he had done came rushing back upon him. When he tried to steal an hour's sleep, he was most vulnerable. He had not digested things that waited in his soul. He had no defense in sleep against his own mind, where all the shocks came back as fresh as scenes in hell. But weariness melted him down into helplessness.

Now at night, in a thick wood, he lay rolled in field hay he had gathered. It was raining hard, dripping inside the hay, but the new woolen cloak was warm.

Memory came rushing without mercy at him and he was too tired now to hold it back...

Holding Florian in the old cemetery woods, they lay together in an old sunken grave among the fallen stones and the cracked slabs under the deadfall. The dark was faintly moon limned, and his eyes pained with the effort to see. Hearing motions first on one side, then something crashing, and more than one man approaching on the other. The enemy was searching the cemetery woods.

Florian held on to him, gravely wounded, telling him the impossible secrets of his own life, of Dietrich his father, of his legacy, and whispering in his ear, begging him to do the unspeakable.

Then there were search lanterns, many more men outside the wood, encircling it. Florian gripped his arm, gasping, trembling, begging him, whispering...

Brother...

The lanterns moved off in another direction and suddenly he had stopped thinking and had done it. Done what he had to do while there was still time.

He had made himself do it as a man forces a boy to do something terrifying.

Then he had gone numb, working quietly to conceal the grave, finally slipping away, easily, once he was alone, escaping through their random line of search...

Bitterly now, as he moved, Lud thought of the lance wound in Florian's side. Ulrich driving hard, recognizing Florian in the battle smoke, and Lud unable to do more than fend off a deathblow.

Ulrich, whom Lud should have killed in the duel long ago, as Dietrich had urged him to do. Ulrich, who had trained in Landsknechts with Florian, and had recognized him. Ulrich, who had shouted in joy, riding hard, his spear piercing Florian before Lud could ride between them...

Lud walked faster.

Lud's hatred helped burn through the fog enshrouding his reason. He moved like a wolf. Always looking farther ahead. Using every rise of ground, scouting, then moving.

The main Imperial Army marched on toward Passau, and Lud drifted far back, days back, in their wake of that army. In the aftermath of great battles, most people avoided the dead wasteland track left behind. Only the pickers went through the human wreckage and then eventually those heartsick ones—mostly children and old folk—searching for the faces of their lost ones, their dead.

To avoid all people he moved at night. The moon came up over one such field of battle and he saw here and there women looking from one face to another with lanterns, bending low, sometimes whispering to the dead, sometimes sobbing. The moon made the land colorless, all black and white and gray, and the lanterns here and there were warm orange spots of life.

Only the living suffered and worried. The dead lay sprawled in their serene disinterest now, their peace undisturbed even by the dogs that tore at them. All the thunders of battle were gone away. All the feelings and love and opinions and ideals and aspirations were gone away.

Lud only passed near a battlefield when the land took sharp rises or water crossings forced him to do so. It was easy to smell such a place miles away, when the wind turned. Vultures were not as good a sign as before, with too many dead in too many places. There were not enough vultures to service so much death. When he was forced to by hunger, Lud used his dagger and searched the dead for bits of bread. Most were stripped but not all. Many bodies were broken by shellfire. All were rigid and hard to turn over. He felt shame when he found a coin and treasured it with relief. Their shrinking faces did not care. All their glimmer was black as coal now. Once in the moonlight he was frightened by a naked man with gleaming eyes standing in his way, but it was only a body impaled upon a stake, like a scarecrow.

He began to see less and less dead, and fewer that lived. The land along the Danube opened up and gave less cover.

Those villeins who had survived all of this, somehow, were heading away from the fields of the dead. They were escaping the Imperial Army, not following it, as Lud was. Soon he saw no more of them, at least no more who lived.

One night on a sheep's path he thought he saw Witter. Lud crouched down in the scrub bushes and saw two shapes moving quietly, not speaking. They passed so close that Lud could have reached out and cut their throats. Perhaps it was someone who looked like Witter—the beard heavier, the hair wilder, but the same awkward shamble of walk, slightly bent as if in perpetual humility. The other one ahead of Witter looked stealthier, warier, like a warrior, and strangely familiar, too, but Lud could not see him well nor place him. He watched their gray shapes disappear into the dark that closed in and then they were gone.

By dawn Lud was no longer sure he had seen them at all. And if it had been Witter, Lud had no wish to help anyone else, when he was driven now by only one thought.

Ulrich was ahead there somewhere, heading for Passau with that army. A captain of cavalry, perhaps promoted for valor, returning to receive the bounties that victories always brought to men of the winning side.

There had formed, out of the fog of his mind, a brightness. A reason. A reason worth living for—to find and kill Ulrich. It did not matter what happened after that. Then it would be finished.

They would be having all their victory feasts and festivals. There would be much drunkenness and revelry and wanton lack of vigilance. They had crushed the villeins.

But one thing cheated them—they could not prove Florian was dead. They could not put someone else's head on the city gate. Too many villeins knew Florian's face.

Brother...

No one would ever find Florian. He felt a broken smile tighten his face, how he had made certain of that. And he smiled, for all those who had fought and died in hopes for a better world. He smiled with deep fondness, without mockery nor pity, for the fields of peaceful dead. Florian lay with hands folded upon his chest, hidden under the stones of an ancient grave, with Dietrich's ring upon his finger where it belonged, where Lud had replaced it after the terrible thing was done.

Now Lud, feeling himself as free as any wild animal, crept through the night, stopping often to watch and to listen. He smiled because, as long as the Imperials could not find Florian's body, Florian lived.

The army only paused one night in the river city of Regensburg, and went on marching toward Passau.

Lud forgot his weariness and hurried now, taking greater risks by staying closer to the Danube. Travel was much faster on more level ground, and he was determined now to reach the city close upon the army's entrance. There would be a riot of festival revelries. The Oberhaus was the famed fortress there and they would fete and bivouac the army. Throughout the city there would be drunkenness and chances. Open gates and huge mingling crowds. And that thought, too, made him smile, made him strong, like the stubby blade of his last little friend, his dagger.

Anything might happen, when an army came home to wallow in its glories and spend its gold.

KRISTINA

The tumbrel cart creaked and bounced on the cobbles and rolled through the packed crowds that parted before it. Its cracked wood floor was stained black by slaughter meat, its last load before this human freight. A standing driver wearing a hood drove the two mules that pulled it. Kristina's hands were bound at her belly but she could hold onto Peter with her fingers and her knees.

Four magistrates, walking in front and behind the wagon, carried clubs, their shoulders wrapped in chains, and the crowd spread open continually and widely avoided them.

Monks rode horses on either side, with crosses in their hands, lifted over the crowd, as if protecting the people from this cartload of human evil.

"Beware, heretics pass here! Make way! Do not speak to them! Do not look in their eyes!"

The little procession moved through the festive street, silencing the revelers wherever it passed.

Kristina's eyes were swollen from weeping, and now she had no more tears. She had tried to sing as her mother had taught her. The fear choked off any lifting of song from her heart. The faces around her—of her brothers Dolf and Symon, and her sister Grit—were washed out, vacant, almost peaceful in their deep sadness. At first they had leaned onto the sides of the cart but some in the crowd had struck them with walking sticks and now they were hunched in the center together. Last night Symon had wept until Dolf had held him like a baby.

"They take us for torments," he said.

"But you will be strong," said Dolf. "You have been racked and you can help the others like me who suffer even more fear, from the unknown."

"It is a lie," said Symon.

"What lie?" Dolf said.

Now they were all staring at the two men. Kristina felt rising contempt, realizing what Symon meant.

"I was never racked," he said, sobbing. "I wanted you all to respect me, and believe I am brave."

Dolf pulled away from Symon as if burnt, staring.

"My joints were never pulled loose," Symon said. "When I was a boy a man broke my leg over his knee, for stealing from his rabbit snares."

"Poor…Symmm…" mouthed Grit.

Kristina looked away from them.

There was no more hope except the life of her child; she held on to him as he had slept, and now he sat awake, between her knees, watching the passing people as if they—not the cart and its human freight— were the spectacle.

Grit lay down and curled up near Kristina's feet like an infant, her face shocked, her jaw swollen; drool trickled from the corners of her wounded mouth. Perhaps she was praying; Kristina thought so. Hoped so. If Grit's spirit broke, nothing was left.

Almost worst than the random haters and mockers were those who looked in with leering curiosity and some with pity. Kristina saw them through the cart slats. They looked back at her with sad, silent faces of compassion, perhaps, and shame.

"May God bless you," several said, and others said, "Christ be with you."

The monks shifted in their saddles, trying to see who had spoken. Their faces showed their anger.

"None speak! They are accused of God!"

Kristina tried to sing within her mind but her mind was crowded with fear too sharp, like broken glass.

A small woman with snow-white hair crossed herself.

"God's mercy upon you all," Kristina heard her say.

The nearest monk twisted quickly in his saddle and saw the white-haired woman.

"Heretic!" he seethed, with a look of triumph that he had finally caught one in the act. "Take her! Seize that woman!"

Kristina gasped as the little woman tried to push back into the crowd, but the magistrates easily caught her, dragged her wailing to the cart, and they did not even open the tailgate. They hefted her up over the rail and threw her in. Dolf tried to catch her as best he could.

"I am Ruta, a good church woman!" she cried out.

"You blessed heretics," said the monk. "We shall discover who and what you are in the pits of the Oberhaus."

The woman crawled to Kristina, obviously wanting to be comforted, and then Kristina and Grit and Peter and the white-haired woman huddled together at one end of the cart.

"This cannot be," the woman said, "this cannot be."

"Say nothing more," Kristina hissed.

She did not want to draw notice from this woman and yet she wanted to hold her and to be held.

"God save us," Ruta kept saying.

A carriage with fine black horses stopped for the cart to slowly pass by. The carriage coachman in blue velvet removed his red top hat, bowing his white-wigged head to the monks. Then, as the cart came closer, Kristina saw the lady perched in the carriage, a perfect delicate face that was staring at her. She was radiant, blonde and very beautiful; a high emerald-green silk collar framed her golden hair, and at her throat were pearls.

Kristina stared at her as if at a painting, out of place here, out of time here. Some in the crowd pointed at the beautiful lady and some even clapped. She lifted her chin, basking.

"Paulina! Paulina!" some called out.

"Fray-derrr?" she heard Grit say through her torn lips.

It was Frieda. It was not possible. Kristina stared through the gap in the slats and her eyes caught Frieda's.

275

Dolf said it, too, much louder, "Frieda?"

The beautiful face of Frieda watched back coldly, then turned away, with no sign of emotion. Her driver flicked the reins at the sleek black horses, blue gleams on their muscles, and then the carriage and cart both moved on.

Kristina saw the massive shadow of the fortress on the high bank above the Danube. There was a causeway. The cart turned onto it and was climbing.

On the great spit of land amid the river junctions stood the main city and in its center arose the spires of the cathedral. She heard the rolling choral of many great bells. They tolled not like a dirge but joyously, and this felt even more crushing to her spirit.

The bells tolled a melody—it was the *Pange Lingua*, she realized, the Gregorian vespers hymn for Corpus Christi. At the convent long ago, with Sister Hannah, she had heard it as a child so many times. A longing arose in her, feeling the emotion within the urging of the bells.

Along the riverside, thousands of people drank ale and danced in crowds. Colored tents of performers of all kinds entertained them. The cart and its warders were like a moving cell of darkness amid so much bright gaiety.

At the ale tents, many men and women together sang the same popular bawdy songs, laughing at their lewd lyrics. Kristina could hear them in the distance. The sense of gaiety felt insane, as if she were being mocked by God himself...

"They drank from Monday on till Saturday night
Three drunken maidens kept pushing the jug about
Here comes bouncing Klara, face as red as a bloom
Move up, my jolly sisters, give your Klara some room
For I can satisfy any man before the night is out!"

Peter began humming now and she recognized that he was imitating the bawdy melody. She wished her hands were free so she could cover his ears from the lewd songs. How could their day be so happy, with this cartload of fear and ugliness passing through it?

There were sword-fight exhibitions and tale-tellers stood on platform retelling the magnificent victories of the Imperial Army over the hordes of blasphemers and criminals. On a field, there were drums and bugles and a glittering parade of cavalry, people cheering.

They came into a narrow street and Ruta, the white-haired woman, now tried to climb out of the back of the cart. The cart shuddered to a stop. The magistrates ran into the shocked crowd and easily caught the woman again, with some in the crowd turning their backs in fear. Her gown was torn open and her wrinkled white body was exposed. The magistrates threw Ruta back inside like a sack of grain.

"Have mercy, I am a seamstress of robes and a good woman of Christ!" Ruta screamed, gripping the cart slats with one hand, pulling her torn gown closed with the other.

Now, Kristina tried to look only at her child, as if all the world had gone mad with lust and rage. So many were dead. Many thousands, dead. And everywhere, people were laughing.

What will my child do without me?

She felt great anger at God.

Why did you create such an evil world? Why are we outcasts? Why will you allow this?

Why will you reward killers so, yet abandon us?

That was when the cart shuddered, the left wheel skidding. She heard shouts and saw the leftmost monk's horse falter and fall and the monk screamed and fell into the crowd. Another monk, still astride his horse, was shouting.

The magistrates all turned and stared in wonder. The crowd moved like a school of fish, trying to see what was happening. A mule coughed and went down. The cart stopped completely. Ruta had been sobbing, but now she ceased. All stared.

Grit tried to speak but her swollen jaw wouldn't let her.

"The beast is stabbed!" Dolf said.

"God delivers us!" said Symon. He crawled up on the cart rails to try to get over them.

Peter sat up, and Kristina heard him giggle.

"Kristina," a hoarse voice said.

A strong hand reached through the tumbrel railing and gripped her arm behind her back and hauled her around.

She twisted and almost cried out.

Then she saw the short dagger urgently sawing on her ropes, and the dark-eyed face of Lud was looking up, anguished and disbelievingly at her.

LUD

He had come to kill Ulrich.

Life had shrunk to this pinpoint of one final desire and all of it was very simple now. He was wild and free and had no other plan and needed nothing more for his life now. He had not planned the kill. Find Ulrich and stay unnoticed and stalk him until it happened. If you did not care whether you escaped, it was much easier to kill anyone. He thought how he had not planned anything much in his whole life, and he thought how this was no different.

The forested mountains opened at the river junction and there was Passau nestled on the hillside. For hours he worked his way down through leveling hillsides.

Now, along the quay, he saw where the rivers joined at the Danube, its wide green breadth disappearing, curling to the east. He heard music of all kinds. Saw tents and performers and stalls of free ale. The bishopric and the league were putting on a big show, and the people were hungry to feel good for a change.

Lud drifted inside the gates of Passau with the crowd, part of the swarm. He wondered how many of these revelers had been crying brotherhood only weeks or months before. Maybe some had fought, like him, in the People's Army. But that was no more. Now they were part of this, as if the other had never happened. There were already many drunks asleep in alleys and doorways.

Broadsheets were posted on walls and posts and pillars: "How God Gave Glory to the Imperials." "Liberation from Apostate Evils." "Infamies of the Villeins." And so on.

Lud drifted past the cathedral, around the edge of the enormous city square, through the vast crowds.

An ox was being roasted over a stone pit, monks handing out free meat for all. Farther on there were sweets stalls and hand bread. Lud had not tasted meat in many days and he took a strip of steaming ox meat and relished the juices as he chewed the rich hot flesh. He thought he might as well enjoy the last day of this life.

He kept visiting the many free ale stalls and he felt his head rising, his thoughts mingling. Many were singing the bawdy songs and he sang along with the wild men and the teasing frisky girls...

I went to market to buy me a cock
And my cock went cock and cock and cock a doodle do,
And after everybody's cock did my cock crow!

It was becoming so clear to him now. Singing along with others—that was the story of his life.

He had always followed the lead of others and never had a strong sense of who he was. He had obeyed Dietrich and then Lady Anna and then Florian and now it was all done. He had loved Kristina but never made her his own, and now she was surely dead somewhere with all the others who were all dead somewhere, and this lost war done now and nothing left. The estate was lost, condemned. He was heir to death. That was all he had inherited.

His name meant nothing. His heritage was empty. To know where he had come from, from Dietrich and Arl, made him even less knowing of himself.

From the beginning, in peace or in killing, he had conceited himself as a man who stood alone, yet he saw now he was nothing but a follower, and now he followed this crowd that droned and drank ale.

It was clear, Lud thought, even to a stupid man, even to a man like him. His life had been a pointless folly from the time of his birth. It was all a waste. A joke.

He felt his grimy scarred face pull tight and realized he was grinning. Then the grin went away.

A woman passed, nursing a baby, and again he thought of Arl... all of her small kindnesses when he was but a raw stable child. It came back to him now how sometimes he had seen her watching him following Dietrich, in the linden tree with other boys, at the well drinking. It seemed impossible she had been Dietrich's lover. It hurt bitterly, realizing that Dietrich could never let the truth be told.

My child...

Too much death had twisted Arl into a thing of war, swallowed her up. As it had him. He would have loved to hold Arl, just once, call her *mother...*

He needed more ale, to quench the fire. More ale, to drown the awareness that churned his thoughts. He joined a swarm of hard young men in Imperial tunics, singing around an ale tent. It was the old tragic song of Hildebrand—

Two people matched from the same blood,
Father and son each trimmed their armor,
They girded their swords of the iron rings,
Father against son, they rode to battle...

Lud saw some there starting to watch him, and he melted away into the crowds.

It was foolish to sing with them like that, but he had nothing left to lose. He knew that. Then he realized that if his life were folly, he had never had anything to lose, never in his whole life. He had been born a beast and he would die a beast. The rest was pretense.

And that made him laugh out loud. He took yet more ale. All was a fog in which he moved from moment to moment. It was easy to be Lud, the Lud who did not give a shit about learning, tallying, stewarding. The Lud who needed no love. The Lud of cunning, Lud the killer.

When someone laughed he laughed. He took free tankards and free bread dipped in pork fat. There were plenty with pockmarked faces here, for Passau had been hit hard in three plagues, and no one cared. The war was over and, for the victors, the sense of abandon was complete.

At an ale stall he saw a broadsheet announcing "The Great Cavalry Victory Parade" and knew Ulrich would be out there, prancing and posing, receiving public honors with many others.

Lud was about to make his way through the mass of excited revelers, out toward the Oberhaus parade grounds. But then he saw the crowd move apart. Four pikemen of foot shoved people aside.

"Make way! Make way! Do not look in their eyes! Beware! Make way!"

Behind the soldiers came two monks on fine horses, perched high and pious with their crosses, mouthing chants over and over with a weary obstinacy. Lud did not want to hear their mumblings. Hearing them made him want to pull them off their horses and kick their teeth in. Their pretense to understand this world, and their assurance of a next world, infuriated him. Their posturing made him feel murderous.

Lud thought of Ulrich and was about to turn and push his way into another street and go to the cavalry parade. It was time to find Ulrich and kill him.

Then, it was as if the world turned upside down. Everything changed. The cart came rumbling by and the crowd spread open enough for him to see what was in it.

Lud stopped dead in his tracks. The fog of ale was torn away and he saw with crystal clarity.

Looking up at the side of the passing cart, through the filthy slats, he saw the face of a child. There should be no child in a heretic cart. He knew that face.

"You there, get back!" a monk shouted.

But Lud hurried, pushing closer.

And then he saw Kristina's face.

WITTER

With Mahmed, Witter stood on a rise of ground and saw, in the distance, the great city and the banks where three rivers joined. His cloak was a rag and his body ached and burned and his shoes were worn almost through and the soles of his feet were bleeding. His face was burned from sun and his hair matted to his skull with filth and sweat.

Along the far river banks, distant crowds flowed toward the city gates. He could hear festive music on the wind.

Witter felt dizzy, as if he had come to the end of his world. Many people down there were laughing as if there were no wrong, no pain, no injustice. He had no understanding of such a world.

Witter's eyes followed the tiny toylike train of wagons that wound down the far road, toward the fortress on the river. He wiped flies from his face.

"Following the army was a mistake," he said. "We should have tried to go ahead of them. Now it is too late."

"You do not even know she is there," said Mahmed. "You do not know if she is even alive."

The spires and towers of Passau seemed to hover in the rising heat shimmers of a hot day. He smelled the smoke of roasting meat and then he heard drums and bugles. There was a sudden thunderclap of celebratory cannonades from a battery of big guns along the river. Many people ducked and then many were cheering and laughing again. Much nearer, along the riverfront, were free ale stalls and much music and dancing. Many people lay on the high grounds above the riverbanks and drank and played together.

"You see," Mahmed said. "Most do not care."

"You misjudge," Witter said.

"Do you not have eyes?"

"Many pretend. Many lose themselves."

"You give people too much credit. Most will hide their true emotions. They shall want things back the way they were before, and bury the rest of their hopes."

Witter moved now, walking down toward the crowd, and Mahmed went with him, arguing.

"Witter, stop. If they live they go into the bowels of the fortress. There is no more hope. The Oberhaus was built during the Crusades to command this fork of three rivers. It is unbreachable, even if we had a great army."

"We have to think of something."

"That is no place for a Jew, nor a Muslim."

They were nearing the crowds, and Mahmed tried to stop him, taking his arm, gripping it hard.

"Witter, they are already dead, or if alive, in God's hands now, and may God have mercy in the manner of their deaths."

"No," Witter said.

Mahmed stared at him.

"If she were dead I would feel it," Witter said.

"Romantic love, straight from the poets. But you love without hope."

Witter said nothing; his whole body filled with a heartsick longing. He hardly knew what he was saying. He had no idea what he could try to do or the sense of futility that he refused to accept.

He tore his arm loose from Mahmed's grasp and was moving again.

"If she still lives and you so love her," said Mahmed, "then leave this place. Leave, before they take her into that square down there and you see her burned alive to smoke and ash. There is nothing more we can try to do."

Witter's mind raced.

"There will be a time of imprisonment and pressure. They will try to force them to renounce. While they live, there is hope."

He saw Mahmed look away now, far away, down past the city spires and walls at the great joining of rivers.

"Witter, hear me. You wished to go east and south, you said. The Danube and all its tributaries go there. Vienna, Belgrade, Bucharest, then the Black Sea. There you will be accepted in my country, if we can find our way alive. Have you changed your mind? Do you not wish to try it with me?"

"Go where you will," Witter said.

"This city was old when the Romans ruled. Your lost love changes nothing."

"She saved my life. She saved your life."

"I know." Mahmed completed the thought. "She has never harmed anyone. She has only tried her best to bring good to this world. And for that she is hated and condemned. But you cannot change that."

"Go where you will," Witter said again.

And then Witter was moving again, down toward the city; toward the split of rivers that looked like a three-toed foot, its bones great edifices of stone commanding the river.

"Witter," Mahmed said, behind him.

He stopped and turned.

Mahmed looked at him, his face stricken, sorrowful, almost childlike with anguish.

"For the Christians and for you and for me, all, Abraham is our father. Yet, I cannot go back into a Christian city. For I wear the face of my people."

Witter said, "And I wear the face of a Jew."

"You do not look so much Jewish."

"How must a Jew look?"

"Like a man. How must a Muslim look?"

"As one who fears God too much to tempt Him. I fear going to Passau, too. But go I must."

"Then listen to me now. Remember this well. If you leave this hellish place, make your way south and east to the fortified border town of Saleh, past Vienna but below Bratislava, where the Marcal

River enters the Danube. I will wait for you at the Marcal outpost where my cavalry was stationed. I will wait to see if you come."

"How long will you wait?"

"Until the snow melts in the high passes and the rivers run full. A new life awaits you in those lands."

"Once, that was my dream, to go there."

"I shall pray for Kristina to be alive, and for you."

"As I shall pray for you," Witter said back.

Mahmed pulled the little dagger from his cloak. It was rusty but deadly-slender, and Witter took a step back from the point. Then Mahmed flipped it around, and he realized that Mahmed was offering the haft to him.

"My friend, you shall need it. Do not forget, the Marcal outpost on the Danube."

Witter took his little dagger back. What a thing. It weighed so little in his hand, yet could find the life of a man through the ribs. Then Mahmed pressed something else into Witter's other palm.

"If ever you see Kristina again in this world, give her this for me."

Witter opened his palm. It was a chess piece of ivory, old and veined, a queen.

"Fare you well, Mahmed," he said. There was so much else he felt, but these words were all he could find.

"*Inshallah*," said Mahmed, and began to walk away.

Witter nodded, and turned on the path. He slipped the small chess piece inside a fold of his cloak.

He looked back once, halfway down that hill, hoping to see Mahmed just behind him. But Mahmed was gone. He realized he still held the dagger in his fist, and slipped it back into its familiar place, under the inner sash of his cloak where it rode on the flesh of his hip.

He had not gone a half hour farther when he was in the crowds, at the ale tents near the fortress, and the groups of ale drinkers were laughing about the crazy man who tried to stop the heretic cart near the Oberhaus.

But there was sadness to their laughter. He sensed it was more pity than mockery. They shook their heads in wonder. Their voices were low, covert, furtive. When Witter passed close by, he could barely hear what they said.

"A dagger?"

"Nothing is strange anymore. Many have gone mad."

"But to stop them with only a dagger?"

KRISTINA

The music was behind them now. The sounds of gaiety were gone. The cathedral bells were no longer tolling.

Nearing the massive gates of the fortress, as the cart rumbled through the staring crowds, she tried very hard to pray. She prayed fiercely but could not reach past her dread. Then she knew she was angry at God for allowing all of this and she knew the prayer had no glimmer, for her anger was leaden upon her prayer, as rage chills the heart. The closer the fortress, the greater her fear and the greater her anger at God.

It could not be him but it was—Lud, one of his arms under a monk's horse, the horse suddenly lurching, bellowing, dropping. The monk was tumbling into the crowd, his cross flying. The crowd was churning and the pikemen were shoving and coming fast.

"Lud!" Peter cried out.

Reaching both hands with his dagger through the cart slats, Lud cut Kristina's ropes.

But then they were on him from behind.

"Jump!" he urged, growling at her. "Jump!"

She stood in the cart and pulled at her child. The boy was struggling and trying to see the fight. Then it was too late. A magistrate climbed over into the cart with them. A sweep of his thick arm slammed her back onto her knees.

Lud fought them with his dagger, going wild. With the long pike shafts they beat him down, one tripping him with a shaft, and then they were kicking him. Lud grabbed a shaft and hauled himself up, pulling the other man down, but two more behind Lud beat him down again.

"Get this cart moving," said a monk. "Into the Oberhaus, move!"

Kristina heard Grit crying, and her slurred voice begging them to stop. And she blurted words from her own mouth in a gush that she herself hardly understood.

Then she could no longer see what happened to Lud, for the cart was moving again. Grit was trying to pray through her ruined mouth and the sound was of a hog at slop. A club beat Symon down from the cart rails and he made a moaning sound deep in his throat and Dolf said nothing, rolling his milk-eye down so that his good eye looked up at the sky one last time before the Oberhaus shadow closed over them.

The white-haired lady sobbed and moaned. Peter's eyes searched up at hers and Kristina did not know how to look, how to console, for in herself there was a growing blindness of desperation now.

"Drunken Klara," Peter said, "drunk as a broom…"

The shadow of the gates enclosed, shutting out the crowd, and then jailers in leather harness came to seize them. The end of the cart slammed down. The jailers reached in and dragged them out. Peter tried to fight them but they grabbed him up by a leg and threw him down hard. Kristina tried to reach her child and she was shoved down so hard on the stones that her head struck and rang like the tolling of bells. She tried to sit up and saw flashes of white light.

"Peter," she said many times; there was no answer.

"Unbind their legs," said a monk. "Kill any who try to run, for that is proof in itself of guilt."

They were shoved down through stone passages. She heard moans where they passed, little cries, begging. They came past an opening that resembled a pit. It was a large cell with many inside, perhaps a hundred or more. She could see many whitish shapes that she knew were faces looking up from down there. They made begging sounds as if they had forgotten how to speak, or their tongues were gone.

"God, nothing stinks like villeins," said a jailer.

"They take too long to starve," said another.

"They have meat in plenty," the first said, and he laughed deeply and disgustedly.

The monk said, "Blindfold these heretics, that the false outside world be lost to them."

And so they were blindfolded. Kristina stole one last look straight down at Peter before the world was shut out by the rag. He was still perfectly silent, but looking up at her with searching eyes.

"This girl had her binds cut," said the voice of one.

"Chain her," said the monk.

Kristina felt chains. Cold and jerking, pinching skin, agonizing her shoulders and wrists.

Then they were moving. She was dragged and shoved and pulled like a field animal.

She felt her chained arms go numb again, and her elbows and shoulders scraped the clammy walls of stone passages. She shuddered from the chill of the deep stone pit and her sobbing for her child did no good.

"Peter," she kept saying until a rag was shoved into her mouth. She gagged, trying to breathe, tasting filth.

She knew they went down in dark passages, she knew they were down deep inside the Oberhaus. They turned, went a ways, turned again, then down steps again, and down still more steps.

Kristina's bare feet tried probing the dark before taking each step. A hand kept shoving her.

"The ale and women will be gone. We are missing all the revelries."

"Please," Kristina tried to say through her gag.

Her feet felt a threshold. She perceived damp air and open space. On the air was a stench.

"Hurry on, you heretic bitch."

The hand shoved hard. She tumbled downward in her chains and her knees smashed into an edge of stone.

Please, God, help me please,...

She plunged forward and knew she was falling through space. For a terrible moment she weighed nothing and then all of her weight struck stone.

KONRAD

I t could not have been a happier, more blessed, day.

St. Stephen's cathedral bells had rung for hours, for Vespers and for celebrations, and for anything else anyone could think of. The Church-state was tolling its triumph from the highest tower over the great Imperial city.

Vienna was magnificent, but Konrad longed to return to his Wurzburg, now that the city was subdued. He had a plan to execute first—a plan that would shape the rest of his life, for the greater glory of God.

In the market square, well away from the cathedral, there had been a morning burning of three heretics and the smoke still drifted on the upper air. From his guest chamber in the castle tower he recognized the sweetly sick stench of burnt roast, the reason for burnings being far removed from places frequented by nobles and lords and clerics. He could smell it vaguely on the linen robe of his elderly body servant.

"Did the people enjoy the burning?" Konrad asked.

The servant was dressing him. Konrad stood with lifted arms.

"Burning, your grace?"

"You were there, I smell it on you. Answer me. Did the people enjoy the spectacle? Did they die well?"

The servant hesitated.

"Answer honestly," said Konrad. "I command you."

"Too well, your grace. They had been starved, and they were marked by tortures. Yet they prayed and sang their own songs together. Songs I had never heard before."

"You make them sound like saints."

"Humans only. The fire made their bodies scream."

"They were heretics, not villeins?"

"The charges said they had advocated against war."

"So they were burned for discouraging war, and not for warring against the Church-state?'

"Yes, your grace. I think. It is too confusing."

"And what of the people, how were they watching?"

"Quietly. With pity, your grace."

"Not jeering?"

"Some jeered. But not as it used to be. There was…"

"There was what?'

"Sadness. Many knelt and crossed themselves. And many said prayers, that God would forgive them."

"Forgive whom? The heretics or those who prayed?"

"I cannot be certain, your grace."

"Perhaps God should forgive the church and state?"

The servant froze and did not speak.

"So the heretics died well," said Konrad.

The old body servant had begun to show fear.

"They burn eternally in damnation, your grace."

"What if I sent you to the stake, for your pity?"

"Your grace?" The old man went to his knees in horror.

"Would you love the church better then?"

"Your grace, I do not understand!"

Konrad dismissed him.

A queasy mix, thought Konrad—heretic pacifists and revolutionary villeins all learning to read. And now came fallow fields and perhaps famine, too, and then the pestilence that ever came on famine's heels.

As a guest, he used the Imperial tailors and was soon dressed in new silks with gold thread brocade, artfully padded within the shoulders as his armor had been. New fine red boots with sole lifts and a gold silk bishopric full-length cape were made to compliment his taller stature. The length of cape and height of collar were determined by rank, and his rank was prince, the closest to emperor.

In Vienna, only Imperial tailors knew precisely how high and long to cut the exquisite material, for maximum sweep when in motion. The cost was ruinous but everything of the postwar empire was presently on credit, and the necessary displays of rank had never come cheap.

The emperor's box at Mass had been a place of honor, and Konrad, as honored guest, had felt his spirit rise into the naves of the great cathedral, with the sweet choir song and the nuns singing in counterpoint. Opposite him was the emperor's closest friend and ally, Ferdinand, the archduke of Austria, bone-thin as a prophet, with his perfectly trimmed beard and his lynx-trimmed waistcoat in the high Spanish style. Magnificent company to keep. And heavy with portent.

Later that day, after the Imperial victory feast and ball, he would lay his plan out to air.

No women were invited into the emperor's private stateroom. It was heavily paneled, dark, the walls covered with hundreds of years of paintings and icons collected by many generations of Hapsburgs.

Maximilian was listening to those who spoke, but not yet speaking his own thoughts. Konrad listened, waiting too, knowing what he would say, but in ambush for the best time to speak. He looked at the painted faces of ancient authority on the walls, men and women; most wore the same arched Hapsburg nose that centered Maximilian's bearded face.

There were celebratory toasts, to valor and honor and God-given victories, and Konrad felt the men of power assessing one another.

Ferdinand, archduke of Austria, pulled his pointed chin beard, looked down his birdlike nose, and said, "The shoe army, I called the villeins, not the People's Army, for we are the people, we here together."

"The shoe is on the other foot," said Maximilian. "But now we must wear it, too. We must use the villeins."

"The Church-state must be seen as strong," the cardinal said. "Villeins must be punished, I say, with years of hangings and burnings and other public examples of God's justice."

"Burnings are a great public tonic," said Maximilian. "Villeins fill our cells and burden our Christian natures. They hide in every field and ditch."

"I say let them starve," the archduke said. "If they do not return to work the fields, there will be famine, and they will come begging on their knees for our stores of wheat and barley. Let them crawl. Let them remember their station."

Said Ferdinand, "Those grain stores are diminished severely by this war."

"Estates cannot pay taxes without harvests," said Maximilian. "Taxes for armies to push the Turks."

"New taxes," said the archduke, "must be serviced by the labor of villeins to pay for the debts of purchasing mercenaries with which the uprising of villeins was crushed."

The gouty bishop smirked, his jowls quivering. "Therefore, our task now is to bring the villeins to pay for their own forced submission," he said.

"The villeins must labor to pay for their own chains."

There was laughter. Only Konrad did not laugh; he saw Maximilian watching him.

"Konrad?" said Maximilian, brow lifted in query.

The others all turned to look. Konrad felt the interest of the emperor, positive, and the irritation of the others, negative. It was a careful weighing to be balanced.

Said Konrad, "Starvation will not pay our debt. It will only rouse the sufferers and they will again be at our throats."

"Pity your poor villeins," said the archduke.

Konrad felt the sting of subtle mockery. As if he were a villein himself. He thought of his cousin Dietrich, something Dietrich had said many years ago; and he wondered what Dietrich would think of these arrogant weak men who held so much power over others.

"I have heard it said that the greatest folly in victory is to kick an enemy who is down, for that might give him the gift of anger, to rise back up and kill you."

"They are crushed," said the archduke.

The cardinal sneered, and said, "Shall we ask their forgiveness?"

Now, open mocking laughter, and Konrad's face reddened.

"Let us hear him," said Maximilian.

Konrad took a long, deep breath before speaking. He leveled his voice to reveal no sign of emotion.

"All commoners," said Konrad, and he had thought upon this and prayed upon it many days "all must see this in a different light—that they labor for a new day of goodness for all men. Or some such thing. We must invent a new convincing truth and publish it."

"For this they would all need to learn to read."

"Then we should see they do," said Konrad.

"And turn the whole world upside down?" said the archduke. "Is that not what they fought us for, in great part?"

Said Konrad, "They must believe they have won something, while being brought to heel."

"When we burn some, the others feel they have won life," said the cardinal. "We have dozens of birds in our cage for burning, and we shall let them out one or two at a time, to keep the people alert and chastised."

"Will a few burnings bring the hordes back to the yoke?" said Maximilian.

Said Konrad, "When I left my city, Wurzburg, I wished to burn them all. But now I have been shown by God a more iron-sure means of bringing them to heel. We must pervert their own will against them, and at the same time, convince them that the war changed us, softened us, made us heed their original list of twelve demands. Then we own them, as we did before, yet better than before, for they will work harder, believing their courage achieved much."

Maximilian smiled, flatteringly with amazement. "Konrad, your years at Wurzburg have put a sharp edge on you. You do surprise."

Konrad felt a thrill of validation, and forced himself not to reveal it. There was much jealousy at this table.

"What of Geyer, your godson, their apostate hero?" said the archduke, hitting a weak spot. "The reward has brought in so many heads that are obviously not his. Your monk in Wurzburg, Basil I believe is his name, pleads to be relieved of viewing heads."

Again, there was laughter. Konrad did not laugh.

"Veritas Press," said Konrad, "with its successes and its failures, was only a beginning. Veritas has taught me much. We must create a story of Florian's death, and be believed."

Maximilian sat forward with obvious interest.

"That would be useful indeed, to bury their late hero. Some still believe Geyer lives. While the hordes believe he lives, some may harbor hope for yet another uprising, instead of returning to work our estates."

"Villeins would not believe us," said the archduke.

"What say you, Konrad?" said Maximilian.

Konrad paused and looked at each of them, one by one.

"We are in the infancy of propaganda. We know now that a small lie is not believed. Also, a lie, to be believed, must carry flaws that put us in a partially unfavorable light. Then hear this...Florian Geyer was lured to a forest with promise of aid in new forces for the villeins rising. There by our treachery he was murdered. Such a great lie will work."

"But do we not sound cowardly that way?" said the cardinal with distaste.

Konrad felt something twist in his chest as he spoke.

"Exactly so. Thereby demonstrating our own honesty in confession, at the same time ending the folk hero story of Florian Geyer, forever."

Said the cardinal, "You offer the carrot but we must also have the stick. We must have fear by example. There are heretics at the bottom of this. We must have burnings."

Konrad thought of Sieger, beautiful gleaming white Sieger, his dead black eyes staring up woefully at him, his head impaled upon the villein's stake.

"In God's name, in every city," said Konrad. "There must also be many burnings."

KRISTINA

Before her mind regained itself, in time and in place, she was in Kunvald, and Berthold was there.

Her blindfold had been removed. She sat on the wooden bench and he was testing her. Berthold questioned her, taking the role of her inquisitor.

"You have been arrested for spreading heresy, and you must search your mind and your heart and respond to my questions. Are you ready to begin?"

Her time of training was almost done. She was leaving soon, and Berthold had worked hard to prepare her for her coming journey to try to bring the light of truth to the people crushed under the blight of ignorance and evil.

"Kristina, if that is your true name and not a lie, this is a court of justice, do you understand?"

She knew that this was only a means to train her, prepare her for what might happen out in the world when she left, but the fear arose in her like scalding heat crawling up into her throat. She had to swallow. Something was wrong. This voice was harsh and deep, deeper than Berthold's.

"A court of justice, or of violence?" she said, trembling, fighting not to show it, clamping her hands in her lap. "Why am I detained and threatened? Have I wronged anyone, do you charge me with murder, or roguery?"

"Your adversaries shall determine that," said another voice. She did not see who had spoken. But it was not Berthold's voice, and she felt startled hearing it.

"Berthold?" she said.

"Your forehead is swollen. Who struck you? Did the bestial men of your hereticals molest you?"

"Will you not obey Christ, and love your brother, love your enemy?" she said. "Why?"

"She seems in delirium."

Their voices were not known to her.

"Are you my adversaries?" she said.

"I am your judge. The emperor is your adversary. You preach in woods and corners and barns, but not openly. You teach reading and print words of heresy. Do you deny that your teachings encouraged villeins to demand equality with the Church and state?"

"God is love. Christ commanded we love one another. War is evil. All war is sin."

"Your stubbornness serves you ill. You and your fellow conspirators have held meetings in this new doctrine, and the emperor has decreed it must not be done."

"God has not authorized the emperor to make such commandments. In this he transcends the power that God hath given him. In this we do not recognize his supremacy."

"Child, we are fresh from a ruinous and evil uprising. If you had ever seen a burning, you would fearfully rue such defiance."

"I have."

"You have what?"

"I have seen…burnings."

Now she felt herself choke.

The more she tried to stop the tears the faster they came. But they were tears of anger, not of terror.

"She is indeed in delirium," said the voice she did not know.

Now Kristina realized she should be sitting on a bench, not at a table. Her head hurt. She had been blindfolded and shoved down stone stairs.

Her vision cleared.

"You are not Berthold," she said.

The man facing her across the table was not Berthold. His head was tonsure-shaved, his face a stark white oval shadow—framed in the black collar of his hood.

"Are you faint?" he said. "Is your mind clear?"

She was not in a barn in Kunvald, being trained. Berthold was dead. Long ago dead.

No...

She was facing a hard ascetic face. A hooded monk. He was questioning her and she was answering back, as she was trained to answer back.

Around her were stone walls and lanterns hung on iron hooks. Water dripped somewhere. The yellow lantern light danced on the wet eyes of men all staring at her.

"She dissembles," one face said. "She evades."

"We have not yet even shown her the instruments."

I have a child named Peter not with me who sings of drunken Klara, her face as red as a bloom...

Awareness came upon her in a hot vicious rush.

I am Kristina and this is not Berthold testing me, these hurting chains are real, and I am alone in a stone room with two monks, and much closer, close enough to smell, is a hairy man in leather harness, a magistrate or jailer. His big hand lies sweaty upon my bare arm. When I move, the hand tightens...

And realizing all of this—remembering who she was, where she was now—Kristina thought she might scream but she felt no strength of will to scream, for she was fainting; she fought it but saw their faces blur and then she felt everything fall away from her.

LUD

"Michael," Lud said.

The two monks were there from the cart. The cart sat empty at one end of the stable and Lud was hanging by his wrists behind him, in strappado, his feet barely touching the hay floor. The magistrates stood around him with their clubs.

"Michael what?"

"Father Michael," Lud said.

They hit him with the club, low in his gut. He stayed doubled up this time. There was nothing left inside him to retch.

"Father Michael," Lud said again.

"You had pox, a long time hence. How so?"

"Tending the victims of the pox." Just what Michael would say and yet be modest of the claim.

"Where so? What city? What monastery or abbey?"

"God is my witness, not you. My reward shall be in heaven, not by the conceit of claiming merits on earth."

"He evades."

They hit him from behind, in his left kidney. The kidney blow shattered his vision and he swayed.

"You say you are a priest?"

"Father Michael," he said.

They hit him again, as he knew they would. His mind worked to externalize this. It was necessary to suffer as if breaking from the pain, so that they would believe the words. Pain was a tunnel through which one must pass to the other side. There was no outside way around it. You could try and make a box around the pain but all boxes would break. You had to let them force you right through the center of the pain to get through it. On the other side was either release or death. There were dull pains and sharp pains. He feared the sharp pains much more than the dull, but they seemed to know this business and would likely save those for the next phase. Fear was the greatest pain of all, and he feared fear the most. He had to convince them he was afraid without truly being afraid.

"Do you know the prisoners?"

"No. Please, no."

"Priests do not attack monks with daggers."

"Have mercy. I did not mistake a monk for a mule. It was a mule that I killed."

They hit again. He vomited blood. It was a deep dull pain that his heart fed with each beat. He did his best to show fear. He begged and twisted and sobbed.

"More will kill him," a magistrate said.

"None asked you," said the monk. "But hold."

Lud swam hard against the fog.

Kristina…

If they found him out he would be put with the prisoners of war for execution. He needed to be put with the heretics. That was all his mind could hold. He was passing through the tunnel to the other side of the pain now. The fog began to smooth away the pain and he refused the relief, refused to fall into the miasma. This he had learned long ago.

Whatever happened, he needed to be with Kristina.

All of his learning time with Father Michael flooded into his head. All of their reading together, all of their debates. All of Michael's thoughts became his own. He forced Lud out of his being, lest he break under the blows.

"Priests do not attempt to free heretics."

"Christ commanded we love one another," Lud said. He said it as he would have put a knife in one of them. Knowing it was a thrust they could not avoid accepting.

"Christ and daggers do not mix," a monk said.

Lud felt Michael's spirit smile at this. He said, "Yet you serve the state, in the name of Christ."

They tore open his shirt.

"Scars. This is a fighting man."

"Or a villein posing as such."

Lud's mind raced to think what Michael had said.

"Defend me from their abominable darkness, O Lord. Let the divine light of Thy glory illuminate us that we may walk in Thy light."

"You dare challenge us?"

"Let Christ be my only judge," said Lud.

"What say you of infant baptism?"

"It is an artifice…" Lud tried to recall the rest.

"Artifice?" said the monk, as if Lud were insane.

Lud's mind found Michael's words more easily this time. "It is an artifice of man, not a communion with God."

"Artifice?" said another monk, aghast.

"It is a rite of the Holy Church," said the first monk, outraged.

And Lud knew he had them now. Like fish on a hook.

"Artifice, I say. Each must find God. No priest can come between."

The first monk took a knife from a magistrate. He came with the knife to Lud who, hanging by his arms, twisted his neck aside. Lud looked away from the monk's face, as one who will be forced looks away from the one who shall force the unspeakable thing.

Lud fell to the straw. His ropes had been cut. He lay gasping, throbbing throughout his being.

The monk with the knife looked down at him. Looking up, Lud could see the black hair curling from his nostrils and ears. The monk handed the knife back to the magistrate.

"If you are a priest, where did you take your vows? What is your order?"

With each beat of his heart, pain hammered through Lud's body. And yet his mind raced. *What would Michael say? What would Grit? Yes, what would Grit say?*

Then he knew. He could hear Grit saying it.

"Preserve us from the enemies of our souls," Lud said. "Do not trust in the flesh, which perishes and abideth not."

The monks stared at him with puzzled disdain.

"This man deceives us, but why? He fights six men with a dagger?"

"Surely he is mad."

"Or a fool. But he is no priest."

Or a fool, thought Lud. *Yes, a fool...*

"Priest or not, he goes down with the others, condemned by his own mouth."

KRISTINA

The cell was lightless to her stunned eyes, all black at first. She stood shakily and could see nothing. A foul stench compelled her to gasp and try to hold her breath, then her body rebelled and breathed it in. In the foulness was underlying bitterness, like rotted fruit turned to poison, the smell of slow death.

Her eyes began to perceive a dim glow from the far end of a long boxlike interior. It was a stone room and she looked up and saw that the light came from a long, narrow niche cut high into the outmost wall. The long niche was a slot for air, and the light of day came from there. It was a wide plank of blue sky suspended there high in the dark, and too small for anyone to crawl through.

Peter, clinging to her leg, said nothing. He reached up and touched her forehead wound and she flinched in pain. He kissed the wound. She held him tight.

This foul hole was nothing like the clean little dry cell beneath the Giebel castle keep. She had been put there by Lud, for her own protection. She remembered how she had thought herself forlorn of God and cast into a hellish pit. She wished she could take her child and be back there now. The hay had been fresh. The water had been clean. The people had protected her. She had been loved.

Here about her was the pit of the world. She forced herself to breathe, despite the stench.

Symon and Dolf helped the white-haired woman. Grit staggered into a corner and all sat down there together. Symon was limping badly now.

"It is a mistake," the white-haired lady's voice kept saying, between her gasping sobs. "A terrible mistake…"

"There is straw here," said Dolf's voice.

"Filthy," said Symon's voice. He was stretching now, limping in a tight circle as if desperate to escape.

Grit said, "Praise Him. Praise God."

For what? thought Kristina.

She reached out with her hands and found the opposite wall. The stones were cracked and uneven and damp. She pulled Peter to the wall and sat down in what felt like clots of greasy straw and strips of rags.

"I am no part of this," sobbed the white-haired woman. Grit tried to put arms around her but she would not be consoled. "I will not be with you. This is a mistake. I only meant to bless you out of God's pity."

Peter pointed up at the slot of air and light. Kristina looked up—surprisingly, she saw a bird there, looking down at her. When her eyes perceived the bird, it seemed to sense her awareness, and it vanished, flew away.

She knew now that the wall faced the south, and if she could look out she would see the Danube River, then the city beyond it. She knew because the fortress was on the north bank of the river and the dim glow thrown upon the floor was afternoon light, slanted to the left.

Her eyes followed the light. As her eyes gradually adjusted, now, she began to perceive something else. Peter saw it, too. He pointed.

Perhaps a dozen figures lay together arm in arm along the far wall. She had passed right by them upon entering. Their eyes glimmered like pearls hanging in the grayness, and they were looking at her.

And as if in the strangest dream of her life, a man's voice began to sing…

"We wander in the forest dark,
With dogs upon our track,"

Then a woman's voice came more sweetly, then another man with her, too…

"And like the captive, silent lamb,
Men drive us, prisoners, back."

Then all of the shadows there were singing…some weakly, some strongly. The melody was vaguely familiar, and then she was certain she had heard it sung in the passing city streets as a popular alehouse bawdy, the farmer bragging about how many times his cock could crow before dawn. But these words were serious, were sacred, were those of a hymn—yet a hymn she had never heard before now…

"They mock at us, amid the throng,
And with their taunts condemn,
And judge us suffer the blazing fires,
Where heretics to heaven do ascend…"

Kristina stared at them. The men were shaggy, bearded. They were all ragged and their faces gray from lack of the light of day. Yet their eyes were bright, somehow.

"Are you of our belief?" one said. "I am Hans."

"What is your belief?" said Dolf warily.

"We are Brethren," answered Hans.

"Brethren?" said Symon suspiciously. "Your accents are strange."

"We are Swiss," said a woman. "I am Elizabeth."

"Swiss!" said the white-haired woman. She got up and went to the cell door and beat upon it with her little fists. "I will report this and they shall release me."

Said Hans, "They know who we are, Sister, we hide nothing nor do we have anything to hide. We are in God's hands. We sing. We create songs of our own words, and trade them in turn, singing one after another, that God may never forget us."

Kristina could see their faces better now. Her eyes had fully adjusted and their faces were bleak from want, and many wore signs of torture, the scars of irons and fire, and she saw hands crippled into knotty lumps like wounds healed upon old trees.

She thought of her mother's last words: *"If ever you become too afraid, sing, and God will hear you."*

So against their fear they too had sung. Their spirits still survived in this unholy place, this evil, filthy place.

Said Hans, "We are farmers from Lake Zurich. Count Zwingli sent us to Moravia for learning, and we were caught here on our way back home from Kunvald,"

"Kunvald?" Dolf said.

"Yes, have you heard of it?"

"Kunvald has been destroyed," said Dolf.

"We were told that, yet hoped it untrue."

"It is true," said Kristina.

Elizabeth crawled forward and said, "Old Johannes?"

"All dead, they say," said Symon.

"We loved him well," said Elizabeth, "and Rita, and so many others."

Kristina stared at her. "You knew them?"

"Kunvald," Elizabeth said. "We were trained there."

"We were also trained there, as you, in Kunvald, and sent out to take the place of another group sent to Mainz, for they were…"

"Burnt?" Hans said.

The word lay on the fetid air for a long time before anyone spoke.

"Yes," Kristina said.

Then they crawled to one another and all embraced for a long time. Many wept. Some laughed with delight.

Said George, "We speak in Moravian here, and sing in Moravian, that our words not be understood."

Many names were exchanged:

Hans, George, Schneider, Elizabeth, Marta, Leonard,

Dolf, Grit, Symon, Kristina, Peter.

In a corner of the cell, Kristina was stunned; it was a homecoming, here in this horrible place. Their joy was alloyed darkly with the tragedy of Kunwald and those they loved there. It was almost too large a thing to absorb. A strange silence filled the gray clammy dimness.

In the stone corner of the cell, Kristina felt Elizabeth's hand gently take hers. Her voice came low, almost a whisper. "You are Kristina. Johannes spoke fondly of you. Where is your husband Berthold? Did he not lead you?"

"Dead, he was killed by man hunters."

Elizabeth squeezed her hand. "We were there after you, and Johannes feared for you, and for his daughter with you."

"Frieda," said Kristina. "We lost Frieda." Not knowing what more to say.

Elizabeth drew in a long deep breath. "I came upon Rita bathing poor Johannes one day, in the stream, and his back was... terrible. I turned to hurry away but they called to me. Johannes enrobed himself and we all sat and ate berries with our feet in the cool water. I asked if he were suffering with the hatred of those who did such things to him. He said that he was lucky, for vengeance is the burden of God to carry. When he felt bitterness or fear, when his back hurt so much he wept, he would thank God for letting him escape, for he feared they would have broken his soul, and his body was of such less concern."

Kristina closed her eyes and shuddered.

"Elder he sometimes called himself, half in jest, but never would Johannes let himself be called bishop. None shall have authority over the wills nor souls of others. Each must stand for what is believed, in one's own faith."

She thought of that fine old man, of his dignity and yet of what he must have suffered, and wondered how well she would endure, how quickly they would break her. Deep in her was hatred of them, strong with fear.

"Pretty Kunvald," Elizabeth said, as if dreaming.

And then, slowly, quietly, there were murmurs, and the singing began, and all now sang, hummed, made whatever sounds they could to the melody, learning the makeshift words as they went along, even Grit making her humming sounds as best she could.

"What can be seen from the air shaft up there?" asked Symon.

"We have tried but it is too high up," said Hans.

Peter went to the wall and was hopping at the bottom of it and Dolf went to the wall and hoisted Peter up as high as he could.

Peter giggled, peering out the long, wide slot. Kristina longed to hear what was out there. She felt a joy that her child could see the light of day, even for a moment.

"What?" said Dolf, "what can you see?"

Peter giggled and hopped down.

"What did you see?"

"River," said Peter.

*River...*such a normal word, so impossibly normal...

Kristina started to tear up, not with joy but with a withering sadness, and a refusal to accept this fate. The stone wall was reality now, and the cruelties inevitably awaiting them.

"Dear sister," whispered Elizabeth, and her trembling hand clumsily found Kristina's. In her palm, Kristina felt that Elizabeth's bony fingertips had no nails, and the little finger was only a stub.

Kristina recoiled and jerked her hand away. Her arms found Peter and she pulled him in close to her, tightly.

"Brothers, Sisters!" some of them kept saying.

"Ah, Brethhhhren!" Grit said, struggling to speak.

I will not let this happen, thought Kristina. Peter tried to pull free but she held on to him.

"Let us sing to poor dear Kunvald," said Hans.

"Yesh," said Grit, "oh yesh." And they began to sing, their voices shaky. The meter of the tavern song was slowed, until it became almost a chant, full of gravitas. With the slowing of the pace, Kristina felt the sincerity of the measures of their voices together...

"Thine holy place they have destroyed,
Thine altar overthrown,
And reaching forth their bloody hands,
Have foully slain Thine own..."

There was a clattering of chains somewhere. The half-seen faces went suddenly silent.

The cell door scraped open. A dull yellow lantern light filled the low stone doorway. There was a shocked silence.

Shrinking back, holding Peter tightly, Kristina glimpsed jailers; she gasped and saw the vague shadow of a man flung inside. The limp shape crashed to the stones in a heap.

"A heretic priest to bless your bawdy songs," said the round-faced monk with the jailers. The door shut behind him, and they were gone.

Some of those who had sung were trying to stir themselves to act, but they seemed unable to move but little. The shape in the middle of the cell floor moaned and stirred and struggled to roll over.

"Brother, who are you?" said Dolf.

Kristina saw the battered face move into the grayish shaft of light from the air vent.

"Father...Michael," said a voice Kristina knew, even as weak and torn as it was.

Lud?

She sat sharply forward, staring, not daring to believe it could be him. Her heart leapt, and still, even now, she was not certain, so torn and swollen was his face.

Lud?

Then her hands were on him and she bent closer and smelled his suffering and saw his eyes swollen shut and his cut lips and the pox scars and the strong, hard, still-unbroken line of his blood-encrusted brow.

WITTER

In the wake of the victory festival, Passau went into a dead time, like a hangover following a drunken spree.

Food shortages made the black market a thriving concern, and people who had hoarded money were hungry for news and novelty. He, too, urgently needed money for lodging and to make bribes, to do whatever he could do for Kristina, even to send word to her if possible.

The Oberhaus fortress towers loomed like the horns of a demon. It was a fearsome edifice commanding the river junction, and if she was there, imprisoned within that stone somewhere with the others, she was unreachable. He knew Mahmed was right—the *donjons*, the towers, were not for common heretics. He felt nauseated, imagining Kristina deep in the dark of some foul pit of terror. It would not be so nice as the clean cell under the castle keep of Giebel.

He walked anxiously and warily along the causeway with the groups of workmen and the trades moving there. He saw paths along the riverbank below the Oberhaus, paths used by many people on those lower slopes. He walked there on a rocky path, and when the sun was in the early morning sky, the shadow of the fortress, massive and moving relentlessly with the sun, came down the sloping bank and fell upon the river, covering the path far ahead and behind.

They were up there, somewhere, behind the ancient, massive, impregnable stone walls. Vaguely he could see air slits in the upper stone levels. They could be inside any one of them. Or already executed. But surely they would not waste them when they could be burned for public show of the might of the Church-state. So he chose to believe that they still lived.

Kristina was up there. If she still lived.

His chest went tight and he felt he could not breathe, staring up at the stone mass so like an enormous mausoleum. Men pushing a cart of firewood came toward him and so he turned away and went back to the city.

He found the Jewish quarter and walked past its gates a dozen times, but did not dare seek help there. It was so like Wurzburg, far removed from the city center of cathedral and castle, and the elders had just unbarred their gate following the quelled insurrection. The uprising had nothing to do with them other than to rob them. Looters had vandalized all their shops in the public alley outside their gates. Like a storm, it had blown through and now they came out, dazed, industriously repairing the broken storefronts and doors.

When he passed there, their faces tracked him warily.

Who am I? Who have I been? Who shall I be now?

The vague chant of prayers from within slowed his step. The faint scents of their food cooking made his mind reel back to his childhood. Despite his longings, Witter was unwilling to risk their suspicions and their rejection, as had happened in Wurzburg. He was not one of them.

Witter hurried his steps away.

Then, later that same day, hungry and without coin or any safe place to sleep, he found what he needed.

Two streets off the market square there was a big print shop.

Witter went to work there the same day that he proved himself to Davo, the print master. The bent-back old man wore silk and had white hair in his ears and brows and nostrils so thick it curled out into his white beard. Davo snored when he breathed and was astonished by how fast Witter could set the movable type and block the sheets for printing. But Davo was far more interested when Witter showed how cleverly he could carve woodcut illustrations.

313

"Good illustrations are gold," said Davo. "Especially for a special edition of another kind. You can sup with us and sleep in the upper rooms with the other printers."

Imperial announcements and proclamations were commissioned and printed by day. Witter was surprised to see the imprint of Veritas Press reborn, even here in Passau, and he wondered if the Veritas imprint had spread to other cities following the war.

"Monasteries Aid Poor Despite Villein Vandalism"—much of it was true, this broadsheet he saw. It was a new kind of propaganda: softer, much more clever than the old style of hellfire and damnation. Everyone saw that the streets were full of displaced homeless people and many children. The monasteries that had given them charity, food, and clothing had been sacked by the hordes. The tract ended with the brotherly love and goodness of the Church-state: *"Let all bear witness to how the villeins let starve the poor who so suffered the unholy war by villeins upon their betters and upon the servants of God..."*

At night, behind locked doors of the press house, Davo had much higher-paying work for Witter. The special edition Davo produced sold best with lurid illustrations. It was printed for the black market, based upon Adam and Eve naked in the garden, illustrating the hideous sexual practices of the serpent upon an unsuspecting Eve. Witter quickly did the woodcuts and earned real gold by creating an incredibly voluptuous young Eve, her flowing long hair just concealing the head of the serpent encircling her thigh, so that minds ran riot with their own heated imaginings.

"Brilliant!" Davo snorted, drooling in his beard.

"What about the Church?" said Witter.

"The monks are my best customers!"

The tract was sold as a "cautionary moral lesson" and many monks were indeed among those with coin who bought out the first edition, always coming to the back door entrance. People who came late begged for a second edition. Davo shared out extra coin.

It was exactly as Judah, his father, had always told him: *In their hungers, people rise or fall, yet never change.*

In the commoner market streets and in black market taverns a hot trade in stolen goods from big houses was done. That trade was dying fast, for the Church-state had girded itself with ranks of new magistrates who trolled relentlessly for arrests where bribes could be extorted.

With coin in his pockets now, Witter found better lodging over a tavern and he bought ale for thirsty talkers. He could find out almost anything that way, he had learned over his years of practicing the survival arts.

Jailers of the Oberhaus, he learned, came to a certain tavern on the riverbank below the Oberhaus causeway—the Raging Cock.

So many villeins were imprisoned now that many rogues of the street had been taken as jailers to tend the cells. There were dozens of them there, and he began to go at night and buy rounds of ale for the house. The serving girls there painted their faces and plumped their bosoms with rags, and groping them was very popular for lowborn men—the drovers and diggers and cutters and raiders and jailers and men of foot—all lonely men who worked hard and drank hard, often fighting one another for a hand up a skirt.

Far from the hurdy-gurdy noise, at a back table, the little jailer with no teeth bragged of the importance of his job. It was easy to get people to talk by flattering them, Witter had learned long ago.

The jailer told Witter that hundreds of prisoners of the vanquished People's Army were imprisoned and many had died of wounds and disease and plain starvation. This was known by the ditch diggers who had been impressed as diggers of mass graves in the forest field terraces beyond the Oberhaus fortress.

"The heretics are a different matter. We keep them much longer, and they try to break them before the burnings so they cringe before the public and repent."

"There were some I heard came recently in a cart."

"Them belong to me."

"A young woman with child among them?"

"Are you husband and father then? Did they run off from you to be heretics, that it?"

"I just saw them in the street, such a sad sight."

"True, true, too true. But heretics, still."

And so, Witter learned that the heretics were still alive, in the lower level of cells on the Danube bank of the Oberhaus, and that they sang every day, many times a day.

"What kind of songs?" asked Witter.

"You think they praise?" The jailer laughed and shook his head. "My heretics, they sing tavern songs, bawdies. Except they sing them slow. Tired and weak, you see?"

"Bawdy songs? Are you certain?"

"My singing heretics, now, that is what I calls them, they been there a long time. The bishopric remembers and burns one of them, from time to time. But you can still sometimes hear them singing, even from the trade river paths below the fortress."

"You can hear them?"

"Sometimes. The air windows carry over the river, when the wind is right. Bawdies sung by heretics. I am a good man of the Holy Church, and their bawdies make me laugh, even if I cannot understand the words. I know them tunes from the taverns, even sung slow."

"You cannot understand the words?"

"They sing in some Swiss tongue, or maybe Moravian. I cannot tell. But the tunes cannot be mistaken. The cock song. The girl's jug song. I laugh and laugh at my heretics."

The jailer grinned, showing his yellow gums, as he peered at Witter with his sly, little red eyes over the clay tankard.

With that, Witter slid a coin under the jailer's hand. "You tell me how and when they sing. And just where they can be heard, as you say. And I want to know their names."

"I do not know the names."

"But you can ask them."

The jailer winked. "Now speak plain. You know them. A father? Brother? Wife, maybe?"

"Nothing like that. I am a good man of the Church."

"I could make trouble for one who knows my heretics."

Witter felt under his cloak for his little dagger. His breath was suddenly hard to draw into his body. But the little man laughed and reached over and slapped Witter's shoulder.

"Jesting you, man, jesting."

"Forget it," said Witter. He started to stand up.

"Stop, man, I was jesting you. I like their funny songs. I listen to them. They lift my black old heart, they do. Sit back down. I want to help you, I do. I would even be persuaded to take them a loaf or two and a blanket even, if one were to make nice."

Witter slid a kreuzer across the wet table.

"Your business is your business. Maybe you got a bad cousin or a runaway wife, or sister. It is none of my affair." The jailer scarfed up the coin and winked and put out his gnarled little hand. "My name is Willy."

"Bruckner," Witter lied, and shook the clammy, bony hand. He wiped his hand on his cloak, under the table. "I have been on that road and heard nothing."

"Which road?" said Willy.

"Right along the river."

"The trade road, with run of broken stone?"

"Yes."

"Wrong path, friend. They do not always sing. And that is not the path I mean. There are many shortcut paths down along the river. I tell you, I am dry again."

Witter slid another coin across the wet wood.

"Strange folk. Me now, I would say anything. I seen what the monks have done to stubborn people."

"Do you assist in the questionings?" Witter asked. He had waited for a lull and tried to frame the question indifferently, but his heart was hammering hard.

"I am no tormentor." Willy shuddered and shook his small shaggy head violently. "Not I. Not that. Those men who give pain, they, well, the monks need a different kind to do that work for them. I tend cell is all."

"Do the tormentors drink here?"

"Not them. They smell of butchery, man. Worse than my cell smells. They are proud bastards, think of it, and do not like being called tormentors either."

"Where do they go for fun?"

"They drink with the knackers in a river tavern near the slaughterhouse, below the city. Anything can be bought down there. Foul people, they. I never look them in the eye if we pass in the Oberhaus. They do give me a fright, and I am honest enough to admit such."

"You said anything can be bought?"

"Depends. Not my heretics now, they are bishopric property. But common men, a boy or a girl, yes. But the streets are full of boys and girls these days."

"That is not what I mean."

"What are you really after then?"

Witter felt within his purse and fingered out three more gold kreuzers. He clinked them upon the table and saw Willy's red-veined eyes narrow with the joy of greed.

"In the prison, you say anything can be bought?"

"For good coin, within reason, if possible."

"What of mercy?"

"Mercy?"

"Can mercy be bought?"

KRISTINA

She had always thought of Lud as unbreakable. Now he was so vulnerable. Lud's life was precious, tender, like an anguish that must be soothed. He was badly battered but no bones were broken nor joints separated. Sometimes he moaned and Kristina was glad he could feel something, anything.

With Lud so deeply stunned, her hands moved upon him, searching for wounds, in a way she would never have done were he fully aware. His body was hard and lean and the cords of his muscles were like iron. He smelled of scorched skin and dried blood. She did her best to wash his wounds using her cloak hem soaked in the water of the bucket, before the water became too fouled each day.

Sometimes his eyes slid open, and once, when Grit was helping her, Kristina realized that Lud saw them cleaning the burn wounds on his chest.

"His eyes," said Grit. "He knows us."

"He is still himself," said Kristina.

Grit leaned toward Lud and whispered, "Lud, is Linhoff alive? Did he survive?"

Lud blinked, and then looked away from Grit and closed his eyes, as if hiding from her. Grit took a deep breath and Kristina saw her face go blank. Grit's mouth tightened. She wet the rag and continued cleaning Lud's wounds. Kristina said nothing. What was there good to say?

The group, which had lived here so long, told many stories of their sufferings—how some others from the group had been taken out for burning, and that those left sang to prepare for the time they too would be burned.

She held Peter and he kissed her forehead wound. It was almost healed now and she could feel a wormlike welt forming there.

"Years we have rotted here," said Elizabeth. She looked feverish, blanched. At noon, when the light shaft was strongest, Kristina thought she could see the bone just beneath Elizabeth's pale, translucent skin, drawn too tight on her skull, as if this were the land of the dead.

"Yet you still sing," said Ruta sadly. She sat alone, in one corner, apart from the others, as if proving she did not belong here. "But in what language is that? You sing them slow, but those are bawdy, vile, lewd tavern melodies."

"As you have heard, we sing in Moravian, and sometimes other languages we all know as well as we do German," said Elizabeth. "The popular melodies are used so they will not know what we sing."

"They would take out our tongues," said George. "Instead, we make them laugh. But we can sing our praises to God and lift our souls."

"From need, from faith, not pride," said George. He was a small man with a large wide face and kind eyes that often blinked when he wished to make a serious point. "We share our faith and our need for one another and for God."

"We have lost three in the past year," said Hans.

Said Elizabeth, "Sometimes they forget us for weeks or months, and then they begin taking us out every day one by one, and try to force us to recant our faith."

"You have lost three?"

"Two by burning. One taken by our merciful Lord during their torments."

"Perhaps we are dead," said Symon, "already in hell."

"Have faith, Brother," several said.

Kristina knew this cell was not hell, for in hell she would not still have her innocent child, and Peter was close with her now, clinging to her always. And she vowed to do anything—anything—to save his life, and to save her own to be with him to the last.

At least once a day, Peter would go to the wall with the air window and beg Dolf to hoist him up to see what was out there. All were hungry to know what the child saw.

"River," was all Peter would ever say.

For the first month—by Kristina's count of light passing to dark and then the slanting light coming again, crossing the floor— a wooden water bucket was replaced when a rock-hard stale loaf of bread was brought every two days. The single bucket served for every purpose of drinking and voiding and they took turns voiding in a corner and covering it with straw as best they could.

"Tell us how you began to sing," said Kristina.

"Yes, do, I want to know," said Dolf.

"As do I," said Grit.

Said Hans, "First, our elders, our old ones, died one by one. We were not singing to them. I wish we had done so."

"Then the children began to die," Elizabeth said.

Said Hans, "That was when we began to sing."

"And the torments?" said Symon.

"Please do not tell of that," said Kristina, almost begging.

"We must learn what we need to know," said Grit.

Said Hans, "George can tell it best. He has suffered most of all of us who still live."

"Torture is worst when it begins," said George. "But have faith, for when you feel you cannot endure it further, relief comes, the blessed hand of God brings relief, and somehow the pain dulls and even lifts. Then the pain is like a dream of pain. They watch your face for that time. They know it well. Then they will stop. For this mercy of God's relief I have made a song of praise."

And so George led the song, and all of them but Ruta, the lady from the street, sang together, learning the words as they went along, singing the phrases many times:

"How frightened I to find myself so yoked
A load about my neck that nearly choked

If thou hadst timely not come high
To bring Thy Grace to that lasting place
Of pain I would have sunk to die..."

Kristina clamped her hands over her ears and still she could hear them. Peter hummed and sang along with them as best he could and pulled her hands from her ears, wanting her to sing with him. At first he was making a singsong sound that she realized was the melody of the makeshift hymns being sung. He was learning their melodies, she realized, and she was grateful that it seemed to soothe him.

Sleep was a gray time of not sleeping and trying to keep her child warm. Her back froze but Peter stayed curled within the inside curve of her body, her knees pulled up under him and her arms around him with her threadbare robe open to take him in. Her shivering was often uncontrollable and woke him, fretting. Those were the times she wept silently, bitterly, to herself.

One dawn when she woke, shuddering, hating her life, her misery, she did not feel her child within her arms.

There was a small bird sitting in the air window of the cell. Peter was crouched under it, looking up, and the bird was singing. Peter suddenly leapt up, trying to catch the bird, far above. She saw a flash of blue wings and realized it had been a bluebird. The bird was gone.

Then she heard what she thought was an angel singing, sweetly, not with words but with sounds only.

It was Peter.

He sat down beside her. She sat up, astonished, as if waking in another world. The others in the cell were waking too, and some were rapt, listening with expressions of wonder. Peter kissed her healing forehead wound.

Kristina felt a rapture of joy pass through her. Peter's clear, impossibly high voice seemed as if it could only come from heaven itself. Perhaps God had sent the bluebird. She needed to believe that. It did not matter how much she doubted now, she needed to believe something good, anything good.

Then, as quickly as Peter had begun, he ceased. His singing ceased, she realized, when her own doubt contested her delight.

Kristina threw her arms around him, crushing him to her, and he squealed with delighted resistance, squirming free. He threw his arms out and spun around and all those entrapped here together reached for him, hoping Peter would run to one of them. Most often, he ran to Grit.

From that day on, whenever anyone sang, Peter sang, too. His voice keened high above all the others like a spirit lingering about the stone ceiling of their cell.

"God is merciful," said Grit, with less difficulty now. Said Symon, "Truly we are blessed."

"Blessed?" Ruta said. "Forsaken, not blessed."

Peter went over and touched Ruta's sorrowful old face, and Ruta broke into tears like a whipped child.

Lud was curled in a corner and for three days did not respond except to take water. Kristina watched him the whole time for signs of awareness, and pressed wet cloth to his torn lips and wet his tongue.

For days, Kristina gave Peter her own daily little broken piece of bread that Hans and Dolf together shared out. But then she was faint, and when Grit offered her own share, Kristina took it and devoured it in shame. It was like placing a stone in the mouth and she could not chew nor swallow her piece until she had waited for it to soften on her tongue.

When the jailer brought the water bucket, Ruta, the white-haired lady was often waiting at the cell door, clawing at it, beating the heavy wood with her little fists and shouting,

"Hear me! I am Ruta, a good woman of the Holy Church, not one of them! I beg you to hear me!'

Elizabeth and Grit crept over to the door but Ruta would not let them drag her away. The jailer said nothing. Ruta tried to clutch his legs but he shoved her back.

The jailer said, "My name is Willy. Sing."

They all stared at him. He had never spoken a word before this moment. He dropped something on the stones.

"Sing your songs," he said. Then he slammed the door. When the door was slammed shut, Kristina crawled to the door and saw that two loaves of fresh bread lay there.

Kristina took them to the pale daylight that filtered down from the air shaft, where dust motes twirled like fireflies, in and out. The bread was dark and fresh and still warm, and the aroma filled the close air around their faces.

"Praise God, it is bread," said Hans.

Elizabeth wept. "Fresh bread. And two loaves. God has heard our prayers."

They feasted that day. And sang longer than usual.

Two days later, the same jailer brought four blankets. He left them without a word. The blankets were wool.

Dolf inspected them. "Both stained with blood."

"Do not discredit such goodly charity," said Hans.

"We have a friend," said Elizabeth.

"But who?" said Hans.

"He said Willy," said Dolf.

"God is…our friend," said Grit, speaking with difficulty. The swelling of her tongue was reduced and her jaw was working again, and her slur not as bad as it had been. "God is good…and has sent bread."

They sang longer again, and the most ill and weak were wrapped in the blankets. When Peter sang his high incredibly sweet notes, even Ruta sang with them now. And Grit sang more and more, as best she could.

Over and over in their slow chanting melodies they sang the same phrases, sometimes adding to them at the turn of the moment. The thoughts were shared by all of them. The meanings were a kind of communion for them together, bonded as one yearning, in this terrible place.

If one ill-treat you for my sake
And daily you to shame awake
Be joyful, your reward is nigh
Prepared for you in heaven on high…

Peter lay against Lud like a pillow and petted his face like petting a big sick dog. The boy sang for Lud and sometimes Lud opened his eyes as if in wonder, blinking in pleased disbelief, then sinking back into himself.

"Father Michael?" said Dolf. "Why did he say that?"

"If he lives we shall ask," said Symon.

"I think he was on the rack," said Hans. "They breathe broken breaths that way, when they come from the rack."

"Will he live?"

"Perhaps. His body is hard and strong. They seem not to have broken his bones nor torn out any of his joints. But he must drink. His throat pipe may be swollen from blows."

Kristina's gloom returned and slowly sank in upon her, and her sense of dread was ever increasing, trapped here with her child, together. And worse, being here with the other condemned group meant only one certain thing. That she would be tortured as the others had so obviously been.

Dolf made up his own words to add to one of the songs:

Of such bad men fear not their will
The body only can they kill...

In a corner, day after day, Kristina tried to soothe Lud. Peter stayed with her the whole time, petting Lud, singing for him. Lud's breathing was much stronger. She made him take water but he could not chew bread so she wet it in her own mouth, softening it, and pressed the soft bits in between his broken teeth. Then, gradually, he would chew, and finally, with a moan, swallow.

"Lud, can you speak?" Kristina said. It was a gray afternoon and rain was blowing in the slit of stone that was their airway. She held a damp rag, wetting Lud's torn lips.

"Father...Michael," Lud said.

Kristina bent closer. "Father Michael?"

"Me," said Lud.

"Did he speak?" said Dolf, crawling to them.

Kristina used a corner of one blanket and water from the bucket and spent hours trying to soothe Lud's face, gently wetting the heavy scabs.

"By God," said Dolf, "you did try to help us."

"Kris..." Lud said.

Then Lud's arms lifted and wrapped around her and Kristina let him pull her close.

"Kristina..."

His quivering arms held on to her and she did not resist him. His face buried itself into the verge of her throat and bosom, and Peter snuggled in under one of Lud's arms close to Kristina and they were as close as one. Peter began to sing, so quietly she could almost not hear him. Lud's pained eyes began to soften as he heard Peter's sweet singing.

Elizabeth began to sing with Peter, and then the others joined in:

"But with thy love
Thou brought me near..."

As they all embraced, Lud's arms tightened, as if to release her and Peter would mean his death. Kristina felt something powerful coming from Lud, something she had never felt before in her life, held this way by him. She did not know what it was, only that she desperately needed to feel it within herself, and that she yearned to feel it more.

Holding them both, Lud shuddered, and then he wept.

They stayed that way a long time.

Then, with the light slanting lower from the window, the cell door clanked and scraped open.

The groomed face of a monk peered inside. Everyone in the cell shrank back and stared at the monk. The door opened wider. The monk had a piece of paper, and Willy the jailer held a lantern high for the monk to read by. A long thick club was in Willy's other fist.

Kristina held her breath, waiting.

The little monk paused a long, terrible time to heighten the fear of what he would say. Then he nodded.

"Foulness upon foulness," the monk said, pinching his nose. "Why would you choose to live this way, sunken into the filth of your bodies, and the darkness of your unrepentant souls?"

No one dared speak.

The monk now looked at the piece of paper, holding it pompously, officiously, obviously enjoying his power.

"The woman Kristina," he said.

Willy pointed at her. "There, with the man and the child."

Kristina felt Lud's arms seize harder upon her, tightening. Nor would Peter release her.

"The woman Kristina," the monk said again, impatiently now. "Fear will not protect you."

"That is her there," said Willy, pointing.

Lud wrenched his arms hard and Kristina felt herself shoved back, Lud pushing her behind him. Peter kept holding on to her.

"With your lies," said Lud to the monk, "you have saddened the hearts of the righteous, whom the Lord hath not deceived."

"What?" said the monk, astonished.

"Spawn of demons," said Lud.

"Who is that?" said the monk, surprised.

"That is Father Michael," said Willy.

Lud spit at him. "So much shit flies from your mouth, does it ever go back in? You and the pope, godless donkey dicks, dwelling up inside the evil monk-filled ass of Satan."

The group filled the cell with their sharp gasps.

Kristina herself was astonished; she had never heard such words.

The monk stared blinking, paralyzed with disbelief, and Lud was crawling toward him, cursing and snarling like a wolf on all fours.

"Unholy servant of Beelzebub, slave-mongering devil…" The monk unfroze and staggered backward with a cry.

Lud was almost on them when Willy shoved the monk back and swung his club down, hard.

WITTER

Even in darkness light dawns for the upright, for those who are gracious and compassionate and righteous.

If only all the beautiful words could be true, thought Witter. If only life permitted belief in such words.

He stood outside the Sweet Charity tavern. Fighting with himself, trying to make himself go inside there. This was nothing like the Raging Cock tavern of the common jailers.

The big slaughterhouse was down the river road, not far. He smelled it before he heard or saw it. Under low sheds, an endless stream of goats and sheep and cattle and hogs were herded by clubmen from different pens, inside through different chutes, one by one. The thuds of hammers and snarls of saw and whacks of axes beat the air. Animal screams of all kinds came in waves, and Witter felt dizzy with nausea. He wanted to turn and run away but would not permit it. This had to be done.

The Sweet Charity's signboard was a naked girl with great breasts and a butcher knife in each hand. The long brick house stood by the slaughterhouse on the river below the city—situated, no doubt, so that the vile animal slime that ran down a trough into the befouled waters of the Danube would not flow past the city.

This was the tavern Willy the jailer had told him about. Where the knackers from the slaughterhouse drank. Where the tormentors from the Oberhaus drank. So alike in their dreadful work.

Witter swallowed and forced himself forward. Just inside, the dimness was full of the smell of slaughter and ale and something

328

else. A hurdy-gurdy played somewhere and he saw men and women dancing in a reddish glare of many candles.

A fat greeter girl with black teeth came out of nowhere, and put a fondling hand upon his groin, startling him. Witter jerked back defensively.

"All needs met here in Sweet Charity," she said.

"Ale and a table," he said.

"Friends table?" she said.

"Willy, from the Oberhaus, a jailer," he said. "I drink with him at the Raging Cock."

"Take care, we got no limp dick jailers here," she said, and led him to a corner table. Her buttocks worked under her thin waist shirt. "Coin makes the man, you ask me."

He sat there and she brought him a jug of ale.

"Nothing else?" she said, bending to pour, and opened her blouse so that a round breast fell out almost in his face. It was powdered, the nipple painted red. "See anything you like?"

"A round for the house," Witter said.

"Big man, but coin first," she said, replacing her bosom.

He gave her two kreuzers, and she announced the round, and the house cheered.

Witter steeled himself, not touching the ale. It was hard to breathe, for the stench got into the very lungs, burning deep as if scalding him inside.

It was not long before they came to his table. Just as he knew it would be.

"I was born dry," said the first man. It was the standard demand for more ale, in barter for information. He was blond and his face was young and surprisingly soft.

Then an older man came. He had colorless eyes set too close together.

The two sat without being asked. It was surprising how ordinary they looked. Witter had somehow expected scar-faced toughs with leering expressions. Both looked like men of some working trade. Perhaps a father and son. It was horrifying to think that their trade was one the world needed and rewarded.

"She says you know old Willy?" said the young one.

"Good friend of mine," Witter lied.

"He is nothing but a jailer."

"Little bitch, Willy."

"Old Willy, he tried to step up to what we do, but no stones. He puked out his guts the first five minutes."

They laughed; low, dark-souled laughs, their eyes watching Witter for reaction. They terrified him and they had done nothing but sit here and talk.

Witter called out to the girl and ordered more ale. The younger man blew his nose on his cloak sleeve and took the big wet jug from the weary serving girl. He reached for her.

"You reek," the painted girl said. Sweat streaked her face paint and her blouse armpits were soaked. She stepped back quickly, and was gone before he could run his hand up inside her skirt.

"Sweet Charity," he said.

"All needs met, my red cock," said the older man.

"It takes coin," the young one said. "They go for the likes of this nice soft one here, who wears nice rags and buys rounds for the house."

Witter felt them staring, appraising him. Their hands on the table looked like the hands of regular human beings. Five fingers on each. Not the hands of monsters.

"Willy said I might find a little business down here," said Witter.

"Not one of them, are you?" said the young one.

"One? Of who?" said Witter.

"You want to be let in, to hide in a corner while we work? You want to watch, do you? That costs dear."

Witter felt a fierce sweat break out, burning his face.

"No, nothing like that."

"What then?"

"You see, I have a very bad thing on my conscience, and my priest in confession told me I need a great absolution for it. He said I need to buy mercy."

"Mercy?"

"Mercy, he says. We are fresh out."

They laughed their low, hard laugh, their eyes darting.

"Buy mercy for what?" said the young one.

"For condemned prisoners under…you know."

"Under questioning," the young one said.

"It is called questioning," said the older one. He was insulted. His close-set icy eyes blinked rapidly. "We are not devils. We do not lust for the torment of others. I do the work of God, nothing less."

"I did not say or think you wrong," Witter fumbled.

"Some call us tormentors," said the young one.

"Not I," said Witter, glad he had not.

"People think we are fearsome, and we are," said the young one. "But it takes a brave man to do the righteous work we do, for the monks and the bishopric. We are soldiers of the Church-state as much as any man."

"I am sure, I am sure," Witter said, fumbling on, as a man stumbles and teeters forward, stumbling faster not to fall on his face.

"You lie, man," said the young one.

"What?" Witter felt a panic.

"Willy told us you have relatives with the heretics, and you paid him to ease up, give them bread and blankets."

Witter's mind raced and saved him, yet again.

"We cannot help who our relatives are."

"True, true, I do not judge. My own brother was a villein in that stupid uprising. Now he is dead. Left a wife and six kids and all on me now."

"We know your heretics," said the younger one. "We hear them singing. They sing bawdy tunes, not hymns. They put foreign words to them but we know the tavern songs they sing."

"But when one of them is alone with us, they sing a different tune," said the older. "Yes, we know them well."

Said the younger, "I say we know them better than anyone who ever lived has ever known them."

The two traded a glance and shared their dark conspiratorial laugh, low and ugly, and now Witter was amazed that he had at first thought them to look ordinary. They did not look ordinary at all. He forced himself to stay seated and not get up and leave.

The serving girl with the black teeth and the big bosom came swishing back, eyeing Witter. She winked and ran a big red tongue across her lips, wetting them, but there was something close to hatred in her eyes.

"More ale?" she asked Witter, adjusting the padding in her bosom and ignoring the others. Witter felt embarrassed for her. She was somebody's daughter, had been a baby once, held lovingly in someone's arms. Now here she was full of spit and spite, pretending to like him.

"More something," said the older man, reaching under the girl's skirt. "This man says he wants to buy mercy. Now you take mercy on me, little sister."

"Go wish," the girl said, "or bring more coin."

She went swishing away, her broad hips grinding like hams. The two tormentors jeered after her.

"She is new. What a fine ass," said the older man.

"You would think the young bitch was Paulina," said the young one, "so high and mighty proud."

"Paulina?" said Witter.

"The great Paulina," said the older man. His eyes went soft. "You new here to Passau? She's the star singer of the rich, the hot lady of the lords, Paulina is. They say the court ladies watch what Paulina wears and dress just like."

"Me," said the young one, "I seen Paulina in her fine carriage once. I stood there when she passed and I like to swooned clean away, hard cock man as I am. She is that beautiful. Married to a cavalry officer, a high-ranker war hero, name of Ulrich, they say."

"Frieda?" said Witter, staring. "Frieda is in Passau?"

"Paulina, not Frieda," said the young one. "Who the cock is Frieda?"

Said the older, his face gone soft and dreamy, "If I had all the gold that ever crossed the sea, and all the silver, too, I would give it all for one hour with Paulina alone."

The serving girl went swishing by, just out of range, like a horse parading and daring to be caught.

The older one leaned across the table at Witter, and said, "You want mercy, mercy takes coin. The more coin the better tricks. But listen—we cannot lessen the anguish, but we can avoid crippling. Our skill is fine at body breach."

Witter stood from the chair. Every fiber was needed to control himself.

"How will I know you give mercy?"

"If they live long enough to be taken out for burning, brother, you know we gave mercy," said the older one.

Witter shuddered throughout his being, and found himself struggling to speak.

"Coin," the young one said, "we want mercy from want of that girl."

Witter pulled out his leather pouch and, in a daze of wonder and anguish, emptied out onto the wet table six more of his kreuzers. His desire to escape this place and these men was less now, as his mind raced with this new knowledge, and all sorts of possibilities suddenly unfolded.

They grabbed up the kreuzers. Some rolled onto the floor and they knelt quickly, grabbing at thee gold disks of metal.

Witter fled the place, out into the open air, heard the animals screaming at the slaughterhouse, and he ran and ran and ran.

LUD

"I am Father Michael, I told you…"

Torture startled the mind with the astonishing surprise of how much worse it was than could be set in expectation. There was the necessity of enduring the first shocks, so that they believed that the prisoner meant to resist. He could not fight back. There was no use in having arms nor hands nor knees nor feet nor teeth. All of those extensions of body were strapped down and manipulated and abused, to send shocks of anguish into the mind. The mind, startled, lost its way. Lud could not let that happen.

The monk's voice was gentle, almost serene. The monk lifted a hand to Lud's face and with two fingers peeled the eyelid back from Lud's eye so that Lud was forced to look into the monk's sad, seeking eyes, where red veins curled like the roots of blood trees.

"You cursed me and the pope. Perhaps once you were a priest. I despise you for forcing me to injure my own being, consorting with you, and with these stockmen, hearing you curse in this vile manner."

"I am Father Michael…"

"Priest? You are indeed a heretic. If you are a priest, convince me better."

They had taken him instead of Kristina. He fought to keep that fact foremost in his mind. They had done what he needed them to do. Taken him instead of Kristina. He had protected Kristina.

He thought, *what would Michael say?*

His mind was charged with all the things he had read and now a rush of words came forth, clearly recalled:

"They take such great delight in the Lord's Prayer, yet we must not forget that this prayer constitutes a part of our own mass...they call themselves brethren and sisters, I cannot recognize as wrong, but wish to God that this mode of address might become common among all Christians..."

"What was that babble?" said one monk.

"Blasphemy," the other said. "It is that Dutch devil Erasmus, his tract defending the rebaptizers."

They began again, doing the things that brought the loudest screams. He knew this is what they would do. But knowing it did not stop it or the sense of it.

Then, when all dignity was gone, when it seemed impossible to endure more, suddenly it was easier, and the mind withdrew from the flesh. They would stop to see if the mind still worked.

"Save your soul. Tell us of other apostates."

That was when the time came to tell them the lies that he knew they wished to hear. He could name his enemies. Their quills scratched paper and they would go arrest them and do to them what had been done to him. Or they would waste much time finding out it was all a lie. But they had to investigate, that was the beauty of it. Confusing the tormentors and turning their torments to his own purpose was the closest to justice that any condemned man would ever find in this world. They could make a person say anything. And that got them nowhere.

"Huber is apostate," said Lud, gasping.

"Who?"

"Huber of Geyer."

"Where can we find this Huber of Geyer?" Quill scratched on paper.

"With the army, scheming to murder the bishops."

"Murder the bishops?"

"Huber swore a blood oath to murder all bishops, one by one, using the army as cover." Lud thought of fat Huber looting and raping with his rogues, and his shock at being arrested in some tavern for heresy. Even in his anguish Lud laughed inside, imagining how Huber would fear these torments.

"Who else?" demanded the monk.

"I cannot say more."

He had to resist to be believed. He smelled the coals where the irons were glowing. He smelled his own suffering.

More pressure was applied.

"No more," he said. "Mercy," he said.

"Mercy is for the compliant of God."

"Goetz. Spy. Ambitious. Plotting new revolts."

"Goetz? He led the Gay Brights until he came to our side. And who else?"

"Ulrich."

"What Ulrich? There are many Ulrichs."

"Ulrich, Landsknecht cavalry."

"How does a priest come to such information?"

"Ulrich. Spy. Plotting with Goetz."

"This man lies. Commander Ulrich is a great popular hero of the suppression of the villeins. I saw him riding foremost in the victory parades."

"Ulrich. Plot to kill all bishops."

It was a beautiful circle. But the trick was that he had to hold on long enough for them to believe him when he finally gave them the lies.

The mind wished to surrender and so he retreated the mind from the hand, the arm, the face, the chest, the nipples, the groin, the fingers and the toes, and all the other extremities where they attacked the flesh. He brought the mind away, all the way up into its own island, and there it was remote from all the rest of what they did. The rest was far away now. The pain far away, like the glimmer of lightning far-off on a storm horizon. The bowels let go but he no longer controlled them.

"He shits," someone said, "we are losing him."

"I forgive you," Lud said, as Michael would have tried to say, knowing it would infuriate them; they wanted fear, not forgiveness. Forgiveness was sanity. He who forgave still controlled his mind, still possessed his soul.

Yes, he screamed. He could not stop that. And they expected it. If he lived, after this, the body might heal.

But Kristina was not here feeling this. That was in the center of it all. That was the rock upon which he stood. The storm raged all around that rock.

"His eyes glaze. He is broken," a monk said. "Evil has yoked him. But all must be investigated. Leave him there with the rest of them, until all is investigated and he can be burned."

KRISTINA

Peter floated beside her, waving his small arms slowly as one who is swimming. He glowed a warm golden glow and his eyes were loving and strangely wise and pearlescent. His hair lifted as in water, haloed in that luminous light.

Looking down, she saw her own body detached below her, asleep on the stone floor in the dimness, and the body of her child was curled within her body's arms there.

She felt her spirit rise, weightless. Painless. A radiance of light without need or fear. Her hair floated above her, and she saw Lud there on the floor and he was now trying to rise from his body. The verge of a glow shimmered about his head and shoulders. Peter was singing as he swam to Lud, and he touched Lud's body and Lud came floating upward. Lud glowed darker than Peter, deeper gold, with stains in his luminosity, but as he came floating upward, his being was cleansing itself, too.

His eyes were intense coals of light. His eyes delved into hers. Lud came swimming upon her, was swirling as one with her, and his light entered her being...all fear was gone and within him she was safe and her child was safe and all the harm of the world dropped away, sinking to earth far below...

Now the others were all arising...

They came twirling and glowing up out of their old husks, angelic, serene, joyous, and all mingled their light together and were singing as angels...they flowed into one light and together they were one radiance flowing out through the slot of the air vent, out into the darkness of night, out beyond the banks of the river, and over the river, lifting into the sky, toward the stars...

Then Lud's moaning awoke her. Reality made her choke, gasp, weep. Her dream had been childish, the escape of a weak mind into fantasy.

The cell around her was a stone trap of filthy straw and stench and vermin and misery, and everything her eyes now saw in the dimness was real.

She awoke slowly, in a dull lethargy from the dream. Then, the waking became a force of dismay, being brought out of heaven back to this place. Her fear came like cold dirty water, flooding up in her in one sudden rush.

Now she sat up and remembered...

The monks had come and called for her but Lud had done wild things to make them take him instead, and she had done nothing to stop it. She had been relieved, smothered in her own dread. When Lud was gone she had grieved. The others had sung but she did not sing with them. She did not deserve the luxury of song nor prayer.

Then, sometime in the deep of the night, the jailer had thrown Lud back into the cell.

"His own fault," said Willy. "I gave the least blow I could, and did not break his skull as I might have done. But the others, they went hard on him. His own fault."

The jailer dropped something on the floor. The door groaned closed. Two bread loaves lay on the stones.

Kristina held Lud, not knowing what else to do. He was limp. Like hard wood steamed by the carpenter, to bend upon a form, Lud's body had no rigidity, no will within itself. But he lived, he breathed.

Dolf crawled over with Symon, and they praised Lud. "You are a man. Indeed a man. I never saw such a one."

"He cannot hear you," said Kristina.

"Is he dying?" said Symon.

"I do not know," Kristina said.

And they had crawled away.

There was a narrow band of yellow morning light filtering down from the air window. She looked up there, the only break in this foul hole of stone.

Why this? Why, God? Why spurn us so? I will no longer believe in you if you are so cruel…

Again, the others began to sing, in their slow chanting drone, the old familiar melodies, sometimes adding new words. Dolf sang them a new bawdy that praised Lud's courage, and they took turns making new songs, and in this way they passed the time and cheated their terror. Peter sang the melodies, not the words, in his high sweet voice.

The next morning they could not wake Ruta. She was curled in her corner like a child asleep, and she was dead.

They prayed for her soul and sang for her soul, and for their own, until Willy came with the water bucket for the day, and they told him.

"She is dead, free, and gone to heaven now."

Willy shook his head, poked Ruta, then took her by her pale little feet. "If they go sick in here they do not last long. No one knows why."

The jailer dragged Ruta by the feet and her dirty gown came up over her legs and Dolf stood angrily.

"Can you not lift her like a man?"

Willy spat, but he lifted Ruta up and took her out.

Said Hans, "What was her crime?"

"'May God bless you,' she said," said Symon. "When our cart passed in the street."

"And for that she has died," said Kristina.

"She died," said Dolf, "because the world is evil."

After that they were very quiet for a long time.

WITTER

"Ibrought my board with ink and paper, but where are we going?" said the man walking beside Witter, down the causeway, across the Danube Bridge. He was Gunther, a lute teacher hardly taller than one of his instruments. Gunther wore a blue velvet suit suitable for a large child, and his stride was so short Witter minced his steps, his gangly legs shuffling to slow his pace. In both arms Gunther carried a writing board with a compartment for ink and pen and he stumbled with an awkward grasp. Witter had his own writing board, too.

"Let me carry your board with mine," said Witter.

"Gratefully." Gunther handed it over. "But I do not understand exactly what you need from me."

"Your ear was good enough to steal the Parisian chansons on one hearing at the theater for printing at our press, and you say you need the money, and I will pay."

"Yes, yes, yes, I will do my best."

They crossed onto the river road where tradesmen moved with their carts and wagons and drays.

Gunther stayed closer to Witter now. "I do not like being jostled here among tradesmen and rough sorts."

"Stay close to me," said Witter.

The Oberhaus loomed ahead.

Said Gunther, "Let us hurry past, please."

"That is where we must wait to listen," said Witter.

"Here? So close to the Oberhaus, with all the smells?"

In the massive shadow of the fortress, at the north corner under the walled towers, Witter found a wide flat rock where they sat just off the road. High above there were air windows, long narrow slots in the stone, and Willy had told him that at this end was where he should wait and listen, for almost every afternoon, they sang and sang and sang.

Witter loosed the leather bindings and opened both writing boards and gave one to Gunther. Then they both waited, boards open on their laps. Witter held the writing board and Gunther shrugged and took out his ink and quills and blank paper. The paper on both boards rippled in the breeze from the big river.

Gunther kept looking up at the great towers and walls of the Oberhaus. "Can we move away, please?"

"No, this is where we must sit."

The afternoon sun was glaring across the river. The passing river barges and fishermen and the passing tradesmen traffic on the road, almost all, glanced up at the fortress in passing.

"What now?" Gunther kept saying.

"We wait and hope to hear singing and you transcribe it and I pay you if we hear it or not."

"Singing? From the road traffic?"

"No, from the fortress above us."

"Who has heart to sing in such a place?"

"Wait and you shall hear. I hope."

Wagons rumbled by, lifting dust. Gunther sat perched on the rock beside Witter, and babbled nervously about music and transcription.

"It is not like reading words, no, not at all. Only professionals understand how music can be notated, paced by the *tactus*, the pace of the human heartbeat. I write in white mensural notation, as do musicians of court and church."

Witter hardly heard him. His ears strained for any sound of song. He heard birds. He heard someone on a passing barge. But for a long time he heard nothing from the walls of the Oberhaus above them. But, just when he was giving up, thinking of leaving, he heard them.

"Is that them?" said Gunther.

Tremulous, earnest, sweet, it came distantly.

"Yes," Witter said, closing his eyes, "that is them."

He imagined them clinging together up there in a hideous stone room knowing torture and death was all they could hope for. Yet their voices came sweetly, bravely, and he felt a bitter regret that their spirit was not in him. Such a spirit had been strong in his father and mother, but not in him. The strength of his mind was not enough.

"Perhaps a dozen different voices," said Gunther, listening. "Not very good. Coarse. All but one female. The high voice rising above the others…"

Witter heard her, too, and without doubt he knew that was Kristina. He had heard her sing often before, through the years, and marveled at the beauty of her song, the childlike innocence and clarity of it. Yet now her high notes sounded wounded, still beautiful yet heavier, like a bird unable to fly, freighted with woe.

And yet she lived. She could still sing.

Gunther's pen began scratching on paper.

"Interesting, a common bawdy melody," said Gunther, "but sung much slower…with a slow tactus and weightier beat to the spirit. And the words are sung in some other language. Not German, I understand only some of them."

"I will fill in the words. Transcribe the melodies."

"Everyone knows that one already. The farmer's cock crows many times before dawn. But it is a challenge to catch their measure of time and beat."

Gunther went on scratching the strange symbols on paper. Witter heard the words being sung, rising and dipping on the air as if falling from the stone wall up there, falling like soft rain, and he knew they were Moravian. He wrote them down.

Carts and road traffic slowed, for others heard them, too. People blinked and harked and looked around and some pointed up at the Oberhaus walls. Some shook their heads in wonder and some just looked away and went on. Some laughed.

"Those are the cells of condemned prisoners, are they not?" Gunther asked, writing. He had a big smile on his face. "So ironic."

"Heretics, fodder for profit," said Witter. "For a novelty broadsheet. Just keep transcribing."

"Heretics singing bawdy songs," said Gunther. "I am sure that will sell fast, when they are burned."

"Exactly," said Witter.

But Witter knew the slow chanting words were hymns.

He knew that they sang of their hope for mercy and their faith in redemption in the next world, even singing of their torments and of the fire that would burn them and send them to eternal rewards. He had heard many of the words in years of singing at Giebel, and he now heard new ones, too.

Hearing their pleas in song, heartfelt and sincere, made Witter feel sick with fear for them.

They were up there, and there was nothing he could do to get them out. Kristina was up there behind that stone mass, and he was down here in the hot sun on this river road, and she might as well have been on the moon.

"Five songs," said Gunther, when the singing had finally ceased. "I got them all. All familiar melodies, but they do sing them with a different tactus, a varied arrangement."

"And you got them all just as they sing them."

"I did, exactly."

"I will pay you one gold kreuzer for every song you transcribe, if you come out here in the afternoons."

"Then I will be out here often."

Witter took Gunther's sheets of transcribed paper and paid him. They went out on the road, avoiding a train of wagons and mules.

On the bridge back to the city, Witter looked around once more at the Oberhaus. He had waited to the last to ask one more question, for it was important, and he was not sure how to inquire without arousing suspicion.

"Have you ever played for Paulina?" Witter asked.

"Me?" Gunther laughed. "I play at the high theater, for lords and ladies, for the likes of Paulina? Dear sir, she is as far above me as an eagle is above a frog. Paulina is noble, you know."

"I did not realize that."

The man sniffed and winked, nodding.

"It is an open secret that Paulina is the child of a duke, from another unnamed country. That gives her the exotic touch, you see. And she married a lowborn man of horse who has risen magnificently through the ranks by valor alone. She even went with him to the war. Did you know she sets the style for dress among the noble ladies? Even the duchess of Passau is seen often in her company."

"Marvelous," said Witter.

"Ah, Paulina," sighed Gunther, "Paulina. If only I were a rich man and could search the land for a Paulina of my own."

"Yes, Paulina," said Witter, carefully placing the music transcriptions into his writing board.

Paulina, so beautiful, with vileness deep in her young eyes, who had threatened to expose him as a heretic.

Paulina, who had promised she would see him castrated and burned should she ever see him again.

Paulina, now married to a renowned and powerful professional soldier, duelist and killer. Paulina, who now consorted with the rulers of this city and set the fashion. Paulina, as fearsome in her way as the Oberhaus itself. Paulina, star of the high theater of Passau.

In the print shop, alone that night, Witter worked through the hours. He matched words to transcription, making sense of it on a woodblock, setting type to finish it out, working the press single-handed. By morning he had what he needed.

Frieda, you vicious bitch, carved from ice…

Good seats for the big weekend performances were a month's pay for a top guildsman, yet were sold out weeks in advance, months in advance. Still, for enough coin on the black market, the best seats could still always be had.

Witter had bought a seat as close to the stage as was possible, without noble rank.

LUD

Earlier that day, Willy the jailer had come to the cell with two monks. When they left, the others gathered around Hans, praying with him, hugging him, sobbing for him.

"Hans is to be burned in three days," explained Elizabeth to everyone. "They offered beheading if he recanted but our good brother is determined. In the city square at the festival of St. Ignatius, he will be freed to rise to heaven and be with Christ our Lord."

Kristina crouched in a corner and wept. Lud tried to reach her and comfort her with his rough, awkward hands, and she sensed he feared touching her too intimately.

"Kristina," whispered Lud, "sing for him. Do not increase his fear by your own fear."

Only Peter would she permit to touch her. Grit tried, and Kristina pushed her away as well.

Lud tried not to look at Hans then. So he was surprised, when Hans came over later and sat with him. The sunset light fell from the air window like a bar of gold metal melting on the filthy stones.

"I came to tell you farewell," said Hans. He was trying to smile and make light of it. Lud saw through that. It was very common, when men wished to mask fear. "They have had enough fun with me. Now they will have a carnival with free ale, tale-tellers of war heroes, wire-walkers, and I will be sent, they think, to hell. But my smoke will go straight to heaven. But first, will you repent? Will you take Christ as your Saviour?"

"Do not do it," said Lud.

"Do not do what?"

"I see your fear. I know why you came to speak with me. It is not to save my soul, or whatever a soul is supposed to be. They will behead you instead of burning, if you recant."

Hans looked appalled, and said, "And go to hell for all eternity?"

"You sing about God being so forgiving. Recant."

"You do not understand, Lud, my brother."

"We are not brothers, but I understand fire and sword, and of those I know that sword is better."

"War has cheapened your spirit. Beware the deceptions of the devil. You have been in much war, I know. Only love lasts. All war is sin."

"Once in war, a man has no choice."

"There is always the choice not to kill."

"Never mind then. Fine." Lud tried to turn away toward the wall. His body ached when he moved and he was stiff, but movement brought jolts of pain. He did not want to have this man near him, this man willing to be burned.

"Lud," said Hans.

"Go preach to someone else."

"Please, I need your help," whispered Hans.

"Go badger your brothers and sisters."

"I do not know how to share it without weakening them when they are already weak from hunger and fear. But I am very afraid of the fire."

"Recant, man," said Lud again, "and be beheaded."

"You know I cannot do that."

"Then what? I see the fear in your eyes. You are a bad example, to be such a hero to these here with you."

Hans frowned. "Bad? By what means am I bad?"

"Your pride in being brave at being burned is a bad example. You take pleasure in it."

Now Hans pressed closer, and rubbed his grimy face with his grimy hands. His beard overflowed his chest and gray hair caught the gold light of sunset.

"You see me well. Help me endure. I do not want the others to hear this, to share my fear."

"You will not listen, man," said Lud bitterly, sick of this, wishing he could knock sense into the man; for he liked Hans, and respected him, and saw bravery in his fear.

"Agony," said Hans, now almost whispering. "I have seen even the best ones suffer so when they burn. I cannot sleep for the fear, now. Fear of the agony."

"Use the smoke," said Lud, his voice low.

"Use what?"

"Drink deep of the smoke," whispered Lud. "Forget your shouts to God and all such ways of distancing fear. Use the smoke."

"I do not take your meaning," Hans said, but his face bent closer and his eyes were eager and questioning.

"When they light the hay beneath the wood, do not turn away and hold your breath. Take it in. Take all the smoke into yourself that you can. It will make you cough but keep taking the smoke deep, for its poisons will pass you out of mind, and your mind will be hidden from the anguish of the body as the flames reach the flesh. Do not waste time singing and acting the hero and shouting your praises to God."

"But it is my last chance to witness my faith."

"Maybe that is another deception of the devil. You claim you shall see God soon enough anyway."

"Take in the smoke?" Hans said hopefully.

Lud felt sorry for Hans now. Hans was in a trap of his own making and needed help getting out. The price of being a hero was always higher than advertised, and then one found there were no heroes in the world anywhere.

Patiently, Lud whispered, "The trick is to hide the mind from the body. Make the body go far away."

"Only love lasts," said Hans.

"Many say that," Lud said.

"Because many know it, even if they cannot live it."

"I would give anything if that were true," said Lud. "But we are trapped and there is no escape, except in fire."

"If you could escape this place, where would you go?"

"Where…I would be wanted."

"You are wanted here," said Hans.

"Drink deep of the smoke," said Lud, "until you are nothing but smoke. And then you are free. Never again can they harm you."

With eyes sad and showing fear, Hans looked at Lud, and then he shook his head and crawled away.

WITTER

With nightfall, the grand high theater of Passau was like a deep bowl with benches in the bottom below a wide stage, where many lanterns hung from chains, throwing a gold light upon tapestries and the lower sections of gilded boxes above the common seats. It thrummed with low, excited voices.

Perhaps it was the noontime burning that had invigorated them all. Or perhaps it was the expectation of Paulina returning to the stage, after her patriotic sojourn with her valiant husband in the Imperial Army crushing the uprising of villeins.

Witter had seen the burning earlier that day.

He sat now in the front row of commoner seats and waited for the curtains to part and the performances to begin. The floor lanterns were all lit. The flames dancing inside the glass made him think again of the spectacle at the stake.

Witter had gone to the carnival in the city square. There were stalls and racks of new broadsheets exploiting all the carnival acts. And the new Veritas Press had its own stall, with prayers for the victims of war. Witter perused some of them, appraising the new tact of the Church-state:

We are all brothers in God and in patriotism, nobles and commoners all, and we long for the day when love triumphs over want, when we all work together again in the harmony that made our people so great...

He had read the execution notices that a heretic was to be burned, and he worried that the heretic to be brought out in a tumbrel cart from the Oberhaus would be Kristina. Standing in the shifting crowd, as it pressed ever deeper, he had been afraid of what he might do if it was her. He would either run away or he would fight his way to the stake. His hand had been inside his cloak, sweaty fingers on his dagger.

Then the cart came and the crowd moaned and he saw who it was. Relief went through him like a flood of wine.

It was not Kristina.

The condemned was a starvation-shrunken bearded man, a wretch bent under chains and humbled by terror that Witter sensed; the man strove to hide fear with all his remaining strength. He was braver than Witter knew a man could ever be. It could not be that the man was resigned and did not care, for knowing of the fire soon to be lit would make anyone care.

"Hans Betz," was the name the monks announced, reading his charges of heresy.

But the vast crowd was strange. They were fresh from the ale stalls and carnival acts—minstrels, jugglers, the fire-breathers and wire-walkers, and, the most popular, the Miracles of the Bible spectacle of half-naked dancing girls of Solomon's Harem. For two kreuzers, people could enter another tent and witness, it was said, the unspeakable carnal practices of Turks upon Christian women captives.

Still, today, the stake was where most people waited.

Witter saw the wood stacked by laborers around the tall oaken stake and then the hay straw packed diligently underneath the stacked layers of wood, with long rods, and he realized that the people around him did not jeer. As time passed, they pitied the man. He was chained there while the hay was packed in. He had a long time to watch and wait. There seemed a collective sadness; reverence, even. The carnival revelry went on in the background at the striped ale tents and show stalls, but it had no effect now. Perhaps it was the nearness of the misery of war, Witter thought. Perhaps it was the sad humility of the man himself.

"May God bless," some scattered ones said, covertly with covered mouths, and the magistrates did not try to arrest any of them.

The monk prayed with a queer officious pity, blessing the condemned man, and the victim shook his head and said something Witter could not hear. The monk nodded to the hooded executioner who lit a taper from a lantern.

When the straw was lit, the crowd gasped, smoke billowed out, screening the man from sight, and when Witter forced himself to look, the flames were coming up but the man hung slack in the chains, head down.

Afterward, Witter heard many in the crowd saying it was a miracle of God's mercy that the staked man seemed to pray with head down. When the smoke billowed, he did not scream and struggle terribly as many others at the stake had been seen to do when the flames burned away cloth and hair and the rest.

Witter could not bear the thought of Kristina at the stake. The sense of urgency, of what he was going to try to do, was driving him harder and harder now.

Now it was night, and he sat in his bench down front in the high theater. He clamped his hands on the leather-clad folder in his lap. All around him, excited people in their best finery chatted, gossiped, and read broadsheets in the lantern light from the stage.

Witter sat there feeling as alone as ever, as isolated as ever, always the stranger pretending to be one of the others. He found solace, thinking of the words of Maimonides, his old friend, the favorite of his father, Judah—

"One should see the world, and see himself as a scale with an equal balance of good and evil. When he does one good deed, the scale is tipped to the good, he and the world are saved. When he does one evil deed, the scale is tipped to the bad, he and the world are destroyed."

As the stage curtains drew open and the crowd laughed and hissed, Witter sat frozen, staring, sickened to his core.

The public burning had been a good opener for the play tonight. Though it was early fall and not Easter, an Easter play was performed. The Easter play from Redentin was not the light comedy of French farce, as Witter had expected.

The performers sang and portrayed Jews in grotesque caricature. They were painted and masked in demonic guises, hooked noses like crow beaks, cringing postures, creeping about and scheming. Paulina was dressed as a spirit of goodliness, a heavenly angel. At first she was harried by the Jews, then she bravely resisted them.

Witter forced himself to sit still and not draw notice. It was not hard to follow the simpleminded propaganda.

The Jews fear that Christ might rise from his grave as predicted by Scripture, proving he is indeed the true Messiah. Pontius Pilate is solicited by the Jews to detail Roman soldiers to guard the grave. At the moment of resurrection, all the mighty prophets appear—warlike and dressed as soldiers of the Church-state—as Paulina the angel summons them with singing. Lucifer, the most powerful Jew, gathers all the Jewish devils around him. A wild struggle ensues between good and evil forces. The good, of course, being the blond folk and the evil being the dark folk. The blond folk are also better singers, no mistaking the good from the bad. And none was more blonde than Paulina herself.

At the climax, the audience cheered most wildly, leaping to their feet, when the Jews were driven out and punished. Paulina, the angel, was foremost in singing and driving out the hideous Jews with the power of her irresistible beauty and her voice.

The applause was interrupted by Paulina herself, bowing, and rising up with a finger to her pretty red lips.

The crowd hushed all at once.

Paulina said, "May God preserve his brave and righteous excellency, the duke, and his greatest treasure, her most beautiful and brilliant excellency, the duchess!"

Now Witter saw everyone looking up at the gilded tier of box seats to the right and above the stage. All around him, people clapped and cheered as a bejeweled couple stood—an unremarkable-looking man and woman, except for their lofty perch and their adornments.

The glittering couple returned Paulina's bow with nods. And the duchess blew Paulina a kiss and Paulina bowed again, more deeply.

Now Paulina beckoned to the audience below the stage front, at her feet, and up stood a man in dress cavalry uniform, red with white piping and high collar. Witter recognized him. It was Ulrich. The applause nearly brought the house down. Even the duke applauded from his box.

Paulina blew a kiss into the air where it seemed to float like a butterfly over the audience, and several men pretended to reach for it and pluck it from the air.

Witter stood with all the rest and stiffly clapped. The leather-clad folder almost fell from his lap, half forgotten, and his hands caught it.

Paulina came back out to great applause and, by demand of many thunderous ovations, she again sang the part of the heavenly angel summoning all the prophets and denouncing the Jews.

And standing there feeling like a fool, Witter thought:

Nothing has changed. Just because people can read now, and the compass navigators have circled the earth, and people have grudgingly accepted that the earth is a ball and not flat, and now know where the sun goes at night, still, nothing has changed. People can read, yet more than ever, they hate and they fear all outside themselves.

Outside the high theater, a light rain was falling. Witter stood with many other men, back from the carriageway entrance, where men hoped to glimpse Paulina up close. But there were not many waiting tonight, knowing her carriage curtains would be drawn against the wet.

Witter kept the leather-clad folder under his cloak. Carriages came out one by one. He knew hers was red. Black horses. Then finally the red one came out, and Witter stepped in the way.

"Hold there!" the driver shouted at him. The black horses stamped, pulled up from running him down, and the iron wheel rings scraped the cobbles.

"Frieda!" shouted Witter.

For a moment, the rain curtains in the coach door parted. Witter caught a flash of Paulina's face staring at him, then the face of Ulrich, frowning. Ulrich was in dress uniform and red sash, Paulina all silk and frills. Her eyes amazed.

"Get away, man," Ulrich said. "My Paulina accepts no gifts in the street."

"Frieda will want this," Witter said, pushing the folder up to the carriage window.

"Frieda? You have the wrong coach. Get away."

"Her name is Frieda and she will want this."

Ulrich opened the carriage door, not taking the folder. The folder fell onto the wet pavers. Ulrich had his hand on his dagger in his red silk sash.

"Witter?" said Frieda, surprised, frowning.

"You know him?" said Ulrich.

"Frieda, hear me, your brothers and sisters are condemned in the pit of the Oberhaus." Witter managed to hurry out the words.

"Who is Frieda?" Ulrich said, his face turning red.

Witter picked up the wet folder and shoved it past Ulrich into the carriage. Ulrich's tight face opened wide with recognition.

"I know you," said Ulrich sharply, eyes wide. "You are the footman of Florian Geyer!"

Witter glimpsed Paulina's face behind Ulrich and he saw surprise there, too, and Ulrich shouted but Witter was already turning and running, slipping on the wet pavers, racing away through the rainy streets.

"Hold, damn you!" Ulrich shouted, far behind.

KRISTINA

Kristina nursed Lud, held Lud, rocking him like a child, and did not sing with the others, but hummed to soothe Lud.

Life brought many strange revelations, and strangest was that, here at the end of her life, she adored every breath that a man took, every exhalation that struggled from his body, and she loved the fact of him in every way.

She wanted to go back into her dream. The dream of bodies of light, without being, free from stone, flowing together, all rising together into one radiance escaping out of this hard, cold world, out of this hellishness…

She only knew she could not let Lud die for her, nor could she lose her child, even if she lost her own life to save them. But her mind could find no good scheme for that. She was worth nothing. And she thought then of her mother. So often she had blamed her mother for leaving, for abandoning her, for not saying anything that would save her to stay here with her children. Was this desperation how her mother had reasoned?

Was this why her mother had gone to the fires? Had she somehow schemed to save her child? But what had she bargained? Her mother had begged nuns to take her child, and then she was gone.

What would nuns do with Peter? Would they love him? Could they? What is the trade that must be made?

Kristina prayed and begged her mother to forgive her. And when the others stirred and shared what little they had, and comforted one another with song, this time Kristina joined them.

Grit came to her, and held her hand. And together again as they had done so often before, they began to sing.

Today, Kristina gave her own thoughts to the melody:

There is no way to heaven for us
But through the fires on earth...
but who shall raise my child,
To walk the good path again?

They did not sing again for a time.

"Will you let Peter see the river?" Kristina asked Dolf.

Peter pulled at Dolf, wanting to be hoisted to the wall. Dolf dragged himself up and wearily obliged.

Peter's head wagged back and forth and Kristina wished she could see whatever of the world of light and space that her child could see, and she was glad he could see it, even a little.

"What do you see?" said Dolf.

"Witter," said Peter.

"What?"

"Witter," said Peter.

WITTER

He waited on the river road under the deep shadow of the Oberhaus fortress. The noon sun passed overhead and the road traffic ground past. He waited and watched for the red carriage and black horses, sometimes sitting on the flat rock, sometimes pacing, waiting as one who has surrendered. He had set the wheels into motion and now all he could do was follow it through to the end.

From the Oberhaus above him, the singing had come only once, earlier, and it was less strong than before. Sweet and hoarse voices together, rising and falling on the river breeze. The voices were weak now, but still they sang on. Then the songs had faded, faded, and finally stopped.

Witter had spent many days writing the story of Frieda, the innocent girl with her beautiful voice, who had left Kunvald with her brother and sister teachers to risk cruel torments and death, to teach reading, that each person might liberate themselves from the darkness of ignorance and hatred and slavery. He wrote of the sweet girl who had been taken in war and fled from magistrates at Wurzburg. Frieda, who had fallen upon hard times, and changed her name to Paulina, who had become a star of song, and married a valiant captain of cavalry, and now set the fashion for even the duchess herself. Her story was the first half of Witter's little folio. The second half was the transcribed hymns of the imprisoned innocents wrongfully punished for heresy, when they were as innocent as the great Paulina herself.

By now, the broadsheets would be hitting the streets of Passau. The only word on the front was "Paulina." Witter's fingers were black with stains from the labors of printing them all, single-handed in the closed print shop, running every stage of the press himself throughout the hours of night. They would go fast.

Witter had staked all his hopes on one play. He paced and waited. His knees felt like jelly. He watched for the famous red carriage and black horses.

Witter sat up sharply. His heart began to hammer in his chest. Past the trade wagons on the road, a horseman rode straight at him, and on the black horse was Ulrich.

There was no red carriage, no Paulina, no Frieda. Witter's heart sank. Now he wanted badly to run. But he did not move. Witter stood by the road watching Ulrich's face harden at the sight of him.

Ulrich rode up to him in road dust and twisted down expertly from the black horse. The horse stood still exactly where Ulrich left it. In Ulrich's fist was one of the broadsheets with "Paulina" on the cover.

"You bastard, you did this?"

"I gave you the first copy last night, that you and Frieda could prepare for it. And I wrote there just for you where I would be waiting today."

Ulrich threw down the broadsheet and came close.

Drovers and workmen of trade on the river road were slowing their wagons, some stopping their animals, staring.

"What are you staring at?" yelled Ulrich at them, and they hurried on.

Ulrich gripped Witter's face in one hand and Witter felt the point of steel suddenly at his throat, pressing up hard enough to prick. Ulrich's face now came so close Witter could smell his meaty onion-and-ale breath and see the red veins in his eyes and the trim of his cropped beard where the red scars ran under the black curls of his long hair, concealing where the ears should be. Ulrich's words came with flecks of spittle.

"I should have killed you at the Landsknechts when I let you and Geyer go free, but I am a man of honor and I had a debt to pay. I am a hero of the war yet rumors fly of my loyalty, from where I know not. And now you do this to my Paulina."

"She must choose who she is," said Witter.

"She told me you are a filthy, dirty, lying heretic who wanted his filthy hands on her."

Witter stood stiffly with the blade at his throat, and he was looking straight back at Ulrich—at his arrogant anger, his assumption of superiority, his physical threat—and something powerful overtook Witter. Witter felt his jaw set hard, and he felt firmer of purpose than ever in his life before this moment. Some transcendent power had overtaken him. It was like the time he had run down the magistrates at the Muntzer rally, and the time outside Giebel at the fight on the road, when he had ridden down the pikemen attacking Lud. It was like those times, this overwhelming joy, yet deeper, far more satisfying. Nothing this bastard could do would stop what had been set in motion.

"You will write a new tract saying it is all lies."

"Kill me. But it is too late to change the truth."

"I can make you do it, I would enjoy taking your balls and the rest piece by piece."

The dagger point came away from Witter's throat and Witter felt the hard point low at his groin now.

"And prove," Witter said, with a fearless clarity that astonished him, "to everyone that what I printed is true."

There were shouts down on the road.

Witter looked past Ulrich's strained face.

The red carriage with the black horses was coming, and a crowd was coming with it up the road. The trade traffic was pulling off the road on both sides to let it pass.

Ulrich's face twisted.

"Goddamn you," Ulrich said. But there was a note of panic in his curse.

The dagger came away from Witter's groin and Ulrich released Witter's face from his grasp. Ulrich stepped sharply away.

"Paulina," said Ulrich, "you do not belong here."

Frieda stood up in her open carriage, her famous red carriage, and the crowd had followed with Witter's broadsheets, no doubt seeing her on the causeway through the city and the bridge.

"I fear nothing," she said.

She was often followed wherever she went, but today was much different. She was beautiful and glowing now, as if moved by Ulrich's hot rage.

"Frieda," said Witter.

"You have printed lies," said Frieda passionately.

"Kristina is up there and has a child. Grit is there and they staked her jaw yet still she tries to sing. Dolf is there and Symon. They loved you. They still do love you."

Frieda visibly hardened her face. Her eyes had softened only for a moment but now she was ice again, colder than ever. Witter stared at her mercurial features and wondered at her talent for drama. She lifted her elegant arms and gestured to the adoring crowd.

"I am Paulina and do not know any Frieda. I come to show the world that I do not hide from heretics."

"Your presence credits this filth too much," said Ulrich.

"Frieda of Kunvald and wife of Ott," said Witter.

"Otty," said Frieda, and closed her eyes for a moment.

Now Ulrich blinked, frowning and confused, and stared at her. "Paulina, dearest?"

The crowd was staring at her, their goddess. She was imperious, used to their worship, and her blonde hair caught the sun like spun gold. Yet she seemed shaken.

Said Ulrich, "Paulina, shall I kill him?"

Witter knew then that it was over. He would die now. He had done his best, played it as well as he knew how, and he had lost. All were lost. Kristina and the others would die at the stake. He would die sooner, but with torments first. He had no will to run. He refused to run from this scum.

Then there was the moment—the kind of moment that makes one believe that God might indeed exist, if only manipulating the world through seeming coincidences—for that moment was when singing came again, down from the Oberhaus.

Frieda's face completely changed. She gasped a little, looking up, hearing it.

Tears spilled now from Frieda's eyes.

She stood in the carriage with the crowd around her but her eyes were fixed on the Oberhaus, and she wept silently, and even Ulrich stared in amazement, for Frieda began to sing with them now. She sang softly at first, and her lips trembled, trying out the words.

She sang the words in German, not Moravian. The crowd moaned with surprise. The words were clear now:

We wander in the forest dark
With dogs upon our track
And like the captive silent lamb
Men bring us, prisoners, back
They point to us amid the throng
And with their taunts offend
And long to light the fiery stake
To heaven our souls ascend…

The crowd listened in wonder, and Witter listened, rapt.

All coldness had drained from Frieda's face. She stood up in her carriage and held on to its rail as if she might faint.

Her voice lifted, higher and higher, and even Witter forgot everything for a magical moment, for Frieda sang like an angel, tears streaming down her anguished face. She was singing strongly along with the weakened voices from the Oberhaus, as if uplifting her brothers and her sisters.

Witter could almost believe that her passion was sincere. And then, as she sang on, from some depth in her that seemed long kept hidden, he finally did believe. And so did all others here, he saw. None could resist. All believed.

LUD

"Witter," Peter said, from his perch on Dolf's shoulders, and they all sat up a little.

"Witter?" said Kristina. "Witter?"

"What is he doing?" said Dolf, shouldering the child.

"Witter," Peter only said.

Lud lay against one wall and Kristina was slumped against him.

"Witter?" said Grit.

"Who is Witter?" said Elizabeth.

Lud felt the scabs on his face crack painfully as he smiled. So Witter was out there, on the other side of this vast wall of stone. Good Witter.

Witter had stayed, whatever he wanted forgotten. And Lud thought, that is a brave man, and a foolish man, for he should be in other lands by now. Yet he loved Witter for being out there, foolish as he was.

Now they gathered themselves and one by one began singing again.

Not a full hour later, as light crossed the floor from the air window, there were loud voices outside the cell door. Their singing ceased. With the sound of the cell door they moved closer together as if to shield each other from being taken.

The cell door rattled and slammed open.

"This is their cell," said Willy the jailer.

Lud looked up and saw Ulrich standing there. He was straining to see in the dimness, but Lud saw him clearly in the light of the cell door. It was impossible. But there he was. Ulrich.

"My God, the stench," said Ulrich.

Now Lud shifted and Ulrich's eyes fixed upon him.

"You?" said Lud.

"That is the priest Father Michael," said Willy.

"That is no priest," said Ulrich.

"You," said Lud, again, his mind inchoate at the sight of Ulrich, here, now. Vaguely he felt Kristina clinging to him, trying to hold on as if protecting him.

"Get up," Ulrich said.

"No," Kristina said.

Lud pried her hands loose, and pushed her away. He was facing Ulrich now.

"You," Lud said, dragging himself to his feet.

With his mind in a fog, Lud looked at the man he had come here to kill—Ulrich, standing there in his dress finery with fire in his arrogant face, and the jailer behind him, both blocking the cell door like taunts against freedom itself. Lud again saw the lance driving into Florian's armor under his left arm and Ulrich shouting in self-praise, triumphant and vile, driving hard from his black horse.

Yet it was strange. Now he did not want to kill Ulrich to revenge Florian. Now he wanted to kill Ulrich to protect Kristina. Lud stood, swaying, and felt Kristina trying to hold him back by his leg. He felt his blood drain from his head, and he sank down again to his knees.

Peter, snarling, went racing fiercely across the cell floor at Ulrich, but Dolf caught him up hard and fast.

"Up," said Ulrich, his hand on his dagger now.

Lud struggled to stand, but before he sank down again, he lunged at Ulrich.

"No!" many cried in the cell.

Ulrich's dagger was out and Lud lurched forward and staggered into Ulrich's arms.

KONRAD

B asil had traveled from Wurzburg through Passau to Vienna with a death list, and Konrad had not yet signed it. Attached to many names were petitions, charges, pleas for clemency, and denouncements by magistrates and clergy. The list covered the cities and estates from Wurzburg to Passau, and all estates within, and was over three hundred sheets long.

To kill them all would devastate those regions. Yet they were all listed as enemies of the Church-state.

So he signed nothing, yet.

Konrad had a date with the emperor, and he meant to use it to the utmost.

The emperor had invited him to go hawking on the heights above Vienna. Konrad looked out upon the wide Danube passing below the towers of Vienna, and he felt the might of the world under his feet. There was nothing he would not do to make solid this land for the glory of God.

The falconers stood well away, and Konrad knew Maximilian had wanted to speak privately. The walls had ears, especially in castles where serving men and women moved silently, always listening, servants being only one step away from their villein relatives. The emperor's favorite mastiffs lay panting, their foaming tongues hanging out and their black wrinkled faces watching everything.

"The whole new world is being divided," said Maximilian. "The globe lays open to conquest. Spain, Portugal, Holland, the Ottomans, even little England, they are already grabbing all they can. Gold, fertile lands, slaves to work them. And here we sit, feeble, without great oceangoing vessels, devastated and divided by this infernal villeins' war."

"People's War," Konrad said.

"People, indeed. They want all to be common," said Maximilian, "The empire lies in ruin. We must have the estates earning and tax them. The whole time we are being left behind. The compass points the way across unknown seas and the new worlds, yet it cannot reveal to me how best to rule the people."

"They wish to be our brothers. That is the key."

"Indeed. I have heard your wisdom in the chambers. No one understands these villeins as you seem to."

"You mean I am more a country fellow than others."

"I mean you have more wisdom, Konrad."

"All wisdom comes from God. And to me, God has made one thing quite clear. The world is driven either by love or by hate. And one must choose."

"Love is stronger, all the poets and priests say so. But we are anything but loved these days. I fear poison with every sup, Konrad. I mean it."

"Love takes time. We keep it safe inside the church. Hate is much easier. Love is much harder to provoke in strangers. Hate is so easy, yet hate can turn upon you as a mad dog turns upon its master. The so-called People's War has proved that only too well. It is a fine art, hate."

"Then what must we do?" said Maximilian. "The people do despise us. They seethe. It is only a matter of time before they catch their breath and are again at our throats."

A falcon hit a dove and a burst of feathers floated down. Maximilian clapped and the falcon brought and dropped the velvety corpse. The dogs snapped at the feathers drifting down. Maximilian offered his gloved wrist. The falcon perched again. Maximilian flung it back into the sky.

"Konrad, dear prince, you see, that is training. We are crushed by the debts of this uprising. We must rebuild our armies. The Turks will attack us, and if they do not, we will attack them if we chance a good opening. We need seaports and ships to cross the oceans if we are to take our rightful share. We must retrain our empire."

"The spirit of our people is lost to us."

"Yes, and I am willing to try anything."

"My chief scribe came through Passau. The crowds there weep at burnings now, and many pray. He saw a common pacifist burned and the hordes were sad, angry at authority, not exultant. He said songs of peace and love are being secretly published and sung all over that city, like a plague. Our people's will is broken by our defeat of them."

A brace of limp doves was handed to him. Their slender legs were thonged like a necklace of velvet bodies. He briefly considered the light upon their silken feathers, and then he tossed them to the dogs.

"Tell me what you need, anything to restore our might."

"We have demonized villeins and rebaptizers to no effect, because they are weak and not worthy of true hatred. The people must fear outsiders, Turks, Jews. They must love us and beg us to save them."

"Love us? They no longer even trust us. Yet you said they wish to become as brothers to us? That is the key?"

"We must win them back to the yoke. No longer discourage reading but encourage reading."

"Encourage reading?"

"I see now that I was in error. Even having my own press, I also worked to resist literacy, instead of fully exploiting it in all classes."

"Persuade me. I doubt you can, but do try."

"That which cannot be stopped, must be supported," said Konrad. "Veritas Press, even with its failures, taught me much. Instead of demonizing Florian Geyer, I made of him a great hero, so much that some still believe he lives and will rise again. With reading we control thoughts, or others control them. Erasmus and Luther are the best-selling writers in all Europe. People read of Suleiman's invasion of Hungary and Rhodes. Tales of gold in the new world, of pagan girl slaves and what have you. Their minds are soft, pliable. They are childlike, ready for stamping."

"Our prisons are packed with them and there is no money to feed them anymore when the fields go fallow."

"We failed before because we did not understand one simple equation of the human mind. To fear is to hate. To fear is to believe. Therefore, to hate is to believe."

"Belief? They still want to believe they are brothers, even equal with lords," Maximilian said. "I shudder at the disastrous implications. All God's order would collapse."

The falcon circled overhead, harking to whistles from the falconers on the slopes below. The great black dogs crunched the doves and watched the falcons.

"Belief is power," said Konrad. "We must create it."

"I do not take your meaning."

"We must help the villeins deceive themselves. I will publish Veritas throughout the empire, to unite us in one thought together."

"Why will they believe us now?"

Konrad had waited for this moment. "Because we shall begin by declaring Jubilee."

"Jubilee?"

"During the Hebrew ritual of Passover, criminals were released, debts forgiven, everyone could start over. All villeins who fear returning to the estates can go home."

"Amnesty? Is that not the road to chaos?"

Konrad thought of Florian suggesting this Jubilee, long before the villeins made this People's War. Perhaps then it would have saved so much misery and cost and power. Florian was a great loss. If only he could have bent him to serve the Church-state the right way somehow.

"Radical times," said Konrad, "require radical measures. We shall give commoners their sense of equality. Let them think all are brothers. Grant them the least of their twelve articles of rights."

"What? After fighting a war over them?"

"Exactly. The villeins must again have something they fear to lose. And the best is this—Jubilee means we owe nothing to money-lenders for the cost of the war."

Maximilian blinked, and then his chinless face brightened with a dawning smile.

"You are frightening me with brilliance. That is pure genius."

"You can at once build up new armies, with no revenues diverted to service old debt. The moneylenders are mostly Jews, anyway. Teach them a lesson in the name of the people. Jews cry foul but always come begging on their knees, in time. If we do not burn them for a while, they are happy. Veritas Press will praise our mercy and warn of terrible dangers from our enemies all around."

"Let me embrace you."

Konrad let Maximilian embrace him. He heard the falconers whistle and looked up into the sky and saw the falcon hit another dove.

"We shall be strong again," said Konrad, "and all the world shall tremble when we rouse ourselves, as never before."

WITTER

Witter looked for Kristina. He stood high, behind some of the watchful crowd, on the rock in the hot sun on the river road, watching the prisoners straggle forth.

Let her live, please let her be alive...

The groups of stunned and weary people came down out of the open Oberhaus gates. In ragged streams they walked, some weeping, very few smiling, dazed by the sunlight and shielding their starved faces. A few crawled and some tried to help those. One or two were blinded and led along by others.

The self-praising Veritas Press broadsheet had announced the amnesty of Jubilee. It touted the generous release of prisoners and debt and proclaimed a new day for the Church-state.

Can you see me now, Father? Have I at last done something worthy?

Under Witter's arm was a folio, leather-clad, containing all the songs his transcriber had notated.

They were glorious, beautiful songs, songs of praise created in prison, songs of faith in life, of love, not hate. They existed here in ink upon paper, his treasure, his proof of what he had done, and he longed to see Kristina's face when he gave them to her. He was hot in the dazzling sun reflecting off the great river, and beginning to sweat, and never had he felt more alive.

For the first time, I love my life.

It seemed all of Passau had turned out to line the river road and causeway and bridge. Many had relatives and friends there. Many no doubt wondered if they still lived.

Watching the prisoners emerging slowly, in their little groups, Witter thought of the release of prisoners from the fall of the Marienberg. He wondered where Mahmed was now.

And then he saw what he had waited for.

Here they came, shambling, trying to hurry away from the shadow of the fortress but too weak to hurry: Kristina and Peter, Grit, Dolf and Symon, and there were others with them, people leaning upon one another, coming in their small group together down the road in the massive shadow of the fortress.

"Kristina!" he called, but many others in the crowd were now shouting, and he was unheard.

He was going to go to Kristina. Tell her what he had done. How he had published their music and confronted Frieda and Ulrich, how he had dared everything for them, for Kristina. With the folio of songs, he stepped off the rock and began pushing through the crowd.

Then he saw...

Lud?

Witter stopped. He knew his eyes must be deceiving him. It could not be Lud; it was someone else.

It is Lud...

He had not known Lud was there. Lud lived after all. The sight of Lud was good, yet he saw Lud leaning upon Kristina and she was helping Lud along with her arm around him. Witter stood stone still, for he saw Kristina's face rise to Lud's. There was no mistake.

Lud...

Witter's heart, so buoyed with joy, now sank. He just stood there and took it like a beating, watching them. They passed by him without ever looking his way.

Lud was faltering, and now Kristina had both arms around him, holding him close, and she kissed Lud full on his scarred dark face, many times. Tears wet her eyes and Lud held on to her like a lifeline, forcing himself along.

People along the river began to cheer and Witter turned and saw Frieda in her carriage, with Ulrich. The crowd was adoring them. There was a larger carriage and the duchess was in that one, waving to the cheering crowd.

A Veritas broadsheet boy came passing through the crowd, handing them out, shouting, "Amnesty! A new day! All Germans are brothers!"

Witter did not move. Sweat trickled inside his jacket. He stared as Lud and Kristina and the others shambled on down the fortress road, out of the heavy Oberhaus shadow, into the sunlight along the great Danube River, and among the cheering people.

LUD

It had happened as in a dream. As he thought of it now, he marveled that he was still alive. He had accepted that to satisfy the spite of the man, Ulrich would kill him, and perhaps not quickly.

"I told your man I would kill you when next I saw you," Ulrich said, and hauled him out through the cell door, out past the jailer, into the cell corridor. "I know you told lies about me in confessions here. They have dared ask me things which insult my name."

"I thought you were the great hero of the Church-state."

"Veritas printed many tales of glory with some featuring me, so they cannot harm me, but instead they give me an estate far north, practically an exile. I should cut your throat, but I want to see you suffer."

"Cut it then," said Lud. "I have no blade."

"You cannot even stand if you had one."

Ulrich shoved him into an empty cell and they were alone then.

"I see from your body that they have worked you up. Torments do not seem to persuade you well."

"Rage and impotence," said Lud, "are not persuasive."

"Yes, people lie, they say anything, then we chase our tails. But what if I cut your girl's throat, instead?"

"Then you would be a coward."

Ulrich knelt so that their faces were close. Now Lud could see the lumps of scar where Ulrich's ears had been, covered somewhat by his dark curls, yet still he knew.

"Your man Witter exposed my Paulina, printed a broadsheet all about her past. The duchess herself intervened with the duke, but it could have been bad. My Paulina tried not to care about you all but now it is as if her heart is broken. For that I blame you. Now she wants me to help you all. She wanted to even come here. I told her I would do nothing if she so much as spoke to any of you, ever. I must protect her from the likes of you filth, by helping you."

"You? Help us how?"

"You tell me one thing, and I forget the duel and the war and the rest, and you all go free."

"Tell you what?"

"Where is Florian Geyer buried? I know he is dead. The body has to be somewhere near the old castle at Ingolstadt."

"How do I know you will let us go free?"

"My word as a gentleman."

"I see no gentleman. I would rather have your word as a villein, the way you were born, your word on the memory of your father."

Ulrich's harsh face softened in a curious smile. He stood.

"And if my father was a drunk villein and beat my mother half to death?"

"You would not tell me if that were so."

"Then, villein to villein, I give you my word, as a villein. Where is Geyer's body?"

"He must not be desecrated. He must have a decent burial."

"How will I know it truly is Geyer?"

"He is hidden just where you hunted for us, and wears the ram's head signet ring of his father, Dietrich."

"Any corpse can be given a ring. That is no proof."

"Then all you have is my word."

"And all you have is mine."

So Lud told him where Florian was buried.

And Ulrich smiled. "Fool. You told me for nothing."

"What do you mean?"

Ulrich reached down and pulled Lud to his feet by the hands. Lud swayed, facing him.

"You were being released anyway. The powers have decided that there is to be an amnesty to bring the horde back into their goodly nest. A festival—ale and all. So you told me for nothing."

"Nothing is for nothing," said Lud. "I am glad that day I did not cut your throat."

"You cheated with grappling," said Ulrich.

"Perhaps to kill another is the greatest cheat," said Lud.

"All your spirit is gone," Ulrich said.

Lud only smiled, saying nothing back. There was no way to explain to Ulrich what it had taken Lud a lifetime to discover. It was not something that could be taught.

And Ulrich had left him unharmed.

That had been some days ago...

Now, Lud stood in the open air, a man alive, with Peter clinging to his hand under the blue sky, and he leaned upon Kristina. The sun was strong and hot. Kristina's arm was soft around the hardness of his ribs, and every step sent sharp pain that made breathing a task.

"Will you go home to Giebel?" said Kristina. "You said you are the heir now. The only one left of Dietrich's blood."

"I do not remember telling you."

"You were feverish, half out of your mind from their cruelties. You said it is all yours now. Lady Anna will be glad to have you rebuild it all. Will you go?"

Peter pulled at his hand. The crowd went past them. They stood like an island, unnoticed. Peter let go and whirled around, his arms out, head back at the sky. Lud stopped and looked at Kristina.

"I am a pockmarked man with anger and too much death behind him. After Dietrich, I was never wanted."

"You are wanted," said Kristina, looking up at him.

"Am I?" Lud looked down into her good face. Her eyes were deep and lustrous. They were both filthy and her hair clung to her skull, and yet he had never seen a woman so beautiful.

"Lud," said Kristina, looking up into his eyes. He felt her hands upon his arms, small firm hands squeezing a little.

"In a rainstorm once, after a battle, many years ago, you told me that I am a hollow man, a killer, a filthy killer bound for hell. You were more right than you know."

"You are a good man," she said.

"I have...always wished to be."

"I love you," she said.

It was impossible yet it was happening. Her eyes were very close to his, and it was as if he could see into her soul. A sweetness poured from her into him. She lifted a hand to his face, touched his face, and pulled his face down to hers. She kissed every scar of his face, the new and the old.

"Then I will go anywhere you go."

They came down to the river quay and Lud felt he would faint with pleasure from the pain that had impelled him with every step. Kristina looked at him, her face like a lovely, impossible dream.

Lud walked as if on air. His pain seemed remote. He hardly saw the crowd or the city skyline. Kristina spoke to him as they walked. Ahead of them went the others. Peter was perched on Dolf's shoulders above the heads of the crowd, and the child pulled Dolf's shaggy hair as if steering him like a mule.

"In Switzerland," said Kristina, "the others say, we may be safe at least for now. They do not burn us. They have farms, good rich land there. Homes. They do share all, and they will share whatever the have equally with us."

"We have no coin. Nothing. How do we go there?"

"God knows," Kristina said, and she squeezed him tighter. He felt pain but it was good pain. She said, "Down the Ilz River, then upon the roads. They say there is free food relief as part of the amnesty. We must pray and try our best to live and travel and go as we can as far as we can."

He said, "If we are together, I do not care."

"We are together, Lud. We are together."

"You cannot love me, such as I am."

"Yet I do. I do love thee."

And she stopped there on the road in the sunlight and held him close.

"Look here," said Elizabeth.

Lud looked and Kristina looked.

Elizabeth held a leather-clad folio. "A tall, thin man gave me this. He said it contains all of our songs."

Pressed into the leather cover were the words, in gilt: *The Book of Gloriously Beautiful Songs.*

"Our songs?"

"Our songs, transcribed, he said."

"Who saiiiid?" Grit, voice slurred, leaning close.

"He did not say his name. Only to give you these."

Kristina took the folio and opened it. Papers rustled in the sunlight—sheets marked with strange symbols in ink.

Then a smaller sheet fell out. Kristina picked it up. It was a note in a beautiful floral hand:

With all my heart, yours always… Samuel, son of Judah of Córdoba…

"Witter," Kristina said softly.

"Samuel?" said Grit.

"And he gave me this," said Elizabeth. Heavily in her frail hand lay a leather purse, the drawstrings open, and Lud saw the glint of gold coin deep in its shadows. She offered the purse to Kristina. "Please, take it."

"All is for all to share," said Kristina.

"Where is Witter?" said Grit.

"He said to tell Lud to take good care of Kristina."

"Witter," said Lud, astonished.

Elizabeth embraced the folio and sobbed.

"All of our songs, those of my Hans, too." She struggled to speak, choked with emotion. "Praise be to God."

"Where is he gone?" said Symon.

"The Ottoman lands welcome Jews," said Grit.

"To be where he is wanted," said Lud.

"As all wish to be wanted," said Kristina, holding Lud.

KRISTINA

With the little purse Witter sent—*no, Samuel, I must ever now recall him, my dear, dear friend, by his true name*—they could hire passage south on the Ilz River barges, Dolf said, all the way to Switzerland. They would have nothing much left for food but they could leave here.

"We pray safe journey for Witter, our brother," said Kristina. Peter ran to her and leapt into her arms.

"For Witter," said Grit. "And for Mahmed."

Lud looked at Elizabeth. "Will it be safe there? Even in Switzerland?"

"All war is sin," said Elizabeth, "therefore all states are in sin, yet we each must live somewhere."

"Switzerland fights many wars," said Dolf.

"They offer land and free speech," Elizabeth said. "When last we were there, they were not burning people."

There were monks on the road giving away broadsheets declaring the amnesty, and many were blessing them and praising them, some falling to their knees and kissing the monks' hands.

"All has changed in one day," said Lud. "The Church-state again has them on their knees. Now it starts all over again."

"But we are alive," Kristina said, and she kissed him.

Now the bells tolled from the city.

"Free ale!" people were shouting.

It was on the river road near the quay, where the barges for hire were all docked, where the crowd was going the other way back toward the city, that Kristina saw the red carriage, and then she saw a face she had not seen in many years. It was still lovely, but with lines of hardness under the powder.

It was Frieda, walking toward them. She wore a rain cloak—plain, cheap market goods—with the hood up.

"Frieda," Kristina said. "Dear Frieda."

"Yes," said Frieda.

"Dear sister," Grit said, recognizing her, too.

"I had to see you before you were gone forever."

"Frieda, bless you. Come with us."

"I cannot. Ulrich does not know I am here."

"Your Ulrich serves a murderous state," said Grit.

"You owe that state your lives," said Frieda.

"We owe all to God," said Grit. "Should we bless a state that wrongly held us, because it then let us go?"

"We go to Switzerland, near Lake Zurich. Come with us, Frieda, be one with us again."

"Ulrich is my husband. A good man, a man of power and wealth now. I belong with him. He loves me and will always protect me. This city loves me."

"This city has devoured you," said Grit. "Come with us, child. Free yourself. Let us pray with you."

"God did not hear me. But the city did." Frieda's beautiful eyes went cold as she spoke. "I wanted your forgiveness, for running away at the river ferry that night. But you judge me instead."

"Never." Kristina put her arms around Frieda.

But Frieda pushed away. She then handed Kristina a red leather wallet.

"Let me share, as once together in Kunvald we shared all in common together. There is coin and some of my jewels."

Kristina pressed it back into Frieda's hands. "Keep this to use for yourself. We have enough. Use them to come to us. Pray on that, Frieda."

Said Grit, "Dear sister, when we left little Kunvald so many years ago, you spoke of the End of Days. Do you remember?"

"I remember." Frieda's eyes softened; she blinked.

"Do not give yourself to this living death," said Grit.

"There are End of Days," Frieda said. "But not for all at once. That is what I have learned in this life. Each one has one's own End of Days. I had mine when I became Paulina."

"Frieda, hear us," said Grit.

"Not Frieda. I am Paulina."

Frieda dropped the hood from her face and her blonde hair flashed in the sunlight. Her eyes flashed, yet were dead somehow. Her stunning face was imperious again, the face of Paulina, and Kristina saw no sweetness of life. Her radiance was like reflecting metal, bright but cold and lifeless.

Instantly many in the crowd recognized her. There was a collective murmur and many stopped to stare. She indeed was Paulina, posing for them, aristocratic and proud.

"Paulina!" they cooed, seeing her.

She blew a kiss into the air the way she did on stage and the crowd murmured with delight.

"You see how they love me," said Frieda. "You mistake me for someone else. Perhaps someone you once knew long ago, when she was nothing more than a frightened girl."

Then Frieda again pressed the red leather wallet back into Kristina's hands and turned suddenly and was gone, back to her red carriage, basking again through the mingling, adoring crowds.

SAMUEL

Alone, yet never truly alone.

No longer would he ever again be Witter. From now on, he would be who he was born to be, his father's son.

Samuel watched them climb upon the Ilz River barge and he did not move until late that day when the barge began to move away, south toward Switzerland, pulled by the mules along the road, and poled by the bargemen. The current took it, and the men on the big rudder strained against the flow.

Then Witter turned his back to them—with his longing for Kristina an ache as physical in him as a blow to the abdomen—and he stepped upon the Danube barge downriver, toward the border of Ottoman territory at the Marcal River, where Mahmed said his outpost would be.

If he reached there, perhaps he would not be killed before he had a chance to prove that he was seeking refuge from the Christian Church-state, that he had indeed helped Mahmed, and that he indeed was a Jew.

Samuel, son of Judah of Córdoba, stood on the deck of the barge and watched the towers of Passau and the mass of the Oberhaus slide away.

Kristina was behind him now, as flowed these waters, and Europe, too. He thought of the rabbi and his beautiful daughter Rachael in Wurzburg, so frightened of him. Perhaps there would be a woman with a sweet soul for him somewhere ahead, if he lived.

He did not know whether Mahmed would be waiting at the outpost on the Marcal, but he was not afraid.

I am the son of you, my father...

Night was falling and the stars came up. The river became a black, glassy plain and slid by, wider and wider, with reflected stars streaming past. A chill came up with the river fog. The bargemen lit lanterns hung high on bow and stern poles, and one blew a horn at intervals.

Witter wrapped his rain cloak tight about him and sat on the bow as the world slid past, briefly lit by the passing lanterns. He could see the vague shapes of the banks as the barge glided past. With the wide bends of river eastward, through the night, the rudder men worked hard to hold the turns of current.

Perhaps, Father, five hundred years from now, for such is but a moment in the infinity of time, if people still exist then and have not yet destroyed one another, perhaps there will be one language, one belief in the good, and all shall live as brothers and sisters, all will read, and know, and love, and worship one God with many names...

Now the voice of his father came back, strong and clear, without reservation, as if they sat together in the garden at Córdoba...

Do not think it will be easy in the Ottoman lands. Remember al-Ma'arri, the great Muhammadan seer whom the overrated Dante admired and imitated, al-Ma'arri, who denounced all religious fanatics, whether Christian, Muslim, or Jews, saying, "The inhabitants of the earth are of two sorts: Those with brains but no religion, and those with religion but no brains." Seek out men of wisdom, my son, and with them find your refuge...

Samuel laughed, delighting in his father's counsel, finding great strength in his father's return. He knew that perhaps he was mad. But he was no longer alone.

Many hours later, when dawn came glowing with all its colors, Samuel was still sitting on the bow of the barge, and he smiled, for a thought suddenly had taken him—one of those twists of irony strung so like stepping stones throughout his years, leading all the way here, to now.

I have spent so many years proving I am not a Jew, and now my life ahead shall depend upon proving that I am, indeed, a Jew...

KONRAD

The black bier on the long black carriage brought the body of Florian Geyer through the gates of Giebel, into the old Geyer estate, and Konrad sat on his new white horse and watched the villeins come out to see it. It was an expensive bier with silver filigree and hinges, paid for by Konrad himself, and Konrad wanted the villeins to be awed and for Lady Anna to feel in his debt.

The monks had prepared Florian as best anyone could. He had lain hidden under stones too long. Konrad knew he should not have looked, and wished he had resisted the impulse, for even the young looked so ancient in death.

The ram's head signet ring of Dietrich was ceremoniously given to Anna. She stiffened, but took it tenderly into her palms.

In another carriage were Basil and the new Veritas publicists. Konrad had instructed them how to frame the story best: *"Prince Konrad, now duke bishop, brings his godson home to rest. In gracious forgiveness for his godson's apostasy in the illegal and tragic uprising, all is forgiven. His grace in good heart was seen to weep, though attempting in his great dignity to conceal such outpouring of true emotion. All villeins returning to the fields are glad to have their good work and homes and food again, and many babies are being born. The courts must be fair to all, high and low. Reading should be embraced by all. We are one people again. Praise God and the Church and the state!"*

And on and on, in that manner of reconciliation. He had even let Mayor Tilman Riemenschneider and the upstart city councilmen all live, with token penalties. Riemenschneider's sculptures and paintings were everywhere. Even the tomb of Lorenz in the cathedral was by Riemenschneider. The expense of replacing them all (were the artist condemned) would be ruinous. So Riemenschneider was given mercy. Only his hands were crushed, so that he could never sculpt nor paint again, lest his works might create subtle propaganda and foment new unrest.

The people needed to feel forgiven, and united.

At the great cathedral, monks were instructed to be lenient in confession. Enormous new choirs were formed, sometimes of boys, sometimes of nuns, and the cathedral was jammed with crowds eager to hear them. The popular pageants of the stations of the cross were brought back.

There was a new war coming. The Imperial spies inferred that Suleiman might attack Austria in the southern borders. Or at least, that would be the pretext to attack them first. The estates were working and the taxes could come in and all the debt absolved.

In a slow rain suitable for the dour ceremony, the remains of Konrad's godson, Florian, were buried beside his favorite cousin, Dietrich.

Hard heads, Konrad was thinking, yet not without fondness, he realized. The fruit had not fallen far from the tree. Now both Dietrich and Florian, father and son, were planted side by side. Yet he missed them both, truly missed them.

Konrad mouthed the sacred words. He was dressed in his plainest red bishopric cape, almost as humble as a country priest, though its collar was ermine, lest anyone mistake who he was, in this backwoods estate. He instructed his personal guard of six magistrates to stay well back that the scene not be harsh. But not so far back that they could not move should some of the gathered villeins lose their wits and attack. Many of them were sobbing now, and Konrad found this remarkable.

They weep for one who led them to slaughter, yet they despise me, I feel it, the one who leads them to the light...

Saying the sacred burial words, he hardly heard them. This place made him drunk with memories. He thought of Dietrich drinking with him by the road after the disastrous battle so many years ago. He wished he could get drunk with Dietrich now and for Dietrich to witness his power as duke, the reuniter of the empire. He wished Florian were alive and he could persuade him to come to heel. He wished Anna were young and fresh and he could somehow persuade her to submit to his bed.

Lady Anna, near the open earth at the grave, stood as still as one of the weathered stone monuments. She wore no veil and the full devastation of her beauty was unhidden. She made no attempt now to conceal it from him; if anything, she seemed to flaunt it at him, even with a perverse pride. Rain dripped from her uncovered hair, woven with silver strands of age. Konrad could not bear to look directly at her, only aside. He felt a sting of curiosity, and wondered whether she would submit to him alone, and thereby crush the last adolescent embers of his desire for her. But he had not the courage to risk her rejection. Nor the courage to confront her disfigurement.

All her debts were forgiven and she would keep the estate. He had come here and found her with a cartload of books, for she had planned to go to the convent she had long supported with her patronage.

"How shall you pass your time?" he asked idly.

"I shall read," she said, "and learn, and help others."

The Geyers were always too generous with anything they had, and Konrad had assured her she need not go to the convent, that the estate needed her.

Some of the villeins were crippled, he saw, by wounds or disease of war. Some were marred of mind.

One had no left leg and walked on a stick, oddly, as if trying to dance. He laughed to himself as if fascinated by a strange secret, and Konrad realized he was mad, for once he shouted: "I am Kaspar, why will no one kill me?"

And most curious of all was one strange woman who nursed something swaddled in a baby blanket. It looked odd, and when the old woman turned Konrad saw it was a short length of firewood at her breast. She was old and Anna called her Arl. Konrad thought for a strange moment how this Arl so resembled the hag called Black Hoffman who had raged up the villeins to attack the Marienberg. But of course this could not be that one. She had been a baby catcher before the war, Anna said—as if that were Konrad's fault—and she had returned home quite mad. Now Anna herself was assisting in birth, Anna said, with her maid Lura. Then he noticed that Anna's hands looked red and chafed as if from common work.

Perhaps they were all mad. Perhaps infirm minds had caused all of this tumult and agony and the ruinous costs of the war. He felt a tinge of pity for the villeins and their miserable lot, their filthy spawn. But then Konrad thought of the head of Sieger, saw the black eyes staring up at him, the beautiful white head impaled upon a stake. His pity hardened to scorn, and then deepened more, to hatred. If they were insane, they should be cleansed. Perhaps there would someday be a way to rid the land of such mentally unstable people. But then, who would do the work?

Konrad looked at Anna. Not directly at her, but his vision askew, enough not to view her ugliness.

"So now you are their equal?" Konrad said slyly.

"I try my best," said Anna in plain retort.

"Are you in danger here with these villeins?" he asked. "I can send a guard to post here, for your safety."

"I fear you and your guard more than any here."

"Do you think yourself a villein now?"

"I think myself a child of God."

Perhaps he could learn the pose of righteousness from her, he thought. With her it was real and true, but if he learned to seem so, perhaps it might gradually become so? Or perhaps her will had broken. Or perhaps she was deluded by the whole thing? Had she gone mad?

Konrad pretended to be deeply affected and humble. It was a hard act to keep up, and by the time his retinue saddled up and was back on the road, he was exhausted and in need of the Marienberg's comforts—a steam bath, a rub, the best wine, and a good fire.

His new horse, Vanquish, could have been Sieger's twin. It was indeed one of Sieger's sons. Konrad rode it everywhere, as sign of the enduring rebirth of the empire.

But he had seen a good number of young women who carried suckling babies at their breasts. God, in his eternal wisdom, saw to it that there would always be a good crop of villeins to fill the ranks of pike and powder in the new wars to come. Of one thing now Konrad was certain—God had clearly revealed to him that neither the new age of gunpowder weapons nor the compass brought righteousness nor omnipotence.

The Church-state fed upon the people's belief.

No force of arms or discovery compared to the power of reading. People must be made to believe. All must learn to read. Lorenz had been so right about that.

What had Lorenz called it?

Enlightenment...

Quadruple its prewar size, Veritas Press would praise the new day, far and wide. There was being created the sense that the People's War had brought real change.

Now, nobles and villeins alike were all brothers in arms, if not equal in born privilege or rank. All must think themselves and their children equal in hope, equal in opportunity and in rights, and in the worship of Jesus Christ, and not mere tools of the Church-state.

The people only had to be made to believe it was true.

LUD

The night was pitch-black except for the stars glittering overhead. Low to the west, the white-blue dog star burned so brightly it almost hurt his eyes.

About him like an unmoored island, the barge moved downriver. Two men stood far back on the rudder, and two others vigilant with lanterns on long poles. They were veteran river men and the barge was the world that fed them.

On its wide, flat foredeck, Lud sat and watched over Kristina and Peter, while they slept curled together. Others from the prison group lay sleeping in vague bundles not far away, but he did not care much about them, except that they promised to share their land in Switzerland. For many years, his stubby dagger had been his only true friend, and that had been taken from him at the Oberhaus. All he wore now was the torn cloak and his bruises and burns.

Once, he might have gone back to Giebel and to the estate. Once, perhaps, he might have helped Lady Anna put things back together, and even pressed his blood claim. He was Dietrich's bastard, but no one else was left.

But Lud cared nothing for Giebel now.

Kristina and Peter were his life. He was wanted and he belonged where he was wanted. He was loved and he belonged where he was loved. Not since the death of Dietrich had he felt he knew where he belonged.

He would try hard to resist the violence that was sometimes necessary, but he would never let harm come to them. Whatever lay ahead in the farming lands of Switzerland, he would build a house and bring new life from the soil to sustain Kristina and Peter. He would pray with Kristina as she wished, and try to believe.

Because that was what it meant, at last, to be loved.

KRISTINA

The waters of the Ilz slid by like a plain of glass, southward toward Switzerland. The morning sunrise was mirrored upon it with all the colors of creation. Sometimes she sang with her weary yet hopeful brothers and sisters. The bargemen working the long rudder and the poles watched them. She sang now not from fear but from peace of heart and mind and soul.

Yet she knew it was still happening.

They were still many river travel days from the Swiss border, and she had learned that no one was ever safe in body, not in this life. Much was illusion. Like the morning she had wakened with the sense she and her child were floating in light, radiant as angels released from the grip of earth, above the stone floor of the cell where the bodies lay still asleep.

She saw Peter leaning over the side of the barge and trailing his fingers in the passing water as if playing a harp. But she did not fear him falling. Lud sat with him, one fist gripping the boy's right leg.

"You will not return to your home, to Giebel?" she said.

"You are my home," he said, looking at her with his eyes warm and loving, no longer distant in his hard face.

Kristina sat with the leather folio of *The Book of Gloriously Beautiful Songs* in her lap, and for a long time she prayed. The strong cloth sacking cover lay in her lap and she felt something small and hard in one corner. Her hand felt inside and out came a small chess piece. An ivory queen. Somehow Witter had passed it from Mahmed to her.

A soft smile parted her lips.

Please God, watch over Mahmed, watch over Witter, no, I mean Samuel, help them in their travels...

The river slid past and she prayed for them to find their homes and their loves, who surely must await them somewhere, for God could not waste such good-hearted men.

She prayed on, for Peter that he might find a full life, and for Lud that he might fully believe in God someday, and for Konrad that he might see the kindness and love of Christ, and for Mahmed that he would safely find his way to his home and never kill again, and for all those of Giebel she could think of, alive or dead, Anna and Arl and Lura and Leta and Merkel and Kaspar and Linhoff and Jakop and Ambrosius and all the others, and she prayed then for all those here, for Grit and Dolf and Symon and the Swiss brothers and sisters, and all of those perished at Kunvald, and her mother and father, and for the souls of all who had been taken by the violence of hatred and greed and intolerance.

But most, she prayed for Peter and for Lud, both of them gifts from God that she treasured.

They were refugees from cruelty. Bound by love. And yet she could not know what awaited them ahead, for wherever she had ever gone in this world, humans were humans and day was day and night was night.

Help us learn to think, O God, she prayed. *And help me always to believe...*

Epilogue

AUSBUND

Today, hymns from the Ausbund are sung at every Amish service. It is the world's oldest songbook in continuous use. Its name—the Ausbund—means "gloriously beautiful songs."

Over the centuries, the Amish and Mennonites have preserved those hauntingly spiritual hymns.

Despite the terrors of torture and horrific death by fire, they are—even for enemies who persecute and torment—songs of love and forgiveness, songs of faith in the power of nonviolence and communal love.

The first 51 hymns in the Ausbund are those composed by the prisoners of the pit in the Passau Oberhaus, over four hundred years ago. Those first hymns survived in early folios, notated in the archaic method of earliest printing.

Who printed those first songs is no longer remembered.

Their tone is not of despair, but of the hope that people everywhere will one day, at last, learn to love one another.

The End

Made in the USA
Monee, IL
30 April 2020